PRAISE FOR *THE SPEAKER*

Kirkus Reviews Best Fiction of 2017

Tor.com Top YA SFF of 2017

★ "Filled with even more magic and intrigue than its predecessor, this is a gripping follow-up that will leave readers speculating and wanting more." —*KIRKUS REVIEWS*, STARRED REVIEW

★ "Rich with twists and turns that will leave readers in constant shock while reminding them that there are no coincidences in this narrative." —*SLJ*, STARRED REVIEW

"Fans will be knocking down the door to read this exciting sequel." —**BOOKLIST**

"Chee has once again created an unforgettable story. Filled with secrets and surprises, this fast-paced storyline draws readers in and keeps them on their toes. As readers uncover the past through Sefia's reading of the Book one story at a time, they catch an intriguing glimpse of a complex mix of past and present that will leave them wanting more." —*VOYA*

"The writing is so beautiful." —**BUTTERMYBOOKS**

"*The Speaker* is a strong and lovely sequel that expands this world and its characters into much greater—and often painful—complexity." —**LOVE IS NOT A TRIANGLE**

"A fantastically lush tale full of all the elements that make a YA fantasy great: charming and eccentric pirates, mysterious assassins, apprentices, magic, and schools." —**BOOKSHELVES AND PAPERBACKS**

ACCLAIM FOR

THE READER

"Most world-building shies away from tackling the question of literacy within fantasy cultures, but here it serves as the beating meta-heart." —NPR, Best Book of the Year

"Masterfully written . . . This is a book you will not soon forget."
—Renée Ahdieh, #1 *New York Times* bestselling author of *The Wrath & the Dawn*

★ "Genuine character growth, mystery, unique world-building, adventure, unyielding bonds of loyalty, and pirates . . . Highly recommended." —*SLJ*, starred review

★ "Commanding storytelling and vivid details . . . the first of what promises to be an enchanting series."
—*Kirkus Reviews*, starred review

★ "An intricate, multilayered reading experience . . . Absorbing." —*Publishers Weekly*, starred review

★ "This is a series fantasy lovers will want to sink their teeth into." —*Booklist*, starred review

"Readers will find themselves lifted out of reality to become totally absorbed in the story." —*Romantic Times*, Top Pick

"An enthralling and beautiful, expansive meditation on the act of reading." —*Chicago Tribune*

"Those looking for complex fantasy will enjoy and look for the next installment." —*SLC*

"Wide scope, a rich mine of overlapping stories and timelines." —*Shelf Awareness*

"'Look closer,' exhorts an inscription at the novel's opening, and readers will feel inspired to look for hidden clues in this intricately and unconventionally structured fantasy novel." —*BookPage*

"Ripe for optioning!" —*The Hollywood Reporter*

"Filled with adventure, friendship, and mystery set in a rich world that won't leave you anytime soon." —BuzzFeed

"For a story about the almost magical power of books, Traci Chee certainly does the tale justice with her own book." —Bustle

"Traci Chee has unleashed a new series that will suck readers in." —Minnesota Public Radio

BY TRACI CHEE

The Speaker

Book Two of the Reader Trilogy

TRACI CHEE

speak

SPEAK
An imprint of Penguin Random House LLC
375 Hudson Street
New York, New York 10014

First published in the United States of America by G. P. Putnam's Sons,
an imprint of Penguin Random House LLC, 2017
Published by Speak, an imprint of Penguin Random House LLC, 2018

THE LIBRARY OF CONGRESS HAS CATALOGED THE G. P. PUTNAM'S SONS EDITION AS FOLLOWS:
Names: Chee, Traci, author. | Schoenherr, Ian, illustrator.
Title: The speaker / Traci Chee ; map and interior illustrations by Ian Schoenherr.
Description: New York, NY : G. P. Putnam's Sons, [2017]. | Series: Sea of ink and gold ; book 2
Summary: "Sefia and Archer's adventure continues as Archer searches for a way to combat his
nightmares of his time with the impressors and Sefia becomes more and more consumed by
her study of the Book"—Provided by publisher.
Identifiers: LCCN 2017016556 | ISBN 9780399176784 (hardback) |
ISBN 9780698410633 (ebook)
Subjects: | CYAC: Books and reading—Fiction. | Nightmares—Fiction. | Adventure and
adventurers—Fiction. | Kidnapping—Fiction. | Orphans—Fiction. | Fantasy.
Classification: LCC PZ7.1.C497 Spe 2016 | DDC [Fic]—dc23
LC record available at https://lccn.loc.gov/2017016556

Speak ISBN 9780147518064

Printed in the United States of America.

1 3 5 7 9 10 8 6 4 2

Photographic elements (or images) courtesy of Shutterstock.
Text set in News Plantin MT Std.

THIS IS A BOOK.
THERE ARE HIDDEN ELEMENTS AND CODES WITHIN ITS DESIGN.
LOOK CLOSER AND HAVE FUN.

For Charles, Zach, and Paul,

who were taken too soon

GORMAN

The NORTHERN REACH

NORTHERN OCEAN

SHAOVINH

UMLAAN

Umlari

CANDARAN OCEAN

LICCARO

EPHYGIAN BAY

CAI

HYE

QIN

Serakeen's Fleet

VRITHI

To the EASTERN EDGE

SEA

Karak

BRANDAAL

Anarra

CHAIGON

CHAIGON OCEAN

Dead Man's Rock

JIHON

ANARRAN SEA

INNER CHAIGON SEA

MASERIN

Akapé

EVERICA

ZHUELIN BAY

Mae

KELANNA

Ian Schoenherr © 2016

CREW OF THE
Current of Faith

CAPTAIN–Cannek Reed

CHIEF MATE

SECOND MATE–Meeks

STEWARD–Aly

COOK–Cooky

CARPENTER–Horse

SURGEON/SAILMAKER–Doc

HELMSMAN–Jaunty

SAILORS

    Jules–chanty leader of the larboard watch

    Theo–chanty leader of the starboard watch

    Goro

    Killian

    Marmalade

THE RED WAR

PHASE I
Conquer
Everica

EVERICA
- Lord Darion Stonegold ~~King~~ (Master Politician)
- General Braca Longatta Terezina III (Master Soldier)

✓ Stonegold & Braca unify provinces under one banner. ~~Rock &
River
Wars~~

✓ Oxscini = common enemy ——→ EXPLOIT THIS.

✓ Begin eliminating outlaw way of life.

PHASE II
Ally with
Liccaro

LICCARO — Rajar (Apprentice Soldier)

✓ Rajar becomes Serakeen.

✓ Serakeen blockades Liccaro & gains power/influence
   over corrupt regency government.

Serakeen uses influence to empower political allies
   to seize control of kingdom!

PHASE III
Ally with
Deliene

DELIENE — ~~X~~ **Arcadimon Detano** (Apprentice Politician)

✓ Build following among provincial nobility.

Assassinate King ~~Leymor~~ **Eduoar** & successors.

Get elected sole regent of kingdom.

PHASE IV
Conquer
Oxscini
& Roku

OXSCINI & ROKU

Everica, Liccaro, & Deliene form the Alliance.

Deliene attacks Oxscini from the north.

Everica & Liccaro attack Oxscini from the east.

Everican forces capture Roku.

First ~~Second~~ Assassin kills Queen Heccata.
   └─ ~~soon to be First!~~

Combined Alliance forces attack Oxscini via Broken Crown.

Oxscini falls.

THE RED WAR IS COMPLETE.
KELANNA IS OURS.

THE ALLIANCE

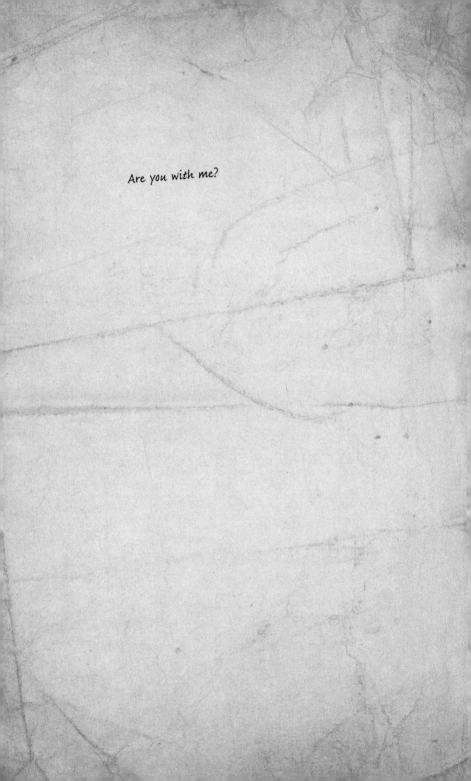

Are you with me?

The Dreams

Archer was dreaming again, and in the dreams he had no name. He didn't remember when he'd lost it, but now the men called him *boy* or *bootlicker* or nothing at all.

He stood in a circle of stones, large and pale as skulls, while men and women jeered at him from outside the ring, their faces turned into hideous masks by torchlight. When he shifted, bits of gravel dug into the bottoms of his bare feet.

"This your new candidate, Hatchet?" a man sneered. He had black deep-set eyes and sallow skin.

"Got him in Jocoxa a couple months back," Hatchet answered. "Been training him up."

Hatchet—stout build, ruddy skin, always picking at half-healed scabs.

The nameless boy touched his neck, fingers grazing the scars at his throat.

Hatchet had burned him.

The sallow man smiled, his teeth sharp and small like a ferret's. "Argo's already put down four underfed whelps like this one."

Turning, the boy with no name found Argo standing on the other side of the ring, the light flickering over four raised burns on his right arm. Through the short coils of his beard, he wore a slack-jawed smile.

The crowd began clapping and whooping. A signal, maybe.

Argo strode toward the nameless boy, who tried to step sideways. But he stumbled.

"Watch it!" Hatchet snapped.

The boy with no name was turning, bewildered, trying to find Hatchet's watery eyes in the crowd when Argo attacked.

His fists were everywhere, raining on the nameless boy's face and head and chest. It got hard to breathe, hard to see.

The blows came faster, heavier, like hail.

The boy with no name doubled over, caught a knee in the face. The ground rose up to meet him.

Dimly, he heard Hatchet shouting, "Get up! Get up, you little—"

But he did not get up.

Argo flipped him onto his back, straddled his chest, and raised a hand to strike.

In that moment, the nameless boy understood: This was the end. He was going to die.

He would cease to breathe. Cease to be. Cease to hurt. It would be easy.

But he didn't want to die.

And knowing that, knowing he wanted to live, however hard it was, however much it hurt, something opened up inside him, something hidden and ugly and powerful.

Argo slowed.

Everything slowed.

As if the seconds were stretching into minutes, the minutes into hours, the boy without a name could see where the fight had begun and every hit he'd taken since, all unfurling before him in perfect detail. He could see bruises and newly healed bones beneath Argo's skin, could sense pressure points in his joints like buds of pain waiting to blossom.

The fist came down, but the nameless boy deflected it into the dirt. He trapped Argo's leg with his own and rolled, pinning his opponent beneath him.

"That's right, boy! Fight back!" Hatchet shouted.

The boy could have struck. But he leapt to his feet and looked around instead.

He could see *everything*. He knew which torches would be easiest to wrench from the ground and how long it would take to reach them. He knew which of the stones lining the ring would make the best weapons. He counted revolvers and hidden knives in the crowd, found loose patches of dirt where the footing would be weakest. He saw it all.

As Argo stood, the nameless boy hit him in the face. The flesh crumpled. He hit Argo again and again, quick and hard, where it would hurt most. Where it would do the most damage.

It was easy.

Natural.

Like breathing.

Argo's kneecap popped. Ligaments snapped. The boy without a name struck him in the collarbone. He could almost see the splinters of bone spring away from each other under the skin.

Argo was crying. He tried to crawl toward the edge of the circle, but his arm and leg were no longer working. His limbs were covered in dirt.

The crowd called for blood.

Kneeling, the nameless boy picked up a rock studded with crags.

It was almost over now. He could see the end. It was very close.

Argo's eyes were wide with fright. His gums were bloody as he pleaded for his life.

But the boy with no name did not listen.

Living meant killing. He saw that now. He knew what he had to do.

He brought the rock down onto Argo's face. He felt the impact, the sudden warping of bone and flesh and beard. There was no more begging.

He raised the rock again.

CHAPTER 1

Quartz and Tiger's Eye

Sefia glanced down at Archer, where he lay in the hidden pocket among the rocks with the rest of their belongings. He stirred once, tossing the blanket from his chest, and went still again. During the two hours since moonrise, he'd already slept and woken so many times, slept and woken, continually pulled under the surface of his dreams until he thrust himself into consciousness again, gasping for air.

Even now, he didn't seem to be resting—brow creased, fingers twitching, lips drawn back in a snarl or a silent cry. She wanted to go to him, to smooth his forehead and uncurl his fists, but since their escape, he'd been different, distant. Their encounter with the Guard had changed him. It had changed how they were together.

It had changed everything.

Perched on a granite boulder, Sefia pulled her blanket closer about her shoulders. She would have preferred her hammock to this niche between the boulders, but her hammock had been left on the floor of Tanin's office with most of her supplies.

And Nin. The aunt she'd sworn to rescue. The aunt she'd failed. A small body beneath a bear-skin cloak.

Sefia shuddered, remembering what had happened next: the gleam of the knife, the way Tanin's skin split beneath the blade. Her second kill.

The Guard would make Sefia pay dearly for that if they found her. Now two of their Directors had been killed by her family.

As she did every few minutes, she narrowed her eyes on the woods. Feeling for that special sense she'd shared with her mother—and her father too—she reached for her magic.

It was always there, always moving, like a powerful ocean beneath a crust of ice. For the world was more than what you could see, or hear, or touch. If you had the gift for it, the world was Illuminated—every object swimming in its own history, every moment accessible if only you knew how to look for it.

She blinked, and her vision came alive with swirling golden currents, millions of tiny bright specks shifting with the wind, the upward inching of the trees, the sigh of decaying matter settling gently into the dirt. In the valley below, not two miles from their camp, the remote alpine city of Cascarra lay along the Olivine River. This close, Sefia could see lamps like golden beads spangling the streets and lumberyards, barges tugging lightly at their moorings, smoke spiraling up from the pointed rooftops. But nothing disturbed the peace.

Sefia blinked again and her Vision—what the Guard called the Sight—faded. She and Archer were safe, for now. The Guard had not come for them yet.

But they would. Just like they had come for her parents.

Lon and Mareah.

At the thought of them, her heart curled up like a leaf in frost. Sometimes she found it difficult to believe they'd been part of a secret society of murderers and kidnappers—not the gentle people who'd raised her, protected her, loved her. But then she'd remember how her mother used to twirl her blades before chopping vegetables. How she'd once killed a coyote among their chickens with one skillfully flung knife. And she'd remember her father at his telescope by the window, studying the ocean. Only now did Sefia understand—he'd been watching for signs of the Guard. For the people who hunted them.

They'd kept so much from her—who they were and what they'd done. Because of their secrets, she'd been forced to run when she might have fought. Forced to hide when she might have been free. Nin was dead because Sefia had been unprepared. No matter how much she loved her parents, she couldn't forgive them for that.

Or herself.

And now she was on the run again.

Five days ago, she and Archer had fled the Guard's trackers by boat, sailing north along the rocky Delienean coast. It wasn't until they spotted another ship behind them, gaining quickly, that they'd risked going ashore, scuttling their craft in an attempt to shake their pursuers.

They'd climbed into the Ridgeline, the high range of mountains leading to the Heartland in the center of the kingdom. There among the peaks, they'd headed toward Cascarra, where they hoped to catch a riverboat back to the sea.

After that, they'd keep running, as long as they could. Hunted the rest of their lives.

Sefia turned her attention to the leather-wrapped object in her lap. Books were rare enough in Kelanna, hoarded by the Guard while everyone else floundered about without reading or writing. But this was more than just any book. This was *the* Book—infinite and full of magic—a record of everything that had ever been or would ever be, all the ages of history spelled out in fine black ink.

As she'd done every night since she began running again, Sefia gingerly pulled back the waterproof leather.

She could find out who her mother and father had *really* been, and why they'd done what they'd done . . . but she could never quite muster the courage to look.

Archer jerked in his sleep, exposing the vicious burns on his neck. Beneath him, dry twigs snapped, like gunshots in the still woods.

Sefia stole another glance at the surrounding forest, but the underbrush was still.

With a sigh, she sat back again. The Book's cover was cracked and stained, with discolored scallops and whorls where there had once been jewels and decorative filigree. But the only traces of precious metal that remained were its clasps and gold-capped corners.

Out of habit, she began tracing the symbol in the center.

Two curves for her parents. A curve for Nin. The straight line for herself. The circle for what she had to do: Learn what the Book was for. Rescue Nin. And if she could, punish the people responsible.

But she still couldn't bring herself to open the Book. Still couldn't face the truth. She was about to replace the leather covering when a branch cracked in the distance.

Tensing, she blinked, and her Sight flooded with gold. To the east, she spotted men descending from the ridge, weaving in and out of the moonlight like black fish in a black pond, fins flashing on the surface before they submerged again.

Trackers.

They must have been on the other side of the mountain when she'd scanned her surroundings, but now they were closing in.

Below her, Archer thrashed, knocking over his pack. The canteen clattered against the scabbard of his sword.

For a second the trackers paused. They turned toward her. In the Illuminated world, their eyes glowed, flicking back and forth in their sockets as they scoured the darkness.

Then they began to advance.

Honed by years on the run, Sefia's instincts kicked in. Swiftly, she wrapped the Book and leapt down among the boulders.

Archer flailed, his outstretched hands raking across the ground. He was so loud. Sefia threw her arms around him, trapping his arms and legs with her own. Beneath them, the fallen pine needles crackled like fire.

His eyes flew open, large and golden. Panic flooded his features. She could feel his heart thundering inside him as his mouth opened and closed, opened and closed, gasping for air.

Then the struggle, like a rabbit caught in a snare. Her grip broke.

"Archer," she whispered.

He shoved her back against the rocks. Pain shot through her.

"Archer." She was pleading now, desperate. "It's okay. It's me. It's Sefia. *Archer.*"

He froze, his breath coming too fast, too loud.

This time he allowed her to wrap him up in her arms, his pulse quick and insistent against her skin. This close, she could feel his breath gliding across her cheek. She bit her lip. Five days since the kiss. Five days and she could still feel the curve of his mouth on hers, still ached to feel it again.

Archer looked up as the sound of footsteps reached them. Sefia knew those noises, had made them herself when hunting with Nin. Stalking paces, interspersed with long listening silences. A hundred feet away? Fifty? Pointing toward the woods, she mouthed, *Trackers.*

He nodded, blinking rapidly. Silent as snow, he drew a piece of quartz from his pocket and began running his thumb along each of its facets in a ritual Sefia had taught him over a month ago, to ward off his panic, to remind him he was safe.

But they *weren't* safe.

Through a gap in the boulders, she watched the shadows shift among the trees. The trackers were all around them now, with starlight on their rifles and shadows in their eyes, searching the ground for footprints.

They'll find us. Anyone with a rudimentary grasp of tracking would recognize the little encampment. Sefia had to force them to move on. And soon.

Summoning her Sight again, she flicked her fingers. In the Illuminated world, the threads of light tightened and sprang back like bowstrings, sending ripples through the bands of gold. Ten yards away, on the slope leading toward Cascarra, a dead branch cracked.

The trackers ducked. Their rifles went up. They were so quiet . . . and so fast.

She did it again, farther away this time.

With a wave, their leader beckoned them toward the river valley, and they began creeping toward the sound of the breaking branches, toward the city, away from Sefia and Archer.

As her pulse slowed, she became aware of Archer's body entangled with her own. He'd stopped rubbing the crystal and was now still as a stone, watching her with his sunken, sleep-deprived eyes. "Did I hurt you?" he whispered.

Even after five days, the timbre of his voice still surprised her, with its layers of fire and darkness, like tiger's eye.

"No." She got to her knees, trying not to wince at the pain between her shoulder blades. They had to keep moving, before the trackers realized they weren't in Cascarra. She grabbed her blanket.

"When I woke up and didn't know where I was . . . when I couldn't move, I thought . . . I'm sorry, I . . ." He sat up, and for a moment she thought he'd continue. But then he closed his mouth and touched the scar around his neck, the burn the impressors gave all their boys, to mark them as candidates. For years the Guard had been searching for the boy they believed would lead them to victory in the bloodiest war Kelanna had ever seen. A killer. A captain. A commander.

Being one of their candidates had taken everything from Archer—his name, his voice, his memory—leaving him a husk of a person.

All of that had come back in their encounter with the Guard. But Archer still hadn't told her his real name, and at times like these she felt like she knew him even less than before.

Just like my parents, she thought bitterly.

"They almost caught us," Archer said, pocketing the piece of quartz.

"I'm sorry. I didn't know they were so close."

"But you could." His gaze fell to the Book. "You could know where they were at all times. We'd always be one step ahead of them."

Sefia stiffened. He was right, of course—the Book contained past, present, future. Every one of the Guard's movements was in there somewhere, buried deep in the layers of history. With it, she and Archer could easily evade the Guard. If they were clever enough, maybe they'd even slip their enemy's grasp for good. And maybe then they'd be free.

But she was afraid. Afraid of what she'd find if she opened it. Afraid of what it would tell her about her family . . . and the horrific things they might have done.

But to keep Archer out of the Guard's hands? Archer, who'd fought for her, who'd gone hungry and sleepless for her? Archer, who, since the return of his memories, somehow seemed even more broken than before?

She met his gaze, steady and solemn. "Okay."

Finding a patch of moonlight, Sefia lifted the Book into her lap and unwrapped its leather casing. Leaning down until her lips almost brushed the ⊖ on the cover, she murmured, "Show me what the Guard is doing right now."

With a deep breath, she unhooked the clasps. The pages rippled beneath her fingers and came to rest like two plains furrowed with ink.

She could feel Archer with her—waiting.

"The bedchamber was a ruin," Sefia read in a whisper, as if the Guard might overhear her. With a shudder, she scanned their surroundings, but the trackers had long since disappeared. They were safe. For now.

She turned back to the Book. "Open volumes and sheaves of paper littered the coverlet, spilling over into stacks of books and pools of parchment . . ." Her gaze skipped ahead. "Oh, no. *No.*"

She'd been wrong.

They'd never been safe. And no matter how far they ran, no matter how well they hid, they'd never be free.

Misinterpretation

The bedchamber was a ruin. Open volumes and sheaves of paper littered the coverlet, spilling over into stacks of books and pools of parchment—a destroyed landscape of questions that led nowhere and answers to riddles she hadn't posed.

At this late hour, Tanin should have been asleep. But she slept little these days.

There was much to do.

Her slender hands shifted across the bedspread, discarding dip-pens and dead-end pages.

This Librarian wrote that the Book was everywhere at once.

Useless.

This one penned corpulent paragraphs describing the paradox of an infinite Book.

Irrelevant.

This Master claimed that fire would visit the Library three times.

Tanin found nothing on the whereabouts of the Book *right now*.

She'd *had* it—cracked leather, crisp pages—exactly as the burned page had foretold.

But she'd lost it too. She'd lost everything—her strength, her voice, even her title.

With shaking hands, she uncorked a new bottle of ink to continue her notes.

Almost immediately, her pulse began to quicken. Her chest seized. Something was wrong. As she fumbled with the pockets of her nightgown, her breath came faster, shallower.

She could have rung for help. In her weakened condition, complications were common. Sometimes victims of near-fatal attacks simply didn't make it.

But this was no complication.

This was an assassination.

Tiny glass bottles of powder and tonic spilled from her trembling fingers as it became harder and harder to breathe, to think, to act. She picked up vial after vial, squinting at their labels as the letters blurred and pain clenched her body.

But this was not the first attempt on her life since her encounter with Sefia, and it would not be the last.

Finally, she found the bottle she needed and broke its neck over the open jar of ink. As the black powder hit the liquid, it hissed and smoked. The faint odor of burned orange peel suffused her senses.

The tightness in Tanin's chest eased. Her heartbeat slowed. The poisoned ink, which emitted a noxious vapor upon contact with the air, had been rendered inert.

You fail again, Stonegold.

Leaning back against her pillows, she took one long breath and, gathering up the remaining vials, she dropped them, tinkling, into her pocket.

Tanin touched her neck, remembering the knife, the hot wet of her own life coursing out of her. If it hadn't been for Rajar, her Apprentice Soldier, slowing the blood loss with Manipulation, she'd be dead.

She might soon be, if she wasn't careful.

It was customary for the five Masters to select an interim from among their ranks if the Director was incapacitated. It was also customary for temporary replacements to assassinate their Directors, making their positions permanent, provided they thought they could get away with it without throwing the rest of the Guard into chaos.

Obviously, the current interim, their Master Politician, Darion Stonegold, King of Everica, thought he could get away with it, at least if he made it look like an accident.

When Edmon was murdered, Stonegold would have been the logical successor. He was a natural leader, and with the help of their Master Soldier, he had already completed Phase I of the Red War—the unification of Everica.

But Erastis had backed Tanin, and where the

Librarian went, the other Guardians followed. So she, the Apprentice Administrator, had been elected Director of the Guard over both Stonegold and her own Master.

The Politician had been waiting decades for an opportunity to kill her, and now her position in the Guard was perilous enough for him to try, although not perilous enough for him to murder her outright. That meant she still had some support among the other Guardians, and she could rally them to her . . . if she retrieved the Book.

But with these assassination attempts, she was running out of time.

Drawing the covers aside, Tanin sat on the edge of the bed, nightgown swaying around her bare ankles. The Library was but a short walk down the hall.

She made it three steps before she fell. Piles of books toppled. A display case came crashing to the floor beside her, showering her with glass. A single sheet of paper, creased and yellowed with age, fluttered to the ground.

For a moment, she lay there, studying the hastily sketched plan, more dream than strategy, with annotations in varying hues of ink, added by different hands over the years.

And at the top, the title, in letters bold as brass:

THE RED WAR

There was a knock.

Tanin opened her mouth to speak, but the movement sent spasms of pain up her throat, like the burning of paper. Instead, she blinked, summoning the Sight, and waved her hand through the currents of gold. Across the room, the door opened.

She picked up the old scrap of parchment, crimping the brittle paper with her fingers. She was not powerless, not by any stretch of the imagination. She'd been a frightened child when she was inducted into the Guard. If she could claw her way up from that, she could recover from anything.

Erastis entered, his velvet robes swishing against the floor as he walked. He was nearly ninety now, his face a topography of wrinkles, his hair—what was left of it—almost completely white, but when he saw her lying on the floor amid the broken glass, he rushed to her side with surprising agility.

Her face reddened as he helped her back to the bed, where she laid Lon's original plan for the Red War on the nightstand.

"I thought I heard a crash," Erastis said, tucking her in. "I know you're itching to leave the room, but you should use this time to regain your strength."

Fumbling for the wooden tray beside her, Tanin smoothed a scrap of parchment and dipped a pen. *Time is short,* she wrote.

Through his spectacles, Erastis squinted at the page. "Another attempt on your life?"

She nodded at the bottle of ink, which he lifted to his nose.

"Poison? You'd think he'd know better than to use a former Administrator's instruments against her. Our Politician must be getting desperate." The Librarian settled into an armchair. "I'll find out who planted the bottle and have them dealt with. Darion must know I won't tolerate assassination attempts in the Main Branch."

Tanin swallowed. Once, Erastis might have stopped Stonegold altogether. But the Master Librarian was old, and his influence was not what it had been.

Aside from the servants, for the past week he'd been her only companion, bringing her manuscripts, helping her search for signs of the Book in the Library's vast collection.

The absence of the other Guardians troubled her. Many were out on assignment, but she'd at least expected Administrator Dotan, her old Master, to have come.

Had he turned on her? Or was he simply preoccupied with Phase II of the war? Her gaze flicked to her bedside table.

LICCARO—Rajar (Apprentice Soldier)
✓ Rajar becomes Serakeen.

✓ *Serakeen blockades Liccaro & gains power/influence over corrupt regency government.*

Serakeen uses influence to empower political allies to seize control of kingdom!

Dipping her pen again, Tanin wrote, **Sefia?**

Erastis folded his hands. "Our trackers are as relentless as you. Have patience. They'll find both children soon."

Tanin scratched out Sefia's name. Last time, they'd been fortunate enough to stumble onto the girl's scribblings. *THIS IS A BOOK* scratched into tree trunks and left in the mud like footprints. They could not count on fortune to strike again.

"She's like her parents, isn't she?" the Master Librarian asked. "Truly Lon and Mareah's daughter."

Once, Tanin had been closer to Lon and Mareah than anyone, except perhaps Rajar. The four of them had been inseparable—Librarian, Assassin, Soldier, Administrator. Years ago, they had conspired to unite all Five Islands under the Guard's control, using war—the Red War—to conquer the kingdoms they could not sway by other means. And to do that, they needed the boy from the legends.

The impressors had even been Lon's idea. "We need a boy with a scar around his throat?" he'd said. "Let's go find him."

"How?" Mareah had asked. "We don't have the personnel."

He'd leaned forward eagerly as he outlined his plan. "We set up an organization that gets us boys with the scars we want. Mar, you can teach them how to spot and train candidates. If we offer sufficient compensation, we'll be sure to have the boy on our side when the rest of the plan falls into place."

Rajar had been the most skeptical. "You can't *make* destiny, Lon. You're good, but no one's *that* good."

Lon had lifted his chin, his dark eyes gleaming like two drops of obsidian. "Not alone. But together we can do anything."

The nib of Tanin's pen punctured the page.

"Still so angry." Erastis sighed.

Aren't you?

With one finger, he touched the sheet of paper on her bedside table, tracing the phases of the Red War, each of the kingdoms they planned to conquer in turn:

PHASE I Conquer Everica

PHASE II Ally with Liccaro

PHASE III Ally with Deliene

PHASE IV Conquer Oxscini & Roku

They'd control the Five Islands. They'd eliminate the outlaws. Kelanna would be theirs. Well . . . not all of theirs. Not anymore.

"Why be angry with the dead?" Erastis murmured.

Because they lied. They told me they loved me. But if they loved me, they would have trusted me. They would have believed in me. And they never would have left.

The Master Librarian shook his head. His hand fell to his side.

Tanin's pen skittered across the paper again: *Have you found any more signs of the Book?*

Leaning forward, Erastis examined the words. "I'm afraid n—"

She interrupted him with a flourish of her pen. Ink spattered the coverlet. *Would you tell me if you had?*

The Master Librarian regarded her sadly.

She swallowed, feeling her guilt burning in her throat. Lon and Mareah may have stolen it. Sefia may have fought for it. But Tanin was the one who'd lost it. And everyone in the Guard knew it.

"My dear." Erastis patted the back of her hand. "I love you like I loved them. More, because you stayed. Do not doubt what friends you have."

Friends, she thought with distaste. Against Darion Stonegold, she needed *allies*.

She believed she could count Erastis and his new Apprentice among them, but what about Rajar? Dotan and his Apprentice Administrator? The First Assassin?

She needed their loyalty and their support, not their love.

Most of all, she needed the Book.

And for that, she had to find Sefia.

Chapter 2

Runners

Sefia stared at the pages, stunned. She'd been so sure she'd killed Tanin—the look of surprise, the rush of blood—so sure she'd avenged her family.

She'd been wrong. She'd been wrong about a lot of things.

"The impressors were your father's idea?" Archer asked. His gaze was hard and broken, like a shard of glass. Inadvertently, her gaze fell to the scar at his throat, the ridges and puckered edges.

Archer's kidnapping. His scar. His nightmares.

Her parents' doing.

All the brandings, the torture, the fights. All those dead boys.

Her parents. The parents she'd loved and admired. How could they be capable of *this*?

For a second she wished Archer would take her in his arms, hold her tight and not let go until the world made sense again.

But she couldn't ask that, not anymore. "I—I'm sorry. I didn't know," she whispered.

A muscle twitched in Archer's jaw. The tendons in his scarred neck pulled taut. "You couldn't have known," he said at last. He didn't tell her it was okay, she noticed. Maybe nothing between them would ever be okay again.

"They didn't tell me. No one did." Folding down the corner of the page, Sefia closed the Book. The symbol on the cover seemed to taunt her. Two curves for her parents. A curve for Nin. The straight line for herself. Answers. Redemption. Revenge.

She'd been so naive. She wanted to rip the cover from its spine, wanted to tear something to shreds. Tanin, for killing Nin. Her parents, for keeping so much from her. The Guard, for causing all of this.

But there was only one thing she could do. Only one thing she'd been trained for. Running. Wrapping the Book in its leather casing, Sefia shoved it deep into her pack and brushed a lock of hair from her eyes. "Are you still with me?"

Archer stared at her so long she could almost see his exhaustion forming bruises beneath his eyes. Did he blame her for what her parents had done? Did he want to leave her, after everything they'd been through?

No, please not that.

Finally, he nodded, but he would no longer look her in the eyes.

"Let's go, then."

Briefly, Archer touched his temple and pointed toward Cascarra. Dawn was nearly upon them, and the streets were beginning to stir with life.

"No, we can't get out of Deliene that way anymore. We'll have to go north."

As they packed their things, she described the Szythian Mountains, poised on the northwestern shores of Deliene. The sharp peaks were home to the occasional shepherd and her flock in the summer, but with fall approaching, soon they would all be gone. No one braved the highlands in the cold months, when food and firewood were scarce and the temperatures plunged below freezing.

"Szythia's not my first choice," she said. "But what other choice do we have?"

There was an uncomfortable silence as they shouldered their packs. Before Archer could speak, she'd spent days in his silence. His silence used to feel comfortable, familiar. She used to wrap herself in it like a cloak.

Now his silence was warped by the truth about her parents, the past he could not share with her, the memory of a kiss.

She thought of what Tanin had said about Lon and Mareah, felt the same sting of their secrets . . . and Archer's. *If you loved me, you would trust me.*

Sefia's hands curled around her pack straps. "Come on," she said.

With swift movements, they replaced the mulch where they'd disturbed it and slipped away as dawn crested the peaks and the daylight chased them through the pointed tips of the pines.

To reach the Szythian Mountains, however, they first had to cross the sprawling Delienean Heartland—rolling hills like waves, an ocean of gold dotted by cattle and rippled by wind—open, exposed, dangerous.

On the last crest of the Ridgeline, Archer raised a hand to his eyes, peering across the stretch of land at the center of the Northern Kingdom.

"Have you seen the Heartland before?" Sefia asked, capping her water canteen.

"I've never left Oxscini before."

She glanced up at him, studying the crooked profile of his nose. So he *was* originally from the Forest Kingdom, where she'd found him over a month ago in a crate marked with the ⊖. She wondered if he was from a family of shipbuilders, or loggers from the interior. Maybe they'd been members of the Royal Navy. He could have even been an orphan, his parents killed five years ago when Everica, the Stone Kingdom to the east, declared war on Oxscini.

Was that part of my father's plans too?

Swallowing, she fastened the canteen to her pack again. "We'll have to stay off the roads if we want to make it to Szythia unnoticed."

Wearily, Archer rubbed his eyes, like he was struggling to tell the difference between asleep and awake. "And then?"

She started northward again. "Hopefully we survive the winter."

"And after that?" he asked. "What will we do?"

"I don't know. Keep running."

But somehow, that didn't seem like enough anymore.

As they meandered through the parched hills, they began following a set of cattle tracks, away from the main roads and prying eyes. But soon it became clear they weren't the only ones hoping to avoid being seen.

There were wheel tracks, divots of horseshoes, and dozens of bootprints among the cracked earth and chips of manure. A group that large was one she didn't want to cross.

Blinking, Sefia summoned the Sight, and flickering streams of gold swam across her vision. She used to get dizzy and overwhelmed by the sheer amount of information in the Illuminated world. An ocean of history, ready to sweep her consciousness away from her body, leaving her an empty shell. But since she'd been training, all she needed to focus her Sight was a mark—a scratch, a dent, a scar—something to anchor her awareness.

Focusing on the dusty footprints, she saw that twenty people—some on foot, some on horseback, some on carts—had passed this way only a few hours earlier.

She inhaled sharply. On the backs of the carts were wooden crates, each branded with the ⊖, the symbol from the Book, the same symbol she'd seen six weeks before, when she rescued Archer from a crate just like these.

She blinked again, and her vision cleared.

Archer touched his fingertips to his forehead, his old way of asking a question. *What is it?*

She could have lied. She could have kept this from him. But she would not let this come between them too.

"Impressors," she whispered.

CHAPTER 3

The Call of Thunder

Impressors. The word dredged up the memories that flooded Archer whenever he closed his eyes: Hatchet, Redbeard, Palo Kanta, the fights, chains, and crates, the branding iron on his upper arm—the sizzle of flesh and the stink of singed hair—each burn a sign of his victory.

Of each of the boys he'd killed.

Of the animal he'd been.

At his feet, the wheel ruts and boot prints blurred together as he stared at the dusty track. He touched his arm, his fingers splaying over the burns the impressors had given him. They'd called it the "count"—an official record of his kills. Fifteen fights overseen by arbitrators. Fifteen deaths for which Hatchet got paid handsome amounts of money. Fifteen burns to get him to the final fighting ring in Jahara, where one more kill would get him an audience with the Guard.

His nails dug into his flesh. He'd killed so many more than that. And now he knew it. In the Guard's office beneath Corabel, Rajar had triggered the return of his memories, and with them had come his voice, his conscience, his guilt.

He closed his eyes, and the dream from that morning came rushing back to him, as vivid as if he were living it all over again. He'd completely obliterated Argo's face—teeth and flakes of bone protruding through layers of muscle and flesh.

There was a roaring in his blood.

"That's right, boy!" Hatchet's face swam before him, ruddy skin and watery eyes. "We're going to make a killing off you!"

He leapt for Hatchet's throat.

"Archer!"

He opened his eyes. Sefia was peering up at him, her face filled with concern.

He staggered back, half-afraid he'd attack her in his delirium. "Did they go west?" His voice came out as a growl, unfamiliar even to himself.

She reached for him. "Archer—"

But he drew back again. His limbs ached, wanting to finish the jump, wanting to grab and fight and wound. His body yearned for it. "Did they go west?" he repeated.

For a moment Sefia studied him, and he saw a flicker of guilt in her teardrop eyes. Her father's eyes, she'd told him once.

He knew it wasn't her fault. She wasn't her parents. She hadn't even been born when they'd done those things. But how could he look at her now without seeing the impressors, the fights, the kills? She'd never look at him with such compassion if she knew what he'd done, what he'd been, what kind of violence still thrashed inside of him.

At last, she nodded.

He gripped the hilt of his sword and headed west, with Sefia, for once, trailing behind.

With each step, dust billowed at his heels. With each step, he drew closer to his enemy. His footfalls became a chant: *Soon. Soon. Soon.* He channeled all his anger into that—the promise of retribution. *Soon.*

Dusk came and went. Stars cluttered the sky. But Archer didn't stop until they found the impressors camped under the moonlight.

His heart took up the refrain. *Soon. Soon. Soon.*

Slinging off their packs, Archer and Sefia crept forward, peering through the leaves.

The camp was positioned between a willow thicket and a series of creeks that gleamed faintly beyond the branches. Men and women lounged about, while sentries patrolled the perimeter, guarding the carts, the horses, and the boys hunkered beside a meager fire.

At the sight of them, his anger lashed inside him like a storm on the rocks. *Soon.* The boys were ragged and dirty, shackled at the hands and ankles. Each one had a burn, pink and taut, around his throat.

Archer's hand went to his own neck, tracing the puckered skin. The boys were like him—candidates to lead the Guard to victory in their Red War.

According to legend, the boy with the scar would be the greatest military commander the world had ever seen. He'd conquer all Five Islands in the bloodiest altercation in living memory.

And he'd die soon after. Alone.

Rajar's voice came back to him, low and harsh: *Who are you, boy? Are you the one we've been looking for?*

The leaves rustled as Sefia shifted beside him. "Seven boys?" she whispered. "I thought impressors only had one at a time."

Archer was already tallying up their weaponry, studying the patterns the sentries made as they paced the edge of the clearing. Inside him, the storm was building—almost ready to break. "Hatchet had five when I was kidnapped," he said, sliding his gun from its holster. "The last of them died weeks before you met me."

Some were killed in training, some in the ring. But once Archer had started winning, displaying a gift for violence that made him feared even among his captors, Hatchet hadn't bothered with any other candidates.

Did he know something I didn't? Archer wondered. *Did he suspect?*

"I'll drive off the impressors," he said. He could feel the fight at his fingertips. *Soon.* "Will you free the boys?"

Sefia touched the pocket of her vest where she kept her lock picks. "That's the least I can do," she said.

Archer watched her try and fail to smile, guilt edging her expression. Reaching out, he traced the green feather she wore in her hair.

He could have kissed her, despite everything. Wanted to kiss her. Because if they didn't make it, he wanted to have done it one last time.

But he didn't deserve her. He knew that now. He was a murderer. An animal who couldn't stop himself from killing. Even if he'd wanted to.

Before she could speak, he launched himself through the branches, letting off two quick gunshots before the impressors could even cry out.

Two men dropped dead.

And like a sudden downpour cleansing him of dust, the fight broke over him—brilliant, purifying, clear—he could see every move, every attack and counterattack, every feint and parry and thrust in exquisite detail. Like magic. Like the *reading* Sefia described.

Terrifying . . . and beautiful.

Shouts went up around the clearing as the impressors grabbed their pistols and swords, but they were too slow. Much too slow.

He ran the nearest man through with his blade, felt the steel shiver as it scraped bone.

His nerves sang with the sensation.

Out of the corner of his eye, he saw Sefia dash toward the group of manacled boys. As she passed an impressor, she flung one of her knives. It pierced his shoulder.

With a snarl, he pulled his revolver.

Archer's first instinct was to protect her. Shield her. But he was too far.

"Sefia!" Her name ripped from his throat.

The gun went off. There was an explosion of powder and flame.

Sefia drew herself up to her full height, her eyes blazing, her hair whipping around her shoulders like black water.

She lifted her fingers and, with nothing more than a flick of her wrist, sent the bullet whizzing into the dirt.

The impressor's jaw dropped. Sefia smirked. Sweeping her hand through the air, she threw him into a tree. Branches snapped. He landed at the base of the trunk, an arm twisted beneath him.

She didn't need protection.

Grinning, Archer turned to the fight again. He slashed a woman across the stomach and ducked, pulling her in front of him as the others peppered them with bullets. Her body jerked at each impact—and then was still. Hot blood ran down his arm, slick and satisfying.

He shoved the corpse at the nearest impressor and rushed in among them, hacking, beating, slashing, like the fight was a dance and he knew all the steps.

But even for him, there were too many. Too many bullets to dodge. Too many hits to avoid. A shot grazed him, then another. Someone cut him across the thigh—a flash of pain.

Across the clearing, Sefia unshackled one of the boys. And another.

A woman struck at Archer's exposed side. He knew the sword was coming, saw the arc of the steel. He wouldn't be quick enough to evade it.

He felt the edge score him. This one would bite deep. He

gritted his teeth, anticipating the pain. But before the impressor could finish the blow, another scarred boy bounded up and cut her head from her body with a heavy curved sword.

For a moment, their gazes locked. The boy had black hair and green eyes, and beneath the layer of dirt, his face had the tan, weathered look of someone who lived along the ice—short summers, blisteringly cold winters. Gormani, maybe, from the northernmost province in Deliene. A deep scar ran down his cheek like a trail of water.

As he and Archer stared at each other, a smile split his face wide open.

Then they were fighting side by side, turning away impressors, fighting and killing, their blades glinting with blood and firelight. Together, they were deadly, terrifying, exultant. Through the melee, Archer could hear the boy laughing, his unfettered joy infectious as they defended each other, blocking, jabbing, like lightning and thunder, two parts of a whole.

Together they fought until the impressors ran off or laid down their arms in surrender. As the thrill of battle seeped out of him, Archer watched them bleeding, helpless, in the gravel. He could have killed them. He *wanted* to kill them.

Dimly, he heard Argo's wet, broken voice: *Please. Don't. Please, I beg you. Please . . .*

And he remembered killing him anyway. The moment the rock struck. The moment the words twisted into garbled moans . . . and lapsed into silence.

Archer's vision spun. His injuries throbbed. His weapons were so heavy, they trembled in his hands.

He wasn't the animal anymore.

But deep inside him, he thought he heard the growl of thunder.

Across the clearing, the other boy was staring at him again, his green eyes glinting with such suppressed glee that Archer, to his surprise, found himself grinning back, as if they were little kids sharing some delicious secret.

As Sefia released the last boy from his chains, she turned to Archer, her face flushed with excitement, and before he knew it they were together, his arms around her like he was a lost ship and she was his mooring.

He slid a stray lock of hair back behind her ear, his fingertips burning where they brushed her forehead, her temple, her neck. Sefia held completely still in his arms, as if she were even afraid to breathe.

Kiss her. The thought gripped him. *Before you remember your anger, your guilt, your violence. Before—*

But a sudden cry from the center of camp thrust them apart.

His hands fell to his sides, cold, aching, empty.

The boys had surrounded the prisoners, jeering, prodding, teasing them with the tips of their scavenged weapons. There was the slap of flesh on flesh, and someone let out a laugh: "All right, bonesuckers, who wants to go first?"

CHAPTER 4

Boys with Scars

As Archer and Sefia started toward the group, the others stepped aside for them, revealing four kneeling prisoners, heads bowed.

"Want to pick your mai-dens fair? Check the co-lor of their hair," one of the boys began in a singsong voice, pricking each of the impressors with the tip of a dagger. *"Gol-den yel-low, not yet there. Brown and dry, be-yond com-pare."*

It was a children's rhyme, for children's games.

But they were not children, and this was no game.

"My mother told me to pick the very best one and you are—"

"What are you doing?" Sefia interrupted.

The corners of Archer's lips quirked upward with a sort of dark humor. *He* knew. And he didn't know if he wanted them to stop.

The boy with the dagger paused. He was tall and dark, with a feral expression accentuated by the white patches at the

37

corners of his mouth and eyebrows. It was like his complexion had flaked off in places, leaving cloud-white skin behind. *"It,"* he finished, leveling the blade at the impressor closest to him.

At the edge of the circle, the green-eyed boy hefted his curved sword. "Sorry, sorcerer," he said with a shrug. "I'm going first." Before Sefia could stop him, he stepped forward.

For a second, Archer wanted to cheer with the others. He wanted to see the prisoner's head part from his body, wanted to hear it strike the ground, wanted to see it *roll*.

But he didn't want to be the boy who wanted these things.

He wanted to be the boy who deserved to stand next to the girl beside him.

As the gleaming blade came down, Archer pulled his own sword, deflecting the other boy's weapon into the gravel. Pebbles sprang into the air and came rattling down again like rain.

The boy glared up at him through a fringe of dark curls. He was shorter than Archer, but no less dangerous—wary and bristling like a cornered animal.

This wasn't his partner from the battle. This was a feral creature deprived of its basic needs. A creature Archer too easily recognized in himself.

His palms tingled. He could picture their next moves— countering, thrusting, slashing, drawing blood. It'd be a brutal fight. Satisfying.

At the thought, his arm dropped.

The other boy straightened. "We owe you our thanks, friend, but if you knew what they did to us, you wouldn't be protecting them."

Archer bit back a reply. He'd been cursed and berated,

prodded and beaten. He'd been made to think he had no other choice but kill or die. Turned into a murderer. An animal. With his free hand, he jerked his collar down, showing the others the blistered scar at his throat.

The boy's eyes widened. "Or maybe you do." He looked to Sefia, as if searching her for the same scar, before turning back to Archer. "What's your name, friend? Where'd you come from?"

"Archer. From Oxscini."

"I'm Kaito. Kemura. From the north." The boy reached for Archer's arm, almost touching the two brands visible beneath the fold of his sleeve. "How many did you—"

Archer's kills flashed through his mind—battered, disfigured, impaled, all of them surprised.

"Too many," he murmured.

The thought flashed across his mind before he could stop it: *And not enough.*

"How about one more?" Kaito waved him toward the impressors. As if on command, the other boys backed away. "You deserve it."

Archer's fingers tightened on his sword. He deserved a lot of things for what he'd done. Did he deserve this, for what had been done to him?

The nearest impressor blinked up at him through eyelashes encrusted with blood.

Watery eyes, like Hatchet's.

It would be easy. It would be *right*.

"Archer," Sefia whispered.

The name brought him back. *His* name, not *boy* or *bootlicker*.

He wasn't back there anymore. He didn't *have* to kill, didn't have to be what they'd made him.

He shook his head.

"Suit yourself," Kaito said, attacking again.

And again, Archer turned the blow aside.

The other boys roared in protest.

Kaito snarled. "I like you, Archer, but do that again and you won't like *me*."

Archer sheathed his sword. He'd fought too many other boys, killed too many, in the past two years. He'd never do it again. "This won't change what they did to you," he said.

"But it'll be fun."

He thought of the way the violence had washed over him like a sudden storm, riotous, inescapable, before retreating again, leaving him dry and thirsting for more. "It'll be temporary," he said.

"Fun's always temporary."

"What about when it's over?"

"Over?" Kaito's eyes flashed, green as glass. "It'll never be over."

"I don't want to believe that," Archer said softly. "For you, or for me."

For a moment it seemed like Kaito would fight him. Would fight anyone or anything for no other reason than that he needed to fight. But then he stepped back, licking his lips. "You saved us, friend, so we owe you this favor," he muttered. "You want responsibility for these bonesuckers? Take it. But don't make me regret giving it to you."

"You won't," Sefia said.

He rubbed the scar on his cheek. "All right." He nodded at the others, and they hauled up the impressors, marching them, not without a little roughness, toward the crates.

As Kaito turned to join them, Archer caught him by the elbow. "Thank you," he said.

"I don't want your thanks." The boy tossed his dark curls out of his eyes. "I want your word that whatever you do with the impressors, it'll be as good as if they were dead."

With a glance at Sefia, Archer nodded.

"Good." In a sudden turn of mood, Kaito slapped him on the shoulder. "Come on, let me introduce you to the others."

A t Sefia's urging, Archer and the others smothered the fires, loaded the carts with the prisoners and supplies, and abandoned the dead. With some of the impressors still out there, they couldn't risk staying.

Astride their stolen horses, they sneaked off into the night.

Now that he no longer had a fight to look forward to, Archer's exhaustion returned. His limbs were leaden. His eyes kept closing. And though he hadn't ridden a horse in over two years, he kept nodding off in the saddle, only to jerk himself awake again, away from his dreams.

He tried to listen for sounds of pursuit, but there was only the gentle lull of hoofbeats, the water, and the whispering of the boys. They were curious about Sefia—who she was, where she got her powers.

She told them little: She and Archer were being hunted by Serakeen's trackers; she'd inherited her powers from her parents. Half-truths, meant to protect them.

Neither she nor Archer mentioned the Book, or the Guard, or her parents' involvement with the impressors.

Archer watched her ride ahead, leading the others through the water. She would have helped them even if she hadn't felt guilty about Lon and Mareah. That was who she was.

When she'd found him, he'd been *nothing*—not a person, barely an animal. He'd had to rebuild himself to become Archer: the boy with no past and a bright future with the girl who'd saved him.

But now that he remembered what he'd done, all the ways he'd done it, he couldn't just be Archer. Or the nameless animal from his memories. Or the boy he'd been before that—the lighthouse keeper who'd never been in a fight in his life.

All he knew was, whoever he was now, he didn't deserve her.

They didn't stop until they were miles from the impressors' camp, where they groomed the horses and put them up for the night. Archer posted sentries. They laid out their bedrolls and blankets. But no one seemed to want to sleep.

Instead, they sat under the stars and talked. They spoke for hours, sharing stories of their kills, mutilations, and captures, the names of their hometowns and of the families who thought they were dead—and whenever they began to tire, they shook themselves awake again and reached for another story.

It was like they needed stories more than they needed sleep or water or air. Like stories would bring them back from wherever they'd had to go these past months—these *years*—to survive.

At first Archer marveled at how much they remembered. But the more he listened, the more he understood: It was because of Kaito. Kaito was their leader, the one who'd kept them whispering to each other when they were shackled in the night, kept them repeating their names so they wouldn't forget. He'd kept them together even as they were forced to hurt each other in training.

He was a born leader, a better brother-in-arms than anyone could've asked for. If Archer had had a friend like Kaito, maybe he would have come through his captivity less broken. If he'd had a friend like Kaito, maybe he still wouldn't have so far to go.

The next time the conversation subsided, Archer cleared his throat and leaned forward. Beside him, Sefia sat up a little straighter. He could feel her arm pressing against his own, like a reminder—*I'm with you.*

"I—" Archer began. "The first boy I—"

But he kept hearing Hatchet's voice and the explosion of the bullet, kept picturing the spray of blood and brain matter, kept feeling it strike his cheeks, hot and wet.

Panic skittered through his veins. His pulse quickened. He couldn't breathe. He could barely see.

Grasping in his pocket for the worry stone, he clasped it so tight its facets dug into his skin. *I'm not back there anymore,* he told himself. *I'm safe.*

Slowly, the refrain brought him back. His body echoed. His blood slowed. *I'm safe. I'm safe.*

But he couldn't tell them what he'd done. If he did, if he brought all the things he did in his nightmares out into the light, where he couldn't look away, it made them real. It made him the monster he already feared he was.

Sefia sat back again. He hated the disappointment etched into her features, hated himself for disappointing her. But he didn't deserve anything but her disappointment, her judgment, her revulsion. He tried to catch her eye, to tell her he was sorry, but she avoided his gaze.

In the silence, Kaito got to his feet. "Come on," he said, beckoning to Archer. "I bet the sentries could use a break."

The sentries had been changed less than an hour before. But now, sensing Archer's discomfort, Kaito was watching out for him, same as any of the others.

When Archer stood, Sefia suddenly became absorbed with her hair, splitting the ends of each strand apart one by one as if there were nothing more important in that moment.

"Don't do that!" Frey, sitting next to her, flicked out a spring-loaded blade and extended it handle first. "You've got to trim it or it'll just get worse. Before my mom died, she used to scold me all the time for ruining my hair. Good thing she taught me how to deal with it before she and my dad were gone, because my brothers could not have cared less . . ."

Frey's voice faded as Archer and Kaito walked into the darkness, where they sent Versil, the boy with the dagger from earlier, and his twin, Aljan, back to the group.

As they began patrolling the clearing with its rocks and willows, so like the one they'd just left, Kaito ran a hand up and down his scarred cheek. "You know, they used to tell us fifteen was a magic number. Fifteen, and we'd go to the Cage. Win there, and it would be over. Win there, and we'd be free."

"Winners get sent to some place called the Academy."

"A school?"

Archer shrugged.

"I didn't believe them, not really." Kaito fidgeted with his sword, drawing it halfway out of his scabbard and letting it slide back again with a sharp *clack*. "But I fought harder. I killed everyone I came up against. Because it wasn't about the freedom, was it? It was about the fighting. And now I *am* free . . . but when I think of those bonesuckers still out there, all I want is to keep fighting."

"You mean the ones we ran off tonight?"

Clack, clack. "And the rest. The other crews in Deliene. The ones in Liccaro and Everica and Oxscini . . . even Roku, probably."

Archer looked up sharply. "How many Delienean crews are there?" he asked.

"Four, including our—including the one we broke up tonight."

Three crews of impressors still in Deliene. Three crews of impressors still kidnapping boys and turning them into killers. Three chances to fight, to strike back against the Guard. And prove he wasn't their monster. He was someone else. Someone new. And if he did this, maybe he'd find out who that was.

Later, as Archer returned to the group, he couldn't stop thinking of it. *Three crews left in Deliene.*

And Kaito's words: *All I want is to keep fighting.*

As he drew near, he heard Frey speaking again: "All these months, they made me . . . They didn't believe me when I . . ."

Frey, Archer had learned, was a girl. That was why Kaito had thought Sefia might have been a candidate too. At first glance,

Frey had had the same straight hips and stubbled jaw as the others, but once she'd donned a blouse and riding skirt she'd found among the impressors' things, she'd started carrying herself in a way that made it impossible to see her as anything other than the girl she was. In fact, sitting beside Sefia, with their black hair and high cheekbones, they looked remarkably like sisters.

Sefia shifted aside for Archer as he sat down again, but she still didn't look at him.

"It was last summer," Frey continued, "and my friends and I were going out swimming. But the impressors caught us before we even made it to the river. We were so afraid. They separated the girls from the boys . . ."

"I don't know what my friend Render thought was going to happen, but when the impressors put me with the other girls and started executing us, he leapt forward. 'That's not a girl!' he shouted. At first they laughed at him, but he kept saying it. 'That's not a girl! That's not a girl!' " She balled her fists.

"Your friend betrayed you?" Sefia asked.

"He *killed* me. In a different way. In a way that hurt worse than one of their bullets. I'd known him my whole life. I trusted him. I thought he . . . Maybe he wanted to protect me, but he should've known . . ." Frey's gaze turned stony. "After a week, he begged me to kill him. And the next time we trained, I did."

Again, Archer heard Hatchet's command, *Fight, or he dies.* Again, he felt the mist of blood on his lips. In his pocket, he clutched the worry stone to stave off his panic. But this time the refrain was different, and it calmed him immediately.

Three crews.

Keep fighting.

Swallowing, Sefia wrapped her arms around her knees. Guilt suffused her features, and he knew she was thinking of her parents. "I'm so sorry," she said. "I'm sorry they took you."

Frey touched her burned throat. Her eyes narrowed to slits. "I wasn't who they were looking for. None of us were."

CHAPTER 5

The Hunters and the Hunted

When Frey and the boys finally retired, Archer and Sefia took over the watch. They climbed up the rocks that overlooked the creek, where they perched on the cold stones, scanning their surroundings for signs of their enemy.

With all her years of practice, Sefia blended into the shadows so perfectly it was like she became part of the rocks and the wild. Watching her, Archer thought of all they'd done—the days in the jungle, the nights on the *Current of Faith*, the Cage, the office of the Guard, the escape, the kiss—all the distance they'd traveled together.

Would she still be with him, in this?

She caught him staring. "That's what you went through?" she asked. "The things the others said?"

Archer nodded.

A flash of hurt crossed her features and she turned away.

He wanted to apologize. He wanted to explain. But he didn't. "About the prisoners . . ." he began.

"We can't let them go. They can't just *get away* with it."

"They won't." He looked out over the horizon, the black silhouettes of hills against the stars. "Not if we turn them over to the law."

Sefia's gaze was piercing even in darkness. "Yeah. I like that. It'll be a nice change before we run again."

Archer ran a finger along the edge of his scar. *Three crews left in Deliene.* "What if we didn't run at all?" he asked. "What if we *fought*?"

"The Guard?" Sefia looked skeptical. "Tanin's coming after us with everything she's got. We can't—"

"The impressors. The people who did this to us." He nodded toward camp, where the others lay under their blankets: Mako, the youngest, sprawled across the ground like he couldn't take up enough space; some, like Kaito, curled up in tight protective balls. "We can fight the impressors and strike back against the Guard. We can *stop* them. We already have, you and me."

"There's got to be hundreds of impressors in Kelanna . . ."

"I know. It might be impossible." His gaze skipped over the willows, the pockets of shadow in the rocks, the shine on the water, before meeting hers at last. "But we can start with Deliene. Kaito said there are still three crews here."

"Rid Deliene of the impressors," Sefia murmured, as though to herself.

"You could use the Book to find them."

"Ha." She laughed humorlessly. "Wouldn't that be fitting? Using the Guard's greatest weapon against them?"

He nodded. "Someone's got to be responsible for stopping them."

And who better than one of their own creations? he thought. To make up for the boys he'd killed? To save the ones who still had a chance?

"Yeah," Sefia muttered grimly, and he knew she wasn't talking about him when she added, *"someone."* In the starlight, she lifted her first two fingers, crossed one over the other.

Their sign. That they were together.

"My family started this," she said. "I'll help you finish it."

He brushed his scar. Through his fingertips, he could feel his own blood pulsing with the promise of fights to come.

"But if we start picking off impressors," she warned him, "Tanin's going to notice. And then she'll know how to hunt us."

Archer nodded, anticipation curling the corners of his lips. "Let her hunt. We've hunting of our own to do."

For the first time in weeks, he didn't dream. Even when Mako woke up shrieking and the others had to calm him down, none of Archer's flashbacks came swooping over him in the darkness. No memories stirred his rest.

As he drifted back into consciousness, Archer could feel all of his cuts and bruises, the little stones beneath his bedroll, and the morning breeze with the kind of clarity he hadn't experienced since his time on the *Current of Faith*.

It was like the violence from the previous night had washed him clean.

He opened his eyes.

Most of the others were already up—walking the perimeter, sorting supplies, rinsing in the creek.

There, Sefia stood calf-deep in the water, her trousers rolled to her knees. As she dipped her fingers and ran them through her hair, drops trickled down her shoulders to the backs of her hands, falling into the water like beads of light.

He would've given anything to trace those rivers along the length of her arms, his touch lingering on the bends of her elbows, her knuckles and nail beds. Or to kneel before her in the cold creek, sliding water up her calves with his cupped palms.

Maybe one day, when he'd stopped enough impressors, when he'd saved enough boys, when he was finally good enough for her, he would.

She glanced up. He knew that look—focused, determined, daring. He'd seen it over and over again as they tracked Hatchet and his impressors through Oxscini. As they'd do again, in Deliene, with Frey and the boys, if he could enlist their help.

He packed away his blanket and made his way to the makeshift kitchen, where two of the boys were sitting. One of them—Griegi, with curly hair and freckles like cinnamon—looked up and smiled, making his round cheeks even rounder. "I started some coffee brewing last night," he said, slathering rolls with jam. "Though I could've done better if we'd had a fire."

Scarza, the boy beside him, set down a piece of the rifle he'd been taking apart. "I can't wait till you actually cook something for us," he said, "and we see if it stands up to all your big talk."

Griegi smiled. "It will."

With a soft chuckle, Scarza began dismantling the gun again. Missing his left hand and the lower part of his left arm, he'd brace the weapon against his elbow or sling it over his shoulder to get it to come apart, his right hand moving so quickly along the stock it was like the pieces came flying off on their own.

"You're good," Archer said, filling two cups with cold coffee.

"At fieldstripping a rifle, or doing it one-handed?"

"Both."

Scarza lifted his eyes briefly. Strong and dark-skinned, he was maybe twenty, the eldest of them all, though not old enough for his close-cropped silver hair. "Been dealing with guns since I could talk. Been one-handed since I was born."

"Guess that means you can shoot too."

Scarza didn't brag, like someone else might have. He just nodded and continued taking the rifle apart, the sharp *click*s of metal rattling around them.

Archer sipped at the coffee. Griegi had added extra ingredients to it—spices, nutmeg maybe. Something deep and rich.

"You brewed this cold?" he asked.

Humming contentedly, Griegi drizzled a sweet-smelling glaze over the rolls. "Yep. It's an old recipe of my grandpa's. Didn't have half the ingredients, but I made do."

"Sometimes Grieg kept us all fed on descriptions of his grandpa's cooking," Scarza said. His hair glinted almost white in the morning sun.

Griegi blushed nearly as red as his curls at the compliment.

In the ensuing silence, Versil, the boy with the dagger, danced up to Archer and relieved him of his second mug. "That for me?" he asked, laughing.

"It was supposed to be Kaito's."

"Oops." The boy wrinkled his nose and the white patches of skin on his face bunched. "Eh. You just tell him Aljan took it."

"I thought you were Versil."

The lanky boy laughed again. "I am. Aljan's over there." He pointed to the creek, where another broomstick-slender boy was sitting in the sand, staring absently into space. Except for the dashes of white on Versil's face and palms, the brothers could have been mirror images of each other.

"I know it's hard to tell us apart," Versil said cheerily. "Just remember, I'm the better-looking one. I'm also taller, smarter, funnier—"

"And you have a bigger mouth," Scarza added wryly.

Beaming, Versil poured another cup of coffee and handed it to Archer with a flourish. "For Kaito."

Tipping the mug at him, Archer left them for the edge of the clearing, where Kaito was making the rounds.

Unlike the others, however, he looked no better for a night of freedom. The skin beneath his eyes was swollen with lack of sleep and a bruise purpled one of his cheeks.

"You look wrecked," Archer said as he joined him.

"Yeah. And I still look better than you."

With a grin, he passed Kaito the second mug and fell into step beside him. Kaito's attention was everywhere, flitting from the willows to the sky to the large blue dragonflies flicking past on translucent wings. The rest of him was always in movement too, plucking leaves from the bushes, scooping up handfuls of stones and skipping them one by one across the water, drumming out frenetic rhythms on the pommel of his sword.

He even drank fast, downing most of Griegi's coffee in a few quick gulps. For a few minutes, it was like they were any other boys, hiking along a creek in search of fish, freshwater roots, or mischief.

"So," he said, wiping his mouth on his sleeve, "you made it all the way to the Cage."

And just like that, Archer was brought back to reality. They *weren't* like other boys. They were a breed apart, bonded by what they'd had to do to survive. Nodding, he turned his cup in his hands.

"Who'd you fight?"

"A boy named Haku and a boy named Gregor." Both of them wounded but alive the last time he saw them, bleeding in the sawdust.

Kaito cursed and ran his fingers through his curls a couple of times. "I knew Gregor," he said. "He killed one of ours."

"I didn't kill him, though."

"Uh-huh. Then you met Serakeen?"

Archer nodded again.

"You lucky dog!" The boy leapt on him, all arms. Coffee splashed the tips of Archer's boots. "What I would've given to be you!"

"I didn't kill *him* either." Shoving Kaito away, Archer couldn't help but laugh at his exuberance. How the boy could switch so easily from one mood to another—pensive, gleeful, hot with fury—was beyond him.

But he liked it.

"Wouldn't expect anything else of a lumberjack," Kaito said. "The only thing Oxscinians are good at killing is trees."

Though it wasn't home anymore, Archer felt a flare of pride in the Forest Kingdom. He roughed up Kaito's hair, and they scuffled good-naturedly for few seconds, kicking up gravel. "Tell that to everybody we conquered in the Expansion," Archer said, pulling the boy into a headlock.

"Never met any!" Kaito declared as he ducked out of Archer's grasp. "You never even got close to Gorman."

Archer allowed himself a grin as they continued their circuit of the perimeter. He'd had friends like this, once, friends to needle and wrestle and banter. Friends who understood you beyond words. He might've known Kaito for less than a day, but it was like they'd been friends their whole lives.

He hoped the boy would come with them.

In fact, Archer couldn't imagine hunting the impressors without him.

At the center of the clearing, most of the others had gathered around the fire, digging into the breakfast Griegi had prepared. Versil stole a roll from his brother's plate, but was soon so distracted by the story he was telling that he stopped eating altogether.

"How quickly they forget," Kaito said.

Before Archer could reply, there was a voice above them, in the willows: "Not all of us."

He looked up to find Frey lounging in the branches, her legs dangling over their heads.

"How long've you been up there?" Kaito asked.

"Long enough to hear you insulting me and all my family," she said, swinging down between them with the grace of someone who'd spent her life in the treetops.

The Gormani boy grinned. "Aw, c'mon, Frey, you know I didn't mean *Shinjai* lumberjacks—"

"Uh-huh." Waving him off, she went to join the others.

"She's from Shinjai?" Archer asked.

"Whole family of lumberjacks. Her parents were killed in a logging accident when she was seven. She was basically raised by her three older brothers." Kaito paused. "I should've known she'd be in a tree. Trees were almost all she talked about when we were in the crates. That's where she went when her parents died, you know. Whenever something bad happened, she'd find a tree to climb. She said it made her feel safe."

They fell silent again, and the shorter boy eyed Archer appraisingly. "So . . ." he began after a moment. "What'd you and the sorcerer decide? Do I get to kill some more impressors today?"

"Not today."

Kaito's expression fell.

"But maybe soon, if you'll join us," Archer said. "There are three crews left in Deliene, after all."

The boy's reaction came immediately—in the widening of his pupils, the lightening of the shadows in his green eyes. It was like he was waking for the first time that morning. "I'm in," he said.

Archer let out a relieved laugh. Of course Kaito was in. "Even if we turn over any survivors to the law?"

Kaito clapped him on the shoulder. "Brother, if you give me even the smallest chance at killing impressors, I'll follow you anywhere."

"It'll be dangerous," Archer said, though he could already anticipate Katio's reply.

The boy bared his teeth in what passed for a grin. "It better be."

As they rejoined the others, the talk died down. Frey and the boys looked up at them expectantly.

Clearing his throat, Archer described their plan: hunt down the remaining impressors in Deliene, free the rest of the boys, and make sure none of the impressors showed their faces in the Northern Kingdom again.

First they had to turn over their current prisoners in the nearest town. After that, there'd be three crews left.

Three crews to fight.

"You should go home, if you can, but if you're like me, well . . ." he paused. "This is the only way forward for me."

Frey and the boys were silent, mulling over what he'd said. What he'd proposed and the purpose he offered them. A purpose, maybe, for their suffering.

Or out of it.

Aljan, the quieter of the twins, glanced nervously at Sefia. "Will the sorcerer be with us?"

When she answered, she wasn't looking at the tall boy but at Archer, her gaze steady as an arrow, ready for flight. "I'm with you," she said.

Archer smiled.

"We're all with you, brother." Standing, Kaito bowed his head and crossed his forearms.

Scarza did the same. One by one, the others joined them.

Startled, Archer recognized the gesture: It was an old Delie-nean salute from the ancient Gormani clans in the north. A sign of respect warriors made when saluting their captains. He'd seen old Goro and some of the other sailors on the *Current* do it to Captain Reed, once or twice.

Turn over the prisoners.

Three crews left.

Bowing his head, he saluted them back.

CHAPTER 6

That's What
You're Remembered For

Liccaro had always been known as the Desert Kingdom—an island crescent of sand dunes and red rock wilderness—but it hadn't always been wretched. Its people hadn't always been stricken by poverty; its regents hadn't always been corrupt; and it hadn't always been prey to pirates like Serakeen, Scourge of the East.

Once, it had been so prosperous you could stroll through its creek beds picking up gemstones and nuggets of gold. People used to come from every corner of Kelanna for the art, the jewelry, the palaces bedecked in mosaics of lapis and malachite.

But everything changed when the last Liccarine monarch, King Fieldspar, seized all his kingdom's amassed wealth and sailed off in a fleet of gilded galleons that would have eclipsed the splendor of Captain Dimarion's *Crux* tenfold.

According to legend, the king's men took a fortnight to bury all the treasure, deep in an underground labyrinth where no one could find it. When they were done, the king ordered all but his own crew into the caves, where he barricaded them inside and left them to rot, their bones standing watch over the Trove for the rest of time.

He scuttled his galleons, sparing only his flagship, the *Desert Gold*, and set off for the capital. But on the return journey, the *Gold* sank in the treacherous waters of the Ephygian Bay. The king and all his sailors were drowned.

Some thought the Trove was lost forever.

Others said the king had inscribed its location inside the bell of the *Desert Gold*, now resting somewhere in the depths of the bay.

For generations, treasure hunters had searched for the bell, braving the maze of sandbars and submerged peaks, searching the wrecks beneath the turquoise waves.

But no one had found it. No one even knew where to begin looking.

Until now.

The bell may have remained with the sunken ship, but the clapper had been carried by the currents all the way across the Central Sea, where it had washed up on some distant shore, a perfect prize for beachcombers and curious children. Since then it had been traded, sold, and traded again, passing from one kingdom to another only to end up in a tavern of liars, where Captain Reed and his crew had stolen it.

For, unbeknownst to any of its previous owners, there was more to the clapper than fine handiwork and verdigris.

The clapper, like many objects in Kelanna, was magic. And when you brought it near its bell, they would call to each other—strike the clapper and the bell would cry out, lonely and wild, for its missing tongue.

After that, all you had to do was follow the sound to the wreck of the *Gold*.

Another man might have wanted the Trove itself—the greatest hoard in Kelanna. Dimarion certainly did. But for Reed it had never been about treasure.

It was about glory. A way to keep his memory alive when his body was nothing but ash.

But after meeting the liars in the Crossbars back in Jahara, he couldn't help but wonder which version of him would survive—Cannek Reed, adventurer and treasure seeker, or some selfish, flamboyant outlaw he wouldn't recognize, face-to-face at high noon?

Was it enough to live on in legend if the legends were lies?

Captain Reed rubbed his wrist, where his bare skin stood out like a bracelet among the tattooed images of ships and storms, skulls and ancient sea creatures. Every adventure he'd ever had was inked on his skin, along his arms and around his torso—except one.

The edge of the world.

The place of the fleshless.

The hairs on the back of Reed's neck rose as he remembered the cold, the way it had sucked the warmth out of him like a leech. Deep in his memory, he heard the echo of voices—inhuman, half-shriek and half-thunder—calling him into the black water.

Could he build a legacy grand enough—when only some of it was true—to overcome *that*?

He tapped his fingers eight times on the edge of the long-boat, listening hard. Navigating the snarls of coral and shifting shallows of the Ephygian Bay was so dangerous they'd taken to the rowboats like mayflies on the water, searching for the *Desert Gold*.

To the west, the *Current* rested easily on the sea, her green hull reflected by the waves, her tree-shaped figurehead spiraling up the bowsprit into the sweltering sky. Beside her lay Dimarion's ship, the *Crux*—a monstrous golden vessel with a diamond at its prow.

From the deck of the *Current* came the tolling of the ship's bell, not its normal bright note, but the knell of lost things—the sound it made when it was struck with the clapper from the bell of the *Desert Gold*.

Reed and the crew in the boat were silent, the sun on their backs and the palms of the nearest desert island undulating with heat.

But they heard no answer from the depths.

Meeks sighed, leaning back against the side of the boat. "Nope, I got nothin'."

Goro held up a hand to silence him.

"What?"

The old sailor nodded at Jules, whose head was still cocked toward the waves. Tattoos of birds and flowers wound along her arms, disappearing around the brown curves of her shoulders. One of their chanty leaders, Jules had a musical voice and a sensitive ear that made her likely to pick up the calling of the *Desert Gold*, if they were close enough. Tossing a wave of black hair out of her eyes, she scowled at Meeks. "You don't have to announce it every time," she said.

"But I didn't hear anything!"

Goro grunted. "That's 'cause you were yappin'."

"So no one else could hear anything either," Jules added.

"Ears are your thing." Meeks shrugged, twisting one of the colored beads woven into his dreadlocks. "I'm here for my eyes." Besides Aly, their steward, their second mate had the sharpest eyes, and could spy a signal flag or spot of trouble long before any of them even noticed a change on the horizon.

Leaning back, Jules kicked lightly at his boot. "That's the good thing about eyes—ears too, come to mention it—you can use 'em without runnin' your trap."

With a flourish, he made a show of snapping his mouth closed.

Jules kicked at him once more, but she didn't hide her smile. On their journey in from Jahara, Meeks had already warned them away from Oxscinian patrols, Everican scouts, and the black-and-yellow hunters of Serakeen's pirate fleet.

Once, you could've sailed the whole Central Sea without worrying about anything more than a pillager or a privateer. Now, Oxscini and Everica were warring in the open ocean, while the Scourge of the East seized entire swaths of Liccarine sea. Kelanna was changing. And not for the better.

Reed took up an oar in his weather-roughened hands. "Maybe we'll hear something from the other side of this island."

But as they rounded the tree-lined shore, the sight on the beach brought them up short.

All along the sand were bits of flotsam, barrels and nets and splintered timbers, a halo of debris circling a beaten, beached ship.

The hull of the wreck was punctured in more places than Reed could count, her sails cut to ribbons, one of her masts snapped. Even her figurehead, a little leaping dog, had pieces missing.

"The *Bad Eye*," Meeks said.

The *One Bad Eye* had always been a scrappy vessel, with a penchant for picking fights and running from them as soon as the tide turned. But her home waters were the Anarran Sea near Everica. Strange for her to be this far north.

Before they could row in, there was a loud *crack* from the beach. A bullet skinned Goro's arm and sank into the water.

They ducked into the boat as a slew of gunfire splintered the wooden siding.

Meeks swore.

Goro clamped his hand over his wound. A trail of blood seeped into the bilgewater at the bottom of the longboat.

Sweeping off his hat, Reed drew the Lady of Mercy from its holster. The revolver's ivory grip warmed in his palm, as if welcoming his touch.

From behind one of the piles of wreckage that littered the beach, there was a flash of movement.

Reed fired. Someone behind the rubble yelped.

Jules ripped off Goro's sleeve and looped it around his arm, knotting it tight over his wound. "Time to use those eyes, Meeks. How many do we got in this bushwhack?"

The second mate peeped over the gunwale. "Captain Bee and four of her crew, with more comin' down the beach."

Bullets struck the boat again, ricocheting off the oarlocks with sharp *ping*s.

"How's the arm, Goro?" Reed asked.

The old salt glowered up at him. "It ain't interferin' with my trigger finger."

"Good." Then, taking a deep breath, the captain bellowed, "Bee!"

The gunfire ceased.

"That the captain of the *Current* I got pinned in that there longboat?" came the reply.

A chorus of laughter rose from behind the debris.

"That cocky little—" Meeks grumbled.

"Pinned?" Reed barked. "I could put all of you down faster'n you could cry mercy!"

His crew exchanged knowing grins. There was only one person faster on the draw than Captain Reed, and she was long-retired.

She'd given him the Lady of Mercy, the exquisite ivory-and-silver revolver he carried now.

"All right, don't get your braies in a bunch," came the response. "Come on in."

Reed and his sailors kept their guns at the ready as they rowed in, but neither Bee nor any of her crew moved to attack.

Captain Bee nodded at them as they reached the island. She was injured, Reed saw now, cuts peppering one half of her body—the kind of wounds you'd get from canister shot, maybe—and a bandage wrapped around her upper thigh.

"Just like you to shoot first and ask questions later," he said. They didn't shake hands, only looked each other up and down like they were studying storm clouds.

The rest of her crew sported injuries too—broken arms, bruised faces. Whoever they'd scrapped with, they were lucky to have come out alive.

Only one of them was freshly wounded, blood running from his ear, staining the collar of his shirt. As the crew of the *Current* approached, he spat in the sand, stopping Reed short.

Meeks and Goro went for their guns, but Captain Reed shook his head.

"Pay him no mind," Bee said, jerking her thumb at her crewman. "His ear didn't do him no good before, or he woulda took cover when I said."

"Looks like you ain't the only one with hearin' problems, Meeks," Jules said.

Bee's injured sailor glared at her, but the second mate laughed.

"Sorry 'bout that," Bee continued, nodding at Goro's bandaged biceps. "After what we been through, I wasn't takin' no chances."

The old sailor flexed his arm and grunted, accepting her apology.

"Exactly what *have* you been through?" Reed asked.

"The Blue Navy," she answered, her voice hard.

"What'd you do? Pick a fight with one of their scouts?"

Her lip curled. "I ain't tangled with them since Stonegold took power five years ago. This was unprovoked."

Captain Reed frowned. The Blue Navy, so-called for its blue and gray colors, was Everica's military force, under the control of King Darion Stonegold. For five years, they'd been preoccupied fighting their rival kingdom, Oxscini. For five years, they'd been picking off outlaws that got caught in their skirmishes, making the Central Sea a little smaller, a little less free.

But they didn't gun down ships without cause.

At least, not until now.

"Them bluejackets show up outta nowhere and tell us we're in their waters. *Their waters.* I thought Serakeen claimin' the seas was bad enough, but now some rock-thumpin' bootlickers want the water too?" Bee's hands strayed to her six-guns and dropped again. She had no one to fight. She'd already been beaten.

Reed squinted at the water. For as long as anyone could remember, the Five Islands had been ruled by infighting kings and queens, by laws and armies and people who craved the stability they provided. The merciless blue sea was supposed to be a place for those who valued freedom above all things. A place for you to go where you liked, where you lived or died on your own talents and the talents of your crew. Even a new king like Stonegold should know better than to lay claim to territory that had been lawless for thousands of years.

Behind him, Meeks muttered under his breath, echoing Reed's own thoughts: "Can't be."

"Believe it, bucko. Any outlaw in the southeast will tell you the same. If there's any of 'em left," Bee said bitterly.

"More casualties?" Reed asked.

Bee ticked off the names of the ships on the tips of her

chapped fingers: "The *Graybird*, the *Pickax*, the *Only Star*, the *Fool's Gold* . . ."

He kept expecting her to stop, but the names kept coming, rattling inside him like buckshot.

"The *Rose* and the *Marilyn*, the *Better Luck Next Time*, the *Water Dog*—"

"The *Beauty*?" he interrupted. The *Black Beauty* was a black ship with black sails and a captain as mean as she was beautiful. She was like a mythic creature—boundless and unbroken, as much legend as she was reality—that you hoped would never be tamed.

She and Reed had been on civil terms last they'd met, but that was before Dimarion and Reed had formed an alliance, racing the *Beauty* for the Trove. He didn't think the captain would be happy when she found out he'd teamed up against her, but he'd rather risk her wrath than never have it light up the water again.

"Nah." Bee shrugged. "I figger she's lyin' low like us. The bluejackets have more firepower than we thought. Even the *Beauty* ain't got the gumption to take on warships like theirs."

"Wouldn't bet on it," Reed said.

Bee looked about to reply when a bell tolled from the other side of the island. Jules tensed, laying a hand on Meeks's arm, as if that would stop him from speaking. He pretended to lock his lips and toss aside a key.

Bee raised an eyebrow at them. "Say, where you anchored? You oughta git the *Current* on the north side of the islands. Seein' as this archipelago's technically part of Liccaro, I don't reckon we'll see any bluejackets up here. But I didn't reckon they'd start chasin' us outta our own seas either."

"Serakeen's on the north side of the islands." Out of the corner of his eye, Reed caught sight of a flicker of gold on the water. A signal flag. One of the *Crux*'s longboats must have heard something—the bell of the *Desert Gold*?

Bee looked from Reed to the water and back. "Somethin' out there, Reed?"

He chuckled. "Something's always out there, Captain." He motioned his crew back to their boat.

"Reed." Bee's voice stopped him. All traces of good humor had left her face, leaving her looking drawn and weary. "We could use your help with the *Bad Eye*."

Behind her, the shipwreck was a blight on the beach—a sorry memory of what she used to be.

In other circumstances he might have helped her. It would've only cost him his time.

But time was something he didn't have. Not if he wanted to stay one step ahead of Dimarion before he double-crossed him. Not if he wanted to outrace the *Black Beauty*, wherever she was, to the Trove. Not if he wanted to make this adventure grand enough to weather the erosions of time and retelling.

"Not this time, Captain."

She started forward, reaching for his arm. "You can take us with you, wherever you're goin'. We don't need no spoils, just enough to keep the old wreck afloat. It ain't safe out there no more, not for a lone ship." She stretched out her hands. "Please. We're sittin' ducks without you."

Reed shrugged. "You're smart. Once you get your ship repaired, you'll be fast. That's all you need."

She held his gaze, and for a moment he thought she'd try to fight him. Her crew outnumbered his, after all.

Reed's hands brushed his guns.

"Please," was all she said.

"Sorry, Captain. We're goin'," he said. He and his crew began backing away. "Best of luck to you."

"You're killin' us," Bee called as they splashed into the shallows. "I hope you remember that, when you're tellin' this tale in taverns all across Kelanna."

Reed stiffened as the words struck him, but he didn't turn back.

As they rowed away from shore, Meeks, Jules, and Goro were solemn.

"Cap, shouldn't we—" Meeks began.

"Bee's shrewd as a snake and twice as sly," Reed interrupted. "She'll make it."

Jules set down her oars. "Since when do you turn your back on folks in need?"

"They ain't my crew."

"Neither was Captain Cat, or Sefia and Archer."

"They was all goin' our way."

"I wasn't," Jules retorted with an unusual sting in her smooth voice, "and you still took me in."

Reed clicked his tongue. Jules had been running from a bad situation when he'd met her, back when he was just a ship's boy on the *Current*. He hadn't thought to ask permission to bring her aboard when she came to him. He just did it, scuttled her away, and when her family came looking, the captain and chief mate had had to deal with them. It'd cost them a couple of sailors, and the rest of the crew had wanted to abandon her, but Reed had fought for her to stay.

"That was different," he said.

Green and gold flags greeted them as they returned to their ship. Whoops of joy filled the air. They'd heard it—the bell of the *Desert Gold*. Soon they'd have the location of the Trove of the King, and they'd be remembered forever as the ones who'd found the greatest treasure in this or any generation.

They'd be *remembered*. And in that way, no matter what happened to their bodies, no matter what happened *after*, they'd never die.

As if she knew what he was thinking, Jules looked over her shoulder, where in the heat her tattoos of water lilies glistened with a sheen of sweat. "You'd better think long and hard about what kinds of stories you want to leave behind, Cap," she said, " 'cause I guarantee you ain't the hero in this one."

Without another word, she followed Goro and Meeks up the side of the *Current*, leaving Reed alone in the boat. He stood there for a moment, with the sea beneath him whispering promises of glory and the crew chattering excitedly above. He had his ship, his crew, and the next leg of his adventure. That was all that mattered.

He spared one last glance over his shoulder for Bee's island—little more than a green smudge on the sea—and began his ascent.

CHAPTER 7

All Is Light

The night before they brought the prisoners to town, Sefia took a lantern from the supplies, retrieved her pack, and sneaked up the hill to a secluded spot overlooking camp, where she pulled out the Book. Drawn by the light, moths began flinging themselves against the warm glass globe, making shadows flicker and jump over the on the cover.

"Show me the impressors," she whispered.

But when she opened the Book, instead of a location, she got images of beatings, burned flesh.

Disgusted, she closed the Book again. Maybe she had to be more specific: "Where are the impressors now?"

But when she turned the pages, all she saw was more stories of torture and mistreatment—her parents' legacy. The reason she was here.

As the hours passed, Sefia tried commands, orders, pleas, anything to get the Book to show her what she wanted.

But the Book would not cooperate.

The paragraphs revealed blood and bruises, scorched skin and scars, but every time she thought she'd found the impressors' whereabouts, the story shifted. It went deeper into the fight, or farther into the past, or switched to another scene entirely.

It was as if the passages in the Book were as fluid as the Illuminated world, ever-shifting, slipping past her like leaves on the surface of a stream.

With a groan, she rubbed her temples. She could master the Book. She had to. For Archer, and for herself. She glared at the cover.

The first time she'd seen someone consult the Book, she'd been in the office of the Guard, deep beneath the city of Corabel.

Taking a deep breath, Sefia whispered the words Tanin had used the last time they'd seen each other: "Show me where the last piece of the Resurrection Amulet is hidden."

As she parted the covers, she gasped.

A page was missing. Only the margin remained—a jagged range of paper peaks.

Was this what Tanin had seen? She'd been furious. *What did you—? Did Lon do this?*

Sefia ran her finger along the torn edge. *Had* her father done it?

There was one way to find out.

She closed her eyes, summoning her sense of the Illuminated world, and when she opened them again her vision was filled with eddies of gold, passing over and through the hills.

When she turned her Sight on the Book, however, she nearly cried out. It was blinding, like staring into the sun, all the brightest fires bursting and expanding, sending out arcs of flame and drawing them in again.

Squinting, she traced the ripped page, using the damage to focus her Sight on the one piece of history she was searching for.

Pain pulsed at her temples. White crept in at the corners of her vision. The Illuminated world pitched and rolled around her in nausea-inducing undulations as images and sounds lurched out of the sea of light: a ship's cabin—night creeping in at the portholes—voices murmuring "We have to" and "It's been written"—the tearing of paper—the splitting of fibers.

A silver ring studded with black stones—slender brown hands speckled with scars—delicate shoulders—black hair pulled into a knot.

Her mother.

Her mother had removed the page.

The Illuminated world grew brighter, narrowing her field of vision to a pinprick. But she did not lose sight of her mother.

It had been eleven years since she'd seen Mareah, and here she was now, perfect, so close Sefia almost felt like she could reach out and touch her.

"Mom," she whispered.

Of course, her mother didn't hear her. She was just a moment in history—one story among billions. The light swelled. This wasn't the sea of gold Sefia was used to. This was pure, excruciating brightness. She couldn't see anything, couldn't get her bearings, and she felt more than saw the riptides of the

Illuminated world flashing past her, carrying her farther from her own time, her own body.

"S-sorcerer?" someone asked.

She was slipping away into torrents of light. She tried to gasp, but she had no lungs. She tried to blink, but she had no eyes.

Then, a distant shout: "Archer! *Archer!*"

Did time pass—seconds, decades, millennia?

Then, the pressure of someone's hand on her cheek.

And a voice, enfolding her, drawing her out of the light: "Sefia."

With a cry, she came plummeting back into her skin, and she shuddered at the shock of air in her chest, the blaze of pain in her head, and the dizzying twist in her stomach. She opened her eyes—

And saw nothing but white. Endless fields of white.

Someone—Archer, she recognized him now—gripped her shoulders. "Sefia, talk to me. Are you okay?"

She rubbed her eyes. Her knuckles were hard. Pink spots appeared in the whiteness. "I can't see."

"You what?"

Before she could explain, a gunshot rent the air, searing her ragged senses. The horses cried out in fear.

"Impressors!" someone shouted below.

Sefia reached blindly for her knife. The smell of gunpowder and frightened animals was thick around her. It was chaos—boys yelling, swords clashing.

"It's the impressors who escaped last night," Archer said.

A gun went off nearby, and for a moment his familiar form left her. Someone screamed. The gun went off a second time. But there was no second scream.

"Aljan. Stay with her." Archer returned to her side. "I'll be back."

She found his face with her hands. "You'd better."

He pulled her near, so close she could feel his breath on her lips.

Kiss me.

Do it.

Then Archer was gone. Bullets ricocheted around her. In the commotion, the prisoners began pounding against the sides of their crates, calling for help.

Somewhere close, a revolver clicked—jammed. There was the crack of knuckles on flesh. She was thrust aside as a body hit the ground nearby. Someone moaned.

"Aljan?" Sefia whispered. Her fingers flexed on her knife as she blinked, straining to see *something*. Anything.

Someone pinned her wrist and wrestled her to the ground. Her blade dropped. She was forced facedown in the dirt.

She flailed with her free hand, grabbing, snatching, but all she caught was air. Without her vision, she couldn't use Illumination.

The man on top of her laughed softly. "You gave us the slip in Cascarra, but we've got you now."

The trackers. They must have joined the ambush.

Her arm was wrenched behind her so hard she gasped with pain.

Her tendons pulled. Her bones creaked. But the brightness

was fading from her vision, revealing the curve of a pebble, the shape of the horizon.

Just a little longer before she could see again.

Just a little longer before she could fight back.

Suddenly, the tracker grunted. The weight on her lifted. There was a rush of air, the *crunch* of bone.

Someone touched her elbow. "Friends of yours?"

Kaito.

"Serakeen's trackers," she said.

Laughing, Kaito pulled her to her feet. "You really are a magnet for trouble, aren't you?" There was the sound of a scuffle. "Aljan, get up. I'm missing the fun."

Then with a whoop he left them.

"Sorry, sorcerer. I couldn't . . . He got me from behind," Aljan muttered.

"Are you okay?"

Something scraped along the ground. When he spoke again, he sounded distracted. "Yes."

The fighting continued for another minute or two before the sounds of battle ceased. Archer's voice reached her, clear and firm, directing the others to secure the new captives, check the dead, see to the wounded.

Then he was with her again, his fingers flitting over her injured wrist, her face. "You're hurt."

"Not much. Kaito stopped them."

He let out a relieved breath. "And your vision?"

"It's coming back. I tried to use the Sight on the Book, but I didn't think it'd be so *bright* . . ." Squinting, she found the blurred features of his face, the orb of the lantern, Aljan's slender figure crouched nearby, the tracker unconscious in the dirt. "Do you see the Book?"

"Aljan," Archer said, nodding.

In the boy's lap, she could just make out the shape of the Book, with its hard, glinting corners. Gingerly, he touched the cover, as if it might burn him.

"This symbol . . ." He looked up, and even with her blurred vision Sefia could see his expression was filled with hurt. "What is this? Are you one of them?"

Sefia flinched. "No . . ." She trailed off, not knowing what to say.

My parents were. They're the reason you were taken. They're the cause of your suffering.

Beside her, she could feel Archer tense up.

If Aljan knew, would he turn on her? Would the others? Would Archer be forced to choose between her and the only people who understood what he'd been through?

He needed them—she knew—maybe even more than he needed to stop the impressors.

"I stole it," she said.

Slowly, Aljan turned the pages, caressing the words as if they were precious things. "Why?"

"It's what we're going to use to beat them." She extended her hands. *Hopefully.*

With only a little reluctance, Aljan passed it to her—hard covers, metal clasps, the only way she could make amends for what her parents had done to Frey and the boys . . . and to Archer.

"*Book,*" Aljan said, testing the word thoughtfully. This was the most animated she'd ever seen him. "A weapon of paper and ink."

Sefia smiled. "Their *greatest* weapon. And we're going to use it against them."

Archer nodded at the tracker's unconscious form. "Take him to Frey, will you, Aljan? She's dealing with the prisoners."

"Yes, Archer." With one last glance at the Book in Sefia's arms, he began hauling the tracker toward camp.

Archer's golden eyes were shining when he turned back to Sefia. "We did it. We got them—the impressors *and* the trackers. No one's out there hunting us."

He looked so exhilarated, hair mussed and tawny skin nicked with cuts and scrapes, not the haunted boy she'd come to expect but someone full of breath and life. But then her gaze fell to his neck, and she was reminded of what her family—the family she still missed, keenly—had done to him. She looked away guiltily.

"You should've seen Frey and the boys," he continued. "They can *fight*. Whatever Tanin throws at us next, we'll be ready."

Rubbing her eyes, she took in their surroundings: the dry hills, the bloodied earth. Aljan and Frey were shackling the prisoners while Scarza stripped the dead bodies, pulling out daggers and spare cartridges and tossing them one-handed to Kaito.

They *had* done it. And after they surrendered the prisoners to the authorities tomorrow, they'd do it again. If she could figure out how to wield the Book.

When Archer returned to camp, Sefia remained on the hillside alone. Sitting back, she smoothed her hand over the Book's cover, listening to the moths beating their papery bodies against the lantern, the cheers as the others welcomed Archer into their ranks.

She could have looked for the impressors again, could have combed through the pages, searching for cities and landmarks.

But she didn't. She sat forward and brought the Book to her lips.

Most of Sefia's memories of her mother were clouded, like images in a tarnished mirror: sculpting creatures out of snow, sipping spiced chocolate at the kitchen table, building words out of alphabet blocks when Lon was working in the garden. She hadn't known how alike their hands were—thin, strong, adorned with dozens of scars—hadn't realized until now just how much she missed her.

"Show me my mother," Sefia whispered. "Please."

Run or Die

Lon & Mareah
—SPRING
—Corabel
—20 years ago?

As the stew bubbled in the cast-iron pot, clouds of
steam fogged the windows, filling the gardening
shed with the smell of brine and vinegar. Outside in the
cold spring air, the vast White Plains were carpeted with
thousands of pale poppies.

In the distance, the terra-cotta rooftops and coral
towers of Corabel, the capital of Deliene, rose behind
the high city walls. But out here, Nin was the only person
for miles, and she preferred it that way.

Smoothing clay into a hinged metal compact, she
placed a leaf of waxed paper inside and snapped it closed.
Dotted with tiny enamel flowers, it looked for all the
world like an ordinary case of powder.

But nothing Nin did was ordinary. Weeks had
gone into the planning of this heist. Through careful

observation and a few well-placed bribes, she'd discovered the location of the safe and the weaknesses of the one man who carried the key. Tomorrow, she'd finally swipe it, make an impression in her compact, and cast a copy with the skill and precision for which she'd earned her name: the Locksmith.

The moniker was uninspired but apt. No lock could stop her. No safe was safe. She prided herself on it.

Placing the compact in her pocket, she patted it once—for luck.

As she turned to the stove, the door opened behind her. Someone shuffled into the shed.

Nin recognized those footsteps—Lon. He never came alone, but the other one was silent and Nin never heard her coming.

They'd first approached her about a job two years ago. Her reputation had preceeded her, they said. No one else could pull off the heist they had planned—no one else could replicate the keys they needed.

They'd offered her a sum that would sustain her for years, but she hadn't done it for the money. She'd done it for the challenge of living up to her own reputation. The first key they'd given her was exquisitely crafted, with ornate wards and multiple-toothed bits so intricate they would have stymied any other craftsman.

But not the Locksmith.

When Lon and Mareah came back for the cast,

they'd promised to return with the second key and the rest of the payment.

That was over a year ago. Nin thought they'd given up. Or gotten caught.

Now here they were. Without turning, she took another two bowls from the shelf.

Lon swung off his pack. "Hello, Nin," he said.

"Finally got me that second key, did you?" She glanced over her shoulder, but Lon didn't look flush with success, as she'd expected.

There was a new scar at his temple, still puckered at the edges where it had been stitched. He had dirt on his boots and the hems of his trousers, and the oversize sweater he wore was beginning to fray. In fact, he looked a bit *frayed* himself.

"What happened?" Nin asked as he pulled something heavy and rectangular from the depths of his pack.

"Ah." Lon ran a hand through his black hair, making it stand up at the ends. "It's a long story."

Nin's gaze shifted to Mareah, standing silently by the window.

The girl—easily in her mid-thirties, but everyone was a child to Nin—stared back solemnly, her hand resting on the hilt of her sword.

"Then start at the beginning." Nin dunked spoons into the bowls and set them on her worktable.

Mareah began pacing the perimeter of the shed,

past the hoes and pointed rakes, the tiny cot with its threadbare quilt.

"We got it." Lon slid the heavy object onto the table and pulled up a stool.

So this was the great treasure they'd wanted her to help them free from the vault—a box. A case for carrying jewels, maybe.

"How?"

"We . . . had to improvise." Lon ate slowly, laboriously, like he could barely sustain the effort it took to hold the spoon. However they'd done it, it had cost him.

Mareah seemed unaffected.

Nin looked from one to the other. "What do you want, then? I didn't copy your second key. Don't want to be paid for a job I didn't do."

Pushing his bowl aside, Lon folded back the leather casing of the box and slid out an object encrusted with gems: amethysts, sapphires, emeralds, cuts of brilliant blue tanzanite and red beryl, cabochons of cat's-eye, rubies and diamonds so perfect they were like cold stars winking among the curling gold filigree.

Nin leaned forward, studying the jewels with an expert eye. The exterior of the box was more valuable by far than the contents of the safe she'd been planning on looting in Corabel.

"Very pretty." She crossed her arms. "But if you've got it, why are you here?"

Lon fiddled with one of the clasps on the box, clicking it open and shut again.

"Lon," Mareah said from the window. Her hand closed around her sword. A sharp silver ring on her finger flashed in the light.

Nin's gaze darted to the acres of poppies outside. "You didn't get away clean."

"No." Lon pushed himself to his feet.

"Stupid boy." Nin began pulling items from the shelves and stuffing them into a sack. All those weeks of work, wasted. "Who's after you?"

"Just believe me when I say they're dangerous. If they find you, they'll do anything to find out what you know." He glanced at Mareah. *"Anything."*

"And you led them here?" Nin buckled her pack and began feeding the rest of her belongings into the stove. "Couldn't just leave me out of it, could you?"

"We had to warn you."

"You haven't told me a rotten—"

"They're here," Mareah interrupted. Her eyes were unfocused, her pupils constricted into pinpricks of darkness in her brown eyes.

"Who's *they*?" Nin patted her pocket, where her case of lock picks thumped against the now-useless compact, and grabbed her bear-skin cloak. "What kind of mess have you dragged me into?"

Lon ran his hands through his hair again. "Anything we tell you could lead them to us."

"You've already led them to *me*," Nin snapped.

While they argued, Mareah drew her sword. The shed filled with the metallic scent of blood.

Nin gagged. Lon grabbed the jeweled box from the table and shoved her toward the corner, placing himself between her and the door.

Through the window, Nin spied figures hurrying across the plains, leaving gray trails of crushed poppies behind them.

Mareah raised her copper blade. Outside, the fields went still.

Then the door flew open. The first attacker barged in. In a single swift motion, Mareah drew a red line across the back of his neck, severing his spine.

The blood on the blade disappeared, absorbed into the steel.

The windows shattered. Assailants leapt through the glass. Mareah was everywhere, a blur of movement between the transparent shards, her sword flashing like copper lightning, seeking blood.

Nin had never seen anything like it. Mareah's movements were so sharp they hurt to watch, so beautiful you couldn't look away.

With a flick of her fingers, she sent a shard of glass flying deep into the throat of one of the attackers.

Magic. Huddled behind Lon, Nin drew a dagger from her boot.

Palming the air, Mareah shoved another opponent

into the wall. The woman's head cracked against a beam and she dropped to the floor like an empty suit of clothing. Mareah fought off another, her sword nicking him in the arms, the chest, the backs of his thighs, until he sank to his knees, his face contorted in pain.

She brought her blade down, parting his head from his body in one seamless movement.

Then the shed was still, the copper-colored sword silently drinking in the last of the blood on its blade.

Mareah looked over her shoulder. "Everyone okay?" she asked.

Nodding, Lon gripped Nin by the elbow and hauled her upright. "You won't need that," he said, gesturing to her dagger.

Nin jerked out of his grasp. *"Sorcerers,"* she spat.

Mareah sheathed her weapon, and the buzzing scent of iron ebbed out of the air.

There was a flash of fire on a distant hill, followed by the *crack* of a gunshot.

Before either Nin or Lon could react, Mareah lifted her fingers. A bullet halted midway through the empty window frame. For a moment, it hovered, turning slowly in the air.

Narrowing her eyes, Mareah turned her wrist and sent the bullet spiraling back into the fields.

Far away, there was a fine mist of blood among the white poppies.

At the table, Lon began prying sapphires and coils

of gold from the jeweled box. Taking Nin's hand, he pressed a handful of gems into her palm. More than enough to compensate her for her wasted time. More than enough to live on for the next few years, if she was careful. And then some.

"You're leaving me?" she demanded. "When I don't even know who's hunting me?"

"The less you know, the safer you'll be." Lon wrapped the box again and stuffed it in his pack. His eyes glinted sadly. "We're sorry. You'll have to lie low. Head into the wilderness. If you're careful, they won't find you."

She dropped the jewels into a coin purse. "For how long?"

"Forever," Mareah said. Her scarred hands flexed at her sides. "You'll never be the Locksmith again. Even a whisper of your whereabouts will draw them to you. You have no choice—you have to run. Run or die."

Nin glared at them. In less than fifteen minutes, they'd taken her safety, her identity, her future. She could imagine the rest of her life now, a harried existence flitting from town to town, as the wanted posters of the Locksmith faded, and she and all her deeds were forgotten.

She wished she'd never met them, never heard the names Lon or Mareah. They had powerful enemies, and now, though she didn't know who they were or what they wanted, those enemies were hers.

Nin flung her bear-skin cloak over her shoulders and looked around. Among the broken glass, the pools of blood, the cooling bodies, Lon found Mareah's hand. Their fingers twined.

"Good-bye, Nin," he said. "Good luck."

"No such thing as luck." Without another word, Nin stalked out the door into the White Plains, leaving Lon and Mareah behind—she hoped—for good.

Chapter 8

Stories Written with
Love and Guilt

Sefia's mind churned with what the Book had shown her.

Nin.

Her parents.

Magic and bloodshed.

For Sefia, the stench of the copper-colored blade would always be linked to loss—of her father, of Nin, and of Harison, the ship's boy from the *Current of Faith*. It wasn't her mother's scent. Not her mother, who had always smelled like earth and fresh greens.

She wondered what had happened to the bloodsword. Maybe it had been buried in the garden, the iron quietly leaching into the soil. Maybe, Sefia thought bitterly, that was why Mareah had spent so much time digging among the furrows—because it reminded her of who she'd been.

While Frey and the boys lit a celebratory bonfire in the camp below, Sefia read and reread the passage, pressing her fingertips to the names like she could reach through the Book and seize her mother's hand, snatch the worn elbow of her father's sleeve, or tug the end of Nin's bear-skin cloak. Like she could take her parents by the shoulders and demand they reveal all the secrets they'd kept from her when they were alive, all the secrets that still kept her in the dark.

One by one, the others crawled under their blankets, but Sefia read until she had memorized every paragraph, every punctuation mark, her emotions grinding against each other until they were nearly indistinguishable: grief, hurt, anger, betrayal, longing.

She hadn't realized Nin had hated Lon and Mareah so much, hadn't realized she'd had to sacrifice everything because of them. But she'd joined the couple eventually, to help them build the house on the hill overlooking the sea, where the three of them had raised a little girl.

It had been an isolated childhood, but Sefia had been protected. And loved.

Glancing at the others, she felt a pinch of guilt for loving the people responsible for ruining their lives. For ruining Nin's life.

And Archer's.

She couldn't reverse the damage her parents had done. But maybe, if she stopped enough impressors, if she saved enough boys, she could make up for their mistakes.

And then, maybe, she could look Archer in the eye without feeling like she was betraying him in her turncoat heart.

A rustling in the grass made her look up. She reached for the Illuminated world, readying for a fight.

But it was just Archer. His lean form was edged in stars,

larger and more grand than his seventeen or eighteen years, than his body muscled with hardship. As he entered the lamplight, his features regained their definition, and he became a boy again, flesh and blood.

"I thought you'd be back sooner," he said.

Placing a stalk of grass between the pages, Sefia set aside the Book, hugging her knees like she could soothe the ache in her chest if only she curled up tight enough. "The Book showed me my parents," she said.

"Oh." Archer sank down beside her, though they didn't touch.

"They kept so much from me." Turning out the lamp, she doused them in inky darkness. "Sometimes I wonder if I ever knew them at all."

He said nothing. She twisted her fingers as each second of silence grew more painful. Blame. Guilt. So much had come between them in the span of a couple days.

"Maybe they didn't know how to tell you," Archer said at last. He pulled out the worry stone, glinting between his fingers. "Maybe they were afraid. Because of what they'd done."

She looked at him then, daring him to argue with her. "I was their daughter. They should have told me."

Trusted me. Believed in me. Tanin's words.

"Would you still have loved them, if you knew?"

"I still love them," she whispered apologetically, "even now."

In the night, Archer's eyes were a dark, searching bronze. She could've looked into those eyes for hours and still not have looked enough. He glanced away, and again she felt that guilt.

Silently, he put his forehead on his knees, completely still except for his thumb, tracing the piece of quartz.

"Do you hate me for that?" she asked.

When he straightened again, the starlight gleamed on the scars that flecked his face and arms. "Sefia." He shook his head. "I could never hate you."

Before she could say anything, before she could even smile, he spoke again: "My first kill was a boy named Oriyah." The words came out in a rush, like if he didn't say them now, he might never get them out. "He was another of Hatchet's candidates, almost as new as I was. Neither of us had fought yet, and Hatchet kept trying to make us train. But we couldn't. I couldn't. Oriyah was younger than I was. They'd broken his arm when they captured him, and it wasn't healing right. I *couldn't* hit him."

Sefia froze, like the story was a spell and if she breathed too loudly it would break.

"When Hatchet realized we wouldn't fight, even for practice, he got another impressor—Redbeard." Archer glanced at her. Redbeard had been the one who burned the newly captured boys. "They tried everything: cursing us, beating us, ordering us to pick up our swords. But we didn't. Oriyah was too scared.

"Then one day, Hatchet brought all six of us boys out of our crates. He gave Oriyah and me each a club and made the others line up." Archer's voice went ragged at the edges, but he didn't stop speaking. "'Fight,' Hatchet said. He put his gun to Oriyah's head. 'Fight, or he dies.'

"Oriyah was in tears. He gave a halfhearted swing. I let him hit me. It didn't hurt much. I wouldn't fight him. I kept thinking, if only I refused long enough, if only I showed them I wasn't what they wanted me to be . . ." Archer shook his head, shuddering. "Hatchet shot him. There was so much blood. I didn't know we had so much blood in us. Oriyah buckled at the knees, and when he hit the ground, he was still.

"Hatchet didn't even bat an eye. 'Fight,' he said, 'or I'll kill another one.'"

Archer swallowed again and again. His fingers were shaking so badly he dropped the quartz point.

Sefia caught it and slid it back into his palm, warm and slightly damp. "Hatchet killed him," she said. "Not you."

"It was my fault. Because I didn't want to . . . Because I couldn't . . ." He took a long quivering breath. "Because I was weak."

"You didn't put the gun to his head. You didn't pull the trigger. Wanting the world to be a better place than it is? That doesn't make you weak. That makes you the kind of person this world needs."

Archer was still for a long time, like an animal crouched in the shadows, waiting for prey. But at last, his posture relaxed, his coiled muscles unwinding. With a sigh, he slipped his arm around her shoulders, and for the first time in over a week, he didn't pull away.

Sefia closed her eyes. He smelled like dust and rain, though they hadn't seen rain in a week, and when she leaned in to him, he made room for her in the crook of his arm, in the curve of his neck.

As the sky lightened above them, Archer reached out,

tentatively, fingers first and then his whole palm. Their hands clasped.

They remained that way, not speaking, while dawn spread across the Delienean Heartland, and Sefia rediscovered the shapes and textures of his hands—the tender flesh on the inside of his wrist, and each of his knuckles, the hills and vales, the crescents of his fingertips.

And when they stood, finally, to stumble back to camp, she picked up the Book and felt the distant reverberation of questions still to be answered, secrets still to be discovered. But those tempests were slumbering. For now.

CHAPTER 9

Nobody Comes Back Unscathed

Eager to be on the road again, Archer roused the others as soon as he and Sefia returned.

Some of them grumbled and pulled their blankets over their heads, but Griegi was up in an instant, whistling happily as he stoked the coals of the previous night's fire.

Archer was about to stop him when Kaito bounded over, seized a pot of water, and upended it over the ashes, which hissed and sent up a cloud of smoke.

"Rotten hulls, Kaito!" Griegi leapt to his feet, coughing. "What's the matter with you?"

"Sorry, Grieg, we've got to get a move on." With a shrug, he jogged away and began pounding on the prisoners' crates. "Wake up, bootlickers! Time to stretch your legs and empty your bladders!"

Griegi looked disappointed. "Archer, come on, please?"

Shaking his head, Archer tossed his pack into the supply

cart. "Kaito's right. We have prisoners to unload," he said. "I promise you can cook your heart out tonight."

The boy's face lit up. "You won't regret it."

Although almost everyone wanted to escort the captives, they agreed it was best to send in as few of them as possible: Archer driving one cart of prisoners, Sefia driving the other, Scarza to bring up the rear on his dun mare, and Kaito to ride ahead.

The nearest town was little more than a handful of weather-worn buildings and a single dusty street. At the north end, the jail was nestled between a general store and the messengers' post.

As they passed the stables, Kaito rode back and forth along the carts, his hands continually going to his weapons as he checked the porches and yellowed curtains for signs of trouble.

When they reached the sheriff's office, Kaito was the first to dismount, followed by Archer, who brushed off his trousers and straightened his cuffs uneasily.

The boy grinned at his discomfort. "Relax, brother. Compared to last night, this'll be easy."

Archer ran his fingers through his hair as the sheriff, a plump woman with a gold star winking at her shoulder, approached. Two deputies with their own silver stars followed behind.

"I'd rather be fighting," he muttered.

Kaito laughed, earning a scowl from the sheriff as she halted in front of them, tucking her thumbs into her belt.

"Sheriff." Archer's voice cracked.

Kaito snickered.

The sheriff raised an eyebrow. "Boys."

Kaito nudged him, and Archer stumbled forward. The sheriff looked unimpressed.

"We'd like to turn over eight criminals we picked up south of here," he said, motioning to Sefia and Scarza, who began unlocking the crates and pulling their prisoners into the light.

The sheriff's gaze traveled over the captives, their bruised faces and wrinkled clothes. Her nostrils flared at the stink of them.

Their unwashed smell brought back Archer's memories of wooden walls, split fingernails, soiled bits of straw.

His chest tightened. His pulse roared in his ears. *Not now.* He grasped for the worry stone. *Not now.*

"What's the matter, boy?" the sheriff demanded.

Boy. He gasped. Tears squeezed from the corners of his eyes as he fought to control his breathing. *I'm not back there anymore. I'm safe. I'm safe. I'm safe.*

"Archer!" Sefia called. "Kaito, help him!"

Then Kaito's hand was on his shoulder, his voice gentler than Archer had ever heard it: "It's all right, brother. I've got you."

At the words, the pounding in Archer's veins eased enough for him to hear the sheriff mutter, "What's wrong with him?"

Archer looked up as his heart slowed. "Nightmares," he croaked.

The sheriff frowned. "I sent my deputies for the warrants. We'll see about these criminals of yours."

He pocketed the worry stone as the deputies came scampering back with sheaves of paper in their arms. Silently, the sheriff began perusing the wanted sketches. Her frown deepened.

"We've got wanted notices for five of your criminals. Assault, highway robbery, kidnapping, a couple are even wanted for murder. Bad folks you've got here," she said. "But these three are clean."

As she pointed at three of the prisoners, one of them adjusted his bandages with a sly grin.

"I can take the others," the sheriff continued, "but not them."

The quartz point dug into Archer's palm. He couldn't let them go. He'd promised Kaito. *Promised.*

Before he could speak, Kaito darted forward. "Let them go?" he growled. He opened his collar, exposing the pink scar at his throat. "Here's what happens if we let them go."

Startled, the sheriff looked up at him, then back to her papers. "Kidnapping," she muttered. Her gaze went to the prisoners and back to Kaito's scar. "Impressors? I thought they were just a story."

Kaito's green eyes gleamed like a coyote's. "Some stories are true."

"We should tell Allannah," one of the deputies murmured.

Who? Archer glanced around. The rooftops and shadowed doorways would have been perfect cover for an ambush. At the rear of the caravan, Scarza adjusted his grip on his rifle.

The sheriff shook her head. "After what they did, why didn't you—" She made a cutting motion across her throat.

"Believe me, I would've, but . . ." Taking a step back, Kaito clapped Archer on the arm. "I owed someone, and I always pay my debts."

The sheriff chewed at her lower lip. "We had a boy go missing about two years ago now. Most folks thought he'd run off, but his aunt, she never believed it."

Allannah. The bereft. The one waiting for a boy who'd probably never come back. "I was taken about two years ago," Archer said.

And there are people waiting for me too. Or rather, waiting for the boy he used to be. But that boy was gone. He'd died in the dirt with Argo.

"His name's Parker," the sheriff added. "Fifteen years old. Yellow hair and blue eyes you almost wouldn't notice behind his glasses. Any of you see him? When you were, you know . . ."

Abruptly, Scarza passed off his captives to Sefia and began leading his mare back down the road.

The sheriff raised her eyebrows.

The scar in Kaito's cheek twitched. "No, sorry. Didn't know him."

"It's all right. It was a lot to hope."

The deputies took the prisoners from Sefia and began tugging them away. Over his shoulder, one of the trackers shot them a last venomous glance.

"You fixing to stay awhile?" the sheriff asked. "Knowing what you did, folks would gladly put you up for the night. Feed you pretty well too."

"Thanks, but we have to keep moving." Archer's restlessness had returned, and all he wanted was to hunt and fight and break things, splintering the impressors crew by crew until they were no more than a dream, distantly remembered. "Got a place to water our horses and fill our canteens?"

She nodded. "You passed the stables on your way in. There's a trough and pump out back."

He tipped his hat to her.

"You're doing good work here, boys. Keep it up."

As they made their way back, Kaito drew up beside Archer's cart. "We did see him," he said.

"Parker?"

"He fought Scarza."

"Oh." The very fact that Scarza was here meant Parker hadn't made it.

At the drinking trough, the silver-haired boy silently stroked his mare's shoulder with his one hand. He had a generous mouth and cheekbones so sharp you could cut your knuckles on them, and over the past couple of days together, Archer had discovered he was quiet too—like a cloud passing over a landscape, so unassuming you didn't realize he was there until he was right beside you.

As if he could sense Archer watching him, Scarza's gaze lifted briefly before dropping again. "Kaito told you," he said.

"Yeah."

"I should've said something. I should've told them I killed him."

"The impressors made you do it."

Scarza laughed bitterly. "Is that what you tell yourself? That they *made you*?"

Archer looked away. They had, hadn't they? Every life he'd taken, he'd done it because he'd had to. Because the choice had been forced on him: kill or die.

Right?

When they started back around the stables, they found a small group of people waiting for them on the main road. Arrayed around them were cloth-wrapped packages, small stoppered kegs, paper parcels tied with string, even a bundle of neatly chopped firewood.

One of the people, a woman with hair the color of straw and large powder-blue eyes, stepped forward. "We heard what you did," she said. "We wanted to thank you."

"Allannah?" Archer asked.

Scarza stared fixedly at the hills in the distance.

She placed a basket in Archer's hands, and he caught a whiff of baked sugar, butter, and lavender. "After Parker's parents died, I was supposed to raise him. I tried, but he . . . we could never seem to get along, you know? But he didn't deserve . . ." She retreated, drawing a pale shawl closer about her shoulders. "Anyway, thank you."

Archer gripped the basket. *We didn't save him,* he wanted to say. Or, *I'm sorry.*

As he searched for the words, Scarza dismounted. He walked up to Allannah and took one of her hands in his. "Don't thank us," he said in his soft voice. "He's never coming home."

Tears formed in her eyes, and she clasped his hand tighter. "Some of you get to. Thank you for that."

Then she embraced him and hurried back to the others, who began loading the empty carts with supplies.

Stunned, Scarza looked up at Archer as if for direction.

They'd hurt so many people. Scarza's right arm had eleven burns—one of them for killing Parker. Kaito's had nine. And

102

every one of the others—even Mako, only twelve years old—had at least two.

Archer had fifteen, though his count was much higher.

He could picture each of their faces when he closed his eyes—boys, impressors, trackers—their jaws gone slack in death, mouths forming questions to which they'd never hear the answers.

Sometimes he felt like the dead would always be with him, hounding his steps, forcing him to keep moving, keep fighting, because if he tried to turn back, the dead would be all he saw.

He'd come back, all right, but neither he nor Scarza nor Kaito, none of them had come back unscathed. Their scars were just an outward sign of it.

But now, maybe they could save enough boys to make up for the ones they'd killed. Maybe they could save enough boys, and maybe when they were done, they'd *deserve* to go home again.

There was a touch at his shoulder, and Sefia's fingers twined in his.

He gripped her hand. They had Frey and the boys. They had the Book. They were *together*. Nothing would stop them until they'd rid Deliene of the impressors.

One crew down.

Three to go.

The Corabelli Curse

O nce there was, and one day there will be. This is the beginning of every story.

Once, before the union of the Delienean kingdom, when the noble houses still battled for scraps of land, the White Plague came out of the cold north. It swept across the land, stealing away the aged and the weak, and when there were no more aged and no more weak, it took the young and the strong as well.

Fearing infection, those who could still walk fled from the north, but they brought the plague with them, and one by one, the lands of the south began to fall.

Only Corabel, the great walled city on a hill, was untouched. To protect his own citizenry, Lord Ortega Corabelli gave the order to close the gates, and behind his high stone walls, he waited for the White Plague to release its grip on the land.

As the seasons turned, citizens from Gorman, from Shinjai

and Ken and Alissar swarmed to the city, but the king would not relent. Refugees died by the thousands, and their funeral pyres choked the sky with smoke.

One day, as the lord stood on the ramparts with his daughter Zunisa, an old woman called up to him, pleading with him to open the gates for the sake of her grandson—the only member of her family untouched by sickness.

The lord refused.

The woman spat in the dirt. "Then I lay a curse on you, Ortega Corabelli. I curse all who share your blood, and all who share their love. All will suffer for the coldness of your heart. Not until your family has been stripped of everything will the curse be broken. Not until you, like us, are bereft and begging for mercy."

For six more months, the plague took life after life, and the rolling green hills around the city grew black with ash. It wasn't until the rains receded and summer returned that Corabel finally opened its gates.

By then, tens of thousands of people had died.

In exchange for aid, Ortega Corabelli demanded allegiance from the other provinces and, faced with the choice to kneel or perish, the rest of the major houses agreed.

Thus, the kingdom of Deliene was formed: with black and white for its colors, and a curse upon the bloodline.

Not a month after he became king, Ortega Corabelli and his wife became the plague's last victims.

The newly crowned Queen Zunisa tried to provide for the people her father had neglected. In honor of the dead, she ordered the plains to be planted with thousands of white poppies. She established medical schools to train healers and doctors, and set up hospitals for the sick.

But before her twin boys were ten years old, she died of consumption she'd contracted while visiting a sanatorium.

Again and again, members of the bloodline floundered and died: victims of murder and sickness and suicide. They died in childhood and childbirth, in fires and hunting accidents. Wives and husbands, childhood sweethearts, mistresses and kept men, all perished, for the love of a Corabelli could kill you.

In each generation, there was always someone who lived long enough to continue the Corabelli line, and their children, too, carried the curse.

Until at last there were only two: Lord Roco Diamar of Shinjai, whose parents were lost at sea, and Eduoar Corabelli II, who was called the Lonely King.

CHAPTER 10

How to Kill a King

Arcadimon's Master, Darion Stonegold, always said there were three ways to kill a king: You could face him with all the force of your military might, and in the end, one of you would fall. You could stab him from behind like a coward, cringing in the shadows. Or you could kill him slowly, from the inside out, so he wouldn't even know until it was too late. If you did your job right, he might even thank you for it.

These were the differences between Soldiers, Assassins, and Politicians. All of them performed their duties in the service of the Guard, but only Politicians did it with a certain flair.

And flair was something Apprentice Politician Arcadimon Detano had in spades.

Peering into the floor-length mirror, he smoothed an errant lock of hair and took a step back to examine his ensemble. Like everyone else in Shinjai Province, he wore mourning white—

spotless and impeccably pressed—with a vest the color of ash and a cravat that matched the forget-me-nots he'd ordered for the funeral pyre. Sharp, attractive, composed—that was how he needed the provincial nobility to see him. He needed to inspire their trust . . . and ultimately, their allegiance.

After all, the death of Lord Roco was an integral part of Phase III of the Red War—bringing Deliene under the control of the Guard.

Which meant he was nearing the one thing he'd been dreading for years.

Killing the Delienean king.

Clicking his polished boots together, Arcadimon strode across the plush carpet toward the king's chamber, which adjoined his own.

At the threshold between their rooms, the captain of the guard stood with one hand on her sword, looking severe in her black uniform. She was small, shorter than Arcadimon by a head, but strong and quick as a steel spring. He'd seen her defeat entire squads of opponents even when she was outweighed, outnumbered, *and* outgunned.

She was the best bodyguard any monarch could have asked for, but she was going to fail. Because the assassination of the king would not come from an opponent, but from a friend.

Arcadimon beamed as he approached the open door. "You're in fine form today, Captain Ignani."

She arched an eyebrow. "Wish I could say the same, Detano. My reflection's missing from your boots today."

"Really?" He looked down, pretending to be appalled. "Must be the angle. I can see myself fine."

"If you get any cheekier, you can see yourself out." But she stepped aside for him all the same.

Arcadimon winked at her. Ignani had been Eduoar's bodyguard since he and Arcadimon were children playing together in the castle at Corabel, and was more familiar to Arcadimon than his own mother, which was why she never suspected a thing.

It was his proximity to the king, in fact, that made him an ideal Apprentice Politician. The Guard had needed someone young, someone close, someone with a margin of talent for Illumination.

They had needed Arcadimon, who, thanks to his father's post in Corabel, had been one of Eduoar's childhood companions for years.

He slipped into the king's room, where Ed was standing by the windows, watching the trees sway in the wind. Eduoar had always been handsome—with that golden skin, that thinness and height, those sad Corabelli eyes—and standing there with the sunlight in his dark hair and the buttons of his shirt undone, exposing his chest, he was every inch a king.

But if you looked closely, you could see his illness in the hollows of his cheeks, in the loose fit of the shirt he'd had tailored not a week before.

Seeing Arcadimon, he brightened. His weariness ebbed away like a tide from a beach, leaving nothing but pristine sparkling sand behind. "Arc," he murmured.

"Hey." Arcadimon grinned. Something inside him eased, the way it always did when he was with Ed. Like breathing deep after a long time struggling for air. "You ready for today?"

"Not really." Eduoar began fumbling with his buttons,

closing up the channel of exposed skin Arc couldn't help but stare at. Today would be the king's first public appearance in over a year. He was supposed to deliver the eulogy for his cousin, the recently deceased Lord Roco Diamar of Shinjai, whose death had left Eduoar the only living Corabelli. The cousin Arcadimon had just killed, albeit indirectly, with a few well-placed bribes and a dram of poison. Roco had always had a fragile heart. It had been easy to make his death appear an accident.

It had been his duty—as killing Eduoar would be his duty. There could be no relatives left in the royal bloodline when Eduoar was gone.

Arcadimon didn't enjoy it, but they all made sacrifices for the greater good. Assassins, he'd heard, had to execute their immediate family to earn their bloodswords.

"Child's play," Darion had said dismissively. "Assassins spend years cultivating their emotional distance. By the time they're sent to kill their kin, they're as good as strangers. You, on the other hand, are a Politician, and you have a much more demanding task. You will have no distance from your victims. You will make them trust you. You will make them love you. And here's the fine edge we walk, Apprentice: You will make them think you love them in return. You will say whatever you must, do whatever you must. But it must *always* be an illusion. These are not your allies. They are not your friends, your kin, your lovers. They are your targets, your tools, your enemies. Sentiment will compromise the mission, and it will get you killed—if not by your rivals, then by me. Do you understand?"

Arcadimon did. And for the last eight years he had crafted a mask of charm and compassion so fine, so lifelike, that he had fooled not only the entire Delienean court, but his own family and closest friend.

"You'll be fine," he said to Eduoar. "You've got me."

"What more could I ask for?"

Although he didn't have to, Arc stepped in to finish buttoning Eduoar's shirt. Beneath his hands, he could feel the king's protruding collarbones, the faint heat of his skin.

Arcadimon drew back abruptly, covering himself with the easy chuckle he'd cultivated over the years he'd spent clawing his way to power among the lesser names of the Delienean court. He'd been inducted into the Guard when he was fourteen, and since then, his Master had guided him as he gained control of the messengers and the newsmen, two of the most powerful guilds in the kingdom, earned the loyalty of most of the minor houses and some of the major, and put himself in position to seize the throne.

"I can think of plenty of things even a king might want," he said lightly. "A cure for warts—"

"I don't have warts!"

Arc continued as if he hadn't heard, ticking off items on his fingers: "—a flying horse, a way to drink coffee without burning your mouth—"

"There's already a way to do that," Eduoar said. "It's called waiting."

From the doorway Ignani grunted—her version of a laugh.

"Lukewarm coffee?" Arc made a face. "I'll take the burning, thank you very much."

The king smiled as Arcadimon retreated to the sideboard,

where he laid the back of his hand against a clay kettle to test its temperature. Finding it cool to the touch, he plucked a silver flask from the inner pocket of his coat and poured the cold tea into it. Then he tipped a few amber drops from a glass vial into the flask before capping it again and shaking it vigorously.

Neither Eduoar nor Ignani moved to stop him.

They thought it was medicine—a special tonic distilled from the bark of a tree that grew only in Everica. His Master, Darion, had presented him with the first vial three years ago. "The Administrators have never concocted a better poison," he'd said. "In small doses it's harmless enough, but once administered, the only way to alleviate its symptoms is the poison itself, and prolonged use will cause fainting spells so frequent our little king won't be able to go a few hours without collapsing."

Unlike the draught Arcadimon had ordered administered to Roco, this poison wouldn't kill the king—not even withdrawal would do that—but it had made him unfit to rule. In the past year, Eduoar had been bedridden more days than he'd been well, locked up in his lonely tower while the seasons swept through his kingdom like a fog from the sea.

And Arcadimon Detano, his childhood friend and most trusted adviser, had stepped in for him. Arcadimon had overseen the courts and councils. Arcadimon had kept the kingdom running, turning himself into a leader they could follow.

As he slipped the vial back into his pocket, Ignani nodded at him approvingly.

Beneath his confident smile, Arc felt a twinge of guilt for fooling her, for fooling all of them.

Sometimes he wondered what his life would have been if the

Guard hadn't found him. Would he and Eduoar have remained friends beyond childhood? Would they, perhaps, have been something more?

Arcadimon shook his head and ran his fingers through his hair. Sometimes his mask of affection was so convincing he fooled even himself. But he was a Guardian before he was a Delienean, adviser, or even friend. He wouldn't waste time dwelling on what might have been.

Eduoar had gone back to staring out the window, idly twisting the signet ring, bearing the Delienean crest, on his finger.

Arcadimon straightened his white jacket and checked his reflection once more: not a curl out of place, not a stray thread to be seen.

"Speaking of coffee," he said, "you don't think they'll mind me taking a mug on the road, do you?"

Ed turned from the window, a wry smile twisting his features. He plucked the flask from Arcadimon's fingers. "It won't go with your outfit."

Arc scoffed as the king took a sip of his poisoned tea. "Coffee goes with every outfit."

Accompanied by the provincial nobility, the minor lords and ladies, and Captain Ignani on her black warhorse, Arcadimon and Eduoar began the slow march around the Lake of Sky, the mirrorlike lake at the center of Shinjai Province. Above the tree line, the Szythian Mountains rose sharp and black as dragon backs, tipped with scales of late-summer snow.

At the sight of the king on his gray horse, the mourners began muttering as they tossed white flowers onto the dirt roads.

The Lonely King. The only one still alive to carry the Corabelli Curse.

If you didn't know the king as well as Arc did, you might not have noticed, but as their whispers reached the funeral procession, the sadness appeared in Eduoar's eyes again, threatening to spill over.

Arcadimon allowed himself a moment of satisfaction. After all, with both the messengers and newsmen under his thumb, he was responsible for spreading rumors about the weakness of the Lonely King, victim to the same melancholia that had consumed his father.

However, he had to admit that spreading the rumors now, freely, in the king's hearing, was crass. Almost vulgar.

He drew up alongside Eduoar. "Bet you wish you had that coffee now," he said.

"Coffee would do nothing to stop them from talking, unfortunately," Ed replied.

"Sure it would." Arcadimon adopted the clipped cadence of his newsmen. "*Clumsy king stains beautiful new jacket!* Or, *Generous king brings coffee for all!*"

"If only we'd thought of that sooner."

"Yeah, a little more foresight on our parts, and we would've been marching to nothing but adulation and slurping." Arcadimon flashed him a smile.

Eduoar swallowed, the lump of his throat visible behind his white cravat, and lifted his chin. The simple show of bravery reminded Arcadimon of the last funeral they'd attended here—the one for Roco's parents, lost at sea.

He and Ed had been eleven; Roco, nine. After spending

a few hours sneaking sips of cordial, they'd wandered off to the Tree of Dreams, the sprawling oak at the center of the castle grounds. Roco used to say that if you slept under it, the branches would catch the nightmares before they reached you.

They'd lit candles inside glass jars and hung them from the highest limbs.

"One for my mother, one for my father," Roco had said. "One for Aunt Miria."

Eduoar's mother, dead from cancer of the pancreas less than six months before.

They'd all lain there, watching the candles flicker out one by one in the dark. "Once the people you love start dying," Roco had said, "they don't stop."

"That's why we've got to love them while they're here," Arcadimon had said.

"Especially in our family," Ed had added.

And Roco had answered, with solemnity beyond his years, "We're Corabellis. For us, love and death are the same."

Now, riding along the rim of the lake, Arc leaned over and with his gloved fingers touched the back of Ed's hand. At the contact, a shiver went through them both, as if they'd been drenched in ice water. The king lifted his gaze, and for a moment, Arc was sure he knew.

For a moment, Arc wanted to tell him.

Hand in hand, they rode on, leaving crushed petals and broken stems in their wake.

At noon, the procession returned to the castle at Edelise. They deposited Roco's body on a floating bier anchored to the marble terrace, where the waves lapped over the polished stone. As members of the procession dispersed across the patio like white foam, Arcadimon flitted among them, dropping a compliment here, a veiled insult there, couching his threats in smiles. In the following days, they'd be meeting to elect Roco's successor, the next leader of Shinjai, and he needed to ensure the person they chose was the person *he* chose—someone who would support his regency when the time came.

Deep in conversation with one of the minor ladies, whom in other circumstances he might have considered taking to bed— he liked a good tumble with a girl as much as a boy, after all—he watched Lady Dinah approach Eduoar.

The leader of Alissar Province, Dinah Alissari had an old name, an empty vault, and the political mind of a rump roast, which had made her loyalty extraordinarily easy to come by.

"Alissar is deeply sorry for your loss, Your Majesty," she declared. The rings on her fingers glittered as she dipped an awkward curtsy. "He was your only family, after all."

Eduoar inclined his head. "My mother's side of the family is alive and well, I'll remind you. Some of them are even here today."

"Oh, don't be coy, sire. You know I meant your *Corabelli* family."

"As if I could forget." Eduoar's courteous expression wavered like sunlight on water, revealing darkness beneath.

Arcadimon bristled at Dinah's foolish prodding. Everyone knew the Corabelli line was ending. Eduoar didn't need it flaunted in front of him, especially not by a bankrupt cow.

Politely, Arcadimon extricated himself from his own conversation and began making his way toward the king.

"It's a shame he never had children," Dinah continued. "If only he'd had an heir, we wouldn't have to go through this tedious business of electing his successor."

"Roco told me once he'd never have children," Eduoar said. "Not with his blood."

"You don't believe that nonsense, do you, sire? When are you going to get married?"

"A good question, Lady Dinah," Arcadimon said, drawing up to them with a smile. He had a wide range of smiles, and this one dimpled his cheeks but didn't reach his eyes. "You've got heirs, haven't you? Old enough to be wed, I believe."

Dinah's face went white beneath its layers of powder and rouge.

As if to greet her, he took Lady Dinah's hand. Her flesh gave slightly under his fingers like an overripe plum.

With a flustered farewell, Dinah slunk away.

"Insufferable woman," Arc muttered.

Ed rubbed his eyes. "Thanks for saving me."

"It's nothing."

The king caught his arm. "It's everything. I know I'm getting worse, Arc. I know it's only a matter of time before . . . I know you'll *always* save me."

Arcadimon tried to smile, but this one faltered and died on his lips like an injured butterfly. Saving Ed would be flinging the flask of poison far into the Lake of Sky. Saving Ed would be taking him by the hand and running back to their horses, riding side by side until they reached the coast, where they'd catch a ship and go sailing into the wild blue sea.

Sentiment, he cautioned himself. Sentiment would get them *both* killed.

Ed licked his lips. "Do you have the medicine on you?"

The request brought the carefully cultivated smile back to Arcadimon's face. "Of course," he said, escorting the king to the edge of the stone terrace, near Roco's body.

The corpse was wrapped in white, floating like a cloud among the blue-and-yellow forget-me-nots. A copper incense bowl sat on his chest, and scribbles of smoke spiraled from the tips of the incense sticks, dissolving into the thin mountain air.

But his face was bare. He looked young, younger than Arcadimon remembered, more like the boy he'd grown up with than the Lord of Shinjai, and at the same time, he didn't look young at all. His flesh had sunken in on itself, like a mask stretched over a scaffolding of bone.

"He always said his weak heart would do him in," Ed murmured with a glance at Arcadimon.

Arc allowed tears to form in his eyes. "I'm sorry he's gone," he said, and to his surprise, it wasn't a lie.

Ed smiled sadly.

Slipping his hand into his vest pocket, Arcadimon withdrew the silver flask. Instead of passing it to the king, however, he hesitated.

"I suppose now's as good a time as any to start drinking," Lady Abiye declared, sweeping up to them in white silk and black obsidian. The leader of Gorman Province, she was old enough to be Arcadimon's grandmother, with a shrewd, strategic nature that had only grown more formidable with age. He'd already secured the allegiance of two of the four provincial leaders. After the election of Roco's successor, only Abiye would be left.

Her silks rustled as she withdrew a carved flask from her robe. "You know what they say: There's no funeral as long as a noble funeral."

"You're a wise woman, my lady," Arcadimon said.

"'Old' is the word you're looking for. But your flattery is noted." She winked and took a long pull, then gestured to the silver flask as he slid it into his pocket. "Well, don't let me stop you."

"No," he said. "I shouldn't." As the words fell, unbidden, from his mouth, he put a hand to his lips.

Eduoar caught his eye and mouthed, *Later?*

I shouldn't. Arcadimon blinked. Again, it was *true.* He knew it from the sweetness on his tongue, like springwater. It was his duty to the Guard to continue poisoning the king, but he *shouldn't.*

And more importantly, he no longer wanted to.

What he *wanted* was to sweep Ed into his arms. What he *wanted* was to run his fingers through his hair. What he *wanted*—

Swaying a little on his feet, Eduoar reached for the edge of the floating bier to steady himself, but before he touched it, his eyes rolled back in his head. His face went slack.

Lady Abiye let out a startled cry as the king pitched forward—right into Arcadimon's waiting arms.

The mourners swarmed them like sharks.

Cradling the king to his chest, Arc sank onto the cool marble.

In sleep, Eduoar's face seemed smoother, somehow, free of cares.

And in that instant Arc finally understood: For all his preparation, for all his masks, he'd been claimed by sentiment.

He didn't know how he hadn't recognized it before, but there it was, like a weed that had taken root in his heart, growing unnoticed in the shadow of all his cunning and all his plans, until it burst into bloom, bright as a star, sudden as an attack.

He *loved* Eduoar.

He loved the boy he was sworn to kill.

Account of the Lion Tamer

Dear Director,
Another report from the messengers, who
have procured additional accounts of
our book thieves. Attached are transcripts
from interviews with members of Lady
Carmine's Traveling Show, which had
been attacked by bandits in the Delienean
Heartland when Sefia and the boy showed
up. Looks like they've been busy since
they turned in the impressors & trackers.
Will keep an ear to the ground.

Ever your Apprentice, A.D.

Yeah, I saw them. They saved us—Lady Carmine and the rest of the Traveling Show—the ones the bandits hadn't already killed, anyway.

I don't think I would've believed it if I hadn't seen it with my own eyes. The storytellers are already fixing to add it to their repertoire—you should talk to them if you haven't already—to let people know what's out there . . . You ever been to a blood-letter, friend? A butcher, maybe? If you have, you can imagine what it was like that day.

They were fast, ruthless—one second, the bandits are threatening to remove the sharpshooter's fingers if anyone else tries to be a hero, and the next, these kids are all around us—shooting, fighting, gutting these men, these rugged, rough-and-tumble criminals, like they're sheep at slaughter. It couldn't have been more than a few minutes before the whole mess was over, and we got a good look at the kids that had saved us.

Boys, most of them, maybe a couple girls. They had those burns you were asking about, like collars. And their leader, he had these golden eyes. Like this cat I saw once, huge, scarred in dozens of places. Maybe someone else had tried to capture him when he was a cub, but that cat was a man-eater waiting to happen. I could see it in his eyes. Put a cat like that in a cage and one day he'll get loose, and then he'll kill you . . . and anybody else in his way.

Best leave a cat like that alone, if you know what's good for you.

Chapter 11

To Pass on a Secret

Wielding the Book proved even more difficult than Sefia had expected; the amount of information was so massive and so little of it was what she needed. But she would not be deterred. She began scavenging scraps of paper from their supplies, filling the pages with names, numbers, details, dates. She kept a record of previous crews, how many candidates they'd captured, which boys were killed and by whom.

The impressors had started out small over twenty years ago, kidnapping a boy here or there, leaving their branded bodies to be found rotting in the mulch halfway across the kingdom. Since then, however, they'd gotten organized, and grown in size—hundreds of boys dead, bystanders executed, loved ones filled with grief and guilt—until *impressors* had become a word you used to threaten misbehaving little boys. The damage they'd done in Deliene alone was vast, and every story she read was another reminder of what she owed to Archer, Frey, and the boys, for what her parents had done.

Soon after their run-in with the bandits at the traveling show, Sefia was sketching a rough map of the Northern Kingdom when Versil came to peer over her shoulder. "What's this?" Without waiting for an answer, he shook his head. "No, no, no, you need my brother. Our pop was a mapmaker, did you know that? Aljan was his apprentice. Hang on, lemme get him—Aljan! *Aljan!*"

As they waited for Aljan to arrive, Versil flashed her a grin. "Pop used to say he was born with a brush in his hand. You know, he was painting before he ever said a word? When we were little, I used to talk for him. 'Aljan wants another candy.' 'Aljan hates asparagus.' Stuff like that. You couldn't blame him, though. Who likes asparagus . . ." His voice trailed off until it went completely silent. Then: "Oh, hey, Aljan." For a moment, Versil looked confused and embarrassed, like he knew he'd forgotten something but didn't know what. "We were just talking about you."

Aljan tried to smile, but it was like he was trying to lift something too heavy for him to carry. "You wanted something?"

"Oh, right. The sorcerer needs your help." Lightly, Versil bounded off again, leaving his brother looking dully after him.

When Aljan remained still, Sefia studied him for a moment. Unlike his twin, he was strangely subdued, like a rabbit awaiting the approach of the fox.

Tapping him on the arm to get his attention, Sefia extended her paintbrush. "I heard you were a mapmaker."

He took it from her, testing its weight and balance with the same quiet care he'd used with the Book the night of the ambush. His resigned expression showed a flicker of life. Then he dipped the brush . . . and everything changed. His eyes brightened. His movements sharpened. A smile tinged his lips.

Without much prompting, he soon began sketching out a map of Deliene. The paintbrush flew across the paper, creating shorelines curling with whitecaps, mountains splashed with shadow, provincial crests exquisitely detailed with miniature bears, harpoons, bulls, and sheaves of wheat. The act of painting so transformed him that Sefia felt like she was seeing a part of Aljan she hadn't known existed.

"This is beautiful," she said.

The boy glanced at her with a hesitant smile, as if he were just remembering his sense of humor. "Paper and ink are my weapons too," he said.

The next morning, after writing down the names and last known locations of the three crews currently in operation, she asked for Aljan's help with the map again. He seemed entranced with her notations, his gaze roving over them with such intense fascination he'd forget he was drawing, until the map was stained here and there by small pools of ink.

"These were in the Book too," he said, tracing the **W** in one of the impressors' names. "What are they?"

"They're letters." Her face twisted as she took the brush from him, rinsing it in a cup of water. That was how the Guard had found her before, by following the scribblings she'd left all over Oxscini like breadcrumbs. She'd been so foolish. But she hadn't known.

"Are they the source of your power?"

"No." She'd been able to sense the Illuminated world long

before she'd learned to read. But reading and writing had sharpened her gift, turned it into a tool she could use. "But they're powerful on their own. That's why Serakeen's kept them a secret all these years."

Thoughtfully, Aljan traced a 𝔚 on the edge of the cart where they were sitting, embellishing it with swoops and dashes that made the letter almost unrecognizable. "Would you share that secret with me?" he asked softly.

Sefia hesitated. Sometimes it felt like her whole life had been a secret: her room in the house on the hill, the Book she'd carried on her back for years, the past Archer was still keeping from her. Secrets were as familiar to her as her own reflection.

But they were her parents' secrets—the Guard's secrets—and they'd already caused so much pain.

Bitterly, she smiled, knowing her father would have said it wasn't safe, knowing Tanin would be furious if she found out. But this was Sefia's secret now, her weapon to wield, and she would use it to defy the Guard and everything they stood for.

"Yes," she said. "I'll do it."

When they began moving again, Sefia sat beside Aljan on one of the carts and explained the alphabet while he drove. Every so often, she wrote a letter on a scrap of paper and held it up for him to study, the wet ink dripping, and he'd trace them over and over on the seat of the cart: the 𝔍s, the 𝔄s.

Occasionally, some of the others would ride alongside them, asking about the markings, but for the most part she and Aljan were left alone.

That night, they sat by the fire and began their work in earnest: their pen, a sharpened stick; their blank page, the dirt at their feet.

By the firelight, she passed him one letter after another like plates of delicacies, and he sampled them all, the 𝕿s and 𝕵s, the 𝕾s and 𝖂s.

He'd string together letter after letter in nonsensical combinations—𝕽, 𝕵, 𝕿—until the whole ring of the campfire was encircled by a complex tapestry Sefia could never have imagined. They were meaningless, as far as words went, but they were enthralling—these explosions of serifs and swashes and versals, like fireworks, full of joy and wonder.

As he wrote, he seemed to come into focus, gaining definition, color, detail, as if he'd finally found a part of himself he'd been missing his whole life and only now—through writing—was he complete.

"Where'd you learn this?" he asked, his wide-set eyes gleaming.

Sefia bit her lip, remembering her mother spelling out her name in wooden blocks. Her mother, who'd taught the impressors to sniff out killers like bloodhounds. "I kind of . . . taught myself."

A half-truth, at best. But she couldn't bring herself to tell him the rest. She didn't know how, without hurting him.

If Aljan suspected her of keeping something from him, he didn't show it. He beamed at her and twirled their stick once before offering it to her. "Can we try the kay again?"

The next day, they continued their lessons while Sefia worked on the map, until a sudden wind whipped the paper out from under their hands and sent it, flapping like an injured bird, across the campsite.

Crying out, Sefia darted after the map with Aljan on her heels, but before either of them could reach it, Frey looked up from where she was practicing with her switchblade and, with the smooth striking movement of a rattlesnake, snatched the paper out of the air.

"Nice catch!" Sefia cried.

Frey flicked her blade closed. "You learn to be fast when you've got three older brothers."

Aljan averted his eyes, like the girl was too bright to look directly at.

"I don't have any siblings," Sefia said, taking the map.

"They're a real pain, but I wouldn't trade them in for anything. Right, Aljan?"

The mapmaker smiled shyly.

Frey sighed, tucking an errant lock of hair behind her ear. "I'm going to get you to talk to me one of these days, if it's the last thing I do."

He just gave her another of those little smiles.

As he and Sefia returned to work, she asked, "You've never talked to Frey? Not even once?"

Aljan shrugged. "No words ever seemed good enough."

Every night, after lessons with Aljan and searching the Book for the impressors, Sefia looked for Lon and Mareah. Sometimes she even read passages aloud to Archer, stories of her father's life as a fortune-teller in Corabel and of her mother's time in Everica, before she was inducted into the Guard.

"My mother's parents were doctors," she said once. "My *grandparents* were doctors. I didn't . . . It never occurred to me that I might still have family out there."

Archer's fingers trailed up and down her arm, sending ripples of heat over her skin, but he said nothing.

He'd told her more, now, about his two years with Hatchet. He'd told her about Oriyah and Argo and other boys he'd known and fought and killed. But he hadn't said a word about who he was before the impressors. Or why he didn't want to go home.

"If you did have family out there," Archer said quietly, "would you want to find them?"

Sefia shrugged. "They wouldn't know me from a stranger on the street."

Archer touched the count the impressors had given him. "After all this," he murmured, "I don't think they'd want to know me."

Reaching up, Sefia traced the furrowed line of his brow. "I want to know you," she said.

His golden eyes glimmered, and for a moment she thought he'd kiss her again, the way he had two weeks ago, on the water. She leaned toward him, willing him to close the last bit of distance between them.

But he pulled away.

As Archer got up to patrol the clearing, Sefia tried to hide her disappointment, looking down at the Book again, blinking to bring the words into focus.

She'd been reading about a crew of impressors led by Obiyagi, a woman with unruly white hair and a toad-like face.

They'd been somewhere to the south in Corabelli Land with seven boys, but recently they'd turned north, traversing the mountain passes of the Ridgeline. If Sefia could find out where they were, or where they would be soon, Archer and the others might be able to intercept them.

Consulting her map, Sefia flipped through the pages of the Book, skimming them for landmarks that would tell her *where* and constellations that would tell her *when*.

She wasn't as powerful as her parents had been. She wasn't as skilled or prepared. But with the Book, she could repair some of the damage they'd done to the world. To Aljan. To Archer. And to their daughter.

Then she looked up, searching the sky for the moon—a waning crescent among the sugar-fine stars.

A triumphant smile crossed her face. She *could* use the Book against the Guard. She *could* help Archer. And maybe if she did that, he would no longer pull away.

Tilting his head, Archer put his fingers to his temple. *What?*

"I found them," she said.

CHAPTER 12

Ambush at the Rock Eater

The next morning, Sefia revealed to the others what she'd learned: In a week, when the moon was a sideways crescent in the morning sky, Obiyagi and her crew would be riding north through the canyons on the Alissari coast. They'd pass a mountain like a kneeling giant—"The Rock Eater," Griegi said, flipping the egg and scallion cake in its cast-iron pan, "that's what we called it back home"—and ride out onto the cliffs beyond, where the plains of the Heartland fell steeply away into the sea.

Archer could almost hear the rhythm of hooves, the report of gunfire. His trigger finger twitched.

Across the campfire, Kaito looked like a little boy with an appetite for trouble. "You promised us impressors, brother. Looks like we've got 'em."

Archer grinned. "Now all we need is a plan to stop them."

The plan took shape as they headed east toward Alissar Province, riding through the last of the summer crops, thick and plentiful in the fields.

At night, Sefia read, and the Book revealed to her kaleidoscopic visions of the future: the cries of men and horses—Frey and the boys darting among the enemy—sprays of blood—dust—a ⊖ splintering—boys, whose faces she didn't recognize, squinting in the morning sun.

She recounted everything she read to Archer, who discussed the coming battle with Kaito as they searched for prey scampering through the orchards and fallow fields.

"Do we know how many there are?" Kaito asked, nocking an arrow to the bow Sefia had lent him for hunting.

"Twenty-six."

"Against the eight of us?" The Gormani boy sighted on a rabbit dashing across the plains. "That's three and a quarter impressors each." He drew back, fired. The rabbit dropped.

Archer dismounted to retrieve their dinner. "Good odds."

"*Killer* odds." It was macabre. But coming from Kaito, it seemed funny.

They spent almost all their time together now. Except for when Archer was with Sefia, he and Kaito ate together, rode together, stood watch together, discussing battle plans, anticipating counterstrikes. When one of them panicked, or nightmared, or needed something thrilling and reckless to forget what had happened to him, the other was there with a comforting word or something to break or a plan to dive off a cliff into a lapis-blue stream so cold and deep they weren't always sure if they'd come out again.

Kaito was like the brother Archer had never had. Even better, he was brilliant, a born tactician. It was his idea to take down Obiyagi and her crew like the highwaymen of old, running down supply wagons in the red Liccarine canyons. "Except we're not out for gold," he added.

Archer swept his hand across the ground, obliterating the map they'd sketched in the dirt. "Nah," he said, "we're out for blood."

Kaito's smile put a crook in the scar on his cheek. "You got that right, brother."

On the morning of the ambush, they mounted their horses and entered the canyon, taking up posts behind bunches of saltbush and shrubs of flowering lupin: Archer with Sefia and the twins on the western slope; Kaito leading Scarza, Frey, and Griegi in the east. In the hills, Mako lay hidden with their supplies.

Beyond the Rock Eater, the grasslands waited.

As the Book had foretold, when the crescent moon rose above the canyon, a cloud of dust appeared in the distance.

The wind whipped past them, and Archer sat forward in his saddle, imagining he could smell axle grease and gunpowder on the air. He licked his lips.

"Hey, sorcerer," Versil said, shifting uncomfortably on the back of his painted horse. "Think I'll miss the battle if I take a minute? Nature's calling."

"If you don't go, you won't miss it." Sefia didn't take her eyes off the canyon, hawk-like in her focus.

Archer's fingers tightened on the reins. They were going to

win. They were going to stop Obiyagi and free the boys from their crates. With the Book to guide them, there was no way they could lose.

Versil shrugged. "All right, but if I wet myself in the middle of the battle, I'm blaming you."

They watched the impressors draw near—four riders with the first cart, where Obiyagi sat with her shotgun and her driver, and the rest of the caravan following in their wake.

Across the canyon, a gunshot cleaved the air. An impressor toppled from his horse.

Scarza. Best rifleman they had.

Cries of alarm went up along the caravan as the impressors closed ranks around the carts.

With a roar, Kaito charged from his hiding place with Frey and Griegi quick behind him, racing down the mountain at breakneck speed. Gunfire flashed at their fingertips, and enemies fell to their bullets like tin cans from a fence line.

But the caravan didn't stop. Ducking shots and returning fire, the impressors charged around the Rock Eater, heading for the grasslands.

Archer bared his teeth—a hunter ready for the chase.

Then they were off, galloping downhill, into the ranks of the enemy. Bullets pinged off rocks, spitting gravel.

As Archer entered the fray, his fighting instincts took over. There was so much to see: the charging horses, manes and tails flying—trigger fingers pulling—bullet cases bouncing in the dust. He could see the whole battle: the trajectory of the caravan—the movements of Frey and the boys—the amount of time they had before they hit the cliffs.

It was loud and awful, and it was glorious.

He rode in among the enemy, pulling impressors from their saddles, plugging them with bullets. He was a bolt of light. He was the *crack* of thunder.

Then Kaito was beside him—there was a feral light in his green eyes, like he didn't care if he lived or died as long as he went out fighting—and they were a terror to behold: riding, shooting, whooping like wild little boys playing outlaws in their backyard, taking one life after another with careless brutality.

Gunfire skimmed Kaito's horse. She startled, eyes white with fear and pain. The boy struggled to keep her in line as a second shot grazed his thigh.

Whirling, Archer put a bullet between the impressor's eyes. She tipped from her cart, reins slipping from her lifeless fingers.

Sefia flung out her hand, catching the reins in her invisible grip, and the cart came skidding to a stop.

Thank you, Archer mouthed.

In the dust, she held up two crossed fingers.

They rode hard as they entered the grasslands, pinning the impressors against the edge of the cliffs. Explosions of gunpowder and blasts of heat surrounded them, and one by one, the enemy fell. Horses escaped. Ahead of them all, Obiyagi and the lead cart rattled on.

Grinning, Kaito gestured to the front of the caravan. "You and me, brother."

They urged their mounts forward. The wind screamed. They were so close.

Turning in her seat, Obiyagi let off a round from her shotgun.

Kaito shot back, his bullet skimming the side of her neck. She ducked.

Cursing, the Gormani boy jerked his head at Archer. "I'll cover you."

Archer sensed Frey riding up behind him. Letting the reins fall, he stood in the stirrups. He felt his mare adjust as his weight shifted, but she didn't break stride.

He jumped—Frey caught the reins before his horse could bolt—and landed in the back of the cart, rolling to avoid a blast from Obiyagi's shotgun. The boards split beneath him.

Behind him, Kaito's six-guns popped, catching the impressor in the shoulder, the ear. She dove back undercover.

As Archer stood, the wheels bucked and skidded on the rough terrain, throwing him into the crates. Clambering over them, he reared over the front of the cart and knocked the driver unconscious with the butt of his gun.

Obiyagi lunged for the reins, then froze. Archer's revolver was pressed to the back of her head. The cart slowed. "All right, boy," she muttered. "You win."

Breath rushed in and out of Archer's lungs. His chest heaved.

He could kill her. A twitch of his finger and she'd be gone. He wanted it. He could almost taste the spray of blood on his lips. His hand shook. *No.* He wouldn't be that boy.

Behind him, Kaito crowed. The boy was standing in his stirrups, arms pumping, head thrown back in an exultant roar. "Rotten hulls, Archer, you did it! You promised us impressors, and you delivered! I'll follow you anywhere, brother, *anywhere*—"

His cries were cut short by the sound of a blunt object on bone. A puff of dust rose as two figures fell to the ground, grappling, flailing. Then Aljan's lanky figure appeared on top of an impressor, lying on his stomach, trying to cover his head with his hands. Over and over the boy's fists struck him, hard, relentless.

Archer leapt from the cart. "Kaito. Kaito! Secure the prisoners."

Aljan was crying, wailing, saliva flying from his lips, blood flying from his fists. But he didn't stop. It was like he couldn't stop. Every time he struck, the impressor's head rocked violently from one side to the other, like a ship's bell in a storm.

Archer raced past Sefia, holding the reins of two of the carts with her magic, but Frey was faster. She ducked one of Aljan's blows and caught his arm, hauling him off the impressor, who lay, unmoving, in the blood-spattered dust. The mapmaker buried his face in her hair, shuddering.

For a moment, everything was still. Archer locked eyes with Sefia.

They'd won.

In the stunned silence, they could hear Aljan sobbing.

Two down, two to go.

CHAPTER 13

The Dead Arise

The impressor Aljan had attacked didn't make it, bringing the death toll to sixteen. Sixteen bodies swaddled in blankets. Sixteen corpses for the flames.

Sefia watched as Frey and all fourteen of the boys took turns touching a torch to the kindling, their faces solemn and hard. Kaito was the last, and he hesitated a long moment, watching the smoke billow from the porous mound of blackrock, before he thrust the torch deep among the logs and returned to Archer's side.

The flames grew higher. The acrid stink of burning hair enveloped them.

Shackled at the wrists and ankles, Obiyagi and the other prisoners stood by. One by one, they repeated the names of the dead.

Sefia knew those names, had read them in the Book. One of them had joined the impressors to prevent her own son from being taken. Another had been a gardener. One had been on the crew of the *Current*, long before Reed became captain. Others were cruel and had reveled in abuse since they were children, plucking the legs off of insects one at a time like flower petals.

None of the boys spoke. There were no speeches, no stories. Quietly, Kaito and Scarza escorted the captives back into their crates.

When they returned, Archer addressed the group: "I know what they've done to us, but when they surrender, we have to stop." There was gravel in his voice, some emotion ground against another deep inside him. His gaze went to Aljan, who had that dull, confused look in his eyes again. "We have to stop, or we become what they wanted. We stop, or they win."

The mapmaker nodded miserably. The others, even Kaito, murmured their agreement.

In the silence that followed, one of the new boys, Keon, a scrawny sixteen-year-old with the sun-streaked hair of a south-coaster, cleared his throat. "We didn't get the chance to thank you, for what you did. When all the commotion started, we— we thought for sure we were dead."

"You were dead." Archer gestured to the others, who touched the scars at their throats. "We all were."

"We were dead," Kaito agreed, saluting with his crossed arms. "But thanks to our chief and our sorcerer, now we rise."

Chief?

Startled, Sefia glanced up at Archer, whose gold eyes flickered with worry—and a darker reaction, like hunger. Until now, the group had been leaderless. Informal. A band of lost boys. But now they'd become something different, something more—a following.

Archer gripped her hand tighter as the others repeated Kaito's words like a rallying cry, to be invoked before some distant battle: "We were dead, but now we rise."

The air crackled. The hair rose on Sefia's arms.

They'd done it again—stopped the impressors, freed the boys—because of the Book. The Guard's greatest weapon turned against them. But what if it was a weapon with a hidden edge? What if, somehow, Sefia was doing exactly what they'd wanted all along?

That night, there was a celebration. Frey and Archer built a bonfire that dwarfed even the twins in height, and when they'd all finished feasting on roasted seabirds and skewers of onions, they took the burning brands of Griegi's cookfire and thrust them into the heap of kindling and driftwood.

The flames leapt skyward, and the boys let out a cheer, their bodies seeming to flicker in the red light. Moving among them, Kaito and Scarza doled out bottles of liquor they'd raided from the impressors' supplies and flasks they'd filched from the bodies of the dead.

On the edge of the firelight, Frey sat with Aljan while he sketched in the dirt. The battle, the beating, had finally gotten him to talk to her. From a distance, Sefia watched their heads tilt toward each other when they spoke, like reeds bowing in the wind.

Giddy with freedom, the others played Ship of Fools and

tossed up shards of broken crockery, which Scarza shot out of the air with a myriad of dazzling one-handed tricks. They told stories and dared each other to stand by the fire, counting the seconds before they danced away from the heat.

And at the center of it all was Archer. Beaming. Beloved. Everywhere he went, the others bowed and crossed their arms, gripped his hand and offered their gratitude.

Eyes bright with excitement, Kaito swaggered up to him. "Why's your cup empty?" He scowled at the others. "Who allowed the chief's cup to go empty? Was it you, Griegi?"

The cook giggled and hid his pink cheeks behind his hands. Laughing, Keon, the skinny south-coaster, pulled his arms down. For a moment, they stared at each other, grinning foolishly, before their lips met in a clumsy kiss. The others whistled.

When they parted, Griegi's face was even redder than before, his smile brighter.

Slinging his arm around Archer's shoulders, Kaito poured a stream of liquor into his cup. "Brother, where I'm from, the first one to stop drinking dishonors his name."

"Your face is a dishonor." Archer clinked their glasses.

Soon they were regaling the others with highlights of their battle. "The way you jumped onto that cart! I thought for sure you were gonna . . . and then Obiyagi—" Kaito mimicked the sound of a shotgun, pretending to jerk back at the recoil. "But that leap! That's the stuff of legends."

Archer shook his head a little too vigorously. "You could've done it, same as me," he said. "You are the best of us, Kaito Kemura." He drew back and raised his cup again. "To Kaito!"

"To Kaito!" the other boys echoed.

The Gormani boy shrugged. "My only regret is not killing more of them before they surrendered."

"No, no, we did good," Archer mumbled. "We did good."

Kaito pressed their foreheads together. "You're a far better person than I, brother."

Through it all, Sefia passed among them mostly unseen—with them, but not one of them. Everywhere she looked, she saw her parents' legacy—in the brands, the scars. She heard her father's words in every story of torture and mistreatment they recounted.

We need a boy with a scar around his throat? Let's go find him.

All this, for one boy. Without meaning to, she found Archer in the crowd. Had it worked? Was she somehow playing right into the Guard's hands? *Could* you, as Lon had claimed, make destiny?

Her thoughts were interrupted as Versil, seeing her approach, beckoned some of the new boys closer and told them in a theatrical whisper how she'd once turned him into a moth for falling asleep on watch. "She restored me to my handsome self by morning, obviously, but see this?" He pointed to the white patches on his face. "Parts of me stayed permanently white."

Sefia rolled her eyes. "I did no such thing."

With an exaggerated wail, Versil prostrated himself at her feet. "Please, sorcerer, don't turn me again!"

She stalked away while he got up again, laughing.

Farther away from the bonfire, she found the remnants of Aljan's letters in the dirt, a mesmerizing pattern of loops and spirals, half-erased. Here and there she picked out a 𝕴, an 𝕰, or an 𝔄—but on the whole they looked more like the necks of some mythic, multiheaded creature than writing as she knew it.

From the other side of the fire, she could hear Kaito's rough tenor leading the others in old Gormani battle songs from his home up north. Grand, haunting melodies for ancient warriors made new and urgent by the boys' untrained voices.

> *Sunrise in the northern sky*
> *Stains the ice and snow with light.*
> *Kiss your children. Raise your weapons.*
> *Through the waves, we ride.*
> *To our deaths, we ride.*
> *Our foes will not forget how we fight.*
>
> *They will know our names,*
> *Our valor, and our blades.*
> *They will tell the world*
> *How we fought this day.*

She could hear Archer trying to follow, but he was always a note off, a word behind, trailing after the melody. But he was from Oxscini. He wouldn't have known these songs.

And he wasn't a warrior. A fighter, yes. A hunter, maybe. But not a leader of men like the generals from the north or even Captain Reed, with his band of outlaws. At least he hadn't been, before today.

She smoothed away the rest of Aljan's letters, lingering at last on a 𝔎 before wiping it out, trying to ignore the twinge of guilt she felt at ruining something so beautiful.

"Sefia?" Archer's low voice startled her out of her thoughts. He was standing at the edge of the firelight, his smile a little more slanted than usual. "Want to get out of here?"

She took his hand, and together they wandered toward the cliffs, the bonfire dwindling to a faint pulse behind them as the night air filled with the sounds of the ocean crashing on stone.

"This is better," Archer said as they settled in the grass. Before them the whole expanse of the Central Sea lay like a vast kingdom of white rooftops and black streets. "Like old times."

Some of the tension eased in her shoulders. "Except the skies are bigger. You don't get skies like this in Oxscini."

He nodded.

"Do you miss it?"

Archer pressed his lips together. "I'm not the boy who belonged there anymore."

"Who are you, then?"

He stroked the inside of her wrist. "I . . . I don't know. Sometimes, I'm one of them." He nodded toward camp, where Frey and the boys were still carrying on. "I have a mission, a purpose. Other times . . . I'm the killer you met in the jungle, the one with no name, and all I want is to break things, to ruin them any way I can, until you can't even tell what they used to be . . . But I don't want to be him."

Every place he touched tingled with warmth, and as he tilted his head toward her, Sefia was suddenly absorbed in the lines of his jaw, of his chin and lips. She could feel his gaze roving back and forth across her face.

"Who do you want to be?" she whispered.

Gently, he traced the curve of her cheek. "I want to be good. I want to be whole. I want to be the boy you deserve."

Heat rippled over her skin. "Archer," she said.

He leaned closer, as if drawn by the way she spoke his name.

She lifted her chin, and their lips touched. It was like the rest of the world was burning away—the grass, the glittering horizon, the guilt and blame—and the only thing keeping them from spiraling off into the darkness was the way they clung to each other.

She gasped, and the shock of them parting brought the world roaring back.

Wordlessly, Archer twined his fingers in her hair and pulled her in again.

She closed her eyes. She didn't want the world. She wanted his mouth on hers. She wanted his hands at her neck, along her back. She wanted Archer, and, at least for tonight, absolutely nothing else.

CHAPTER 14

Bell of the *Desert Gold*

Once they'd heard the bell of the *Desert Gold* crying out over the Ephygian Bay, they'd used the clapper to home in on the bell's location, and now it and the *Gold* lay directly beneath them, more than fifty feet below the surface, with the map to the greatest treasure Kelanna had ever known. Captain Reed tapped his fingers impatiently, while Horse, the ship's carpenter, and his assistants roved over the great wooden framework they'd erected on the deck of the *Current*, tightening bolts and checking pulleys, attending to the air pumps and long lengths of hose.

Horse's diving bell was a wonder to behold: A dome of iron with an open bottom and portholes to let in the light, it would lower into the sea, using the water pressure to trap a pocket of air inside. As long as you continued to pump in fresh air through the leather tubes, you could swim in and out of the iron chamber as often as you pleased.

Nearby, the *Crux* lay at anchor too, her gold hull brilliant in the beating sun. On her decks, Dimarion's crew prepared a diving bell of their own.

The chief mate sidled up next to Reed, all grizzled features and gray hair. "I don't like you going down there after what Bee said about the Blue Navy," he said.

Hundreds of outlaws blown out of the water. Hundreds of names lost. King Stonegold and the Evericans were obliterating their way of life, one ship at a time.

Reed touched the blank circle of skin on his wrist.

But some deeds were so great they couldn't be contained by ships and mortal men. Some deeds were so great they'd outlast everything else—little kings, lies, and his own mistakes.

He hoped.

Reed removed his hat. "This far into Liccarine waters, you oughta worry more about Serakeen."

"Oh, I do." The mate pinched the bridge of his nose, between his dead gray eyes. He could sense everything that occurred on the ship, picking out rats nesting in the bilge as easily as he could pinpoint leaks. But sometimes, especially when he was anxious, all that sensory information gave him searing headaches.

"It's a big stretch of water. If Serakeen's pirates show their ugly mugs, you've got plenty of time to warn us down there." Captain Reed unbuckled his gun holsters and stripped off the rest of his clothing piece by piece until he was in nothing but his braies.

"Anything happens, and we'll literally be caught with our trousers down," the chief mate warned.

"Don't need trousers to fight off pirates."

"Don't *need* them. But you might want them."

Reed clapped him on the shoulder. "Don't worry. It ain't today."

The mate grunted, but as it always did, the answer satisfied him.

Captain Reed was one of a few people in Kelanna who knew how they were going to die. Folks said the water had told him while he was caught in a maelstrom that had nearly peeled the skin from his bones.

When he died, there'd be one last breath of salty wet air. A black gun. A bright dandelion on the deck. The timbers of the ship bursting. And darkness.

But it wasn't this day.

Together they descended to the main deck, where Jules was waiting. She'd been a pearl diver before joining up with the *Current*, and still had the lungs for it, though thanks to Reed she'd left that life behind a long time ago. Today she wore braies and a leather bandeau that exposed her tattooed arms, and her skin was bronzy in the hot sun, except where a few silver scars, decades old, ran laterally along her rib cage, half-hidden beneath her top.

There was a cheer as the diving bell submerged.

Captain Reed glanced over at the *Crux*. Though they were allies now, for all intents and purposes, they'd been enemies for much longer, and there was no telling when the gold ship might turn on them.

"I know we're supposed to be on the same side and all,"

Jules said in her velvety drawl, "but if we don't get that bell first, we're gonna have trouble."

"We'll get it." Reed flashed her a grin. "We've got you."

With a great leap, they dived over the side of the ship, striking the water like arrows. Kicking and thrusting, Reed came up in the chamber of the bell, which was equipped with seats and footholds, safety lines and hooks, and a long umbilical of tubing connecting their air pocket to the bellows on the deck of the ship.

Jules surfaced beside him, and they hauled themselves onto the seats. As they knotted the safety lines to their waists, she picked up a small hammer tied to the wall and glanced inquiringly at him.

He nodded. "Go on."

She struck the hammer against the inside of the bell. The sound reverberated around them and traveled through the water.

Distantly, there was an answer from the ship and a slight tug on the line before the diving bell began to sink deeper into the sea.

Through the portholes, the water turned turquoise and teal and green as they traveled farther from the surface. The bell echoed with the steady *whoosh* of air from the hose, the quiet splash of the sea dripping from their fingers and toes.

Every so often there was a toll from above, like a question: *All right down there?*

And they'd rap the side of the bell with the hammer: *All right.*

Then the hulk of the *Desert Gold* appeared before them.

The ship had tipped sideways in the sand, her masts snapped, her flanks encrusted with coral. Blue fish like spearheads darted through the gun ports, and algae fuzzed the ancient decks.

But she was a beautiful ship, festooned with the exquisite craftsmanship that had once made Liccaro the richest kingdom in Kelanna. Even now, at the bottom of the sea, Reed spied precious metals, gems, and cabochons the size of his fist adorning the rotten rails.

As they neared the seafloor, he struck the diving bell twice to halt their descent.

There was an answering ring from the surface, and they eased to a stop above the warped decks. "All right, Cap." Jules's lilting voice echoed around them. "Show me what you've got."

Reed flicked her a quick salute and, taking a breath, submerged.

Water closed over his head as he swam toward the *Gold*, the safety line at his waist unreeling behind him. Where the decks had collapsed, the crisp fans of sea scallops lay among elaborately carved doorways, and fish flicked through the ruins, waving ethereal white fins.

Reaching down, he collected a chipped tea saucer and scraped algae from its surface, revealing the gilded crest of Liccaro—a desert flower in full bloom.

He looked around. Faintly, he thought he could make out the massive shadow of the *Crux*'s diving bell hovering over the prow.

They had to move fast.

Dropping the saucer, Reed launched himself upward again.

He emerged in the air pocket, gasping. "Two minutes," Jules said approvingly. "Not bad."

Coughing, he hauled himself back onto his seat, still trying to catch his breath.

Jules laughed at him. "I'm on it, Cap. You rest your lungs a bit."

He kicked water at her.

Slipping easily into the sea, Jules ducked beneath the surface, leaving him alone in the iron chamber. He shut his eyes, listening to the waves.

It was as if he could hear the ocean murmuring to him, telling him of nearby coral reefs and basins empty of everything but sand, of the *Crux*'s divers exploring the wreck, of the *Current* above and other ships on the surface, cutting through the water.

Jules came up beneath him. "I found it, Cap. Only . . . I think you oughta take a look yourself."

They switched places, Jules settling into the seat again and him dipping into the water. He swam toward the fractured remnants of the ship's helm, where a skeleton, picked clean by scavengers, stared up at him from the deck, its jawless face unsmiling. Nearby, the ship's brass bell lay on its side.

Brushing aside silver minnows that fluttered once around his hands before dispersing, Reed pulled the bell upright. It was inscribed with the insignia of the *Desert Gold*—a sun rising over a flat desert—but that was all.

No map.

No key to the location of the Trove.

Frowning, he peered inside the bell.

There, half-obscured by a crust of verdigris and limpets, were words.

Words.

His hand went to his chest. He recognized those uniform shapes, like the prints of snakes in the sand. Like the marks in Sefia's book. Like the tattoos that had been forced on him when he was sixteen.

Legend said the clapper would lead to the bell, and the bell would lead to the long-lost hoard. It hadn't mentioned *words*.

Suddenly, the water filled with the sound of the *Current*'s bell clanging over and over, ringing all around him, making the sea shiver with noise.

The alarm. Something had gone wrong above.

Leaving the deck of the *Gold*, Reed resurfaced at Jules's feet.

She grabbed a hook from the hangers on the ceiling. "We need that bell." Before he could protest, she dove into the water and kicked toward the deck below.

The diving bell jerked and rose a few feet. Cursing, Reed scrambled onto the seat and rapped the hammer against the side of the bell.

Stop.

But the alarm was growing more frantic with every second. He waited a breath and signaled them again.

Stop.

"Come on, Jules," he muttered, staring down at the water. On the side of his thigh, he nervously traced two interconnected circles—once, twice, three times, four . . .

She didn't resurface.

The diving bell lurched again and began to ascend. Jules's safety line tightened. If they went up too quickly, even a strong swimmer like her wouldn't be able to catch up. She'd drown, her body pulled along by the rising bell.

Captain Reed grabbed the second hook and dove after her.

He found her wrestling with the bell of the *Desert Gold*, trying to tie it to the hook and line. Her head jerked up as Reed hit the deck beside her, and she nodded briefly before they continued securing their prize.

Without warning, the alarm ceased. The ocean went silent.

Reed cursed. Bubbles burst from his lips. This would have been the time to tell Horse to stop the ascent.

Above them, the diving bell began to shoot through the water. Their safety lines went taut. Reed and Jules launched themselves upward. Below, the bell of the *Gold* was pulled from the decks.

Reed swam as hard as he could, but it wasn't hard enough. They'd run out of air before they caught up. His chest burned. *Almost there.* He coughed. Water flooded his throat.

Jules grabbed his arm and hauled him upward.

Just as spots began to whirl before Reed's eyes, he and Jules surfaced inside the diving bell. Air rushed into his lungs. Jules pulled herself onto a seat, dragging him after.

"Thanks," he wheezed.

"It ain't every day you get to rescue Cannek Reed," she said. "I'll be milking this story for a long time yet. Might even make a song about it."

The light changed again—blue to teal to cyan—and the

diving bell halted. Sky shone in the portholes. They'd made it. Unlooping their safety lines, Reed and Jules dropped through the opening at the bottom of the bell and resurfaced in the shadow of the *Current*.

"Cap!" Marmalade cried as soon as he came up again. *"It's Serakeen!"*

On deck, Horse and his assistants threw their weight into the winch, and the diving bell rose out of the water like the head of some enormous sea creature. Behind it came the smaller bell of the *Gold*. While Marmalade and Killian, a sailor from the larboard watch, secured their find, Captain Reed and Jules climbed back onto the *Current*.

Shedding water, Reed bounded up the steps to the quarter-deck, where Aly, his steward, pressed a spyglass into his hands. "How many and how far off?" he demanded.

"Four," she chirped in response. "Three scouts and a double-decker."

He tossed the glass back to her. "Keep an eye on 'em for me, kid."

With a nod, she flicked her blond braids over her shoulder and dashed away.

Across the water, the decks of the *Crux* were swarming with activity as Dimarion's crew hoisted their own diving bell out of the water, drew up the anchors, and unfurled their gold-embroidered sails. Oars appeared from her sides like the legs of a water centipede.

Dimarion's mountainous form appeared on his quarter-deck. "Did you get our bell?" he called in his great basso profundo.

"What kinda treasure hunter you think I am?" Reed hollered back.

"We'll split off, draw some of them away from you."

For a moment, Reed thought he'd misheard. The *Crux* was going to draw fire for them?

"Meet east of Hye," Dimarion continued. "You know the place?"

The last time they'd joined forces, Captain Dimarion had stranded him on a sandbar east of the island of Hye—a betrayal that had brought them to a standoff inside a roaring maelstrom and sparked five long years of competition and hostility.

And now Dimarion was sticking his neck out for the *Current*. What had changed?

"Couldn't forget if I tried," Reed said.

The diamond rings on Dimarion's fingers flashed as he raised a hand in salute. "If they catch you, make sure they remember your name."

"They won't catch me."

With a laugh, the captain of the *Crux* disappeared from the rail.

The chief mate appeared at Reed's side. "The wind's flat. Can we outrun them?"

Reed scanned the water for signs of a current, but the surface was still as a lake. "We've gotta try."

The mate pivoted on his heel, bellowing orders. The crew ran to their posts.

Reed pulled on his trousers and stuffed his feet into his boots, buckling on his holsters as he squinted at the horizon. The ships were closer now—close enough to count their sails.

He leapt down to the helm, where Jaunty, his stringy, taciturn helmsman, was already maneuvering them to catch the stale breeze. "Get us outta here, Jaunty."

The helmsman grunted.

"Make clear for engagement!" Reed cried.

The sailors scurried down to the magazine and back up again, bringing rammers and sponges, crows and handspikes, powder horns and cases of shot. Dripping seawater, Jules joined them, calling out instructions over the din. They loaded rifles and mounted swivel guns to the rails, and between the cannons they set tubs of seawater and swabs for battling fires.

Every minute the enemy ships were gaining on them, growing larger and more fearsome on the horizon. Their black-and-yellow hulls made them appear like wasps, with thorns of weaponry along their flanks.

Serakeen's pirates. For over a decade they'd besieged Liccaro: plundering cities that opposed them; attacking incoming merchants, military ships, privateers; sparing only those that funneled resources to their corrupt allies in the regency. They were a disgrace to outlaws everywhere—they were men of land and war, not men of water and freedom.

Off to starboard, the *Crux* edged to the northwest, propelled by the oars of Dimarion's galley slaves.

There was an explosion behind the *Current*.

Reed's crew flung themselves against the decks.

The cannonball struck the edge of the quarterdeck, chewing out a corner of the rail and falling into the water with a *splash*.

The mate let out a string of curses that could've seared a side of beef.

Reed threw himself against the rail, scanning the sea. If there was a way out of this, he'd find it. He had to. He wouldn't die today.

Behind them, two of Serakeen's ships peeled off in pursuit of the *Crux*.

That left two quick scouts and the *Current of Faith*. Poor odds.

Captain Reed blinked spray out of his eyes.

It was as if he could see the pull of the moon, the rising of the tide, and the swirling storms out there on the Central Sea, the wakes of ships and the rumbling of volcanoes in the deep.

He began counting. Always to eight. Never more. His favorite number. It kept him focused. Eight after eight after eight.

Then he found it: a break in the waves, like a channel through the crests. A rip current.

If they made it there before Serakeen's ships caught them, they just might escape.

"There!" he yelled to Jaunty. "Off the port bow!"

The helmsman nodded once and turned the wheel. Serakeen's ships were close now, the flags of the Scourge of the East flying from each of the yards, with the fore guns thundering one after another.

At the stern, Cooky and Aly crouched with their rifles, popping up every so often to let off a round.

On the deck, the gun crews prepared the broadsides, readying for battle.

Reed gripped the rail so hard his fingernails dug into the wood.

Then they hit the current. The waters surged up around

them, carrying them rapidly over the troughs. Spray washed over the forecastle.

Serakeen's ships fell behind as their helmsmen tried to adjust. Jaunty cackled, pointing the ship into the fast water. The aft gunners cheered.

The *Current of Faith* drew ahead. The distance between them and the enemy increased.

They were going to make it. The currents would sweep them out of range, and Serakeen's scouts would flounder while the *Current* skimmed the surface, speeding out of the Ephygian Bay into the Central Sea.

As his crew let out a cheer, Captain Reed began pacing the quarterdeck. They'd gotten what they'd come for. They'd gotten away. But now they had a riddle to solve.

He only knew one person who could decipher the marks inside the ship's bell, and the last time he'd seen her, she'd been striding into the maze of Jahara's Central Port with a boy who fought like a wild beast.

Picking up his shirt, Reed scooped a folded scrap of canvas from the breast pocket and traced the letters written there: **REED**.

Words meant trouble, and not the good kind.

Because of words, an assassin had come prowling onto his ship, seeking them out the way the Executioner sought blood.

Harison, the ship's boy, had died.

And long before that, when Reed was only sixteen, he'd been kidnapped and laid flat while words were carved into him, letter by letter, line by line. The memory of it lanced through his chest, and he put his hand over his drumming heart, where beneath the years of ink and glory those first tattoos lay hidden.

He didn't know who'd done it.

He didn't know why.

But with the way words kept circling back to him, he suspected he'd soon find out.

Account of the Second Child

Dear Director,

Troubling reports from the messengers. Sefia must be teaching the candidates to write. Loose ends have been clipped, but the knot remains. Instructions?

Your loyal Apprentice, A.D.

We saw them on the riverbank that morning, but Mama said to stay away, so we didn't go to the river until after lunch.

All the boys were gone by then, and they took their horses too. They left footprints in the mud—big ones, like this—and we kept trying to walk in them, like we were spies who couldn't leave any tracks.

That's when we found it drawn in the mud. It was all rubbed

away, like someone tried to hide it, except for this one part. I thought it was pretty, and so did Amilee. She said it was an old crest from an ancient magical kingdom, and it hadn't been seen for thousands of years. It only showed itself to royalty, she said, so we must have been long-lost princesses.

We copied it lots of times in the mud—did you see?—to make a line between the goblin kingdom and ours, because goblins can't cross a magic border . . .

It's probably all washed away by now, isn't it? In the rain?

You don't think that means the goblins got in, do you? You don't think they got Amilee? You don't think we brought them here by doing it, did we? We just wanted to keep our side of the river safe . . .

Where's Amilee?

When can I go home?

CHAPTER 15

The Loyalty and Cowardice of Dogs

he greenhouse smelled of earth and late-summer fruit ripening in the trees. Through the glass wall that joined the greenhouse and Library, Tanin could see Erastis and his Apprentice, June, leaning over the curved tables, turning pages on a series of Fragments while they searched for patterns in the text.

Her health had improved enough to increase her reach to the primary levels of the Main Branch, where the servants carted her about in her elaborate wheeled chair. But she had not been reinstated as Director, and had to resort to spies and subterfuge for any information at all.

Pocketing Detano's report to Stonegold, Tanin rested her elbow on the arm of her chair and flicked her fingers, chopping tiny daisies from their stems in the grass. The intercepted documents were troubling indeed. Sefia was spreading the written word. *Children* were replicating it. And Stonegold seemed to be doing nothing.

Her spies told her Stonegold was engrossed in Phase II of the Red War: securing Liccaro's allegiance to Everica, and therefore to the Guard. In other circumstances, she might have been equally absorbed. But while Stonegold's attempts on her life had decreased in frequency, they had not ceased altogether, and in her fragile state, she was a Guardian without rank and without work.

Except for finding Sefia and the boy, who seemed to be building an army, of sorts.

Deftly, Tanin sliced the head from a flower. It tumbled onto the lawn, its petals creasing on impact.

The air shivered.

She looked up. *Another attack?* Unlikely, with Erastis nearby. Unless he was privy to it. She narrowed her eyes as he smiled at something June had said. Around her, the leaves began bobbing and dancing in an increasing frenzy as a breeze whipped through the enclosed greenhouse. As Tanin summoned the Sight, preparing to defend herself, Rajar appeared in a cloud of salty air, smelling of tar and smoke.

She blinked. He had changed drastically since he'd begun masquerading as Serakeen. As one of the Guard's Soldiers, he was trained in military strategy, battle tactics, naval maneuvers. But Lon's plan had required an agent in Liccaro to push the Guard's agenda. So Rajar had taken the name Serakeen, joined a pirate crew, fought his way to captaincy, and earned the fear and loyalty of an entire fleet of outlaws.

The years of cruelty had hardened him—he'd witnessed the most brutal of crimes, participated in them, goaded others to commit them in his name. His piercing ice-blue eyes had a feral glint to them now, like that of a wild dog, and a twisted purple scar marred the left side of his otherwise handsome face.

But his sacrifices had been worth it. As Serakeen, Scourge of the East, his dominion was so complete that he'd obliterated the Liccarine regents who wouldn't bow to his demands, and the ones that remained were both afraid to defy him and desperate to appease him. Now the regency would grant him anything, including an alliance between Liccaro and Everica. Phase II of the Red War.

As the tails of his aubergine coat fluttered and came to rest behind him, Rajar took her hand and brushed her knuckles in the softest of kisses.

"Tanin," he purred.

She didn't miss the slight—he used to call her *Director*. Passing her tongue over her lips, she whispered, "Rajar."

The voice she had prided herself on, the voice she had been able to manipulate like a blade or a riding crop or the soft curve of her hand, was gone. Now her voice brought tears to her eyes.

"Dear heart." Rajar sighed—his breath smelled faintly of cigars and charred meat—and took her smooth hands in his weathered ones. "Don't cry."

"I was expecting you yesterday."

In fact, she'd summoned him two days before. One day she could have excused, but two days showed disrespect, and she was determined to discover just how deep his lack of deference went. With her life and her title at stake, she had to know whom she could trust.

"I came as soon as I could." Stuffing his hands in his pockets, he appeared a blunt instrument among delicate statuary, like he might destroy something simply by touching it. "I miss this place."

The greenhouse had been Lon and Mareah's favorite part of the Main Branch, where they'd stolen away to meet, to talk, to practice more and more advanced forms of Illumination. When Rajar wasn't off on assignment, they'd brought him here too. And Tanin, after she'd become the Apprentice Administrator.

Flicking back his coattails, Rajar sat beside her and inhaled deeply, as if all the scents and fond memories of the greenhouse could whisk him into the past again, before Lon and Mareah had left, before he'd thrown himself headfirst into the role of Serakeen.

He splayed his fingers in the grass, carefully avoiding the daisies peeping through the greenery. "Do you remember when Lon turned the glass a dozen different shades of green?"

Tanin's mouth twisted. Of course she did. He'd been practicing Transformation, the third tier of Illumination. *Green-house*, he'd said, laughing. *Get it?*

He'd always liked wordplay. He'd take any opportunity to prove himself cleverer than everyone else—except when Mareah cut him with one of her looks.

Tanin missed them both, despite what they'd done. Despite what she'd done to them. You could still love the people who hurt you most.

She blinked away the memory. "How is Phase II progressing?"

"Well enough."

"Hmm."

Ignoring her displeased expression, Rajar began picking at

the grass, clearing space around the flowers so they could reach the light more easily. "Did you hear my scouts recently ran the *Current* and the *Crux* out of the Ephygian Bay?"

Eradicating the outlaws and their way of life was essential to gaining control of Kelanna. Stonegold and Serakeen were destroying all pirates they found in eastern waters.

"Did they have the bell?" she asked.

"If they didn't, they'll be back, I'm sure."

Her fingers curled. She would have liked for Reed and Dimarion to continue their search for the Trove, but she'd been waiting months for them to locate the treasure hoard and the Resurrection Amulet. She could wait months more if she had to.

Patience was a virtue she was learning. Slowly.

"Your friends are nothing if not persistent," Rajar added.

"They aren't friends."

"Oh?"

"Friendship isn't a luxury we can afford. Surely you understand that, Serakeen."

He winced at her use of the name. "You and I are friends."

"Indeed?" She lifted an eyebrow. "Then you won't mind lending me a few of your ships."

"What would you need my ships for?"

"Apparently there's a rogue group of boys roaming across Deliene, killing your impressors," she said, brandishing the stolen reports.

Rajar grimaced as he finished making space in the grass for his daisies. "They're not *my* impressors."

"People say there's a sorcerer traveling with them," she continued.

Rajar touched the petals of one of his flowers. "She was so much like them, wasn't she? Seeing her was like seeing them all over again . . ." He sighed. "I don't blame you for what you did."

"What I—"

"Some of the others do. I'm sure you're aware."

Some of the others, she thought. Stonegold and Braca, the Guard's Master Soldier. She was Stonegold's attack dog down to her bones. She'd protested hotly when Tanin was elected Director instead of Stonegold, and she hadn't made contact with Tanin at all since her incapacitation.

Who else? Tanin wondered.

"Letting her come to us on her own terms? Trying to get her to join us? I would have done the same." Rajar shrugged. "You weren't the only one who loved her parents, you know."

For years the four of them had planned on being the ones to bring the Red War to pass, to bring all of Kelanna under one rule—*their* rule. Over and over, they'd promised one another this.

Then Lon and Mareah had changed their minds, their hearts, their allegiances. When they left, Rajar had retreated into his role as Serakeen. He'd spent more and more time with his cutthroat fleet, as if being at the Main Branch, where they'd all pledged their loyalty to the Guard, to *one another*, was too painful. He'd run from their betrayal, but Tanin had stayed to pick up the pieces.

She could do it all again, if she had to.

"I need three of your ships," she whispered. "Sefia and the boy are hunting impressors, so we know exactly where they'll be. Your pirates should make short work of a few lost boys and their *sorcerer*."

Rajar stood. The leather of his coat creaked. He didn't make eye contact with her when he said, "I'll have to run it by my Director."

Liar.

Traitor.

Prevaricator.

Tanin didn't know if she'd lost his loyalty when she was attacked or if it had been trickling out of her grasp ever since Lon and Mareah had abandoned them, but she knew it was gone. She glared at Rajar in disgust. "And you called yourself my friend."

"I am. I just . . ." Still avoiding her gaze, he traced the hems of his pockets. "All the years of being a pirate, all the things I've done in the name of *Serakeen* . . . Darion—the *Director*—has offered me the one thing you never have: the chance to be a Soldier again, a true Soldier. When Liccaro joins the Alliance, my fleet will become a proper military. After all this time."

"I could have done that for you."

Rajar shook his head. "No, I think you liked Serakeen too much to ever let him go."

Serakeen had been a savage creation. A top dog the impressors would fetch for and a mongrel to hound the weak Liccarine regency . . . but he'd been *her* dog, *her* mongrel.

Rajar leaned down, clutching the arms of her chair. The smell of tar and cigar smoke surrounded her, and she fought the instinct to lean away. "Recover your health. Let me talk to Darion. With the death of the Second, we're short a Guardian.

There can still be a place for you, if you want. We're nearly there—all of Kelanna will be under *our* rule. Exactly what we promised ourselves all those years ago."

"Not exactly," she said bitterly. Lon and Mareah wouldn't be with her, and now neither would Rajar.

He planted a kiss on her forehead and straightened. As if he could read her thoughts, he said, "Forget them, dear heart. They're gone. But we're still here."

Tanin glared up at him. "There is no 'we.'"

Hurt dimpled his expression, and his blue eyes seemed weary as he turned toward the Library. He flung open the greenhouse doors and she heard Erastis's surprised exclamation, followed by Rajar's laughter, tinged only faintly by sadness.

Striking out with her hands, Tanin lopped the heads off all of Rajar's carefully exposed daisies. They popped into the air and fell back again, dead.

She'd gotten what she wanted: an assessment of the Apprentice Soldier's loyalty. It was better to know than to wonder.

The Administrators, the Librarians, her agents secreted among the outlaws and in Rajar's own fleet—these were her allies. These were the tools she had to help her wrest control of the Guard away from Stonegold and his dogs.

The first step was setting a trap for Sefia. Without Rajar's support, it would take a little longer. But patience was a virtue she was learning.

CHAPTER 16

The Secret Keepers

Sefia found the next crew before they'd even turned in Obiyagi and the other prisoners. The impressors were in Gorman, fleeing south from the cold with five boys in tow.

When he heard the news, Archer swept her into his arms and kissed her, teasing her bottom lip with his teeth. After waiting for him for so long, she still ached at his touch.

They turned north again, with weeks of riding ahead. The days shortened. Fog settled in the dales, and dew blanketed the fields at dawn. Nights grew chill as rain swept over the Heartland. During rest stops on the road, Sefia and Archer would find each other—sneaking kisses behind the carts, fingers roving along waists and exposed collarbones—until Griegi came in search of apples for his campfire cobbler or Kaito came to ask when they'd get a move on, and they'd spring apart again, breathless.

In the evenings, Frey and the boys began to spar—Kaito's idea, to sharpen them up. Everyone fought everyone, and unless one of them was fighting Archer, you didn't know who'd come out on top.

Only Kaito, if he was lucky, could best Archer.

One time the Gormani boy wrenched Archer's arms behind his back and wrestled him into the dirt. "Gotcha!"

Watching from the sidelines, Sefia saw Archer's eyes glaze over. He struggled—not like the fighter she'd come to know but like an animal in a steel trap. He flailed. He spat. He clawed and gasped. Surprised, Kaito backed off immediately, but instead of standing, Archer curled up on his side. He couldn't seem to breathe. It was like something had shattered inside him that couldn't be pieced back together.

Sefia rushed to him, drew his hand gently to his neck, where the worry stone now hung from a leather cord. He hadn't had an attack like this in weeks, not since their battle with Obiyagi. "You're not back there," she whispered, smoothing his hair away from his forehead. "You're safe."

I'm safe, he mouthed. But he couldn't seem to find his voice.

When he was calm enough, Kaito helped him to his feet. "I'm sorry, brother. I didn't know."

They embraced swiftly, all arms and chests. "It happens to all of us," Archer murmured.

After that, Sefia didn't watch the fights. It was like Archer and the others were addicted to violence, the thrill of it maybe, no matter how much it hurt them.

When the skirmishes were over, Archer would come find

her, wherever she was, alone with the Book. He'd be scraped and bruised, with skin peeling from his knuckles, and he'd explain how everyone was coming along. He'd tell her how Frey could hold her own against boys twice her size. How if Griegi got a hold on you he wouldn't let go. How one time Versil wouldn't stop dancing, laughing, around the ring until he let his guard down and Scarza hit him so hard it knocked his smile askew.

Archer was *happy*—happier than she'd seen him since the *Current of Faith*.

Sometimes they'd pass the rest of the watch together—Sefia leaning into him while she read, his fingers trailing gently through her hair. Sometimes he didn't appear until she was walking back in the rain, and he'd catch her and kiss her in the downpour, water coursing down their faces, making their mouths slick and their fingers stray.

Sometimes his lips tasted of blood.

Later, when Archer returned to the tent he shared with Kaito and Sefia retreated to hers and Frey's, Frey would be waiting up for her, whittling wooden utensils for Griegi or sharpening her switchblade, and she'd eagerly demand details.

"It took almost a year to get Aljan to talk to me," she said once, flipping her blade from one hand to the other. "It'd better not take that long for him to kiss me."

"I waited sixteen years for my first kiss," Sefia said, settling into her cot.

Frey twirled her knife in one hand before snapping it closed again. "I waited fourteen."

"Who was it?"

"Render." The boy who'd given her up to the impressors. The boy she'd killed.

"Oh."

"This was his switchblade," Frey said. "I took it back from the impressors the night you found us."

Sefia turned onto her side, watching the other girl in the darkness. "Do you think he would've wanted you to have it?"

"I hated him, and I loved him, and I killed him." She slipped the knife beneath her pillow before she crawled under the blanket. "I don't keep it for him. I keep it for me."

Sefia reached over the side of her cot, where the green feather lay with her other personal items. As she caressed the vane, she remembered the night Archer had given it to her. The way its colors flashed. The shapes his fingers made in the starlight. How close they'd been without even touching.

So much had changed since then.

Archer still talked to her often about the impressors, the Book, her parents, but he had stopped telling her about the boys he'd killed. He had stopped telling her about his nightmares, if he still had them.

"It's done," he'd say. Or, "It's over. And there's so much else to look forward to now."

In fact, the more he fought, the less he shared, and the happier he seemed, like fighting was a tide that washed away his past, his grief, his guilt.

Until the tide came in again.

As Archer spent more time sparring with the others, Sefia spent more time with the Book. She combed the pages for information about her parents—their lives before the Guard, their inductions, their Apprenticeships. She even watched them fall in love: from their first confrontation in the Library over the skull, through all their clandestine meetings in the greenhouse, to their first kiss under the frosted glass.

She learned so much about Illumination from reading about them, gleaning tricks for the Sight and Manipulation she never would have discovered on her own.

Often, while Archer and the others ran drills for the coming battle, she practiced lifting stones, throwing darts, watching decades revolve past her in golden circles while she remained rooted to the spot.

Lon and Mareah had been so powerful.

And now, through the Book, they were teaching her to be powerful too.

The next night, after hours of reading, Sefia hefted the Book in her arms and headed back to her tent. Canvas domes dotted the campsite, leaking light and conversation through the cracks, and she meandered among them, listening idly to discussions to which she didn't belong.

Except for the watch, Archer and Kaito were the only ones still up and about, prodding the embers of the dwindling campfire and laughing like little kids as sparks flew into the air.

As Sefia passed the twins' tent, she stopped. Through the flaps, she could just make out Frey and Aljan sitting crosslegged on his cot, their knees nearly touching. Across from them was Scarza, practicing sailors' knots Keon had taught him. He'd never been across the sea, and wanted to be prepared in case they left Deliene. Versil paced between them, up and down the center of the tent with his restless energy.

"Sounds like a joke, right?" he asked. "How many boys does it take to win an imaginary war?"

"That's not a joke," Frey said, plaiting her hair and pinning it up. "It's a riddle with no answer."

The tall boy drummed a quick *ratatat* on one of the tent poles. "My money's on Archer."

Outside in the shadows, Sefia went cold. *No, it can't be Archer.*

"What about Kaito?" Scarza tightened a knot with his teeth and lifted it to examine his handiwork. He'd missed a half-hitch, but he must have been satisfied because he allowed himself a shadow of a smile.

"Kaito, yeah," Versil said. "But he's not the chief. He gave that up the night after we caught Obiyagi at the Rock Eater."

The rifleman shrugged, the lamplight gleaming on his silver hair. "He kept us alive."

"Archer's keeping us alive now."

"It's not Archer," Frey said. "The boy dies in the Red War, remember? Sefia would never let that happen."

Suddenly the Book felt heavy, as if Sefia were carrying all of Kelanna between her hands, all of destiny, including Archer's. Not for the first time since the ambush at the Rock Eater, she wondered if she truly was striking back against the Guard, or if she was as much their pawn as one of the impressors.

Versil's mood darkened abruptly. He clenched and unclenched his fists, his white palms flashing. "This next crew of impressors, they're the ones who give their boys a second brand, aren't they? Here." He pointed to his narrow chest.

Boys. They never called themselves *candidates*, Sefia had

175

noticed, as if by using the term, they'd be giving the impressors power over them.

"Like everything else they did to us wasn't enough. Remember the kid of theirs I fought? The kid I . . . he was younger than Mako."

Scarza nodded once and began undoing his knot with one hand. "I remember."

"He didn't stand a chance. He was never going to win against guys as big as you or me. They shouldn't have taken him."

"They shouldn't have taken any of us," Frey added.

Without warning, Versil struck one of the tent poles with his fist. The canvas shuddered. Sefia jumped, clutching the Book to her fast-beating heart.

"Who *does* this? Who *does* something like this?" Each time he spoke, the tall boy hit the pole again. The wood splintered. His knuckles bled.

Sefia shrank back, as if he might see her, who she really was, what her family had done.

Versil was always the happy-go-lucky twin, always the one making jokes. He never let her see this part of him. He was supposed to have been a Historian, Aljan had told her. Their parents had been so proud when he'd gotten his apprenticeship. But after the impressors, he couldn't focus, couldn't get his memory to hold on to anything. He'd always be a jester and a storyteller, but he'd never be a Historian now.

The impressors had changed that.

Her parents had changed that.

"Who does this? *Who does this?*" he demanded. The pole cracked. Tears crept into his voice. "Who's so sick they—"

"Brother," Aljan said quietly.

Versil whirled on him, the pale patches of skin above his eyes making them appear wider, wilder. "*One* boy. They wanted *one* boy. For some stupid war that'll never even come." When he laughed, it came out like a sob. He punched the tent pole again. Something cracked, and he reared back, cursing and cradling his bloodied hand.

Aljan was already there, enfolding his brother in his arms, and for a few moments they stood in the center of the tent, silent except for Versil's soft crying.

Guiltily, Sefia crept away. She couldn't watch them anymore, or listen to their questions when she could have answered them all.

My father did this.

My mother did this.

My family did this.

The secret sat inside her like a stone, cold and heavy in her gut.

She knew the frustration, the confusion, the anger, felt them every time she thought of Lon and Mareah, every time Archer avoided her questions with a laugh and a kiss.

She looked for him now, but he was nowhere to be seen. The embers were cold. The camp was dark and empty. And she'd get no answers from Archer anyway, she knew.

Alone in her tent, she turned to the Book. The gilt-edged pages flashed in the moonlight.

She descended through the paragraphs, taking one after another like rungs on a ladder. Goose bumps rose on her arms. A chill trickled between her shoulder blades. When she looked up, she half-expected to see snowflakes come gusting under the tent flaps.

The Book had taken her back to the winter before her parents found Nin on the plains outside Corabel, before they told her to run.

Family

Lon & Mareah
—WINTER
—Gorman?
—20 years ago

Mist rose from a stand of black pines along the lake, obscuring and revealing the snow-veined mountains and the early periwinkle sky. Crouched behind a driftwood log stuck fast in the ice, Tanin shivered in her furs. She'd been waiting on the shore since before dawn, watching the trail of smoke coiling from the cabin's stovepipe, certain this was where she was supposed to be, terrified of knowing for sure.

A fur-wrapped figure opened the cabin door and stepped out into the trees. She stood in the shadows for a moment, staring intently across the ice, before stalking to the frozen shore. On the sharp bits of shale, she barely made a sound.

It *was* her. It had to be her.

But it wasn't until the woman knelt, brushing frost

from the lining of her hood, that Tanin's suspicions were confirmed.

Her brown cheeks were windburned, but there was no mistaking her pointed chin, her dark eyes and whip-like lashes.

Mareah—the Second Assassin—who'd been like a sister to Tanin ever since she'd been inducted into the Guard.

She remembered standing in the Great Hall, with its marble columns and stained glass ceiling, impossibly high. She remembered her own voice distorted by the pale stone and curving vaults, echoing the final words of her oath: "For today I am a Guardian, and so shall I be to the end."

She remembered her loneliness as Master Dotan led her to the Administrator's Office deep in the mountain, and the way her tears dampened the pillow.

And she remembered Mareah's voice in the darkness, rousing her from sleep: "Don't be scared." The light of a match flaring in Mareah's eyes. The strength in her grip as she took Tanin's hand and led her up the winding staircases to the greenhouse, where Lon and Rajar were waiting.

On the edge of the lake, Tanin stood.

Mareah looked up. Her eyes widened.

With fear? Tanin wondered. The thought skewered her. She'd never wanted anything from Mareah but affection and pride.

And now, answers.

What Lon and Mareah had done to Director Edmon was awful; their theft of the Book, even worse. But deep inside, Tanin still hoped she could return them both to the fold, if only they would tell her *why*.

Mareah's hood fell back, and her black hair streamed around her shoulders, across her face. "You shouldn't be here," she said.

Tanin's voice wavered in the chill air. "I had to come. You'd have come too, if you were me."

How many times had they helped each other? How many times had Mareah tutored her in Manipulation? How many poisons had Tanin brought her from the laboratory, to dip her blades in or tip her darts with? How many wounds had Tanin slathered with ointment or stitched up so expertly they never left a scar?

"Go home to your Guard," Mareah said.

"It was your Guard too, once."

"Not anymore."

Tanin took an unsteady step forward. "*Why?* What made you do this?"

Mareah sighed. A cloud of condensation bloomed from her mouth. "You wouldn't understand."

"I would, if you just explained—"

Before Mareah could answer, Lon emerged from the trees. Even now, his clothing was too big for him, making him seem small, young. But none of them were children anymore.

"How'd you find us?" He blinked, using the Sight to search the white-capped ridges that surrounded the mountain lake.

"One of the Fragments in the Library," Tanin said. Someone had known they'd come here. Someone had copied out the location perfectly, down to every peak and promontory, the hunting cabin, the couple whispering within. "Come back. We can explain to everyone—"

"We can never go back," Mareah interrupted.

"You *can*. We're family."

Family. That was what they'd called themselves—Lon and Mareah and she and Rajar. The new Guard. The greatest in generations.

Lon and Mareah exchanged one of their looks, indecipherable to anyone but them.

"You and I were never family," Mareah said.

Moisture gathered at the corners of Tanin's eyes, freezing in the cold. She knew then that she had not come to take them in. She had not come to punish them for what they'd done to Edmon. She hadn't even come to retrieve the Book.

She'd come for their secrets. For their trust . . . and their love. She might even have abandoned the Guard with them, if they'd believed in her.

But she knew now that they would share nothing. And somehow, that was worse. The not knowing. The questions. The confusion and the doubt and the fear that maybe there was something wrong with *her*, something defective that she couldn't see.

Tanin took another step forward. "What am I supposed to do now?" To her surprise, her voice no longer quivered. "I looked up to you. I *loved* you. What about me?"

"What about you?" Mareah's words burned like ice.

Tanin felt sick.

"Mareah!" Lon cried.

Quickly, the Assassin scanned their surroundings. When she looked back at Tanin, her expression was so full of venom that Tanin staggered back onto the ice.

"You," Mareah snapped.

Tanin glanced over her shoulder. On the far shore, the dark figures of the trackers were racing across the lake. She looked back at Mareah. "What else was I supposed to do?"

"You led them here." Raising her hand, Mareah cut the air.

Tanin scrambled backward. Again and again, she dodged, until at last her feet went out from under her. She landed on her back on the frozen surface of the lake.

Gunshots echoed off the peaks.

Lon lifted his hand. The bullets sank into the snow around him, hissing on impact.

Tanin stood shakily, though her voice remained steady. "You brought this on yourself."

Mareah flung out her hand. Great fissures appeared in the ice, spiderwebbing through the frozen surface.

Halfway across the lake, the trackers skidded to a stop. Their cries of alarm rose like spurts of flame in the frosty morning.

And then Tanin was no longer confused or doubtful or afraid. She was hurt, and she was angry. They should have trusted her. "You'll regret this," she muttered, "one day."

Lon took Mareah's hand. "Come *on*," he said.

Tanin's chest burned. Heat flared up her neck, down to her arms and hands and the tips of her fingers. She blinked. The Illuminated world sprang to life behind her eyes, sparking with gold. In an instant, she narrowed in on the whitened logs on the beach, saw their seams, the way they were woven together with brittle threads of light.

She lifted her hands.

The logs exploded, sending shards in all directions. Mareah flicked her wrist, deflecting the fragments.

But she didn't get all of them. A spear of wood lanced toward Lon. It tore along the side of his face.

Tanin blinked. Her vision returned to normal. She'd struck Lon. Hurt Lon. Who'd welcomed her and trained her and encouraged her all those years. She regretted it as soon as she saw the blood, red and steaming in the morning air, pouring from his head. She hadn't wanted to hurt him, not really, had only wanted them to listen. To stay. To let her in.

But that would never happen now. Some things you couldn't come back from.

Mareah palmed the air. Spars of ice jutted up around Tanin. The lake was fracturing, sending up pops and groans.

On the ice, Tanin swayed. The trackers shouted in fear.

Mareah spoke. Not loudly, but hard and cold as steel. "If you follow us," she said, "I'll kill you."

Taking Lon's hand, she hauled him toward the woods. At the edge of the trees, she raised her hands once more.

Beneath the ice, the lake water swelled. Tanin lost her balance, and she got one last look at the back of Mareah's head before plummeting into the freezing water.

CHAPTER 17

If You'd Been There

*T**anin really did love them,* Sefia thought, closing the Book. *The way* I *loved them.*

Deep in thought, she flicked the clasps again and again. She still hated Tanin for everything she'd done to her family, but for the first time Sefia felt like she understood her.

The questions *were* worse—Tanin's, Versil's, her own.

Sefia thought she was protecting Frey and the boys, protecting Archer. But was it kindness or cowardice? For their protection or hers?

Shaking her head, Sefia closed the clasps. She stepped into the damp night air, threading through the tents until she found Archer and Kaito's.

Beneath his blanket, the Gormani boy whimpered. In sleep, he seemed so young. Vulnerable.

Crossing the tent, she knelt beside Archer's cot as he began to thrash, his hands becoming fists.

"He's dreaming," someone whispered.

Sefia turned to find Kaito, awake and watching her like a wild thing in the darkness.

"He always dreams like this," he continued. "Quiet. Never makes a sound."

"When I met him, he couldn't talk," she whispered back. "Did he ever tell you that?"

Kaito shook his head, his curls rustling against the pillow. "We all lost something to the impressors."

"What'd you lose?"

"My future."

Archer lashed out suddenly, striking the side of the canvas tent with a sharp *thwack*.

"I could've been chief of my clan up north, like my mother, and her father before her," Kaito said. "I'd been preparing for it my whole life. But now . . ."

"Can't you go back?"

"I *could*." He regarded her for a long moment. This was the stillest she'd ever seen him, with the focus of a hawk before the dive. It was unnerving, almost frightening. Then he rolled over in his cot, pulling the blanket over his head. "But I don't want to."

Crouched in the darkness, Sefia waited for him to explain, to laugh—something—but he didn't stir again. Turning, she laid a hand on Archer's shoulder.

His body jerked. His eyes flew open.

For a second, the panic was there—his confusion, his urge to fight blistering beneath his skin. But as his eyes adjusted to the darkness, he stilled.

"Come with me," she whispered.

Pulling a shirt over his head, Archer followed her out into the night. They retreated to the edge of camp, climbing onto one of the carts.

"You were dreaming," Sefia said as Archer slid onto the seat beside her, thigh to thigh.

He nodded, fingering the piece of quartz at his throat.

"What about?"

"Same thing as always."

She caught his hand in hers, twining their fingers. "One day, you're going to tell me what that is."

A sad smile flitted across his features. "What did you want to talk about?"

"I think we should tell the others what's really going on."

"The Guard?"

"The Book. My parents. Everything." She explained what she'd read and what she hoped to do, and for a while, with Archer listening as intently as he ever had, she was reminded of how comforting his silence had once been, not a gap but an invisible tether, connecting them.

"Why?" he asked when she was done.

She nudged the Book, sliding it farther away on the seat of the cart. "Isn't it worse not knowing?"

"Not always," he said quietly.

Sefia reached up then, angling his face toward hers. For a moment, she stared into his golden eyes. "Whatever you're afraid of," she said, "don't be." Then she kissed him, long and hard, like she could finally convince him that she was with him, and she was not going anywhere.

When at last they parted, breath smoking between them, she

put her fingertips to the worry stone gleaming at his throat, felt him stiffen as she grazed his damaged skin. Slowly, she leaned in and kissed the edge of his scar. Archer shivered beneath her touch.

"They're going to hate me," she said, laying her head on his shoulder. "But it's better if they know."

His arm went around her. "They won't hate you."

A cold wind rushed over them suddenly, making Sefia shudder.

Then, more to himself than her, Archer added, "I won't let them."

When Sefia woke in the morning, it was still dark. Frey must have been on watch—her cot was empty—but there was someone else in the tent, standing motionless at the threshold.

"Archer?" Sefia whispered, rubbing her eyes.

He let out a gasp, like he was drowning and struggling for air. "You're alive." He was at her side in a second. "You were so still, I thought—" He reached for her cheek, as if to reassure himself she was real. A small sob left him when his fingertips touched her skin.

"What happened?" she asked, sitting up. "What's wrong?"

"I dreamed you were in the ring with me. I had to fight *you*. I had to kill—but it wasn't the impressors who put you there, it was Kaito and Frey and the boys. They wanted your *blood*, and I . . . I . . ."

"It wasn't real." She pulled him toward her. "You're safe. *I'm* safe."

"I couldn't stop after that. I kept seeing you, whenever I closed my eyes . . ." He studied her face for a moment, as if searching for injuries, and then he kissed her, his mouth urgent, insistent, against hers.

Gently, Sefia drew him onto the cot beside her, murmuring, "It wasn't real. We're safe."

He kissed her again and again, touching her face, her throat, her shoulders, his hand sliding down her arm to squeeze her hand, as if he still wasn't sure she was safe. "Don't tell them," he whispered. "Please. I don't know what'll happen . . . I don't know if I can stop them."

She stroked the side of his face. "I'll never forgive myself if I don't tell them."

He squeezed his eyes shut. "What if *they* don't forgive you?"

"You forgave me."

"There was nothing to forgive." Archer licked his lips. "But I—"

"Whoa, what—" Frey's voice interrupted them. *"Chief?"*

Sefia's cheeks went hot as Archer scrambled up, straightening his clothes. Frey looked amused as he slid past her, awkwardly bumping into the tent pole. But before he left, he said, "Sefia, please, just think about it, okay?" The canvas closed behind him.

Laying down her weapons and kicking off her boots, Frey gave Sefia a pointed look.

"I'm so sorry," Sefia mumbled, hiding her face in the blanket.

Frey laughed softly as she flopped onto her own cot. "For years, I lived in a house with three boys and no parents. Trust me, you and Archer, that was nothing." She propped herself up on her elbow, cocking an eyebrow. "Well, not *nothing*. Details, please."

Despite Archer's fears, however, Sefia had not changed her mind by the time Griegi called everyone in for breakfast. The haggard look in Archer's eyes was more pronounced in daylight, evidence of just how little rest he'd gotten, worrying for her. But she couldn't run from the truth anymore. Or her guilt.

Gathered around Sefia, Frey and the boys leaned forward as she unwrapped the leather casing and held up the Book for all of them to see. In the light of the campfire, the ⊖ on the cover seemed almost alive, flickering with magic and intent.

"This is a book," she said.

She told them about the Guard, Serakeen and his impressors, her parents. She told them how she'd found Archer in the crate, how they'd tracked Hatchet through Oxscini—two kids blundering into a conspiracy decades in the making. She told them about her father's murder, and Nin's, and how that same fate awaited them all now, if they weren't careful—and maybe even if they were.

"The Guard?" Kaito asked when she was done. "That's who wants us?"

"Yes."

"And your parents were part of it?"

Sefia nodded, sensing Archer's edginess. He'd buckled on his weapons this morning, and his hands hung loose and ready at his sides.

"But they turned on their masters," Kaito said.

"Yes."

"And now they're dead."

"Yes."

He whirled on Archer, who flinched. "You knew?"

Archer nodded.

"You're one of us, brother. Didn't you think we had a right to know?"

"It's not his fault," Sefia said. "*I* was scared. I didn't know what you'd do if—"

"You should've given us a little credit, Sefia." Frey flicked her switchblade from hand to hand, the steel turning and twisting in deadly arcs between her palms.

"I'm sorry." Sefia shifted the Book's weight in her arms, not daring to meet anyone's gaze. "I wanted to tell you. I—I hope it's not too late."

"She got you out," Archer snapped, taking her hand. His fingers were cold, but strong. "She got all of us out. All she's ever done is try to protect us."

With a glare, Frey closed her knife and thrust it into her back pocket.

Kaito rubbed his scarred cheek as he paced before the fire like a caged creature. "You can't undo what they did, you know that, right? You can't unkidnap us, can't unburn us, can't bring the dead back. It still happened. It was still their fault."

Sefia glanced up at Archer, who looked back at her with his sunken sleep-deprived eyes. "I know," she said, "and I'm still their daughter. But I'm here, aren't I? Trying to fix what they did?"

Kaito's eyes flashed. There was a moment when she thought he might attack, all his rage and resentment unleashed, but then his lips pulled back from his teeth in a vicious smile. "I'm glad they're dead then," he said, "because that means you're on our side."

It was as good an acceptance as Sefia was going to get, so she nodded solemnly.

As the others began muttering among themselves, stealing glances in her direction, Archer dropped her hand. Without a word, he walked away, smoke curling around his head and shoulders as he crossed the campsite.

He still had not let go of his weapons.

While she wondered at Archer's mood changes, Versil came up to her. "Sorcerer," he said.

She squinted, trying to read his expression, but for once his white-speckled features gave nothing away. "Is it better?" she asked. "Now that you know?"

"Yeah. And it's worse. Because they were your . . . because you knew . . ." He shook his head and went silent.

Frey made a disgusted sound in the back of her throat and stalked off.

"She's pissed," said Versil, coming back to himself.

"I'm sorry," Sefia said.

"I know. That's why I'll get over it, eventually." He gestured at Frey's retreating form. "But sorry's not enough for everyone."

Sefia jogged after her, trying to ignore the stares and whispers of the others. But then Frey whirled on her just before they reached the tent, her voice drawing everyone's attention.

"How could you not tell me?" she demanded. "All this time, I've been sharing a tent with the daughter of the people who dreamed up *this*." She jabbed a finger at her scarred throat.

Not knowing what else to do, Sefia gripped the Book tighter. "I'm sorry."

Frey dashed tears from her eyes. "You didn't think I'd been betrayed enough by people I love? You had to betray me too?"

"I didn't mean to—"

"No one ever *means* to. But they still do." Then, as if she couldn't stand to look at Sefia anymore, she swept into the tent, which closed behind her with the sudden *slap* of wet canvas. Dew misted Sefia's cheeks, her hands, the Book's leather casing.

She didn't go in after her.

When they struck out again, the mood remained tense. No one would speak to her, not even Frey or Aljan. Miserably, Sefia shivered in her oil skin cloak as a cold drizzle drenched the land.

Archer rode at the front of their caravan, stiff in the saddle with the rainwater running off him. It was as if he was the same haunted boy he'd been a season ago, harried by his nightmares.

When she tried to ask him what was wrong, he said nothing for a long while. The muddy track sucked at their horses' hooves. Then he spoke: "I can't let anything happen to you."

"I know you wo—"

"No, you don't get it. I'd have done it. I'd have done it in an instant. Don't you see? If you'd been there with me, I would've killed you without a second thought."

She reached for his arm. "You'd never—"

"*No.*" He jerked away so suddenly the horses started. His eyes flashed like lightning. "I *know.* Sefia, I can't . . . you don't understand."

She fell back then, and allowed the others to pass. Archer did not look back for her.

That evening, when everyone else gathered to spar, Archer watched them from the edge of the group, so wound up you could almost see the urge to fight crawling under his skin.

Ordinarily, one of the boys might have wanted to fight him—they did that from time to time, to test their mettle—but that night they let him alone, like wolves avoiding their pack leader.

Except Kaito.

Maybe he wanted to challenge himself with an opponent at his most perilous.

Maybe he knew Archer needed a fight the way some people needed a drink.

It was brutal. Archer was too quick, too strong, too good. It was like he was channeling the whole force of his fear and guilt into his fists. The Gormani boy didn't stand a chance.

When it was over, Archer stood over him like a conqueror, back and shoulders slick with sweat, breath heaving in his chest.

Kaito staggered to his feet. One of his eyes was swollen shut, and blood dripped from his knuckles as he raised his fist toward the black sky.

"Chief!" he cried.

"Chief!" The others took up the chant. "Chief! Chief! Chief! Chief!"

Archer grinned.

Later, Sefia cornered him while he was washing up, dabbing at his cuts with a damp cloth. "What happened? You could've really hurt him," she said.

Anger touched his lips as he tossed the bloodied cloth back into the bowl of warm water. "You're just figuring that out now? I'm *dangerous*, Sefia."

"I know what you are," she said, frustrated. "And I know you'd never hurt me."

Before he could answer, Kaito ran up and hugged him from behind. "You were pulling your punches."

Chuckling, Archer shoved the other boy away, his mood swing so sudden it made Sefia dizzy. "You'd be out cold if I hadn't."

"When I beat you, I don't want to beat you because you went easy on me. I want to beat you because I'm better than you."

"What if you're not better than me?" Archer raised an eyebrow.

The Gormani boy glanced at Sefia. "You're luckier than me. That's all."

"I wouldn't call us lucky," she said.

"Luckier than some, sorcerer." With a grin, Kaito punched Archer in the arm and ran off again.

There was an awkward silence as Sefia waited for Archer to say something, but he just shook his head and walked away.

Heavy with dread, Sefia watched Frey and the boys the next morning, running drills as the sun pierced the overcast skies, lighting on frosted shards of grass and flashing sword points. The air was filled with the sounds of battle—metal ringing against metal, yelling and grunting, boots stamping in the mud. While Kaito called out commands, Archer wove in and out of the ranks like an eel, smooth and sinuous, avoiding thrusts and adjusting stances as if it were the most natural thing in the world.

He looked so comfortable among the flickering blades and ranks of boys. But surrounded by bodies and sharp edges, he no longer looked like someone she knew.

Gradually, the others began to forgive her. Griegi stopped feeding her cold leftovers. Mako gave her a hug. Aljan took up his lessons with her again. She taught him to write, and he taught her to write beautifully, pouring all their guilt and forgiveness and sorrow into the 𝔐s, 𝔈s, 𝔖s, and 𝔗s they carved into the ground.

One cool night as Aljan looked across the campfire at Frey, sitting watch on one of the carts, he asked how to write her name. At the rim of the darkness, the twists of Frey's braids and the curves of her cheeks were blue with starlight, as if she were one part human and one part sky.

She hadn't said a word to Sefia in days. She didn't even use their tent anymore. Aljan told her she was sleeping in the trees, bundled up in the branches with her blanket.

With a sigh, Sefia wrote Frey's name in the soil with their sharpened stick.

Aljan was silent as he studied the letters.

On the other side of camp, Scarza patiently led Versil to the stack of pots and pans left over from dinner. They often had to do that for him, or his chores would never get done. Grinning cheekily, the tall boy took up the scrub brush.

"Well?" Sefia asked.

Aljan's only answer was a smile.

Abruptly, Versil plopped down between them, his hands dripping with suds. "Stop moping and go to her, brother."

The mapmaker wiped away the letters, giving Sefia a look like, *Can you believe this?*

Her gaze drifted to Archer, sitting with Kaito as they planned their attack. It had been two days since they'd spoken of anything but their next battle, and she could feel the distance growing between them.

"Actually," Sefia said, "I agree with him."

"Huh?" Versil frowned, as if in the brief pause he'd forgotten what they were talking about. "Of course you do. See, Aljan? If the sorcerer says I'm right, I'm right."

Aljan made a face. "Shouldn't you be scrubbing a pot or something?"

"Oh, right." Versil's smile seemed broader for the patches of white at the corners of his mouth. Leaping to his feet, he danced toward the unwashed dishes. "You two are just more fun."

Aljan didn't approach Frey that night, but on the trail two days later, as they headed out of Shinjai into Gorman, he passed her a pleated sheet of paper inked with flowers—his version of a bouquet.

Sefia was watching her when Frey glanced up. Their eyes met, and there was a little less anger in her face than there'd been the day before. She lifted the piece of paper and smiled, ever so slightly.

It wasn't much, but it was something.

As Frey tucked the flowers away, Sefia reached for the green feather she still wore in her hair.

The vane was tattered; the barbs were bent. She tried to smooth it between her fingers, but some things, once damaged, couldn't go back to what they used to be.

Ahead of her, Archer rode on, stiff and broad-shouldered in the saddle.

She slipped the feather between the pages of the Book and closed it with a sigh.

CHAPTER 18

The Shrinking Sea

After three days waiting among the islands east of Hye, searching for signs of the *Crux*, the *Current of Faith* spotted smoke on the horizon, like a poisonous bloom above the turquoise seas.

In the haze, Captain Reed saw flashes of orange and explosions of powder—two frigates the size of the *Current* fighting something much bigger . . . something with a gold hull.

Serakeen's ships must have caught the *Crux*. What a prize they must have thought her, with those gem-studded rails, the plunder in the holds, the slaves belowdecks.

Reed knew he could leave them to their fate. A bejeweled brawler of a ship, the *Crux* had passable odds of survival. And if she didn't make it, no one would know the *Current* could've saved her. Reed and his crew would have the Trove to themselves. All the treasure. All the glory.

But Dimarion had put his ship and his crew on the line to

give the *Current* a chance to escape. What kind of person would Reed be if he abandoned them now?

Not the kind of person he wanted to be remembered as.

Not the kind of person who deserved to be remembered.

"Prepare for battle!" he cried, and the crew sprang into action, securing the portholes and readying the great guns. In his carpentry workshop, Horse prepared shot plugs and lead sheets to reinforce the bulkheads. Marmalade, the ship's girl, went skipping across the deck, bringing armfuls of weapons up from the magazine.

As they neared the fighting ships, the noise of the battle struck them: the booms of cannons, the report of rifles, the shouts of men rising over the tumult of the sea.

Then the *Current* was in the smoke. Close enough to smell the gunpowder.

The *Crux* was surrounded, her gold hull pitted, her masts broken, her cannons sputtering as she fought off two ships half her size: one of Serakeen's black-and-yellow scouts . . . and a blue frigate flying the flags of the Everican Navy.

Reed's chest tightened. Serakeen and the Blue Navy? If they'd formed an alliance, they'd smother the east, and outlaws—true outlaws that had called the seas home for generations—would be driven out and hunted down like game.

"It's just like Bee told us," Jules said, pausing at the rail beside him.

He shook his head. "You were right. We should've helped Bee and the *Bad Eye* when we had the chance."

Jules's voice was soft as velvet when she said, "Can I put that in my song about you, Cap?"

For a moment, they exchanged sad smiles. Then with a quick salute, she dashed back to her watch.

Captain Reed scanned the waters, sizing up the action. The frigates were going to flank the *Crux*, pinning her between them. With cannon fire coming at her from both sides, it'd be a bloodbath.

To stop them, the *Current* would have to sail behind them, fire on the Evericans, reload, and fire again on Serakeen's scout. She'd have to be quick.

But in these parts, there was no one quicker.

"Gun crews, prepare to fire!"

They sliced through the seas clean as a knife.

The Evericans didn't even see them coming. The windows of the officers' quarters gleamed, exposed, at the stern of the blue frigate.

Then the cannons of the *Current of Faith* let loose.

Shot soared through the air and went battering into the enemy vessel, shattering glass, splitting beams like kindling. The rudder snapped. One cannonball grazed the lower gun deck, opening up a gaping hole along the port side, revealing blood, bodies, and iron.

The *Crux* let off a broadside of her own, demolishing the Everican hull. A mast snapped. Men screamed.

The crew of the *Current* prepared the next volley.

But Serakeen's scout was ready for them. Fire spewed from their aft guns.

"Incoming!" someone cried.

The crew ducked behind the gunwale as scrap shot splintered the side of the *Current*.

Reed flinched as a bit of shrapnel cut into his cheek. "Fire!" he shouted.

The black-and-yellow ship took the explosions all along her stern, large chunks of iron raking her fore and aft, revealing her innards.

A killing blow. No ship could recover from that.

"Jules!" Marmalade's thin voice pierced the air. "No, no, *no*!"

Fear clenched Reed's guts.

Jules?

Not Jules.

Not his chanty leader, his runner, his brawler, his singer, his conscience, his friend. Not *Jules*.

He bounded down to the main deck as the *Crux* fired on Serakeen's ship. Heat and flame rippled the air, nearly throwing him off balance.

He skidded to a stop beside his chanty leader, where she was laid out among the cases of shot, blood darkening her clothing in a dozen different places. Glass and nails spiked her left side, and a shard of rusted iron protruded three finger lengths from her stomach.

Doc was already there, cleaning wounds, removing shrapnel. Captain Reed knelt beside them.

"She saved me," Marmalade said, shuddering in Horse's enormous arms. "She saved me."

"Not quick enough to save myself, though." Jules coughed, grimacing at the pain.

Doc glanced up for half a second, long enough for Reed to see the grim expression behind her spectacles. But she didn't stop suturing.

Across the water, flames spewed from the black-and-yellow ship. Sailors screamed and pitched themselves, burning, into the waves.

The blood wouldn't stop. Reed felt it puddle around his knees.

Jules was ashen. "I never got to make that song about you," she whispered, her strong, musical voice reduced to a mere thread. "Now no one's gonna know I saved your life."

He gripped her hand, but her skin was going cold. "We'll tell 'em," he said. "We'll tell everyone."

She tried to smile, but tears leaked from the corners of her eyes. "Make it a song, will you, Cap? Something to sing when the sun goes down in the west—" Blood came bubbling up in her mouth, and her next words were a wet, suffocating gasp. "Don't forget, okay? Don't forget . . ."

"Never," Reed whispered. "You're my crew, now and always."

Always, she mouthed, but her voice was already gone.

Then she closed her eyes, and didn't open them again.

That evening, while the *Current* and the *Crux* lay at anchor in the shelter of a cove, their crews gathered on the beach to burn the bodies of the dead.

Together, they sent six funeral pyres flaming onto the water. Three for Dimarion's crew, two for his slaves, and one for Jules.

The *Current*'s other chanty leader, Theo, sang one of her favorite songs. Though his baritone was strong, Reed couldn't help missing the way Jules had sung it—hard and raw, like an open wound.

But she'd never sing again.

"You miss a man so much," Horse said. In the crook of his arm, Doc laid her head against his chest.

Marmalade hadn't stopped crying since Jules went still, sometimes whimpering, sometimes sobbing so hard it was like her grief would rip her in half.

Later, when they gathered to eat and drink and tell stories about the dead, Reed stood apart, barefoot in the surf, feeling each wave flood around his ankles and recede again like an intake of breath.

He closed his eyes, immersing himself in the sounds of the ocean, the babble of the shallows and the growl of the deep. The water spoke to him of danger. Of navies amassing off the coast of Everica and of outlaws fleeing like fish before a great blue heron. Of pirates circling Liccaro like sharks. Of blockades and fierce armadas and invaders in the Central Sea.

Of Jules, her body reduced to ash.

Of red lights in the west.

He'd tried. He'd tried to be someone worth remembering. And it had cost Jules everything.

At his ankles, the rhythm of the waves changed—faster, deeper. Opening his eyes, Reed found Dimarion standing beside him like an oaken mast, swaying slightly in the breeze. A silk scarf almost hid the bandage around his head, and a fine linen shirt almost covered the bruises at his collarbone, but he couldn't disguise his limp or the carved mahogany cane at his side.

That he could have snuck up on Reed in his condition was a remarkable feat of grace.

In one of his hands, two glasses of brandy flashed like spheres of topaz. Passing one to Reed, he lifted the other in his splinted fingers. "We owe you our lives, Captain. Whatever you want, it's yours, as long as it's in my power to give. The hammer of the Thunder Gong? Take it, and let bygones be bygones."

Reed raised an eyebrow. So Dimarion had the mallet. He'd thought it'd been lost in the maelstrom five years ago. Ordinarily, he would've leapt at the opportunity. But treasure and great deeds didn't hold the same allure as they once had. Not today.

Slinging back his drink, Reed wiped his mouth and pulled a piece of paper from his front pocket. "That's what's inside the bell of the *Desert Gold*."

It had been Meeks's idea to make a charcoal rubbing of the inscription—a perfect copy of the words that Reed hoped would tell them where to find the Trove of the King.

Taking the sheet of parchment, Dimarion turned it sideways. "Is it a map?"

"It's writin'."

"It's riding what?"

Reed shook his head. He'd made a similar mistake, not long ago. "I met a kid on my way to Jahara," he said, explaining about Sefia, the book, how she could read it.

"Like you and the sea," Dimarion said, nodding.

"Yeah."

"And she's the only one who can locate the Trove?"

Captain Reed scratched his chest, remembering his first

tattoos, the words he'd buried beneath more ink as soon as he got the chance. "The only one I trust," he said, shrugging. "Look . . . you try to find someone to decipher them marks if you like, but I can't go with you."

Dimarion tucked the rubbing into his shirt. "You're planning something, aren't you? You're going to do something so dangerous, so illustrious, that it'll make the rest of us curdle with envy."

"Dangerous, yes. Illustrious, no," Reed said, staring hard at their ships in the sunset. "I lost a sailor today. Her name was Jules."

The captain of the *Crux* raised his glass.

"How many others have we lost already?"

The ships Bee had listed came rushing back to him: the *Graybird*, the *Pickax*, the *Only Star* . . .

"We're outlaws, Captain. Unless we're on the same crew, there is no 'we.'"

. . . the *Fool's Gold*, the *Rose*, the *Marilyn* . . .

"Maybe there should be. Maybe outlaws need to start lookin' out for each other."

Dimarion scoffed. "Outlaws, banding together? You'd have an easier time catching minnows with your pinkies."

. . . the *Better Luck Next Time*, the *Water Dog*, maybe even the *One Bad Eye* . . .

"I know," Reed said. "But if someone doesn't try, we're all as good as dead."

"Who, you? You're the worst of them. 'No authority but the gun and the sea,' remember?"

Reed patted his silver revolver. "It ain't my gun they'd be answerin' to."

Dimarion's dark eyes gleamed. "The Lady? Is she still alive? Where has she been all these years?"

"A little place called Haven."

A hidden island surrounded by riptides and rocks, Haven was home to Adeline Osono and Isabella Behn, two of the toughest people Reed had ever met. In her younger days, Adeline had been sheriff of an outpost in the Central Sea, where she'd kept order in a lawless territory. She had quicker trigger fingers than anyone, even Reed, and once her name had commanded the respect of every smuggler, slaver, and cutthroat in Kelanna.

She was the Lady of Mercy, the original owner of Reed's legendary gun. If anyone could keep a community of fighting, thieving outlaws from killing one another, it was her.

"This will be challenging," Dimarion said.

"Yep."

"Painstaking."

"Yep."

"And small."

"Yep."

Dimarion dug his cane deeper into the sand. "I've known you a long time, Captain. You don't *do* small. Small deeds aren't the ones you'll be remembered for."

"I know." Reed thought of Jules—getting a tattoo to remember each of her family members until her arms were a tangle of songbirds and jungle flowers; making up little ditties during the morning watch; saving Marmalade from cannon fire. "But they make you the kind of person who should be remembered."

"So you're done with trying to live forever, are you?"

Captain Reed hesitated. He'd dedicated *years* of his life to immortality. To finding artifacts that promised him eternal life. To collecting adventures so impressive you couldn't resist re-telling them. It had been a good dream, but some dreams you had to let go.

"It ain't worth livin' forever if you're just livin' for yourself."

"Right." Dimarion sighed. "So when do we start?"

"We?" Captain Reed asked, startled.

"'We' indeed, if you'll have me. It might be a nice change of pace to achieve something that isn't motivated *entirely* by self-interest."

Dimarion was a plunderer and a pillager who kept slaves as spoils. He was probably the last among all the outlaws Reed might have asked for help.

"I mean it, Cannek. If you do this, I'm with you."

"The Lady won't like it one bit if I sail in with a ship full of slaves," Reed said flatly. "In fact, she might even have my head for showin' you the way."

Dimarion rolled his eyes. "I don't *beat* them, if that's what you're thinking. They're probably better cared for than some of your own crew. They're certainly better clothed—"

"You said you'd give me anything in your power to give," Reed interrupted. "You don't get to be a slave-owner *and* a hero."

Dimarion curled and uncurled his fingers so many times Reed thought for sure he'd hit him.

Well, try to hit him.

"Give up my slaves—or give up my word and my honor." The captain of the *Crux* slung a heavy arm around Reed's shoulders. Harder than he needed to. His smile was half-snarl. "Fine. We have a deal. You're too clever for your own good, you know that?"

Captain Reed smirked. "Seems like I'm just clever enough."

"You'd better be, if you hope to pull this off." Deftly, Dimarion steered him back toward the bonfires, where the silhouettes of their sailors were black as burned matchsticks against the flames. "We've already lost sailors. We're bound to lose more, before this is over."

CHAPTER 19

Strange Marks

It's said that all legends start small, and the legend of Cannek Reed was no exception. He was sixteen when he left his home in the Everican interior—a skinny kid with hunched shoulders and an awkward gait that gave little indication of the greatness inside him.

Except for his eyes—those striking blue eyes, the color of the water on a clear day.

His mother's eyes, though she was long gone.

There had been one last beating the night before he left. Shouting: his father's wet voice washing up against the windows, seeping through the cracks into the still black night.

His father had struck him. More than once.

More than twice.

The pain had spread across his cheek, his back, the side of his head, like the splatter of water on flagstone.

Eventually his father's anger eroded, as it always did, into drunken sleep. So it was quiet when Reed left.

His footsteps were drenched with dew.

His heart was filled with the sounds of the ocean.

He didn't look back.

In Kelanna, folks said you'd never been home until you'd been to sea. At sixteen, however, Reed had never even seen the ocean. His father had forbidden it. Reed's mother had left his father for it, or for a Gormani sailor—the stories differed depending on who you asked—and for Cannek the water had always been out of reach beyond the ridges that insulated his country from the Central Sea.

But he'd felt the water calling to him his whole life—streams, brooks, little rivers—chattering to him as they ran down to the sea.

It took him a few days and a few moments of doubt before he crossed the mountains, but when he finally saw the ocean it was worth it.

The sea was a magnificent tempestuous creature, bluer than the sky, with silver crests and wings of spray and mist. Its voices were white birds with black-tipped wings and the deep *thrum* of water on rock.

But in the little port town, he couldn't get anyone to hire him. "Can't hire a sailor who can't sail," they said, laughing.

But he had to be out there. The water was waiting for him.

He stowed away in the bowels of a passenger ship and sailed off in the stinking darkness of the bilge.

Days passed. Three nights of sneaking out, filching handfuls of food and a few gulps of fresh air before retreating into hiding again. He would have made it all the way to Liccaro if not for the tailors.

They weren't actually tailors, of course, but he'd never learned who they really were.

They were on deck one night when he popped up from the main hatch for a glimpse of the sky. It was overcast, but the moon floated through the clouds, its light an oil slick in the darkness.

"Isn't there anywhere else we can hide it?" the woman asked. Reed couldn't make out her features, but she wore a sharp silver ring on one of her fingers.

The man shook his head. "What is ridden comes to pass."

Clutching the lip of the hatch, Reed blinked in confusion. He was about to duck out of sight when the woman turned, her dark eyes fixed on him, as if she'd known he was there all along. She raised her hand, and something struck him in the neck.

He collapsed.

The man and woman stalked toward him.

He couldn't move. He couldn't even open his mouth to scream.

"We're sorry," the woman said, plucking a dart from his throat.

The rest of the memory was fragmented, as full of holes as a rusted bucket: the man carrying Reed belowdecks—the weave of an oversize sweater beneath his cheek—quarters packed with bolts of cloth and needles sharp as spines—in the ceiling, a knot of wood shaped like an eye.

Reed couldn't be sure, but he thought the woman may have smoothed his hair from his forehead. Maybe he was reminded of his own mother, except for the odd tang of copper at the back of his throat.

Over the years he must have blocked out most of what happened, but he still remembered the worst of it: the man uncorking a bottle of ink—the woman lifting a scrap of parchment decorated with dots and curious designs the like of which Reed had never seen.

The man dipped a needle into the ink and began piercing the flesh of Reed's chest over and over and over. Reed tried to scream. Tried to flinch or wince or cry. But the paralysis held him fast.

He didn't know how long he lay there or what else they did to him, but he remembered the pain folding over itself again and again as the man deepened the tattoos, making sure they would never fade.

They mopped up the blood—or did they?

The man washed his hands, he thought.

The woman set the sheet of paper on fire and dropped it into a metal bowl.

Maybe she withdrew a bottle of amber liquid from her bag. Maybe she pinched his nose shut to get him to swallow, or maybe she injected him. All he remembered was falling back into darkness, which closed over his head like ink.

Shivering and wet, he awoke to salt water splashing into his face, up his nose, and down his throat. He gagged, recoiling. He could move again.

His chest ached. His legs were numb. Raising his head, he looked around.

He was tied to a barrel—floating in a turquoise sea with sandbars peeping up from beneath the water. The passenger ship was nowhere in sight.

The morning sun blazed down on him. Every now and then a faint thread of blood leaked from the tattoos on his chest, drawing white water snakes that circled him, curiously, their tongues flicking in and out, testing for blood.

He fumbled with the ropes, but they'd swollen in the water. His shriveled fingers couldn't undo them.

He attacked the fibers with his teeth, pricking his lips and gums on the rough cord.

Black-tipped sharks emerged beneath him. Pain surged through his calf as one of them sunk its teeth into him. Reed kicked out, but the shark had already circled away. Blood streamed from the bite.

Something flashed in the waves—another triangular fin, another tipped tail. The creatures were all around him now, darting in to nip at his body and darting out again. Panic gripped him.

Was this how he was going to die?

It couldn't be. He'd waited sixteen years to see the ocean. It couldn't betray him like this.

There was a gunshot. Water sprayed up around him. A white snake split in half, its pieces snapped up by sharks before they'd even begun to sink.

A shadow fell over him—a ship with white sails, a green hull, and a figurehead shaped like a tree.

There were more shots. Someone whooping, "Lookee what we got here!" Laughter. Bullets sank into the waves around him, scattering the open-water predators.

People lowered themselves over the rails. Reed's bonds parted beneath their knives, and he slipped under the surface, flailing and coughing. He'd never learned to swim.

The sailors lifted him up by the armpits, remarking on his strange tattoos, and hoisted him onto the deck, where he collapsed, limbs throbbing, chest stinging.

"What're you doing out here, boy?" someone asked.

In answer, Reed vomited up seawater.

"Easy," the man said, hunkering down beside him. He had a severe face with dead gray eyes and a notch on the bridge of his nose. "You're safe now. You're on the *Current of Faith*."

Chapter 20

Bloodletters

Whenever Archer closed his eyes now, he dreamed of Sefia. Every night, as soon as he drifted off, there she was. She was Argo, missing a face. She was Oriyah, with Hatchet's gun to the back of her skull. She was in the ring, or in the crates, or on a funeral pyre. It was inevitable—retribution for the pain he'd caused—and it'd be Sefia who paid the price.

He wasn't the boy from the crate anymore. He was worse—he lived and breathed violence like a shark in water. It was all around him, and those closest to him would drown.

When he dreamed, he saw himself killing dozens and dozens of people, felt the thunder drumming in his chest, and when he woke, he wasn't always sure if they were memories or something else.

Fights yet to be fought. Battles yet to be won.

"There's a word for that, brother," Kaito said, sharpening his curved sword. "Bloodlust."

Archer began counting down the days until they reached the next crew of impressors.

Five days.

Four days.

Three.

With two days left, they turned northwest into the Szythian Mountains, riding into the high plains while the jagged ridges rose around them and groves of naked aspen rattled like bones along the slopes. When the winds blew, Archer imagined he could smell the smoke from the impressors' camp on the air.

That afternoon, they passed a split-rail fence and a small herd of cattle grazing among the sage. Beyond lay a log cabin and a barn, with a few figures wandering between them, hauling bales of hay.

It must be a peaceful life, Archer thought as he watched a group of men on horseback ride toward the cabin, dust drifting up behind them.

His gaze went to Sefia, where she sat on one of the carts beside Aljan, teaching him to read. Maybe there'd been a brief time, on the *Current*, when Archer imagined he could go anywhere, do anything, be anyone. They could've spent their days working alongside Reed's crew, and their nights, clasped, breathless, in the crow's nest while the watch passed over the decks below. But he wasn't that boy either.

Not anymore.

Half of the riders dismounted in the yard. Chickens dodged out from under their boots as they threw back their dusters, revealing six-guns glinting at their waists.

Archer straightened in the saddle.

Something called inside him, like distant thunder, warning of a storm.

He was already turning toward the riders when the gunshot shattered the air. There was a cry from inside the barn.

A fight. His blood surged.

Without a second's pause, Archer urged his horse over the fence. Behind him, Kaito let out a whoop.

Then they were riding hard through the sagebrush, roaring with anticipation.

Two women staggered out of the barn. The men on horseback closed in.

Archer drew his revolver. Around him, he could sense Frey and the boys pouring over the plain like a deadly tide. Only a few more breaths before they reached the yard. He pulled the trigger.

One of the men collapsed. Blood arced from his skull.

Before the first drop hit the ground, Archer was in the yard, shooting, fighting, pulling riders from their shrieking horses.

Frey shot out the kneecap of one man. Versil thrust another to the ground. Scarza ducked a bullet, which skimmed his silver hair, and raked his knife across a robber's side. The man collapsed. Blood ran through his hands like water through the cracks of a crumbling dam.

Archer was thrown from his horse. He hit the ground and came up on his feet again, cutting, jabbing, nicking arteries and severing hamstrings, feeling his revolver kick back in his hand as each of his bullets reached their targets.

In the chaos he found Kaito—streaks of blood on his brow, blade flashing in his hands—and they came together like wind and rain, furious, driving, demolishing anyone who stood in their path. This was what they were meant for. *This* was where they were home.

While they cut and carved, shot and battered, two little girls ran into the fray.

One of the robbers turned, his revolver gleaming in the weak autumn sun.

Archer shot. So did Kaito. Three bullets sped through the air. One hit the man in the back, making him grunt with pain.

Kaito was on top of him in an instant, his face seamed with savage joy. In one quick motion, he slit the man's throat. Blood splashed Kaito's chest and neck and lips. The robber fell, choking, gasping, still.

A cold wind, smelling of earth and sage, blew across the plain.

All the robbers were dead.

Blood drenched the ground, turning the hard-packed dirt of the yard to mud.

Someone screamed. They screamed and screamed.

One of the girls was crumpled on the ground. She was small, so small. She couldn't have been more than ten. The other girl kept shaking her, making her dark brown hair fall into her face, across her unblinking eyes.

A wound gaped on the side of her head.

Archer felt like his insides had been carved out. He ran for them, but the ranchers made it there first, knocking him aside. They were crying, gathering the girls into their arms—a single body of grief.

"I'm sorry," he said. "I'm sorry. Is she—" But he didn't need to ask.

His revolver fell from his hand. Mud spattered its wooden grip.

His bullet or Kaito's? Kaito's or the robber's? All three had fired their guns.

"Archer?" Sefia's voice seemed to echo around him. "Archer, look at me. What happened?"

He shook his head, tried to push her away. He'd been right about him and violence, hadn't he? *My bullet or Kaito's? Kaito's or the robber's?* "She's dead," he croaked.

"You killed her!" One of the ranchers launched herself at him, striking him over and over with her fists. "You killed her!"

He didn't try to defend himself. Cuts opened up on his brow, his cheek. A blow to the stomach made him double over, wheezing. The ground tilted beneath him. He saw spots of blood on his boots. The rancher didn't stop wailing even when the others pulled her off him.

Red streaked the sky as they left the ranch, leaving the grieving family, the bloody yard. The air, no longer smelling of cattle and sage, was thick with ash.

At the head of the group, Archer rode alone. He hadn't allowed anyone to touch him, hadn't wanted to be touched, and now his fingers were stiff on the reins, glazed in other people's blood.

His bullet or Kaito's? Kaito's or the robber's? He kept picturing it over and over in his head—three pops of gunfire, the man crimping as one of the rounds struck him, Kaito finishing him off, and then the screaming. The screaming. No matter how many times he reimagined it, he still didn't know.

His bullet or Kaito's? Kaito's or the robber's?

"The ranchers said the Delieneans have a name for us," Kaito said, trotting up beside him. When Archer didn't reply, he continued: "*Bloodletters.* Can you believe that? They've been talking about us up and down the kingdom, the things we've done, the people we've saved."

"Now they'll talk about the people we didn't."

Kaito tried to hit him lightly on the shoulder, but he smacked the boy's hand away, hard. Kaito sat back, dismayed. "Come on, brother, don't be like that. If it weren't for us, they'd *all* be dead."

"She was just a kid," Archer snapped.

"So what? We've all killed kids before."

"She was innocent!"

"So were we!"

Archer didn't want to hear Kaito's casual disregard, like one dead girl was nothing, was to be *expected*, because deep down, he was afraid. Afraid of forgetting the wound, the limp neck, the screaming. Afraid of them just becoming another set of nightmares, to be fought off in the dark.

And because deep down, all he wanted was to hurt someone else, someone who *deserved* to hurt, so he could forget all the other hurts he'd caused.

He grabbed Kaito by the collar, nearly pulling him off his horse. "What's the matter with you?" he demanded. "It could've been your bullet that hit her."

Kaito shoved him back, spitting. "It could've been his. Or yours. *It doesn't matter.* People die, brother. That's what we do. Why do you think they call us 'bloodletters'?"

"We're not *murderers.*"

Kaito laughed in his face. "We kill people and we get people killed. You better come to terms with that now if you're going to lead us."

"And turn out like you? I don't want to be a *butcher*, Kaito. *I'm* better than that." As soon as the words left his mouth, Archer knew he didn't mean them. Kaito was the best of them. A better warrior, a better brother, than Archer would ever be.

He *needed* Kaito, the bloodletters, the battles, the mission. They were who he was.

A killer. A captain. A commander.

Clack. Clack. The Gormani boy drew his sword a handspan out of its scabbard and let it fall back again. *Clack.* The sounds ricocheted around them like gunshots, making Archer flinch.

"Kaito, I'm sor—"

Before he could finish, the Gormani boy cut him off. "I'm going to find us a place to camp. If that's all right with you, *chief.*" Clicking his tongue, he kneed his horse into the darkness, which quickly swallowed them up.

The Suicide King

I t's the same with stories as it is with people. They get better as they get older. But not every story is remembered, and not all people grow old.

Like many in his family, Leymor Corabelli always had a touch of melancholia—a side effect of a cursed bloodline, or so they said. In a mere five years, a heart attack had claimed his father; a hunting accident, his uncle; pneumonia, his aunt; fever, his six-year-old cousin; and by the time he took the throne, his mother was losing her wits to dementia.

Perhaps it was his melancholia that attracted Miria Imani to him. She was a noblewoman from Gorman and its islands of snow and stone. Her people had always been fond of sorrowful things—the transience of spring, the forlorn isle battered by waves—and Miria was a true lady of the north, strong and enduring as the Reach.

Despite her family's protests, she took the Corabelli name and soon brought a beautiful, dark-eyed son into the world. She and Leymor called him Eduoar, and for eight years they were content, if solemn, with the curse always hovering over their heads like the executioner's ax.

Then, one day in early spring, Miria was diagnosed with cancer of the pancreas. In the following months, she grew thin as a rail. Her skin became waxy and yellow.

She fought. She was a fighter, like all of her kin, and she didn't slip quietly into death.

But death took her all the same.

After she died, Leymor didn't leave his chambers for a month. His son, Eduoar, saw him only once, early on, and what he remembered was the shape of his father's body under the coverlet, like a corpse in the snow.

When the king finally returned to court, he had retreated so far into his grief that it was as if he were still asleep, and all the people of his kingdom, all the servants in his castle, even his own son, were but a passing dream.

Eduoar was twelve when he found his father dead in the royal chambers. The shades had been drawn, and a single flake of sunlight sparkled on the carpet. The room had been so cold. Walking in had been like wading into a pool of ice.

But Eduoar had to do it.

"Why?" Arcadimon asked once.

"I just had to," Eduoar replied.

Because he'd already known.

Because he'd had to know for certain.

Clutching a vial of poison, Leymor was curled up in a corner against the back wall, as if he hadn't wanted to be found. His flesh was cold to the touch.

Stiff.

For years after, Eduoar was afraid of dark corners.

For years after, he felt like he'd never be warm again.

For years, whenever he looked in the mirror, he saw his father's eyes. His father's sadness. His father's weakness. But whenever he stood on the ledge of his lonely tower, looking down at the flagstones below, he could never quite bring himself to jump. Could never pull the trigger. Or put the stones in his pockets and walk slowly into the sea.

Until the poison was handed to him.

CHAPTER 21

The White Plains

The black-and-white marble was cold beneath his cheek when Eduoar woke on the floor of the portrait gallery. Sitting up, he prodded his head for bruises. "Ow," he muttered, finding a lump above his ear. "Why didn't anyone tell me dying hurt so much?"

In their gilded frames, the portraits of his Corabelli ancestors glared at him, unamused.

With a grimace, he hoisted himself onto the bench in the center of the room. Since his rather public collapse at Roco's funeral in Edelise, his health had declined significantly. He was weaker. Fainting spells struck him with increasing frequency.

To everyone's surprise except his, however, his mood had improved. He was no less sad, no less empty, but he felt *lighter*, as if he were a kite tethered by a single thread, and when it finally snapped, he would be whisked up into the thin blue air—weightless and free.

He wondered if death would be like that: a rushing away from the ground, leaving behind the castle courtyards, the terra-cotta rooftops, the undulating fields of poppies.

Just him and the endless blue sky.

It would be a relief. A release from the curse that had claimed everyone he had ever loved, and the sadness that came with it.

Turning the signet ring on his finger, he stared up at his own portrait.

The painting had been commissioned five years ago, when Eduoar had ascended to the throne. He'd been healthier than he was now, but he still seemed small in his embroidered robes, looking out of the frame with those sad dark eyes.

Every portrait in the room had those same eyes.

Though there'd been little doubt of his illness before, his collapse had confirmed to all the provincial nobility that his condition was worse than they'd suspected. The following morning, the newsmen were reporting it as "the fall of the Lonely King." Appropriately foreboding, Eduoar thought.

In the days that followed, Arcadimon had presided over the selection of Shinjai's next lord. He'd issued statements and pacified the concerned citizenry.

Eduoar had let him. After all, Arcadimon needed more practice than he did, if he was to rule when Eduoar was gone.

He could just imagine Arc decked out in the black suit and silver trim of the Delienean high court, with the ivory circlet of a regent in his brown curls and an easy smile dimpling his cheeks.

There was a small tug in Eduoar's chest. Part of him wished he would see it.

But he shoved that part of him down again where it would never see the light of day.

His gaze slid to the portrait of his father, Leymor Corabelli, the Suicide King. He'd been painted at the window of the royal chambers, with the morning light limning his edges, as if he were already disappearing from the world.

Mother's death was just an excuse to do it, Eduoar thought bitterly.

"You should never have married her," he said to his father's portrait.

Not all Corabellis had the melancholia. Before the fall that had taken his life, Eduoar's great-grandfather, his namesake, had been robust and full of life, hunting, feasting, taking a myriad of lovers—servants and stableboys and ladies of the court.

All of them had died—childbirth, fever, housefire, and so on and so forth.

When his mother passed away, Eduoar had promised himself he'd never curse someone he cared for, not a boy he wished to spend his life with nor a child he made his heir. It didn't matter whom he loved, but if he loved them, they'd surely die.

No, the Corabelli line would come to an end with him. And so would the curse.

Some days—he called them "dead days"—the sadness and loneliness would be unbearable. Eduoar would lie in bed for hours, eyes closed, willing himself to sleep again because he couldn't face another day waiting for the inevitable.

Sometimes Arc would arrive and throw open the curtains and cajole him from under the covers with jokes and amusing anecdotes from his visits to the provinces.

The worst days were the ones when Arcadimon was away.

As if on cue, his friend entered dressed in his riding gear—boots and jacket and pants that showed off his well-proportioned form.

Eduoar's hand went to his chest, feeling the familiar flutter of his heart beneath his fingertips. Did Arcadimon's blue eyes brighten upon seeing him—or was that a trick of the light?

Ever since they'd returned from Shinjai, Arc had been different. More attentive. It was like he was absorbing every gesture, every inflection in Eduoar's voice, committing each moment to memory as if he were chiseling it in stone.

Maybe because he knew it would happen soon.

"Glad that's over with," Arcadimon announced, dusting off his immaculately clean hands. "You're lucky you're so sick you don't have to sit through court anymore."

Ed allowed himself a smile. "Yeah. Lucky."

As he'd grown weaker over the past three years, Eduoar had delegated more and more of his responsibilities to Arcadimon. At first, some members of the court had protested, but Arc had proven himself such an efficient leader that soon the court was operating more smoothly than it had since Eduoar's grandmother had been queen.

"Want to go for a ride?"

"A ride?" Eduoar glanced at the glass ceiling, where the sky was gray as wet wool. "My physicians wouldn't approve."

"Your physicians are concerned with your body, not with your mood. Come on, it'll be fun." Arc grinned, as if he knew Ed would never say no to that smile of his.

Maybe it's today, Eduoar thought. *Maybe it'll be a fall from my horse, like my great-grandfather.*

He imagined the pain in his neck, the *crack* that would be the last sound he'd ever hear.

He would have preferred a less painful death. But at least he'd be with the person he trusted most. The only person he trusted to end his life.

Arcadimon didn't think he suspected. But Eduoar had known within months that the "cure" for his illness was really the cause of it. And he'd been grateful. Because of the curse, he'd been wanting a way out of his life since he was a teenager, and Arc was giving it to him tied with a silver bow.

For a while Eduoar had been worried Arc was responsible for Roco's death. The timing was too convenient. But Ed knew Arcadimon had loved Roco like a little brother, and at the funeral, his grief had been so raw. You couldn't grieve like that for someone you'd just killed. It wasn't possible. Not for Arc. Not for anyone.

Now Arcadimon would avoid the war of succession Eduoar had been dreading. He'd be elected regent of Deliene, gaining custody of the kingdom to which he'd devoted his entire political career.

He was good at it, and he enjoyed it—the council meetings, the trade agreements, the political maneuverings. If Ed could trust Arc to end his life, he could trust him with his people.

All he had to suffer through was a few fainting spells and a touch of fatigue. It wasn't much worse than his melancholia, to be honest. But Arcadimon couldn't be caught killing a king.

He had to make Eduoar's death look natural to avoid casting suspicion on himself.

So Ed took the poison whenever Arc offered. Sometimes he even requested the flask himself.

They charged from the city gates—Eduoar on his gray gelding and Arcadimon on his white mare—out onto the White Plains, where the fields of snowy flowers rippled away from them like water.

Frog, Ed's favorite dog, went racing ahead of them, her quick lithe form practically flying over the earth, paws barely touching the ground before launching off again.

It felt like winter already—that wet chill in the air, that breeze like a knife. But Ed could hear Arc laughing as they crested each rise, and that was all he needed for warmth.

The minutes filled with the sounds of hooves and breath and wind.

Catching Eduoar staring, Arc winked and galloped ahead, daring him to catch up.

Ed laughed. His laughter startled even him, foreign as it was to his own ears, and he laughed again, surprised at the clear sound of it.

They didn't stop until they were miles from Corabel—the city little more than a blemish on the horizon—when Eduoar's fatigue finally got the best of him. He slowed his horse.

Arcadimon pulled up beside him. "It's been a while since I've ridden so hard."

Ed's smile was a faded thing. "Your horse is doing all the work."

"Tell that to my sore ass." Dismounting, Arc grimaced. "Actually, don't. My ass would prefer to be left in peace."

Eduoar chuckled—a sorry rendition of his earlier laughter. He whistled for Frog, and she bolted back to them, leaving trampled poppies in her wake.

As he slid clumsily from his saddle, he half-expected Arcadimon to offer him the flask of poison.

But his friend only led the way through the flowers to a barren oak in the center of the field. Frog came loping back, tongue lolling from the side of her mouth.

Ed gave her head a rub—behind the ears, just as she liked. She licked his hand.

They tied their horses to one of the tree branches, and Eduoar sank shakily to the ground. Frog lay down beside him, panting.

Arcadimon stretched, showing off the broad expanse of his shoulders, but still didn't offer Eduoar the flask.

"Hey, Arc?"

"Mmhmm?"

Eduoar licked his lips. "My tea?"

Arc patted his riding jacket a few times. "Sorry, I must have left it at the castle."

"That's not like you."

"Maybe I'm changing." Arcadimon paused. "Think you can make it until we get back?"

Ed lay back with a sigh. "I suppose I'll have to." In this position, he couldn't see Arc anymore, but he could feel him near, could smell his familiar scent—like wind and snow.

"I could stay here forever," Arcadimon said after a long moment. "Except for that whole eating-and-sleeping-and-surviving thing."

Ed shrugged. "Survival is overrated."

"Is it?" His friend sounded so sad. Eduoar craned his neck to look at him, but Arc was watching the curtains of rain out at sea.

"Living is messy," Ed said, attempting to lighten the mood the way Arc usually did. "Lots of smells. And fluids."

A shadow of a smile crossed Arc's lips. "I guess I could do without the smelly fluids. But there are good fluids too. Like coffee."

"Ha. Coffee. How could I forget."

"Coconut water. Oxscinian spiced chocolate. Whiskey."

"I don't like whiskey."

"No wonder you think survival is overrated. A life without whiskey is a sorry life indeed."

Ed ran his hand along Frog's back. "Sorrier some days than others," he said quietly.

"Not today, though." Arc leaned over to peer down at him.

Eduoar's breath caught at the sight of Arcadimon's face: bright eyes, dimples, stubble along the planes of his jaw.

A wind whipped off the sea, rushing over the poppy fields like a wave, the flower heads bending and tossing as the air barreled over them. Ed closed his eyes as the breeze blew his hair across his forehead.

"No," he murmured. "Not today."

At a touch on his temple, he looked up to find Arc fondling

one of his curls. He moved as if to stop him, though all he did was hold Arcadimon's fingers there, against his temple.

Arc's face eclipsed the whole sky. Cocooned by the noise of the wind, the distant waves, and the soft nickering of the horses, it was like nothing else existed but the two of them.

No dead days.

No dead fathers.

No curse.

Just them.

Arc leaned in. Their lips met. Startled, Eduoar opened his eyes wide for a second, before he let his eyelids flutter closed again.

Arcadimon's hands passed through Ed's hair, down the sides of his face to his jaw.

Eduoar had shared kisses before. Arc had too. But he knew in his bones that nothing either of them had done had ever felt like this.

Like everything in the world could be found in the points of contact between them: all the ins and outs of the tides, the pulsations of stars in the sky, and the running of wolves across the cold north—all part of the same rhythm.

This one.

Theirs.

Eduoar wished for a second that this would go on forever, this connection of lips and tongues, of heartbeats and breath.

But it couldn't.

He was cursed.

And he couldn't let anyone, *especially* not Arc, die because of him.

Eduoar pulled away. "I'm sorry, I can't—"

"I'm sorry," Arcadimon said at the same time. He was blushing, smiling, giddy. "Was that—"

"I need my tea." Eduoar stood, stumbling back to the gray gelding.

Arcadimon's confusion showed in the way he mussed his curls. Green stained his elbows and the legs of his trousers. "Ed, wait," he said, tripping over his own steps.

Frog hopped up, eager to run again, as Eduoar struggled into the saddle, his vision listing sideways. He was weaker than he'd thought.

Weaker in every way.

"I need my tea," he repeated.

"Sure, we'll get your tea, but slow down. You're going to fall." Concern wrinkled Arcadimon's normally smooth features, and he laid his hand on Eduoar's thigh.

The contact burned, sending surges of longing up his legs to his chest.

I won't let you die. Eduoar jerked away and set off toward Corabel at a brisk trot. Eyes fixed on the city on the hill, he didn't look back. He *couldn't* look back, or he'd go racing toward Arcadimon like a bullet, taking them both to the ground for good.

CHAPTER 22

Gauntlets of Ink

The night after their run-in with the robbers, Kaito challenged Archer to a fight.

Archer *wanted* to fight, certainly, had the desire in his fingers and bones, craved the respite it would give him, and the forgetting, however temporary. But he was afraid too, afraid of what it would make him.

So he refused, and Kaito's features warped with hurt. He tried to mask it with a grin, but his smile didn't reach his eyes—green and flat. "What's the matter, brother?" he demanded. "Afraid I'll beat you?"

Archer almost stepped forward. He almost laughed and threw an easy punch for the Gormani boy to dodge, knowing how it would escalate. It might've been okay, if only they'd fought. Fighting was the language they shared. No one spoke it better.

But then he saw Sefia watching him from outside the ring. She wasn't wearing the green feather in her hair anymore. Had she lost it? Or was he losing *her*?

"Rest up," he said, and Kaito's eyes flared with hurt and disappointment. "The real fight's in two days."

Something in Archer's chest twisted, pulling him toward Kaito, but he ignored it.

The others parted as he made his way to Sefia, who led him to her tent, where, piece by piece, she peeled away his bloodspattered clothing, finding wounds he hadn't even noticed on his legs, his arms. He could still hear the woman screaming, *You killed her! You killed her!*, could still hear Kaito laughing in his face. But slowly, as Sefia applied a wet cloth to his skin, wiping his fingers, his knuckles, the noise inside him faded, until all he heard was the trickle of bloodied water being wrung from the rag.

When she brought the cloth to a cut on his arm, he put his hand over hers. She looked up at him.

And in that moment she was perfect: midnight hair and onyx eyes, compassion and strength.

"I can't lose you," he said.

Setting the rag aside, she crawled into his lap. She cupped his face with her wet hands and looked deep into his eyes. "You won't," she said.

Gingerly, he touched her wrists as water trailed down his neck, over his chest and his thundering heart.

Each night after that, he dreamed. He wept. He panicked. It was worse than it'd been since his memories had first returned. He would've liked nothing more than to spar, to pick a fight, to drown someone in violence. It would've helped, he knew, would've made him feel like himself again. Only he was afraid of being himself now.

So he waited. He waited until they were crouched on the hill above the impressors' camp, where the cabins and the cross-shaped canteen nearly touched the frost-spiked shore. Beyond lay a sheltered inlet, with the Northern Ocean a steel cut along the horizon.

Sefia and the bloodletters—a term they'd seized upon as eagerly as Kaito had—huddled around Archer as he arranged rocks and pinecones in a rough approximation of the enemy camp. "The boys are being held here, on the south side," he said, tapping one of the stones.

Thanks to the Book, they were already familiar with the number and movements of their enemies, and this close to the evening meal, most were in the canteen, with a few others in the surrounding cabins.

"Scarza, you and your squad will take the north cabins. Frey, the south."

He glanced at Kaito, who'd wanted to be part of the main assault on the canteen. Despite the friction of the past two days, Archer would have liked for the Gormani boy to join them; he was their best fighter, after all. But according to the Book, Kaito was supposed to help Sefia free the imprisoned boys, and the rest of the bloodletters wouldn't hear of trying to change things.

"Don't worry, brother." Kaito's voice was rough with bitterness. "With the sorcerer on our side, we can't fail."

Sefia shot him a glare.

"What is written comes to pass," Aljan murmured.

Archer could feel the battle racing toward him, dark and furious, so close he could almost taste it.

He wanted it. He *needed* it. If he didn't get it, he'd explode.

"Let's go," he said.

Squads of bloodletters split off and went stalking into the dark, fanning out among the cabins as Archer led the rest of them toward the canteen.

Creeping up the steps, he glanced around. The others were in place. Everyone was ready.

As he reached for the doorknob, a single snowflake fluttered down, landing on his wrist—perfect, fragile, fleeting. Flurries of white spiraled out of the sky as if by magic.

The first snow of the season.

The first snow of his life.

The camp went deathly quiet.

He thrust open the door. Gunfire skittered through the air like chips of ice on a hot stove.

It had been less than two days since their battle at the ranch, but to Archer fighting felt like a long drink after a week in the desert. He slit throats, punctured skulls, cut tendons, and wrenched bones from their sockets. Every movement was crisp, clean, like silk rippling in water.

It felt *good*.

It felt *right*.

The bloodletters fought with the same vicious abandon. Anything to do the most damage. Anything to inflict the most pain. Nothing could withstand them.

All of a sudden, Kaito was there too—roaring, slashing, venting his fury on any impressor who crossed his path.

Archer scanned the room: corpses, mangled bodies. No Sefia. He grabbed Kaito by the elbow. "Where is she?"

The boy shook him off. "She's fine!" Pulling his revolver, he shot someone behind Archer. Blood spattered the back of his neck.

In that moment, Archer knew he could have left. He could have let Kaito finish the battle in the canteen to make sure Sefia was safe.

He didn't. He chose the fight instead.

Kaito grinned.

In the heat of battle it was like nothing had changed between them. They were together again, and it was joyous, comforting, perfect—they were *home*. They moved through the canteen with ruthless efficiency, their movements so well-timed it was as if they shared the same violent heartbeat. In and out, they ducked and dodged, feinted and fired. Around them the bloodletters danced like marionettes in a theater, perfectly choreographed, always deadly.

And then—too soon, it seemed—it was over. There was blood everywhere, splashed on his jaw, slicked across the floor. Frey and Scarza returned with their squads to let him know: All the bloodletters had survived.

Sefia appeared in the doorway. Her clothing was torn, her hair coming loose from its ties, and there was a bruise forming on one of her cheeks.

Guilt split Archer's insides. He should've gone to her. He should've left the fight to help her. He could've lost her.

Catching him staring, she held up three fingers.

Three down.

Trembling, Archer raised his trigger finger.

One to go.

Night fell as celebrations began in the canteen. Finishing up bowls of Griegi's fish stew, the bloodletters sang and drank their pilfered barley wine and told stories to remember the boys who hadn't made it to freedom. They looked so happy, Archer would have liked to join them.

But then Kaito raised his cup and declared, "We were dead, but now we rise!"

The others stood too, their benches scraping against the newly scrubbed floor. "We were dead, but now we rise!" As one, they drank.

And Archer knew—maybe he wasn't free either.

The noise in the canteen swelled. They sang their victory songs and recounted their battles. Frey pushed Aljan into a corner, one hand on his chest, and there, with the old fishing nets dangling from the rafters like wisteria, she kissed him. His arms went around her, hesitantly, like he couldn't quite believe she was real. The food and the liquor and the heat of all their bodies made the room feel cramped, until Archer felt like rushing to the shuttered windows and flinging them open for a breath of fresh air.

Sefia found him by himself, hunched over an empty mug. "Want to get out of here?" she asked, extending her hand. The skin under her left eye was swollen and purple.

Faintly, he nodded.

They'd almost made it to the door when someone grabbed Archer's shoulder.

Kaito. His cheeks were red with drink and he was smiling, but he looked more cross than cheerful, more desperate than drunk.

"Hey, the party's just getting started," he said.

Archer shrugged on his cold-weather gear. "I just need some air."

The Gormani boy looked from him to Sefia and back again. His eyes were unfocused. "C'mon, brother, you're our *leader*. You're one of us. Stay."

Archer hesitated. He could've stayed to drink with Kaito and sing his songs and be his friend and brother. But then he remembered the ranchers' screaming. He remembered the bruises on Sefia's face. He liked Kaito, but he didn't want to *be* like him.

"Sorry," he said, pulling up his hood. "Not tonight."

"You could be great, you know?" the Gormani boy called, his expression contorted by hurt and betrayal and anger. "If you weren't such a coward."

Archer cringed at the words as he stumbled down the steps into the yard. The fallen snow glinted sharply on the frozen ground.

"He's just drunk," Sefia said. "He didn't mean it."

"I know," Archer answered. *But it's true.* He was at war inside himself, daily, sometimes moment by moment, and he was too afraid to choose: the weakling who'd gotten himself kidnapped, the animal, the chief . . .

They crossed to the nearest cabin, where Sefia peeled off her coat and sat down on a cot. "So," she said, tracing the weave of the blanket. "One crew left."

Archer couldn't figure out what to do with his arms, so he settled for crossing them over his chest as he leaned against one of the support beams. "Yeah," he murmured. "One."

"And then?" She tilted her head. "D'you think we'll continue? To stop the rest of the impressors in Kelanna?"

He closed his eyes. As if on command, the faces of the men he'd just killed flashed before him. They went by so quickly they soon became unrecognizable, muddled combinations of eyes and mouths and broken noses, bruises, cuts, and bullet wounds.

Nightmares or dreams. Fears or desires. He couldn't tell anymore.

"I don't know," he said, opening his eyes again.

Sefia bit her lip. "Do you want to?"

"Yes." Archer sat beside her, feeling the cot shift beneath them. "But I'm afraid." He lifted his hand, sweeping her hair behind her ear. As his fingers grazed her bruise, she winced. "Of this," he whispered. *Of hurting you. Of losing you.*

"You should see the other guy." She attempted a smile, but at the look on his face, she frowned. "I'm fine, really."

"I'm sorry," he whispered.

Cradling the sides of his face, she kissed him. "One day, all of this will be over. One day, we're going to be free."

She tasted like salt and sweetgrass and a hint of the wine she'd drunk in the canteen, and for a moment he forgot about the mission. For a moment all that mattered was the way Sefia pulled him toward her; the way she sighed as his lips found the hollow of her throat and she fumbled with the buttons of her shirt, exposing her collarbones, her chest; the way she looked at him with such trust as they lay back on the cot, half-undressed, and kissed each other until their lips grew tender and he forgot everything else but her.

Cruel dreams, filled with jeering and shouting, startled Archer awake, but the sounds of his nightmares did not fade. Sometime during the night, the celebration in the canteen had become pure noise—hollering and laughing and the rhythm of fists on tables.

Sefia bolted upright beside him, her eyes unfocused, her cheek creased by the pillow. "What is it?" she asked, sliding back into her shirt.

"I don't know." Archer shook his head. "But I don't think it's anything good."

Struggling into their outerwear, they flung open the door.

The cold bit, stinging Archer's lips, reminding him of the push and pull of Sefia's mouth on his own.

When they reached the canteen, they were swamped with light and heat, the smell of medicinal alcohol and warm bodies and iron. Strewn along the dining tables were needles, candles, rags spotted with ink, and empty cups. Seeing Archer and Sefia, a few of the boys jumped up, cheering.

"Archer!" Kaito greeted him with open arms. Sweat damp-ened his hairline, and his green eyes shone bright as stars. "I'm sorry, okay? I'm sorry. You are my chief, and you are my brother, and one day I will prove I am good enough for you."

Archer didn't move, transfixed by the tattoos that coiled

around Kaito's forearms. They had the thick swooping slashes of Aljan's work—a fine mesh of lines and barbed stars.

Writing.

One by one, the others stood and crossed their arms. Even the newest bloodletters wore the marks.

Kaito beamed at him expectantly.

We were dead, but now we rise.

"'We were dead, but now we rise,'" Sefia read, turning his left arm. And the right, "'What is written comes to pass.'" With each word, her voice grew heavier, and softer.

What is written comes to pass.

The boys had quieted now. Archer stared at them—at their flushed, fervent expressions—and at Kaito, who looked at him like an eager dog that doesn't know it's about to be kicked.

"Why would you do this?" Archer asked.

Kaito tried to smile, but it came out half-formed. "Because we're bloodletters. We're *your* bloodletters," he said, sounding confused and hurt. He glanced around. Then, as if he didn't know what else to do, he bowed his head and crossed his arms. "We offer you our allegiance."

In that moment the tattoos seemed to blaze like black flames. Frey and the boys looked like warriors from some far-off battlefield, from some far-off myth. And Archer was their great leader.

At last, it hit him, *really* hit him: the following he was building, his gift for killing, the way destiny seemed to guide their blades.

What is written comes to pass.

Was it him? Was he the boy with the scar? What if, all this time, they'd thought they were fighting the Guard, when in reality they'd been doing exactly as fate had prescribed? As the Book had prescribed?

"Brother." Kaito's voice was soft, high, the voice of a scared little boy. "Are you with us?"

Shaking his head, Archer took a step back. "No." *It can't be me.*

And Kaito, thinking he was being rejected, for all his service, for all his loyalty, shot Archer a look so black it could have curdled darkness.

Archer fled. Over the threshold and down the steps, he stumbled into the yard, feeling the lamplight on his heels and destiny breathing down his neck.

"Chief!"

"Come back!"

But he didn't go back.

He reached the edge of the bay, where his feet slipped on the icy stones. He pitched forward.

Then Sefia was there beside him, her breath warm against his cheek. "I've got you. It's okay."

But nothing was okay, and he finally admitted it.

He clutched her to him, burying his face in her hood. Her mittened hands cradled the small of his back, her touch muted by their fur-lined coats.

"Is it me?" he whispered.

His next questions came to him before he could stop them: *How many do I kill in the war?* And: *Why do I die alone?*

Out on the water, the moonlight shifted over the whitecaps.

"I don't want it to be you," Sefia said, but her voice was filled with doubt.

Inside, he crumpled.

He should have run away with Sefia when they'd had the chance, before they'd ever met Kaito or Scarza or any of the others. They should have picked a direction and kept going, over the ocean, until they hit some foreign land where they could have started fresh.

Alone. Uncomplicated. Free.

But he wasn't free.

Maybe he'd never been free in his life.

Because even now, knowing what he was becoming, what his thirst for violence was turning him into, he couldn't stop. Not now, with only one crew of impressors to go.

Maybe never.

CHAPTER 23

Once Damaged

On the stony beach, Archer and Sefia watched as Kaito came staggering after them. In his hurry he'd left his coat, and his tattoos stood out on his pale skin like charcoal in snow. "You think you're so much better than us, don't you?" He shoved Archer, hard, in the chest.

Archer shrugged him off. "Leave me alone, Kaito."

"No." The Gormani boy grabbed his arm. "You don't get to walk away from this. You don't get to walk away from *us*."

Archer almost broke his grip. They almost fought, punching, grappling, pushing each other into the frigid water of the bay.

But before either of them could move, an invisible force thrust them apart. Sefia. "Stop it," she said.

"You chose this, remember?" Kaito shouted, struggling against her magic. "When you asked us to follow you."

Ducking Sefia's grasp, Archer started toward him. "I wanted to help people! I wanted to do something *good*—"

Kaito laughed, loud and bitter. "You wanted to kill people, same as me. I've *seen* you, Archer. I know what's inside of you. You're not a savior. You're a cold-blooded killer, just like the rest of us."

"That's just it. I'm *not* like the rest of you." Archer tried to explain. *I'm a* leader. *I have a* following. *What if* I'm *the boy the Guard wants?* "I'm—"

"No. You're worse." Kaito's eyes flashed like the last light at sunset. "You're a killer *and* a coward, and you've got no right to be chief."

"I didn't ask to be chief!" Archer cried, grabbing Kaito by the shoulders, hoping the fear in his eyes would say what he couldn't. "I didn't ask for any of this!"

The Gormani boy sneered. "No, you got lucky."

Archer's grip loosened. *"Lucky?"* After the kidnapping, the abuse, the blood on his hands? After being broken and piecing himself together and still feeling the cracks? He almost laughed. Almost cried.

Coldly, Kaito jerked his head at Sefia. "Because of *her*. She's the reason they follow you. *She's* what makes you special."

For a second, Archer met Sefia's gaze. *Was* she what made him special? Would things have been different if, when she'd pried open that crate three and a half months ago, she'd found Kaito, or Scarza, instead of Archer? Would one of them be leading the bloodletters now, becoming the boy the Guard wanted?

Kaito pushed him away. "You didn't ask for *her* either, I bet.

You didn't ask for any of this." His voice dripped scorn. "But I don't see you giving any of it up."

Archer balled his fists. He'd had enough of Kaito's derision and jealousy. His anger, his disappointment, his always goading Archer to be a warrior, a killer, a boy from a legend. "What do you *want* from me?" Archer's knuckles burned. His limbs tingled with the urge to fight. "The bloodletters? Take them. *Be their chief.* Kill as many innocent people as you like. I'm *done* with you."

For a moment it looked like the Gormani boy might lunge at him. Archer half-hoped he would. They'd fight, and all their frustration with each other would be pulverized under their feet, elbows, fists. Then they'd laugh and embrace, and in the morning they'd be friends, brothers again.

When Kaito finally spoke, his words were quiet and sharp, like a knife between the ribs. "I know what you are, Archer. You *can't* be done with us." With a last spiteful glare, he prowled back to the canteen.

The distance between them pulled, achingly, at Archer's chest. He was tempted to run to him, like he was a shard of iron and Kaito was his lodestone. But he did not move.

The gravel crunched as Sefia found her way to Archer's side. "Should you go after him?" she asked.

Archer slipped his hand into hers. "No," he said shakily. "We'll be fine."

But they weren't fine.

Massive storms struck the camp the next morning, bringing biting downpours of snow and sleet that rattled the cabins and iced the yard. As Archer entered the canteen, shaking slush out of his collar, some of the boys saluted with their tattooed arms.

He nodded at them uncomfortably as he made his way toward the kitchen, where Aljan was talking with Griegi over the pot of coffee.

As Archer approached, the cook let out a little yelp and scurried back to the stove, where he hastily began stoking the coals. Nervously, Aljan poured another cup of coffee and offered it to Archer.

"Chief." The boy's face was swollen with bruises and lack of sleep. "I—I'm sorry."

"For what?"

The mapmaker gestured wearily to his wrists, black with ink. "I don't know if it was my idea or Kaito's, but I'm the one who taught everyone else how to do it. I thought it'd be—I thought you'd like it."

Archer stared at the tattoos, like knife cuts or bullet wounds, trying to make sense of them. *Is it me?*

"But then you ran," Aljan said.

Through his mug, Archer could feel the heat of the coffee begin to scald his fingers. "Do you believe the legends, Aljan, about the boy with the scar?"

The mapmaker touched his right arm—*What is written comes to pass.* "I don't know. But I know you'd never help the Guard, and that means it can't be you."

It can't be me. Archer clung to the words.

"They were supposed to be beautiful. They were supposed

to bring us closer together." Miserably, Aljan hung his head. "I'm sorry I ever made them."

Archer gripped his shoulder, knowing he should say something comforting, but he didn't know what.

As they sat down to eat, Kaito climbed onto one of the tables, kicking aside an empty bowl. "You'd better get comfortable," he announced, "because with the weather as it is, we're gonna be stuck here for a while, until the roads are safe to travel again."

Some of the others groaned.

Kaito ignored them, staring Archer down. "That all right with you, chief?"

Chief.

Not *brother.*

Not *Archer.*

Chief.

Archer swallowed painfully. "Whatever you think is best," he said.

The answer must not have satisfied Kaito, because he leapt down from the table and stalked to the door, which he threw open and slammed behind him again. The walls of the canteen shuddered.

Archer cringed.

"Looks like Dad and Dad are still fighting," Versil said.

No one laughed.

Without impressors to hunt, the bloodletters grew restless. There were only so many stories they could tell, so many rounds of Ship of Fools they could play, before their boredom drove them to more violent pursuits. They began sparring more often, testing their quickness and strength.

Whenever it was Archer's turn to fight, Kaito volunteered.

Maybe it was his way of apologizing, as if they'd find their friendship where they'd always found it before.

Maybe he felt like he had something to prove.

Archer welcomed it. Because fighting was the only way he forgot the dead who haunted his nightmares. It was the only way he could escape his past, his fears about the future, his problems with Kaito. It was the only thing that made him feel normal. He hated that about himself. But fighting helped him forget that too, at least for a while.

And Kaito was there. Almost as if he knew. Almost as if he had the same need for it.

They fought nearly every night, in the mud and sleet, and neither of them pulled their punches. They left their fights battered and bleeding and gasping for air.

But fighting didn't help. They didn't laugh when it was over or recount their favorite strikes. In fact, they barely said a word to each other, barely touched.

Every time, after they fought, the Gormani boy held out his hand and said, "Well fought, chief."

Every time, the title was a dart, an arrow, a wound. A reminder of their broken friendship, dangling, limp and festering, in the space between them.

"My brothers used to fight like this," Frey said, practicing with her switchblade while Sefia read and Archer changed his bandages. "They'd beat the piss out of each other. Tried to get me to join them."

"But you didn't?" Sefia asked. Since the battle at the ranch, she and Frey had been mending their friendship, little by little, exchanging a few words, bringing each other pastries filched from Griegi's stores. Now they were sharing a cabin again, and things between them were almost as they had been.

Archer longed for that with Kaito, but every time he considered apologizing, he thought of Kaito's stubbornness, his wrath, and it made him more determined not to be the one to break first.

"Nah." Frey twirled her knife with a flourish. "A lady solves her problems in more civilized ways."

"Did they ever stop?" Archer asked.

"Not until they *grew up.*"

"Ha." He wound a scrap of cloth over his knuckles. "Tell me what you really think."

Frey's smile flattened. "You're our leader, Archer. You're the one everyone else looks up to. *Fix* this."

But he didn't know how. Kaito didn't even set foot in their cabin anymore. For all Archer knew, he slept in the snow. Or in the stables with the horses. The Gormani boy seemed to go out of his way to avoid him, except when it was time to fight.

So they kept fighting, and the rest of the bloodletters grew more and more uneasy.

At dusk one evening, Archer and Scarza lay downwind of a game trail, waiting with their rifles at their shoulders. The snow was falling heavily when the rifleman spoke up. "I'm not saying he's right."

Archer jumped at the soft scrape of his voice. The boy hadn't said a word since they left camp.

"But he's stubborn, and in his mind, that's as good as being right."

"Kaito?" Archer asked.

"But he loves you. And we love him."

Archer traced his rifle stock with his thumb. There was dried blood under his fingernail.

"If you don't work this out, it's going to tear the rest of us apart." A branch creaked. The wind whispered in the trees. Scarza lifted the barrel of his rifle with his short arm, searching the shadows. After a moment, he relaxed again. "Don't make us choose, Archer."

As the sun set, the silver-haired boy shouldered his rifle and began heading back. As they reached the cabins, Archer halted. "Hey," he said, "have you talked to Kaito about this?"

"Yeah."

"What'd you say?"

A wisp of a smile crossed Scarza's face. "That you're stubborn. But you love him."

Except you keep doing this to each other," Sefia said later that night, after he'd fought Kaito yet again. "He's not the one you want to be fighting."

He watched her daub his cuts with a cloth. She was right. He loved Kaito. He missed him. But the people he wanted to be fighting—the impressors, Serakeen, the Guard—weren't here. And Kaito was.

"Any luck finding the next crew?" he asked.

Sefia sat back suddenly. "No, I—I assumed we were done."

"But there's one more crew of impressors in Deliene."

"I thought you were worried about being—"

"I am."

"Then why—"

"Because there are more boys we could save."

She looked up at him fiercely. "There's only one boy I care about saving right now."

Taking her hand, Archer kissed the crown of her head. "I'll be all right, Sef."

"Not if you're the boy the Guard wants."

But it couldn't be him, could it? Despite his talent for bloodshed, his following of bloodletters? Because Aljan had been right—he'd *never* fight for the Guard. And they had a way to prove it. "Ask," Archer said suddenly. "Ask the Book if it's me. Then we'll know for sure."

Sefia shook her head. "Will we? Tanin thought she was going to get the Book back. *It was written.* And look how wrong she was."

"Tanin had one page. You have the whole Book. You've never been wrong, not once."

"And what if it is you?" she whispered. "What if you are building your army?"

"We'll stop," he lied. He couldn't stop until he'd finished what he'd started, until the impressors were nothing but a story meant to frighten Delienean children. "But if it's not me, we have to save those boys."

She narrowed her eyes, and he wondered if she could see the truth lurking somewhere deep inside him. But she just sighed and said, "Okay."

The Book lay on the table, stuffed with scraps of paper and

scribbled markings, bookmarks made of leaves and twine and blades of grass from the Heartland. Among them, Archer spied the tip of the feather he'd given her—a little frayed now, but as green as the Oxscinian jungle where he'd found it.

Sefia laid the Book in her lap and looked up at him again, her eyes burning like drops of coal.

Archer nodded. *It's not me. It can't be me.*

"Is it Archer?" she whispered. "Is he the boy who will win the Red War . . . and die shortly after?"

What if it is *me?* He closed his eyes, and in the time it took him to blink, he saw them all—the dead—Oriyah, Argo and the boys he'd killed in the ring, impressors, trackers, bandits, the girl at the ranch—so many, and still, somehow, not enough.

Silently, Sefia began to read.

The Lighthouse Keeper

Soon—too soon, it seemed, for all of them—Annabel had to return home. In comfortable silence, she and Archer walked back along the trail until they reached the jungle, when she sighed happily. "I've missed your family."

Archer cocked his head at her. "Don't you see them all the time?"

Annabel trailed her fingers through the undergrowth beside the path, the backs of her nails tapping softly against the stiff leaves and autumn flowers. "I did at first, after you disappeared . . . But then your mom found Eriadin, and Aden and I . . ."

He looked away. "Right."

"You found someone too, didn't you?" she asked. "Sefia?"

Found her and lost her. He nodded.

Annabel gave him the simple, curious smile that used to make him spill all his secrets—who'd given him a black eye, what he'd gotten for her birthday. But he was not the boy he'd been—now his secrets were deep and painful.

But he wouldn't think about that. He wasn't the chief of the bloodletters anymore. He was someone different, he told himself, someone who wanted to stay.

"Why isn't she here?" Annabel asked.

They stepped from the path, wandering through the trees until they found the cliff, where they could see the village of Jocoxa along the eastern curve of the bay.

"It's . . . complicated," Archer said.

Annabel sat down among the sprawling roots of an old tree, which made a sort of bench near the edge of the bluff.

"With her, nothing was ever easy," he continued. "Not like it was with—"

"Us."

"Yeah." He shrugged. "Except there is no 'us' anymore."

"Could there be?"

He looked out toward the village, where the lamps glowed yellow through the curtained windows and the sailboats bobbed softly at their moorings.

This had been home once. Could it be again? If he could forget Sefia, the bloodletters, the guilt, the violence, the way his longing for it remained kindled even now, like a candle flame floating in the vast black ocean?

"I don't know," he said.

Annabel bit the inside of her cheek. "I didn't invite Aden tonight," she confessed.

"I figured."

"You did?"

Archer chuckled. "You haven't changed a bit, Bel. I can still read you like a book."

"Like a what?"

"Sorry. Nothing."

"Where is she, Sefia?" Annabel asked.

He sighed and sat beside her, placing the empty cake box between them. "Deliene, I think. I don't know for sure." Again, he felt the absence of the worry stone at his throat.

"Do you want her to come back?" Annabel pleated the folds of her dress, not daring to look at him.

"Bel . . ." he began.

She leaned over, mimicking him. "Cal . . ."

He almost didn't say anything. But he must not have been as immune to her charms as he thought, because the wall inside him cracked. "That's not my name," he said, surprised to hear the truth on his lips.

"That's always been your name," she chided him.

"Not anymore," he said, holding her gaze, needing her to believe.

"That's okay." A smile dimpled her round face. "I don't mind getting to know you again."

He buried his face in his hands so he couldn't see her bright-eyed earnestness anymore. "I don't think you'd say that, if you knew."

"Knew what?"

And because he couldn't resist her, even now, the wall he'd so painstakingly built came crumbling down. "I've killed people, Bel," he began, and once he started it was like he couldn't stop. It all came flooding out of him, all the things he'd tried to keep hidden, all the things he'd tried to forget. "I've killed so many people I've lost count. Some because I had to. Some because I wanted to. Some because I couldn't tell the difference anymore. I couldn't stop. I'm afraid I still can't. I'm not *Calvin* anymore. I'll never be him again."

"I know," Annabel said, so matter-of-factly, he looked up, surprised. She bit her lip. "I mean, I didn't know all of that, but I knew you weren't the same. How could you be? But I still believe in you, whatever you've done, whatever your name is now."

He swallowed. "Archer."

"Archer, then." She extended her hand. "I'm Annabel."

He took it.

"Nice to meet you." She leaned in, and for a second he thought she was going to kiss him, and it scared him, because he wanted it. Missed it. Longed for it. Although he could not help thinking of Sefia and their last kiss on the cliff, with the wind buffeting around them.

Wild.

Complicated.

Thrilling.

Instead, Annabel kissed him on the cheek, her soft

pink lips lingering on his skin. And he wanted so badly to turn, to put his mouth on hers, to gather her up in his arms.

Maybe that would drive out his memories of Sefia. Maybe that would help him let go. Maybe if he kissed Annabel, they'd slide back into the love they used to share, simple and straightforward. Maybe with her, he wouldn't need walls, and he could be all the different boys he'd been, all of them at once—the lighthouse keeper, the animal, the killer, the captain, the commander, the lover—and maybe . . . maybe he'd finally be home.

CHAPTER 24

After

Tears filmed Sefia's eyes, blurring the final word of the passage.

Home.

For months, she'd been asking Archer where he'd come from. For months, he'd refused to answer. But now she knew.

Home was a seaside village in Oxscini.

Home was a family awaiting his return.

Home was a girl named Annabel—his past and his future.

"Well?" Archer leaned forward. "What did it say?"

In the lamplight, his gold eyes were so bright he looked almost feverish. She'd thought she knew him. The set of his shoulders. The curves his body made in battle. The jolt of delight and guilt that went through him when he made a kill. She knew the freckles that tipped his ears. She knew the texture of his hair between her fingers. She knew the whisper of his breath against her neck.

But she didn't know him at all, did she? Didn't know his friends or his parents, his childhood aspirations, his phobias, or his greatest loves.

She hadn't even known his name.

Calvin.

She should have been relieved that his life wouldn't be shortened by war. In part, she was. Whoever he was, *Calvin* wasn't the boy from the legends. *Calvin* wasn't the one the Guard wanted.

Calvin got to go home. Calvin got to live.

But he did it without her.

Marking the page, Sefia closed the Book. What would he do if she told him? Would he go running back to Annabel, now that he knew she'd take him back? Would he promise Sefia he'd never leave her, and hurt her worse when he did?

Or would he use this as an excuse to keep hunting, keep fighting, until he'd gone so far down the path to being the boy with the scar he couldn't come back?

"It isn't you," she said.

For a second he continued to stare at her, as if waiting for lightning to strike.

"It isn't?" A smile touched the corners of his mouth, but his voice was laced with disappointment.

She took his hand, while it was still hers to take. "You're going to be happy," she said, as if she could convince them both this was what they wanted. "You're going to leave all this behind."

You're going to leave me *behind.*

His lips parted. His canines flashed. "Then you'll help me find the last crew of impressors?"

He wanted her. He needed her. And yet she'd never felt farther from him.

Suddenly, Sefia shoved the Book aside. Whatever the future held, they were here, now, together. Grabbing him by the neck, she kissed him, rough, teeth knocking, lips bruising. He responded eagerly as she pulled him down beside her, hands climbing under her shirt, up her back. "I'll help you," she murmured, her words melting on his lips like snow.

But then what? she wondered even as he kissed her. *How will I lose you?*

O nce the roads finally cleared, Sefia announced to the bloodletters that she'd found their next target.

There was a flooded ocean-side quarry on the west side of Ken, an old pit of slate tiers and blue-green salt water, and in less than a month, the last Delienean impressors would be there, camped in the few stone buildings that remained.

While she spoke, Kaito sat against the back wall, tapping out uneven rhythms on the bench beside him. His right eye and the bridge of his nose were swollen, and there was a gash on his cheek where Archer's knuckles had cut him.

"What about after?" he demanded when Sefia had finished speaking.

Archer frowned. "After?"

The Gormani boy stood. Boys shuffled out of his way as he stalked forward. "Yeah. After we finish off the last of the impressors in Deliene. Are we done? Do we all go back to our homes and wait for Serakeen to retaliate?" He glanced at Sefia out of his good eye. "Or do we keep going, until we've rid all of Kelanna of those bonesuckers?"

Sefia and Archer exchanged glances.

She knew what he'd do—who he'd go home to—even if he didn't know it himself yet. She just didn't know why. Or where she'd be when it happened.

Archer turned back to Kaito. "I think that's something we'll each have to choose for ourselves."

The Gormani boy took a hesitant step forward, like he was testing the ice to see if it'd hold. "But you're with us. Until the mission is over."

"I've always been with you." Archer extended his hand.

Kaito pulled him into a hug so quickly the sound of their hands on each other's backs was like a clap of thunder. Sefia hadn't even realized how incomplete they'd looked without each other. Now they were like two broken halves, chipped and raw at the edges, made smooth and strong and whole again. The Gormani boy murmured something into Archer's shoulder.

They held each other for so long Versil jumped up and thrust them apart with a laugh. "Take it easy, boys, or the sorcerer's going to get jealous."

Sefia tried to laugh, but inwardly she knew Kaito wasn't the person she was jealous of.

Encumbered by poor weather and plunging temperatures, they began the journey south. The ground thawed. Hail became rain.

It almost seemed as if things had gone back to normal. For the next three weeks, the bloodletters drilled and skirmished;

Sefia searched the Book for descriptions of the coming battle; and Archer and Kaito spent long hours planning for their assault on the quarry and the twenty-one impressors within.

Aljan continued his lessons from Sefia in the tent she shared with Frey, who sat on her cot watching while they made words from movement and ink.

"What are you going to do when the mission's over?" Frey asked Aljan once, watching the mapmaker practice his Ơs and Ƥs.

"I thought I might go home. Become a mapmaker again."

"In Alissar?" She sounded disappointed.

Aljan added a stroke on the Ä he was painting.

In the awkward silence, Versil caught Sefia's eye and mouthed, *Wait for it.*

The mapmaker glanced at Frey shyly. "Would you come with me?"

Laughing, she elbowed him, smudging the ink on an Ꞩ. "Only if you come to Shinjai first. I bet my brothers would love to put the screws to you for a bit."

"Sounds appealing."

"Not me. I'm not going home," Versil said, crossing his hands behind his head as he lounged on Sefia's cot. "The world's too big to go back to someplace you've already been."

"Where would you go, then?" she asked.

"I'd hop a ship out of Jahara. Maybe to see the palaces of Umlaan, and the abandoned gem mines of Shaovinh. I hear Everica's nice, when they're not warmongering. And maybe I could check out Zhuelin Bay. I bet the ruins are something, if you don't mind the rain . . ."

He rambled on and on, sometimes losing his train of thought only to pick it up again minutes later, about searching for dragons in Roku and visiting the Sister Islands in southern Oxscini, climbing the Cloud Pillars and bathing in incense at the top, and while the others dreamed about their futures beyond fighting impressors, Sefia kept wondering about Archer and his hometown, Archer and Annabel, Archer without her.

What would happen to her after they'd defeated the last crew of impressors in Deliene?

Where would she go?

Why would Archer leave her?

She glanced at her pack, which held the Book, and a thought sparked inside her: *I could ask.*

I could know for sure.

Later, when they'd burned their practice letters and the twins had retired to their tent, Frey blew out her lamp and curled up under her blankets. Sefia remained awake with the Book in her lap, tracing the ⊖ while she waited for Frey's breathing to even out. When she was sure the girl was asleep, she ran her fingers nervously along the edges of the cover.

Licking her lips, she whispered, "Why aren't I in Archer's future?"

Look to
the Horizon

Poised on the deck of the *Current of Faith*, Sefia watched the sun sink into the waves. Night spread across the sky like spilled ink, dripping into the golden sea below.

While the songs and conversations of the crew arose from belowdecks, Meeks crept up beside her. "Look to the horizon, remember?" he said. "That's where the adventures are."

She was glad of the company, though she didn't take her eyes off the water. "I've had enough adventure to last the rest of my life. I don't need any more."

He shook his head, making the shells and beads in his dreadlocks clink together—small sounds like raindrops. "There's all sorts of adventures, Sef," he said.

The light in the water dimmed, all the gold overwhelmed by the black. In the east, the constellation of the great whale was rising out of the ocean, spangled with stars.

"You had to let him go," Meeks said.

"Did I?" Her voice cracked.

He put a hand on her shoulder. "It was supposed to happen from the beginning, wasn't it?" His warm brown eyes sought hers in the darkness. "Because it was written?"

"And 'What is written always comes to pass,'" she whispered.

With a sigh, Meeks let his hand fall. Leaning down, he planted his elbows on the rail and put his chin on his fists. "He'd want you to move on, I think."

"I know."

The warm glow of the sun disappeared, and soon they were awash in the cool light of the stars, twinkling distantly overhead.

For a long time after, Meeks remained beside her, uncharacteristically silent, watching the horizon.

CHAPTER 25

Before the Inevitable Comes

Aboard the *Current of Faith*, life wasn't the same without Jules. She'd been the heartbeat of the larboard watch, whose voice kept them together as they hoisted the sails or hauled up the anchors. When Jules called, you answered.

When Jules sang, you listened.

Now the sounds of the ship seemed thin, like a piece of music missing its harmony, its rhythm, its lead—stripped down and skeletal.

Jules would have said this was the right thing to do—getting outlaws together to establish a safe harbor from the war between the kingdoms. But Reed had not forgotten Dimarion's words—*We're bound to lose more, before this is over.* What would doing the right thing cost him? he wondered, rubbing the unmarked skin of his wrist. What would it cost the people who looked to him, the people he loved?

From a distance Haven appeared perfectly circular, its steep sides providing no mooring for ships that made it through the savage currents, the fog, the swells and stone monoliths. But Captain Reed, who understood the ocean the way Sefia understood writing—the way Jules had understood music—knew there was more to the island than that.

The tides buffeted the *Current* this way and that, tipping it precariously close to the cliffs as Jaunty maneuvered them toward the island's secret entrance—a narrow channel to the heart of Haven.

After a few nail-biting close calls, the waterway opened up. The mist rolled back. And the center of Haven was laid bare before them: white beaches, teal waters, jungles teeming with birds and bright flowers. An isolated paradise perfect for harboring outlaws.

Reed just hoped Adeline and Isabella would be willing to help them.

By the time they anchored the *Current* in the center of the lagoon, two figures had appeared on the beach. The first, lean as a whip, with hands resting easily by her gun holsters—Adeline. The second, tall and soft, with full skirts and a double-barreled shotgun on her shoulder—Isabella, the gunsmith who'd crafted Reed's silver-and-ivory revolver.

"Is that them?" Marmalade asked in a hushed voice. "Is that the Lady?"

Reed smiled down at her. Sometimes she still cried at night, curled up in her hammock with Jules's old mandolin. Sometimes she'd pluck a string, and the sound would reverberate all through the *Current* like a ripple in water.

"That's them, kid," he said.

Adeline and Isabella were as close as you got to royalty out here. In her prime, Adeline had earned the nickname the Lady of Mercy—the only authority in the whole Central Sea to which every outlaw answered—and the title Lady had become a sign of respect.

Hoisting a longboat over the side of the ship, Captain Reed and a dozen of his crew struck off for the beach.

He'd met Adeline and Isabella when he was seventeen, not long after he'd joined the crew of the *Current*. Five years, numerous adventures, and the death of a captain later, he'd brought them to Haven to retire, spry sixty-year-olds eager to settle down in peace.

Now Adeline's short blond hair had gone white as snow, and as they neared the beach, Reed thought he saw a tremor in one of her liver-spotted hands. Isabella had aged too—her thundercloud of hair was more gray than black now, and her sagging skin had made a few more folds in her smile.

As they splashed into the shallows, hauling the boat onto the sand, Adeline nodded at him. "Cannek Reed," she drawled. "I've never known you to go visitin' when there's adventure to be had."

"Visitin' you's always an adventure." Reed tipped his hat to them. "Good to see you both alive and kickin'."

Isabella laughed. At least that was the same—clear and resonant as a bell. "We're alive. I wouldn't say we've done much kicking lately."

Adeline watched Reed thoughtfully with her rheumy eyes. "I suspect there's time for that yet."

Isabella scanned the crew, her expression brightening as she recognized sailors she knew. But then she frowned and turned to Reed. "Say, this is a nice landing party and all, lots of old faces and some new," she said, winking at Marmalade, who blushed. "But where's Jules? You didn't make her stay on the ship, did you, Cannek?"

The others shifted uncomfortably. Marmalade's already pale face went even whiter. Always steadfast, Horse hugged her to his side.

"Well," Reed said softly, "that's part of why we're here."

Striking off for Adeline and Isabella's home in the jungle, Captain Reed told them what had been happening in Kelanna the past twenty years: the war against Oxscini, the Everican-Liccarine Alliance, the way outlaws were being exterminated like rats, how Jules had lost her life. By the time they reached the compound, Reed had related the whole plan.

But once he got a look at their little patch of land, he began to doubt.

Their compound had fallen into disrepair. The wide porch that wrapped around their house had caved in at one end. The roof was rotting, and the garden was quickly losing ground to the jungle. The barn, the splintering gazebos, the weedy walkways, everything had the look of decay.

"It all started coming apart a few years ago," Isabella said as she escorted them into the yard. Though she didn't seem troubled by the shotgun resting on her shoulder, her bad leg seemed to have finally gotten the best of her, and each step was like a hiccup of pain. "But honestly we thought we'd be gone by now, so we figured why bother fixing something that no one would use when we were dead?"

Adeline picked up a broken piece of fence. "If we do this, we'll have to build. Docks, barracks, land to till, barns for livestock."

Build? How could they build when they couldn't even maintain what they had?

Reed must have looked as worried as he felt because she chucked the rotten board at him. It hit him square in the ribs and crumbled into dust. Her aim was still true, at least.

"Don't look at me like that, Cannek," she said.

He brushed at his shirt. "Just wonderin' how you'll get pirates to tend a field."

"Same way I ever did anything." She patted the revolver holstered at her side. "They do what I tell them, or they'll see just how much mercy I have left."

Reed tried to grin, but he couldn't help wondering how long it would take for some conniving pirate captain to kill Adeline and seize Haven for himself. In the past, the Lady had held her own against dozens of bandits. Somehow, he doubted she'd be up to it now.

For a moment, he imagined both old women in their deteriorating garden, their bodies riddled with bullet holes, their blood soaking the earth. Even if they lived through the war, they'd be giving their last years to a cause that wasn't their own.

How could he ask that of them, knowing where they'd be going? How could he live with himself, knowing he'd be sending them there quicker?

Sun baked the compound that afternoon as the entire crew of the *Current* turned out to offer their services to Adeline and Isabella. Horse and his carpenters set to work on the house, sawing and hammering, repairing rotten beams and holes in the roof, while the rest of the sailors mucked out the pigpen and patched up the barn, weeded the garden and hacked at the jungle encroaching on the fences.

"The world's changed," Adeline said as she sat on the porch, supervising the repairs.

Reed nodded.

"You've changed." The Lady scratched at the paint peeling from the arm of her rocking chair. In their silence, they could hear Isabella chatting with Doc, who was inspecting her bad leg. "For the better, I reckon."

"Hope so," Reed said. He'd lived close to danger his entire life, demanding his crew do the same, and spit in death's eye if they ever got the chance. But it'd always been with the promise that the things they did would be recounted so many times they'd never be lost.

Collecting outlaws fleeing from the Alliance would be dangerous, yes, but it'd be forgettable. If they died, they'd be a drop in the ocean, utterly unremarkable in the grand scheme of the war. They'd have nothing—no legacy, perhaps not even anyone to remember the way they went down.

Nothing but red lights and black water.

"Cannek?" Adeline's voice startled him from his thoughts. "What's eatin' you?"

"Is this a good idea?" he asked. "Am I doin' the right thing?"

"*Right?*" Adeline flicked a paint chip into a broken flower pot on the porch rail. "The hard questions ain't got a *right*. They only got what you think you can live with, at the time."

Just then, Isabella came limping out of the house.

"How's the leg, my love?" the Lady asked.

"Painful," Isabella said, kissing Adeline gently on the lips. "But I'll live."

"You'd better." As Isabella settled in her own rocking chair, the Lady touched her sleeve, fingering the cotton as if it were made precious simply by being on Isabella's person. "I plan on you outlivin' me for a good few years, at least."

With a smile, Isabella clasped her hand, squeezed it once.

Around them, the work continued.

By nightfall, Adeline and Isabella were set up in their rocking chairs again: Adeline nursing a glass of some potent gold liquid Cooky had dug out of his pantry; Isabella fanning herself with a wide leaf. Below in the yard, Cooky and Aly dished out crispy cuts of pork and curried lentils while the rest of the crew regaled the two old women with tales of what they'd done since they'd parted ways: chasing dragons with the *Black Beauty*, finding the Lady Delune in her garden, braving the maelstrom for the Thunder Gong, Captain Cat and her cannibal crew, the floating island, Sefia and Archer and the hunt for the Trove.

Every so often, Theo, the chanty leader of the starboard watch, would pick up his violin and play a tune. Sometimes Harison's red lory, perched on Theo's shoulder, would even whistle along.

They tried not to think of Jules, but she was everywhere—in the stories they told, in the songs they sung.

Those that had been to the place of the fleshless didn't mention what they'd found at the edge of the world.

They didn't want to think of her out there, robbed of her voice.

But Reed couldn't help thinking of it, couldn't help thinking of Adeline or Isabella out there too, of Meeks or Doc or Marmalade or any of his crew out there, one day soon.

They had to know. They had to know what would happen to them, what they were running toward, since they'd given up on immortality. They deserved to live however they wanted before the inevitable came for them.

He stood, rubbing his wrist. "I got a story," he said. "'The Red Waters.'"

The others fell silent. Adeline raised an eyebrow. Isabella's fanning slowed.

Meeks swallowed. "But that's a story we never tell."

"It ain't right keepin' it to ourselves anymore," he said. "C'mon, we'll tell it together."

Marmalade and some of the new crew members looked around uneasily. To them, the Red Waters was only a name they'd heard in passing, meant as a warning. The sailors who'd been there drew in, like they could already feel the cold closing in on them.

Meeks inhaled deeply—the breath before the plunge. "There's a story no one tells, for those who know it don't want to remember it," he began. "But it's a story we'll never forget.

The story of what we found at the edge of the world, when we passed through the sun into the black place beyond. The place of the fleshless."

Reed shivered as the second mate's words pulled him back there, into the dark.

"It was cold, so cold frost crept up the hull of the ship, spiking the running lines and silvering the decks. So cold our throats seized up, and our breath was brittle in our mouths. Deep in the water, the red lights blinked, innumerable, goin' back as far as anyone could see. And that sound . . ." Shuddering, Meeks covered his ears with his hands.

Adjusting his spectacles, Theo took up the story in Meeks's stead: "It was like whisperin' and chitterin' and mad laughter. Voices, or the tollin' of funeral bells, or glaciers cleavin' in two. It was like cliffs crumblin' to dust. Like the last rattlin' gasp of the dyin'." On his shoulder, the red bird let out a low whistle. "The most terrible sound in a world of terrible sounds. The kind of sound that haunts you in the late hours of the night when the darkness closes in and the cold creeps into you through the cracks. 'Cause we knew, didn't we? We knew where we were. We didn't know how we knew it. But we recognized those red lights in the water."

"The red eyes of the dead," Reed said.

Adeline glanced at him sharply. In Kelanna, they didn't believe in an afterlife. Didn't believe you were anything more than a story once you were gone.

But Captain Reed knew the truth.

And now, so would Adeline and Isabella and all of his crew.

The sun had been a gateway, a portal from the living world to the place of the dead. They'd managed to blunder through it at dusk, when the sun touched the water. But the sun had left them, sinking through the waves, and it wouldn't return until the following day.

"The dead rose from the water," Meeks continued, "more monsters than men, with two red lights where their eyes should have been. They looked like the people we knew, more or less. Sometimes their faces were clear as day. Sometimes they were hazy, like we were seein' 'em through frosted glass.

"They wanted us to join 'em, see. They used the voices of people who'd died. We wanted to go to 'em. I would've given anything to . . . But when they touched us . . ."

Goro made a sound like he'd been punched. "But every time they touched us, their fingers went right through us, takin' a little of our warmth, a little of our life."

"Some of the crew started pitchin' themselves over the rails," Meeks said, "like they'd be united with loved ones they never thought they'd see again. But when they hit the water, the red lights swarmed 'em. The waves seemed to form faces and hands. I'll never forget the shriekin'. Over and over they screamed as the shadows ripped into them, stealing away their life."

"I saw my brother out there," Jaunty said hollowly, rubbing his tattooed knuckles. "My brother. Hadn't seen him for twenty years. Was sure I'd never see him again. But there he was, lookin' almost as scruffy as I remembered. Can you imagine? I thought I could hold him again. I thought I could tell him I was sorry. For not bein' a better brother. For not payin' enough attention. For not knowin' he was gonna climb onto the bowsprit one night and eat his gun. My *brother*."

"But it wasn't his brother." Meeks shook his head. "'Cause when you die, you become a shadow of who you were. Empty. Starvin'. A monster.

"We couldn't fight 'em. Couldn't shoot 'em. Our bullets passed through 'em like they were made of smoke. We kept losin' folks who jumped over the side, or who got touched one too many times and just curled up and died. It's a miracle we lasted the night."

"That was Doc's doin'," Horse said, putting his arm around the surgeon. "She thought to stop our ears with wax so we couldn't hear 'em callin' us."

"And the light," Theo added, fixated on the flaming coals, "the light kept 'em away."

"We passed that fearful darkness together, while the shades of our friends and kin hovered just beyond the reach of the light. We couldn't hear their words anymore, but we felt their chill in our hearts and our bones. And when the sun returned, descending out of the starless sky, Cap roused us. It woulda been easier to stay out there and let the fleshless take us, but Cap made us get up. He got us out of there, and the warmth returned to our bones. We unstoppered our ears. Never in my life have I been so grateful for the sounds of water and sails.

"But some of us never returned to normal, like the fleshless had stolen too much of them, and they just sort of faded away on the journey home. Sometimes we'd find their bodies still and cold in their bunks. Sometimes they'd simply be gone. Lost overboard during the night watches.

"We held the funerals. We said the words. But we knew. Death ain't the end." Meeks glanced around at the others, who avoided his gaze. "It's worse."

In the silence, Marmalade began to cry. "So she's out there, then? That's what happened to her?"

Reed gripped her shoulder. "That's what happens to all of us."

On the porch, Adeline and Isabella had clasped hands. "This a warning, Cannek?" the Lady asked.

He shook his head. "We ain't gettin' any glory for this one, folks. Might be all we get is grief and nothingness. I thought everyone oughta know the truth before they chose to throw in their lot."

Isabella smiled ruefully. "We knew the second you showed up in our lagoon you'd ask us to do something that'd probably get us killed. We let you come ashore anyway."

"And now?" Reed asked. "Even knowing . . ."

Adeline turned to Isabella, and as if to some unspoken question, some secret language they'd developed over the years between the two of them, she nodded. "If we all become monsters in the end, best we do something that makes us better humans while we're still here," she said.

"I'll still do it," Marmalade added in a quavering voice. "Just like Jules would've."

Meeks raised his glass.

Everyone drank.

Later, long after the others had turned in for the night, Reed joined the two women on the porch and slid the silver revolver into Adeline's hands.

She trailed her fingers across the engravings of cottonwood leaves, the mother-of-pearl inlay. "When I gave this to you, I never thought I'd see it again," she said. Her hand closed over the grip, and it was as if a part of her had been missing all this time, and only now, with the gun in her hand, was she made whole again.

Isabella nodded. "That's good work, that," she said. "Some of my best."

"You only do the best work," the Lady chided her.

She preened, touching the crackling waves of her hair.

"Much obliged, Cannek." Adeline tucked the revolver into her waistband. "Sounds like I'll need this."

"Don't you think I'm letting you go without a replacement." Isabella glanced at the black grip of the Executioner with distaste. "You need a gun, not a monstrosity." She limped off into the house and came back with a cloth-wrapped bundle.

Gingerly, he folded back the fabric, revealing the most beautiful revolver he'd ever laid eyes on. It was longer in the barrel than the Lady of Mercy, but while the silver gun was a moonbeam on the dunes, this weapon was the great dark ocean itself—crafted of deep blue steel with silver crests and an ebony grip as black as the depths of the sea.

"This is too fine." Reed tried to hand it back.

"Nonsense." Isabella swatted him in the shoulder. "I made it with you in mind, Cannek. It was always meant to be yours."

He spun the cylinder, studying the light through the chambers. The revolver fit as perfectly in his hand as the Lady of Mercy fit Adeline. Isabella had been right, as she always was when it came to firearms—there was no weapon more perfect for him.

"Any idea what you'll call it?" Adeline asked.

With a turn of his wrist, Reed flicked the cylinder closed. "How about the Singer?"

"Cry of the Watchman"

JULES'S FAVORITE SONG

My love, where did you go
    Since last you spoke my name?
To skies above or seas below,
    In darkness, both the same?

My love, where do you sleep
    Without me by your side?
A bed of tears, or gloam you reap
    From willows that have died?

My love, where is the light
    You promised me would rake
The barren reaches of the night
    When dreamers start awake?

My love, I'll help you find
  The way, though it be long.
My love, oh love, give me a sign
  If you can hear my song.

CHAPTER 26

Lies of Omission

Sefia didn't belong in Archer's future. Of this, she was certain.

He would end up back in Jocoxa with Annabel.

She'd end up on the *Current of Faith* with Captain Reed and his crew of outlaws.

Maybe it wasn't what she'd always imagined for them. But like Meeks had said—or would say, one day—she had to let that go. She had to let *him* go.

It was written, after all. She'd seen it with her own eyes. And what was written always came to pass.

As they rode into Ken, down the outer curve of the kingdom, she tried to resign herself to it. Archer would be in Jocoxa. He'd be happy. He'd get to live.

But why couldn't he do that with her? Why couldn't she be the one he brought home, the one he opened his life to, the one he woke up to each morning with the sounds of waves outside their window?

They found the quarry exactly as the Book had predicted: a flooded pit, twenty-one impressors, six boys locked in cages, and one autumn storm charging in from the Northern Ocean. But on the morning of the attack, they discovered something the Book had not shown them.

Beyond the inlet, a single black-and-yellow ship rocked in the restless water, sails trimmed for the coming storm. Along the gun decks, the cold cylinders of cannons protruded like thorns.

While Archer sent scouts to see what else had changed in the quarry below, Sefia lay on the cliff, shredding stalks of grass. *Why didn't the Book warn me about this? What else has it kept from me?*

"Whose ship is that?" Archer whispered beside her.

"One of Serakeen's," she answered. On their travels, she and Nin had encountered the pirate's fleet only once, but she could not forget those hornets' colors, the *boom* of the chase guns, the whispering of the other children and the gleam of the lamplight on the opium vials in their parents' hands.

Nin had patted Sefia's shoulder in a rare moment of affection. "Better dead than plunder for pirates."

"This wasn't in the Book?" Archer's voice brought her back to the present.

"No." She ripped up another blade of grass. She'd combed through those pages. She knew the impressors' fighting styles, their weaknesses and favorite weapons. She'd been so thorough she knew how much they'd racked up in gambling debts. But not once had she seen a word about Serakeen's pirates. "The Book withheld it from me."

He glanced at her sharply, surprised. "I didn't know it could do that."

"Neither did I."

If it could omit a detail as important as this, what else could it do?

More importantly, *why*?

Blinking, she summoned her sense of the Illuminated world. Gold eddied across her vision, sweeping over the quarry and streaking toward the center of the bay. She scanned the ship, the crew, the great guns.

"It's called the *Artax*," she reported, blinking again. "Serakeen must have finally sent a ship to stop us."

"Serakeen?" Kaito repeated as he crawled up beside them. Sefia could feel his muscles tense, as if preparing to catapult him from the cliff.

"Don't get too excited," Archer said wryly. "It's one of his ships, not the man himself."

Kaito gave him a wicked grin. "I'll take whatever I can get."

A corner of Archer's mouth twitched, but the worried creases in his brow remained.

"We're not prepared for this." The tremor in Sefia's voice betrayed her uncertainty. "We should delay the attack."

"Wait? No way." Kaito looked to Archer. "C'mon, brother, we can't hesitate. Not now."

She tried to catch Archer's eye, but he was staring off into the distance, at the dark bank of clouds on the horizon, head cocked, as if listening for thunder.

Before he could respond, however, their scouts returned, slinking through the grass like predators.

"Pretty much everything's like the sorcerer said it'd be," Versil reported. "Two-man watch in the wood shack on the upper tier. Boys in cages below that, with another three guards nearby. The rest of them are on watch by the ramp or holed up near the water."

"Did you see any pirates?" Kaito asked eagerly.

"The captain and seventeen of her crew. They're mean-looking bonesuckers. Came up in boats. We overheard them saying the rest would join them when the storm cleared."

A cold smile curved Archer's lips.

"I don't like this," Sefia said, touching his arm. "There's something else the Book's keeping from me. Something's going to go wrong. I can feel it. Give me time to figure it out."

Archer squinted at the darkening sky. "You've got until the storm breaks. The weather will give us enough time to escape before the rest of the pirates come ashore."

Sefia drew back angrily. "You can't do this without me."

"We won't," he shot back. "It's been written. But we'll start without you, if we have to." His gold eyes flashed, and for a second he looked like a stranger to her.

"C'mon, sorcerer," Versil said. "You can't lead wolves to their prey and expect them not to hunt."

"Not when they're hungry," Kaito added.

While the bloodletters prepared for battle, Sefia fled to her tent. Slamming the Book on her table, she demanded information about the *Artax*, the pirates, the fight. She tore through the pages, scouring the paragraphs for details she'd missed, but the Book stubbornly refused to help her.

It showed her darkness—wall after wall of rain—Archer's teeth seamed with blood—a gunshot.

Over and over she saw the gunshot. She saw the trigger finger beaded with rain. She saw the tongue of fire and the tail of smoke. She saw the bullet spiraling through the air.

It was like the Book suddenly had a will of its own.

Or had it always had a will of its own?

Had it been manipulating her this whole time, showing her only what she needed to see in order to continue down whatever path the Book had chosen for her?

Or for Archer?

It was like trying to see the future through a fractured spyglass. She didn't have enough to go on. She needed more time.

But by afternoon, the storm had come. The skies turned black. The winds ripped at the cliffs. The rain fell hard, soaking Sefia and the bloodletters as they assembled on the cliff.

Out on the water, the *Artax* plummeted in the waves as lightning flashed on the sea behind her.

In the quarry, a sentry paced back and forth across the highest tier. Once every hour, he traded positions with his partner in the shack, leaving the upper level unguarded.

That was when the bloodletters struck.

They descended from the cliffs above, finding slippery handholds in the weather-beaten slate. Down the rocks they came like spiders, alighting on the highest tier, where they dispersed into squads.

Sefia reached for Archer's hand. The water slid over their fingers.

"It's not too late," she said.

The seconds flicked by in a tracery of lightning. Sparks flared deep in his eyes, and she knew he needed this battle, needed the violence, needed to hurt and kill.

He's the boy, she thought. *He's the one they want.*

The Book had told her differently, but she didn't know if she could believe the Book anymore.

"One more," he said, "and Deliene is done." With a wave of his hand, he directed Frey and Aljan toward the wooden shack.

As they burst in on the sentries, the storm masking the shouts, the gunfire, Sefia hooked her fingers into Archer's collar. Rain coursed down his face, over his lips. "You can still leave this behind," she whispered. "You can be happy. You can live." Fiercely, almost viciously, she kissed him. Whatever happened next, she wanted to make sure he remembered her—her lips, her tongue, her body in his arms—and what they'd meant to each other, once.

They parted.

Archer staggered back, surprise and longing written all over his face. He touched his lips.

Then Frey and Aljan emerged from the shack. From the edge of the tier, Kaito said, "Let's go, brother." With one final glance at Sefia, Archer motioned his bloodletters toward the bottom of the quarry.

Alone, Sefia and Griegi approached the north wall, where the cages were positioned on the tier below. Hands slipping, feet scuffling along the rocks, they clambered down the slope.

The row of cages had been built against the cliff wall, with scrap wood laid over the top, though the rotten boards didn't stop the rain from trickling inside. As Griegi dispatched the guards, she made quick work of the locks, and soon the rescued boys were scrambling up the storm-washed stones to freedom.

On the upper level of the quarry, Sefia paused to survey the action below. Through the rain, she could see bodies on the bottom level of the pit. Flashes of gunfire. Skirmishes in the gravel.

As she watched, three figures dashed from behind the buildings. Too big to be boys, they had to be impressors or pirates. Lightning cracked overhead, dousing the quarry with brilliant white light. The runners picked up speed. They didn't look back.

Cowards, Sefia thought.

Another figure broke from the fighting and raced after them.

Fear bolted through her. That wasn't part of the plan. That was never part of the plan. Was this what the Book had been hiding?

Sefia blinked, and her vision went gold. In the Illuminated world, she learned who it was.

Kaito.

Of course. She scanned him, retracing his steps, reading his story:

He'd been leading his squad against the impressors, sprinting along the quarry wall, past the ramp, where they'd gathered at the corner of a long stone building.

The heat and excitement of battle rippled through his limbs. He cast a glance at his squad and raised his right arm. Flashes of light-ning licked at his exposed tattoos. What is written comes to pass.

Thunder called overhead. His heart answered.

Behind him, Versil grinned, rain streaming down his face.

They burst in on the impressors with bright rounds of gunfire and the slashing arcs of their blades. One after another, their enemies fell like fields to scythe and flame.

They cleared the first building and were approaching the next when Kaito saw three men dash into the yard. He narrowed his eyes. They had the heavy weaponry and weather-beaten skin of pirates—Serakeen's pirates.

Serakeen. *The word sang inside him. His weapons burned in his hands, begging for blood.*

He raced after them, ignoring Versil's startled cry.

Now, water splashed under Kaito's boots. Gravel skidded out from under him. There was nothing but him and the black sky, and one way or another, either he or his enemies would die tonight.

Sefia blinked again, and the physical world came falling back into place around her.

That must have been what she'd been missing. Kaito. Archer's brother in arms. The gunshot she'd seen was meant for him.

"Sorcerer?" Griegi asked.

"Kaito went after the pirates alone," she said. "Get the boys to safety. I'm going down there."

Obediently, Griegi returned to the bewildered boys. Over the noise of the storm, she could hear him shouting instructions.

She raced past the wooden shack and down the narrow steps to the floor of the quarry. She had to stop Kaito, had to stop the pirates from killing him, had to stop the bullet. Archer couldn't lose him now, not when they'd only just found each other again. She dashed into the open stretch of yard, where the storm-tossed waves rushed onto the jagged slate shore.

The bloodletters were winning. The battle was almost over.

From behind her, there was a roar. Griegi and the boys from the cages were skidding down the slope to the bottom of the quarry, stealing weapons from corpses.

She had almost made it to the edge of the yard when she saw it happen.

In the dim light, Versil was fighting one of the impressors—a dark-haired man named Arz whom Sefia recognized from the Book—the boy's slender form skipping and ducking in the rain, his sword flicking in and out like the tongue of a snake. He was laughing.

A pistol slid from the impressor's sleeve. There was a puff of smoke.

Versil twisted, but the bullet caught him in the thigh. Blood burst from the wound. He stumbled.

Sefia gasped.

The point of Arz's sword emerged from Versil's back. The boy went limp.

Sneering, the impressor tossed the body aside.

On instinct, Sefia summoned her magic. Arz froze where he stood, his arms useless at his sides.

She'd been wrong. She'd been so focused on Kaito she'd missed it entirely.

The single bullet that had cost Versil his life.

The battle was over. Frey and the boys looked up from their defeated opponents.

Aljan let out a cry. As he ran, his legs buckled underneath him, until he was half-scrambling, half-crawling to his brother's body. Gathering Versil up in his arms, he began to scream.

Sefia wiped her eyes with her free hand. The others were shivering, shifting as they exchanged uneasy glances. Since joining up with Archer, they'd been injured, certainly, but none of them had *died*.

As Frey knelt beside Aljan, Sefia looked for Archer. But he had not appeared.

Kaito joined them, sauntering back over the rocks with a triumphant smirk. His hands and tattooed forearms were covered in a weak mixture of blood and rain.

His smile faded from his lips when he saw Aljan holding Versil's corpse.

He looked from the twins to the impressor, still frozen, the bloody sword useless in his hand.

Kaito's face twisted. He pulled his revolver. "You did this?" He drew back the hammer.

CHAPTER 27

Brothers

As if the battle were a piece of music and he its conductor, Archer could sense the rhythm of the fight charging toward its conclusion. Arcs of bloodshed. Clashes of steel. The thrill of things dying in his hands.

A grand crescendo of violence and then—

The stillness of the dead.

The groans of the wounded.

Panting, he surveyed the stone building where they had brought the battle to a close. Tables were upturned. Chairs were broken. Their enemies were scissored on the floor. He could almost feel the reverberations of their last cries and the soft, pulpy impacts of their bodies hitting the ground.

Four down.

None to go.

He should have felt relieved. After tonight, there would be no more impressors in Deliene.

But all he could think of was continuing the mission—in Oxscini, in Everica, Liccaro, and Roku. Hunting impressors, saving boys, and building his army.

Archer's sword clattered against the floor as his squad began securing prisoners.

"You?" one of the impressors said as the bloodletters tied her wrists. "*You're* the leader of the bloodletters? I should've known."

Half of her face was purpled with bruises, but Archer recognized her from the Cage in Jahara, where he'd once fought for an audience with Serakeen. A whale-tooth pendant still hung from her neck.

"Lavinia?" Archer asked, sliding his revolver back into its holster.

"In the flesh." She bared her broken teeth. "For now."

"Is Gregor here too?" Last he'd seen, the black-haired boy had been moaning, bloody, in the sawdust.

"You beat him." The woman made a *tsk*ing sound. "What do you think?"

He should never have left Gregor and Haku once they'd been defeated. He should have known. But he hadn't thought. And now they were dead. He advanced on her.

Lavinia glared at him out of her good eye, daring him to strike. "It's *you*, isn't it? I should have known as soon as I saw you fight. Serakeen's sure got a surprise coming for him."

You're wrong, he wanted to say. *It's not me.*

But Lavinia saw in him what he'd been trying to deny for weeks, the same thing Kaito had seen in him all along. His taste and talent for violence. His inability to stop. A shiver ran through him.

Then Aljan began to scream.

Archer ran to the door, where he took in the scene in the yard—Versil's body in his brother's arms, Sefia holding the impressor in place, Kaito's helpless fury.

Versil was dead. He was dead.

Sefia had warned him, but he hadn't listened. He'd been impatient. Reckless.

And Versil had paid for it.

Archer knew he'd dream about this for the rest of his life—the sound of Aljan's screams, the spatter of the rain on Versil's upturned face. Another dead boy.

And it was his fault. For not stopping. For not listening. For leading them into this.

His hand was on his revolver. He wanted to fight. To kill. To drown himself in violence so he wouldn't have to think of this, deal with this, feel this.

Kaito put his gun to the impressor's temple.

He'd kill him. He'd kill a defenseless man, and after that, he'd never be able to come back. He'd be wild, his thirst uncontrollable, all-consuming, destroying himself and everyone who loved him.

In that split second, Archer was afraid.

For Kaito. And for himself.

"Stop!" he cried, splashing into the downpour. In the puddles, his footsteps beat out another rhythm: *Versil is dead. Versil is dead.*

Kaito's eyes were bloodshot. He could barely get his words out: "He killed Versil."

Archer fought the urge to look back at Frey and Aljan huddled in the mud. "Give me the gun, Kaito," he said.

Kaito stepped back. His hands were shaking. "Versil's dead. He's *dead*. And you want to let his killer *live*? Get out of my way."

"He can't hurt anyone anymore."

"You were his *leader*. He *trusted* you." Kaito's words were loud and choked with tears. "You were supposed to be there. You were supposed to protect him. *Where were you?*"

Archer flinched.

The sound of Aljan's screams.

The spatter of rain on Versil's upturned face.

"Move." Brushing Archer aside, Kaito pointed the gun at the impressor and pulled the trigger.

But Archer was faster. He'd always been faster. His hand slammed into Kaito's wrist, and the bullet went speeding harmlessly into the darkness.

The gun dropped. Dingy water splashed Archer's boots.

Bending to retrieve the revolver, he caught a knee in the face. Suns exploded behind his eyes.

Then Kaito was on top of him.

But oh, he *welcomed* it. The way his vision sharpened. The way he could sense every raindrop striking the slate. The way he could forget he'd never hear Versil's laughter again. The way he could lose himself. The way he could forget.

He and Kaito fought without weapons, their fists and elbows making dull impacts in the rain. It was like practice all over again.

Except for the grief. And the guilt.

Except for that.

"Stop!" Sefia cried. Archer felt her try to thrust them apart with magic, but he slipped her grasp.

Griegi tried to stop him next, pulling him to the ground. If Griegi found a hold, he wouldn't let go.

Archer elbowed him in the nose. Something crunched, and the boy let go. Archer vaulted up again.

Sefia had frozen Kaito, who was struggling against her magic like a rabbit caught in a snare—eyes wild, saliva flying from his lips.

Archer charged him. As they fell to the ground, Sefia's invisible grip loosened. Kaito was free. They scrambled to their feet, circling again.

Scarza grabbed Kaito from behind. Seizing the opportunity, Archer got in a few hits before the Gormani boy threw them both off.

Around and around they went in the gravel, their hands slippery, their faces bruised.

With Griegi trying to stanch his bleeding nose and Scarza stunned on the ground, none of the other bloodletters tried to stop them.

The end came quick after that. With a grunt, Archer threw Kaito into the gravel. Lightning flashed. The green-eyed boy lay on his back, gasping.

Archer wiped at his lower lip with his sleeve. Everything hurt. His head. His knuckles. His heart.

Versil was still dead.

In the stillness, his grief and guilt came rushing back.

But as Archer pressed his hands to his aching chest, Kaito got up and attacked again.

Archer tried to dodge, but the Gormani boy grabbed his arm and wrenched him back. They went at it again—circling, grappling, throwing punches—and this time it was different. It wasn't because they wanted to practice. It wasn't because they wanted to forget.

It was because they wanted to hurt someone—anyone—the way they were already hurting.

Again and again, Archer threw Kaito to the ground, and again and again, Kaito got up. Even Sefia could no longer intervene, her magic shaky enough as it was, holding the impressor in place so long.

At last, Archer hit Kaito so hard his knees gave out. His face hit the gravel, his fingers curling around sharp bits of stone.

The bloodletters were silent. It was as if they knew Kaito was beaten.

Archer's whole body hurt, but inside he finally felt numb. Blissfully, mercifully numb. No guilt. No grief. Nothing. Even knowing Aljan was still sitting there whimpering.

The rain spattered against the rocks as Archer leaned over Kaito. "Enough," he said. "It's over." Blood sprayed from between his teeth.

"It'll never be over." Kaito pushed himself off the quarry floor like a creature of rock and mud and rain. "Something has to change. Something has to be different. It's not fair. He shouldn't have died. You didn't deserve him. You don't deserve any of this."

Archer turned. Kaito flung gravel at him, the pebbles rattling harmlessly off his back.

Behind him, Sefia ordered the bloodletters to bind the prisoner's hands. As he walked away, Archer tripped on the wet stone. Everything that didn't sting ached. Blood and water dribbled from his fingertips.

And then—"Archer!"—Aljan's voice. Aljan, whose brother was dead in his arms.

Archer spun. He saw it all in a flash: Kaito with the gun. Kaito pulling back the hammer. Kaito's finger on the trigger.

Archer didn't think. He didn't have to.

The revolver was already in his hands. The bullet was already leaving the chamber.

Kaito Kemura was already dead.

For a split second, Archer thought he saw Kaito's horror . . . and his regret.

Then the bullet hit him between the eyes.

The boy dropped. His arms and legs crumpled under him. His face—green eyes going dark and anger fading from his lips—looked completely unsurprised.

CHAPTER 28

Love and Death

After two weeks in the north, trying to gain a foothold with Abiye in Gorman Province, Arcadimon returned to the capital with spatters of mud still clinging to his clothing. No matter. No one would notice in the wet weather.

Autumn had taken root in Corabel. Every afternoon, the rain came up from the south, drenching the city, the cliffs, the miles of white poppies bobbing on their stems. Everything from the sand-colored stones to the red rooftops of the city had a faint gleam, as if touched by magic.

Arcadimon traversed the lower halls, passing in and out of the milky light from the windows as the rain beat down on the glass.

He was looking forward to seeing Ed again. Ever since the kiss on the White Plains, Eduoar had been distant. And the more Arcadimon tried to talk to him, the more he shied away, spending long days in his rooms when even Arcadimon couldn't coax him out.

They had to address the kiss.

And maybe repeat it.

The thought glimmered like a flame in his chest, but it was extinguished just as quickly when he remembered his duty to the Guard. *Kiss him or kill him. You can't have both.*

Brushing the thought aside, Arcadimon took the steps to the throne room two at a time, his feet skipping over the stairs. But the room was empty.

Not unusual.

Except the attendants hadn't seen Eduoar.

Captain Ignani and her guards hadn't seen him either.

A king missing in his own castle.

Arcadimon raced to the kennels, where as a kid Eduoar used to spend his afternoons. He patted Frog and the other dogs as they came bounding around his legs, but Ed wasn't there either.

Not in his bedchamber.

Not in the council rooms.

Not in the kitchens.

Among the rain-splashed flagstones of the courtyard, Arcadimon paused, squinting toward the gray skies as the damp seeped into his clothes. His gaze roved from window to window, searching for Eduoar's slim figure behind the curtains, for his face in the glass.

He almost skipped over the royal bedchamber. It hadn't been used since Eduoar found the Suicide King dead in a corner, and over the years it had been passed over so often it had nearly been forgotten.

But Eduoar hadn't forgotten it. You don't forget something like that.

Cold gripped Arcadimon's heart.

He dashed up to the second level of the castle, to the third, until he was racing down the corridors calling for help, calling wildly for Ignani, the guards, the doctors, for anyone in earshot.

He reached the hallway to the royal chamber, cluttered with covered statues and rolled-up rugs.

The door was locked.

"Ed!" He hammered on the door, but there was no response. "Eduoar!"

Nothing.

Arcadimon rammed his shoulder into the door, but it didn't budge. He wasn't strong enough for something that had been built to withstand a riot. Sneaking a glance around the empty hallway, he summoned his sense of the Illuminated world.

Gold sputtered in his vision. He'd never had to live at the Main Branch, so he'd never been as well trained in magic as the other Apprentices—the realm of the Politicians was bribery and threats and governance, after all—but Ed's life depended on him now.

He palmed the air. The fine metalwork warped. The door cracked. But it didn't open.

He struck out again. Boards fractured.

Come on.

There were voices in the stairwell. Arcadimon swept his

hands at the door—and then it was open, breaking as he stumbled into the room.

The royal bedchamber hadn't been touched in over a decade. White cloths draped the canopied bed, the chairs and tables, the portraits on the walls. The rugs had all been stored in the corners, and dust floated from the stone floor as Arcadimon dashed inside, rushing past the white sheets, his passage exposing the arm of a chair, the corner of a table.

It was empty.

His stomach dropped. He spun, checking the bed, the hearth.

No.

No.

No.

Then Arcadimon saw him—Eduoar—curled in a corner of the room, as if he hadn't wanted to be found.

"Ed!" The word broke from Arcadimon's mouth as he flung himself down. Eduoar was pale and cold, with a sheen of sweat on his face and neck.

"Ed," Arcadimon repeated, softer.

There was so much blood. It was everywhere. On his boots and shins and knees. On his hands. Arcadimon ripped a sheet from the nearest table and wrapped the wounds on Eduoar's wrists.

"Help!" he called. "In here!"

There was some Manipulation that would slow the bleeding. That was how Rajar had saved Tanin. But Arcadimon could barely break down a door. He couldn't do something as delicate as this.

Cradling Eduoar's body against his chest, he pressed hard against the blood-soaked sheets. "What have you done?" he whispered, his lips moving against the king's damp hair.

Eduoar had followed in his father's footsteps.

Just like the Guard had wanted.

For a moment Arcadimon let up on Eduoar's wrists. This was what he'd been planning for, all this time.

The death of the king.

A tragedy, just like his father.

Darion would want him to let Eduoar die. The timing was off—he still needed the support of Gorman Province if he was to succeed in his coup—but he couldn't have asked for a better opportunity.

Eduoar's eyelids fluttered. "I couldn't let the curse get you."

Arcadimon clamped down on his wrists again. "I'm not a Corabelli, you fool."

"You have the love of a Corabelli," Ed whispered. "For us, love and death are the same."

People flooded into the room. Guards. Servants. A doctor, maybe. The sounds of their footsteps mingled with the sounds of the rain. They were speaking. They were trying to pull Arcadimon away.

He hugged Eduoar tighter in his arms.

Someone was nudging Arcadimon aside. Someone was putting pressure on the king's wrists. They were taking him.

"Besides," Eduoar murmured faintly, "you were taking too long."

Arcadimon's grip went slack. The king's fingers slid from his own.

Eduoar knew about the poison—*How long? All this time?*—and he'd taken it anyway.

They whisked Eduoar's body out of the room, and Arcadimon was left sitting in a pool of the king's blood, alone.

You were taking too long.

CHAPTER 29

Born for This

While the rain hammered the quarry outside, Archer leaned over the table and sketched out a plan for attacking the *Artax*.

A two-pronged assault, like they'd done to Obiyagi and her caravan at the Rock Eater. As soon as the storm dried up, before the pirates could gather their bearings, they'd take the rowboats and hit the *Artax* from both port and starboard, pinning their enemy amidships.

"It has to be soon," he said, "before they realize what's happened. Before they can escape."

Archer was surprised by the even keel of his own voice—pragmatic, confident, the voice of a leader in total control of himself. Not the voice of a leader who had just killed one of their best, one of their brothers.

He found it hard to believe the bloodletters had shown up at all, trickling in a few at a time, leaving wet splotches on the floor as they took up positions around the table, against the stone walls: Scarza, brooding in the back; Frey, sitting beside Aljan, clasping his hand.

Archer tried not to look at him. Whenever he looked at Aljan, he saw Versil—eyes open, mouth slack, never to speak again.

Archer traced the edge of the table, his thumbnail digging grooves in the wood.

He kept experiencing it—the gun in his hand—the widening of Kaito's eyes as he realized he was going to die—the recoil shuddering along his arm.

Why didn't you stay down?

Archer dug out another crescent of wood from the tabletop.

"Why?" Griegi said, interrupting his thoughts. "We already got the boys out. The mission's over."

It'll never be over.

"Not for me." Archer looked down at his hands so he wouldn't have to look at Aljan. Blood darkened the undersides of his fingernails. Slivers of wood littered the table. "Not after what they did to Versil."

"That was one man," Griegi protested, "and we got him. The pirates on the *Artax* have done nothing to us."

"They did, actually," one of the newest boys said quietly. "They executed one of us as soon as they got here. He'd been injured in a fight and . . . well, I guess they didn't want him in that condition."

Archer nodded. "Those are *Serakeen's* pirates. Strike now, and we'll be doing the world a favor."

The bloodletters shifted uncomfortably, muttering among themselves.

Across the crowded room, Sefia's dark eyes met Archer's. "You sound like Kaito," she said.

The others went silent.

He stared at her for a moment. She could've stopped him, he knew. Could've stopped the bullet. He'd seen her do it dozens of times. But when it had really counted, she hadn't even tried.

"Maybe Kaito was right," he said. "He wouldn't have passed up this chance, and neither will I."

"He *can't* take this chance." Her voice was a knife. "He's dead."

"I know." Archer's eyes burned. "Don't you think I know? I'm the one who did it. I'm the one who killed him."

Kaito had known as soon as he'd pulled his weapon that it was a mistake. He hadn't wanted Archer dead, not really. Archer had seen it in his eyes, a split second before the bullet struck.

But by then it had been too late.

Archer gouged out another chunk of table. He had to *fight*, to make things *hurt*, to make things *end*. If he didn't fight, all the things he felt would break him, bit by bit, from the inside, splintering his bones. He'd do anything not to feel like that. Anything to forget.

"We all saw him draw on you. He would've killed you," Scarza said softly. "And the sorcerer is right. He would've wanted to attack the *Artax* too. He would've been first to the boats."

"I'll go with you," Aljan said hoarsely.

Archer forced himself to look at the mapmaker.

313

"Someone needs to pay for what happened to my brother." His voice was low, and he had the same hysterical light in his eyes as when he'd beaten a man to death in the shadow of the Rock Eater. "Since you won't let me kill the bonesucker that did it, this is good enough."

"You're not going alone." Frey squeezed his hand.

"I'll go too," Scarza added. "For Kaito."

Archer stood as the bloodletters began to nod, agreement passing through them like a quake through stone. He didn't care about their reasons for joining them. He cared that their blades were sharp. He cared that their chambers were full and their enemies were within reach.

"My brother is dead," Aljan said. "But when I fight, he will rise."

"We were dead, but now we rise." The bloodletters' voices echoed around him. "We were dead, but now we rise."

Without another word, Sefia walked out the door and into the rain.

Archer should have been relieved that the bloodletters were with him. He should have been disappointed Sefia wasn't.

He should have been afraid more of them would die.

But with battle so near, it was as if all of his emotions had shrunk to pinpoints no bigger than flecks of blood, and he felt nothing but his desire to rip and rend and smother.

He was a bloodletter. He was a killer.

And for once, that didn't bother him at all.

The bloodletters assembled after midnight, as the storm abated with a few last growls of thunder. They'd blackened their clothes and shining bits of weaponry, pulled up their hoods and covered their faces, but they'd left their forearms bare, tattooed letters exposed.

Archer stood in the gravel, watching them.

His bloodletters. His army, made for killing.

At his signal, the bloodletters began loading into the boats. Wind beat about their ears. Waves gnashed at the prows.

As Archer was about to climb in with them, there was a touch at his wrist.

"Archer."

Sefia was here. He hadn't known if she'd show up, but she was here. Her hand slid up his arm. She tipped her face toward his. Their lips touched.

He almost pulled back, but his body would not obey.

It was a reminder: *I know you, even if you've forgotten.*

It was a declaration: *I'm with you, even in this.*

The words went unsaid, but he felt them there, between their teeth.

She broke contact so suddenly it was like she'd stolen the breath from his lungs. When she turned toward the boats, he saw the green feather, the only splash of color on the entire rocky shore, glinting in her hair.

He remembered giving it to her—the simplicity of it, the way she'd described the birthday party she'd never had, the sad beauty of her face, the way her eyes brightened as she ran the feather through her fingers. Everything had seemed so simple then.

But nothing would be that simple again.

They seized their oars and shoved away from the beach:

Archer, Sefia, and twenty bloodletters, the ones who weren't guarding the prisoners or too injured to fight again.

Silent as sharks, they paddled out onto the water, pushing through the swells as the tides threatened to throw them onto the rocks. No one spoke.

They passed the breakers. Soon it was only them and the black water and the charcoal skies. Out on the bay, the *Artax* bucked at anchor like a startled bull.

The closer they got, the calmer Archer felt, knowing his next fight was at his fingertips.

Paddling up to the waist of the ship, they ditched their oars and began to climb.

The mad scramble, swift and silent, hand over foot along the side, hauling themselves up by rings and wales, ornamentations and anchor cables, anything to reach the rails before they were spotted.

But they were spotted.

There was a cry. The *crack* of a gun.

One of the boys—one they'd just rescued, Archer didn't even know his name—shrieked and plummeted into the water below.

And then chaos.

Terrible, gorgeous chaos.

Boys hoisting themselves over the rails. Pirates striking at them with curved swords and shots of powder. Archer leapt into the melee, his sword carving arcs of silver and blood.

Months after he'd gotten his voice and his memories back, he'd finally figured out who he was. A killer. A butcher. An artist with severed sinew and bone.

As Sefia reached the deck, she flung out her hands. One by one, the lanterns of the *Artax* broke, popping, their lights snuffing out in blossoms of glass and flame.

The bloodletters surged forward. Screams filled the air as the crew of the *Artax* toppled like fence posts in a flood.

Archer wove through the battle, his blade finding throats and hamstrings, the vulnerable places between ribs, the chamber of his revolver cycling as each bullet found a target.

Somewhere inside him, he remembered being horrified. This bloodshed.

The pirates might not have attacked. They might have sailed away, leaving the bloodletters alone.

These deaths weren't *necessary*—they wouldn't stop the impressors—but they made him forget.

They made him empty.

They made him whole.

Archer fought his way to the captain's quarters, where he cut down the woman who had barricaded herself inside. She tried to fight back, but he could see every move she made before she made it—in the direction of her gaze, the bunching of her muscles, the tilt of her wrist.

She collapsed facedown on the rug and was still.

Outside, the din of the battle died to a whimper.

The *Artax* was theirs.

In the cast-iron stove, the embers seethed. An uneven bloodstain appeared beneath the woman's body, nudging the tips of his boots.

How many dead were out there?

How many more boys had lost their lives?

How come he couldn't stop thinking of doing it again? To stop himself from feeling this?

From feeling anything?

Archer flung his weapons away. His sword hit the baseboard. A sharp point appeared in the wood, like an arrowhead.

He collapsed on the bunk with his head in his hands, feeling the worry stone swinging at his throat.

The door opened. A gust of cold air shook him.

"Archer?" Sefia sounded so far away.

"How bad is it out there?" he asked.

The door clicked shut. "Two of the bloodletters are dead. Seven are injured. We took twenty-nine prisoners." A pause. The mattress shifted as she sat beside him. "Most of them are badly wounded. I don't know how many will live to see morning."

Archer closed his eyes.

The battle on the *Artax* was already a blur inside him, but he couldn't stop seeing Kaito's face again. His curls slick with rain. His brow and cheek and lip split open. The way he'd known, moments before the end, that he'd gone too far.

Then the resistance of the trigger. The explosion of sound and fire.

There was so much blood in a human skull.

Kaito was dead.

Archer had killed him.

He hadn't been able to stop himself.

He kept remembering the words Kaito had murmured to him the day they decided to go after the last Delienean impressors: *You're born for this, brother. You may not think so. You may try to deny it. But one day you're going to realize you never had a choice at all.*

When he opened his eyes, the bloodstain had seeped beneath his boots.

"Archer?" Sefia touched his shoulder, lightly, as if he'd crumble at the slightest breath.

He blinked at her. Her features were soft, unfocused, wet. *Am I crying?*

"I killed him," he said. "I tried not to. But then he . . . and I did it anyway."

"I'm sorry," she whispered. "I know you loved him."

"I used to kill boys for the impressors. I tell myself they made me. I tell myself I was an animal. I tell myself I'm different now. But I'm not different at all, am I?"

Sefia wiped his cheeks. "You *are* different. You're not the boy I met four months ago."

"You're right. I'm not." His voice fractured. "I know you said I wasn't the boy from the legends, but I *feel* like him. I feel myself turning into him, and I can't stop. I see what's happening. I see what I'm doing. But I can't stop. I can't stop. I can't . . ."

His words lodged in his throat, no longer sentences but sobs. He felt her arms go around him, felt her take his weight. He brought up his knees and curled against her, and she held him tight while all the things he hadn't allowed himself to feel finally came pouring out of him.

CHAPTER 30

Assassination Is a Slow Dance

Eduoar was alive.

And he was disappointed.

Every time he began to stir, he shut his eyes and resubmerged himself in sleep. But like a glass buoy, his consciousness kept floating up, bobbing to the surface of his dreams. In those brief moments of awareness, he discovered his wrists thick with bandages, his aching body, and Arcadimon.

A glimpse of brown curls streaked with gold, a stubbled cheek, blue eyes with long lashes that caught the sunlight.

Time passed. Eduoar didn't know how long.

But when sleep finally washed him ashore, he woke to the smell of Arcadimon, the smell of wind and snow. In the window, the curtains swayed like slow dancers.

His hand spread over the coverlet, studying the weave.

"So . . ." Arcadimon's voice interrupted him. "How long have you known?"

Painfully, Eduoar turned. Arc was seated at the bedside, his clothes rumpled, his hair standing up where he'd run his fingers through it too many times.

"Years." A weak grin crossed Eduoar's face. "What, did you think it was that easy to kill a king?"

Arcadimon fidgeted with a stray thread on one of his cuffs. "If you knew, why'd you let me . . . ?"

Eduoar looked away. "It was for the good of the kingdom, wasn't it? I thought you'd . . ." His voice trailed off as he studied the room. It was immaculate. No clothes littered the floor. No wardrobe doors were ajar. Arcadimon's doing, though his friend obviously hadn't taken the same care with his own appearance. "That's why I let you take over my duties. So you'd know how to run things when I was—"

"You *wanted* me to take your kingdom from you?"

Eduoar shrugged. "I decided a long time ago that Corabelli rule in Deliene was going to end with me. I just thought this way, I'd know it'd be in good hands."

His friend sat back, scouring his face with his palms. "The hands of someone who tried to kill you?"

"Well, I mean, a part of me thought you knew I wanted . . . You *had* to have known, right?" Grimacing, Ed plucked at the sheets. "All those rumors? That I was like my father?"

"I didn't think you'd actually do it!" Arcadimon stood abruptly, pacing the bedchamber.

Eduoar frowned. "That's what I don't get, Arc. This was what you wanted. Why'd you stop me?"

His friend stalked to the window, staring down at something in the courtyard below. As if on their own, his fingers tugged at his cuff again, unraveling the thread further. "If you knew about the poison, why'd you try to kill yourself at all?" He turned. "Why didn't you just wait?"

"Because of what happened on the White Plains," Eduoar answered softly.

"Oh." A touch of pink rose in Arcadimon's cheeks.

"The curse claims anyone I love," Ed interrupted. *"Anyone."*

"But I—"

"Don't say it. If you say it, I won't be able to stop myself. And then you'll die." A sad smile crossed his lips. "Don't tell me you weren't going to say it either. That's a heartbreak I'd rather avoid."

Arcadimon ran his hands through his hair, tousling it so perfectly Ed wanted to mess it up just to see him do it again. "So if you weren't cursed—" he began.

If I could have family, friends, and someone to share my life with? Ed's heart whispered. *If I could have you?*

He might still have his sadness. But if he wasn't so afraid of loving someone, of letting them in, of hurting them the way he'd been hurt, having to watch so many of his family suffer and die . . . perhaps he might want to live. Perhaps he *could* live, in a way he'd never allowed himself to before.

"I'm a direct descendant of Ortega Corabelli," Eduoar said grimly. "I *am* cursed."

Arc didn't answer. Instead he crossed the room and slumped into his chair, arms dangling over the sides. Ed almost laughed. Arcadimon Detano didn't *slouch*. "So what do we do now?" Arc asked. "Just continue on like nothing's changed?"

Eduoar pressed his cheek against the pillow. "That depends on why you didn't let me die."

Arcadimon stared at him for a long moment, long enough for Eduoar to study the veins of gold in his blue eyes and watch doubt and longing pass over his features like the shadows of creatures in the deep.

"Because I'm not ready," Arcadimon said at last. "I don't have Abiye's support, and if you go, she could make a good case for the crown."

If there was more to it, Eduoar didn't want to ask. Instead he nodded. Lady Abiye was his great-aunt on his mother's side. Ruler of Gorman Province, she was a capable leader and a formidable enemy. If she wanted to rule after the end of the Corabelli line, she and Arcadimon could split the kingdom in civil war.

"I'll take care of it," Eduoar said.

"You'll what?" Arcadimon straightened. He looked almost like his old self, except for the wrinkles in his clothes and the surprise in his expression.

Ed almost chuckled. It wasn't every day he got to surprise his friend. But their days together were coming to an end. "I'll make sure she'll support a regency government, with you to lead it," he said, sobering. "And then . . ."

"Ed . . ."

"And then you'll help me?" he asked. Begged. "As my friend?"

Pain flickered across Arcadimon's handsome features.

"Come on, Arc."

Arcadimon shook his head and pasted on a grin. "All right, all right." He tugged at his shirt, all bravado. "Just don't fall in love with me or anything first, okay?"

Eduoar grinned. "Stop looking so good and I'll try."

CHAPTER 31

As All Fools Must Do

One of them was going to die, Arcadimon was certain of it. He just didn't know which.

Me or Eduoar?

He charged down the stairs, lower and lower, to the deepest levels of the castle.

Ed or me?

If he didn't go through with the assassination, the Guard would kill him. His Master, Darion, might even do it himself. And if that happened, Eduoar would end up dead all the same.

But I love him. Maybe Ed couldn't admit it, but Arcadimon could no longer ignore it.

He passed into the cellars, winding between barrels of spirits and wheels of ripening cheese.

I can't kill him.

Reaching for an iron sconce, Arcadimon gave it a hard yank. The stones rumbled, and a section of wall slid aside. He squeezed into the winding stairwell that led deep under the city, to one of the Guard's branches beneath Corabel. Like a smaller version of the Main Branch, the Corabelli Branch contained a library of its own, dungeons for prisoners, living quarters, and an office for Directors to conduct business when they were in town.

It also contained a portal to the Main Branch, so he could communicate with the other Guardians. He'd been using it to sneak in and out of the city since he was fourteen.

One of us is going to die. His mind turned over the thought like it was a shining piece of glass. *Unless I find a way to keep us both alive.*

Maybe with Ed on his side, he didn't need to be regent. With Ed on his side, they could still join the Alliance with Everica and Liccaro. They could still unite the kingdoms under one rule and establish peace in Kelanna that would last for generations.

For the briefest of seconds, Arcadimon imagined him and Eduoar sitting side by side in the courtroom, decked out in white and black and silver as if they'd been cut out of the firmament.

He shook his head. He couldn't allow himself to dream when he had to plan instead.

As Arc sneaked into the office of the Corabelli Branch, past the tapestried walls and unlit chandeliers, he drew a finger along the surface of Tanin's desk. It left a streak of jet black in the dust. With Tanin out of commission and Darion firmly ensconced in Everica, no one had been here in months.

If he could convince Darion that they had Eduoar's support, the Guard could let them both live.

It was a long shot.

But it was the only shot they had.

Unlocking a small, unobtrusive door, Arcadimon entered a small, equally unobtrusive room. All it held was a single floor-length mirror with a frame carved with scenes from the Library—the portal.

Politicians weren't trained in the upper tiers of Illumination like other Guardians, so he'd never learned to teleport like the Soldiers or the Assassins. Like his Master, he needed portals to traverse the long distances between Corabel, the Main Branch, and Darion's stronghold in the Everican capital.

To his surprise, however, the room was not empty.

A woman stood before the portal, her silver-streaked black hair trailing down the back of her ivory blouse and leather vest. A lantern sat on the floor beside her.

"Tanin." Arcadimon stopped short. "I didn't expect to see you here."

In the mirror, her eyes met his. As if in challenge, she lifted her chin, giving him a look at the injury that had almost taken her life. The scar had the perfect curve of a parenthesis, with impeccable edges.

"Nice to see you after so long, Detano," she whispered, using his surname like an insult. Of all the Guardians, Politicians were selected more for their connections than their aptitude for Illumination, so only Politicians got to keep their last names. "You look a little flustered. Something ruffle your feathers?"

Suddenly aware of his rumpled clothes, Arcadimon resisted the urge to tuck in his shirt. Instead, he flashed her a smile that would have made anyone else weak at the knees. "Nothing I can't smooth over."

The words sounded more confident than he felt. After all, he was going to bargain for the life of the boy he loved.

Against the man who'd taught him to bargain in the first place.

Tanin turned, fixing him with a stare so cold it made him shiver. "So there is trouble in the Northern Kingdom."

Inwardly, Arc berated himself for revealing anything to her. He wasn't supposed to make mistakes—not with his words. He was a *Politician*. He needed to do better than that if he wanted to face off with Darion over Ed's life.

"Is it the girl? Or something else?" she asked, tilting her head. "Resistance from Gorman? Don't tell me that old bat Abiye is immune to your charms."

Arcadimon couldn't help being impressed. She was good, or her spies were good. No wonder she'd been made Director straight out of her Apprenticeship.

But all those problems were already on their way to being resolved.

And the one problem that remained was between him and Ed alone.

I love him. I can't kill him.

Arcadimon smiled more broadly. "You think a lot about the girl, don't you? I suppose that's why you sent three ships to fetch her."

Tanin was quick to cover her surprise, but Arcadimon was also quick enough to see it.

"Someone should have told you," he continued. "One ship arrived yesterday."

Her voice wavered. "Only one?"

"You're lucky the Director gave you that much, after what you did."

Tanin's eyes narrowed. "I'm grateful for the *Director's* generosity. After all, he gives very little." She advanced on him so suddenly he flinched. At this show of weakness, she smiled, and it was not kind. "So tell me, Detano, what are you flying off so quickly to ask him for?"

She blinked.

She was going to use the Sight on him.

Quickly, Arcadimon took stock of his appearance. He'd changed out of his bloodstained clothes. He'd washed his hands and face. There were no marks to betray him or what had transpired in the royal chambers, when he'd decided to save Eduoar's life.

Were there?

Tanin's gaze traveled to his sleeve, and his stomach sank.

The stray thread, like a question mark, curling from the cuff of his sleeve. He'd been pulling at it in Eduoar's room while they discussed the assassination.

And even though neither he nor the king had said it aloud, reading that moment, Tanin knew.

I love him. I can't kill him.

Arcadimon saw it in her eyes, her triumphant smile.

"Sentiment makes fools of us all," she whispered, blinking again to dispel the Sight. "But if there's one thing Stonegold lacks, it's sentiment."

Arc ducked around her, edging along the wall toward the

portal. "It's not sentiment to keep Eduoar alive. It's strategy."
His words sounded small and naive, even to himself. He'd never
convince Darion like this.

Tanin shrugged. "I loved once. Lon and Mareah. I loved
them dearly, and when they left I had to choose: love or duty.
You'll have to choose one day too, Detano—your Master or
your King, your mission or your heart—as all of us fools must
do."

Arcadimon swallowed as his back struck the portal's gilded
frame. "Are you going to tell him?"

"I thought that's what you were going to do." She smiled
again, thin as her scar, more menacing than a poisoned blade.
"But if you're having second thoughts, your secret's safe with
me."

Turning, he fled through the mirror, her hoarse laughter following on his heels.

CHAPTER 32

The Dead Were All He Saw

After the battle, Archer dreamed of Versil—the slack jaw, splatters of rain on his white patches of skin—and of Kaito—the lightning in his green eyes, the anger, the betrayal, how his expression changed once Archer drew his gun.

The fear. The complete lack of surprise.

"He didn't look surprised," Archer said once, staring across the tent at Sefia, curled up on Kaito's cot. "Everyone looks surprised. But not him."

At first, when he nightmared, she tried to comfort him, tried to curl around him and stroke his hair, but he'd pull away. He'd turn his back. So now, night after night, she watched him dream from the other side of the tent. Watched him thrash and wake and dream again.

He dreamed of the fountain of blood and the way Kaito's head went back.

"How many times can you kill your brother?"

Sefia said nothing. They both knew the answer—five, ten, twenty, as many times as it took for the sun to rise, to chase the dreams away.

And she stayed with him, in Kaito's cot, hoping her presence was enough to let him know that he was not alone.

In the morning, the rain returned, sweeping over the grasslands in gentle, even strokes.

In subdued silence, the bloodletters built their pyres of wood and blackrock. Sefia collected flowers for Frey, who circled the four bodies they'd wrapped in white linen, weaving clover and thistles into the kindling.

Archer stood beneath the arms of an oak tree, his features distorted by his injuries. Water dripped from his hair and the tips of his ears, and his sodden clothes seemed as ill-fitting as the ones Sefia had stolen for him back in Oxscini.

He was no longer the lost boy from the crate, but he seemed lost without Kaito, without his brother.

When it was time for the funeral, Aljan appeared from his tent with two white spots of paint above the corners of his eyes.

The bloodletters gathered beneath the tree, listening to the whisper of rain on the leaves, the hiss and crackle of the smoking torches.

They patted Aljan on the back. They embraced him and said the comforting words, but when they were done they scuttled away again, their gazes sloughing off their bereaved brother like water.

It was funny, Sefia thought, how your grief could isolate you when it united everyone else. Like tragedy was an explosion, and the closer you were to it, the hotter and whiter you burned, until no one could look directly at you without the risk of being burned themselves.

They didn't look at Archer either.

Whether it was out of respect or fear or discomfort, Sefia didn't know.

The bloodletters took turns speaking of Versil's bravery, his laughter, his jokes. Griegi told them how when they were prisoners, Versil had fed them stories: "Sometimes he'd talk all night. He'd tell us jokes, nursery rhymes, anything to give us something to hold on to, something to nourish us . . ."

They talked about Kaito too—his ferocity, his loyalty, his leadership—and when it seemed like no one else had anything to add, they all turned to Archer.

At first he said nothing. His face, bruised and patched as it was, remained impassive.

Sefia almost stepped forward, but after a moment he straightened. His gaze traveled over the bloodletters, the corpses on the funeral biers, finally coming to rest on Kaito—or what had once been Kaito.

"He was my brother, and I loved him." Archer's voice splintered. "Even at the end."

Sefia found his hand, tracing the bandages, the scabbed knuckles.

Aljan stepped forward. Drops of water ran down his forehead, over the white paint at the corners of his brows, as he pulled a sheet of paper from his pocket.

Sefia caught a glimpse of black marks, maybe an $\mathcal{S}$, but Aljan didn't read the letter. Leaning across the top of the bier, he tucked the piece of paper into the folds of cloth that swaddled his brother's body—a painting, a message, a secret.

Taking a torch, the mapmaker touched the flame to the funeral pyre.

"We were dead," Frey said, "but now we rise."

As if on some unspoken signal, the bloodletters crossed their arms and bowed their heads.

Archer did not.

He wandered over the cliffs toward the sea, where he stood on the edge with his hands in his pockets, watching the *Artax* rock gently at its mooring.

Sefia joined him a short time later. "We can't keep hunting impressors, not after this," she said.

"What else can we do?" His voice was raw.

"Run."

"Where?"

"I don't know. Anywhere. Roku, maybe." With its sulfurous volcanic shores, the littlest of the island kingdoms, in the deep south, might be remote enough. The Guard might take years to find them there.

Archer glanced at her. "You once told me no one goes to Roku."

"We could be the first." She managed a faint smile. "No one's stopping us. The others could come with us, if they wanted."

A journey to Roku wasn't what the Book had shown her. But the Book was a fickle oracle, and couldn't be trusted.

Maybe there was a reason they weren't together in the future. Maybe violence and revenge were the glowing core of their relationship, and when that was scooped out, everything they had built together would collapse.

She'd been over Archer's future again and again, but she couldn't be sure exactly when he'd return to Jocoxa. Maybe he'd return home in a few years, not a few weeks.

And maybe the *him* the Book had told her to let go of wasn't Archer at all. Maybe it was someone else.

Maybe once they parted, they'd find each other again.

"Roku, huh?" Archer said, interrupting her thoughts. He seemed so tired. Maybe he, like her, was tired of fighting too.

"Why not?"

His fingers found the crystal at his neck. "Roku it is, then," he murmured.

It was a strange time in camp.

Despite their victories, there was less an air of celebration than of sadness and uncertainty. Archer gave instructions to Scarza, his new second-in-command, to deliver the prisoners to the nearest town, and most of the bloodletters, needing something to occupy them, went along.

"When are you going to tell them we're stopping?" Sefia asked.

"Soon," was all Archer said.

At night, he dreamed. He woke. He looked for her in the darkness. He dreamed. He woke. He said little.

"I wish I was someone else," he whispered once. "Someone better. If I was someone else, maybe Kaito would still be alive."

Turning to face him, Sefia tucked her hands beneath her cheek. "I don't want anyone else."

During the day, Archer began to work on the *Artax*, preparing for the voyage south. His first move was to toss the whips and weapons of Serakeen's pirates overboard, where their instruments of torture sank into the sea.

Sefia joined him. It was nice to work beside him again, like they used to do on the *Current of Faith*. Together they washed the decks, scouring the bloodstains until the brushes turned red.

Once Archer scrubbed so hard, he wore the bristles down to nubs. Sefia had to take the brush out of his quivering hands and straighten his fingers, one at a time, from their gnarled positions.

"I'm sorry," he mumbled.

"Don't be."

Every so often, when he was working, Archer sat up and looked around. Then his eyes would harden, and he'd return to the work again.

Although he didn't say so, Sefia suspected he kept forgetting Kaito was dead, kept looking for him, kept having to remind himself.

He'd killed Kaito.

When Scarza returned from town with the rest of the blood-letters, they took up the work too. They painted the *Artax*, obliterating Serakeen's yellow-and-black with a pattern of red and white.

Aljan renamed the ship the *Brother*.

"You've got to tell them we're finished with the mission," Sefia kept telling Archer.

But all he'd say was, "Soon."

Sefia didn't consult the Book. After Versil's and Kaito's deaths, it remained sealed inside her pack, beneath Kaito's cot, where it couldn't mislead her again. The past had caused her nothing but confusion. The future had given her nothing but grief.

For now, the present—and the promise of freedom—was enough.

One evening, she found Archer sitting in the crow's nest, watching the sun melt into the water. Scaling the rigging, she dropped down beside him, leaning against the rail.

A cold breeze tousled Archer's hair, tugging at his sleeves and the legs of his trousers. His bruises were beginning to fade, but the purplish-green shadows of his sleepless, grief-stricken nights remained.

"Did you know Versil wanted to see Roku too?" she asked. "He wanted to go dragon-hunting. Not to kill them. Just to see them with his own two eyes, to prove to himself they weren't ex—"

"I can't go to Roku," Archer said abruptly.

Sefia leaned back. A deep sense of foreboding opened inside her. "Why not?"

Behind him, the water turned gold and amber in the sunset. His face was in shadow, except for his eyes, which had the predatory glint of a hunting cat. "Oxscini's closer," he said. "And we already know we can find impressors there."

Hatchet was in Oxscini. Annabel was in Oxscini.

"I thought you were done," Sefia said. "I thought *we* were done."

"How can we be done when there are still boys to save?

With you and the Book, we can—" She shook her head, but he kept going. "We won't rely on the Book this time, if that's what you're afraid of. We just need you to locate the impressors. We'll make quick work of the rest."

"Stop. Stop, Archer. You can't. Not after what happened to Versil, to *Kaito*—"

"I'm doing this for Kaito. Don't you see? This is how I make it up to him. This is how I honor him. This is what he'd do for me, if *I* was dead and he was still here."

"But it's supposed to be over!"

His eyes flashed, and for a second it was like he *was* Kaito. "It'll never be over," Archer said. The words were almost a growl.

Sefia could see it now. He and the bloodletters would tear through Oxscini—killing impressors, amassing followers—and then they'd move on to Liccaro, or Everica, or Roku. They'd lose some boys along the way, of course, but every time it would hurt a little less, would take a little less out of them, because there'd be less and less to take.

Eventually, the boy she knew would be gone. He might still be called Archer, but he'd be someone else. Someone with an army.

And a bloody destiny.

"Are you with me?" He reached for her hand.

Sefia pulled out of his grasp, searching his face for signs of doubt, for some indication that she could talk to him, reason with him, change his mind.

But all she saw was grief and grim resolve.

Archer had been right.

He *couldn't* stop.

He was the boy from the legends, the boy the Guard wanted for the Red War.

That night, he outlined his plan for the bloodletters and told them to give him their decisions in the morning. Doubt flickered in some of their faces, but it was like most of them had already known they would follow him wherever he went. He was their chief, after all.

While he slept, she dragged out her pack. Inside, the Book was just as she'd left it, swathed in its waterproof wrapping.

Folding back the leather casing, she traced the ⊖ on the cover: Two curves for her parents. One for Nin. The straight line for herself. The circle for what she had to do.

Except there was only one thing she had to do now.

"Tell me how to stop him," she whispered. "Tell me how to keep him safe."

She opened the Book, and there she found her answer. Not in the future, but in the past.

A past she hadn't known existed.

A past that had been erased.

The Last Scribe

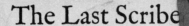

O nce there was, but it would not always be. This is
the ending of every story.

Once there was a world called Kelanna, a wonderful
and terrible world of water and ships and magic. The
people of Kelanna were unremarkable in many ways—
they spoke and worked and loved and died—but they
were different in one very important respect: for them,
reading and writing were magic.

They practiced spells for creating light without
flint and tinder, for peering into the future, for turning
salt into gold. They recorded their histories in immense
tomes—their mathematics and philosophies, all their
secrets and discoveries—amassing so much knowledge
so quickly their halls overflowed with books, and when
they slept they curled under sheets of paper inked with
incantations, dreaming of inventions yet to be invented,
breakthroughs yet to be broken.

Most exalted among the literate were those who
belonged to an elite society of readers known as the
Guard, which possessed the First Book.

Guardians toiled over it generation after generation, poring over its pages and copying them down, harvesting knowledge like sheaves of wheat. For years, they circulated their findings, teaching the people, feeding their desire for more knowledge, more power. Their magic proliferated so quickly Kelanna was overrun with it, as a beach is overrun by the tide.

And as with the tide, some drowned.

Kingdoms fought. Orchards burned. Cities crumbled. The very geography of the Five Islands was transformed by the violence of their conflicts.

Five of the Guard's divisions—Librarians, Politicians, Soldiers, Assassins, and Administrators—struggled in vain to control the explosion of magic, but Kelanna was already glutted with it, sick and corrupt with the power of the written word.

So the Guardians turned to their sixth and last division: the Scribes, who made their home in an abbey deep in the frozen Northern Reach.

Scribes were more powerful than any of the other Guardians, for they knew how to rewrite the world. With the stroke of a quill, they could erase a man from history, inscribe new stars into the firmament, alter the currents in the vast blue sea.

When the Master Scribe learned of the disorder in the Islands, she knew she had a choice before her—the most difficult choice any Guardian would ever have to make.

The word was beautiful, precious, capable of molding the very fabric of the world into exquisite, transcendent forms.

It was also dangerous, insidious, capable of corrupting even the most honorable with an insatiable desire for knowledge and power.

The Master Scribe gathered together her servants and Apprentices and put this choice before them:

Destroy the word and preserve the world?

Or preserve the word, and in so doing, destroy the world?

The Scribes deliberated for many months, and at the end of the deliberation, they all took up their quills.

Using a deep and ancient magic, they revised the Illuminated world itself, in inks of gold and light. They eradicated literacy from Kelanna, erasing alphabets, books, enchantments, libraries, universities, all the institutions built upon foundations of reading and writing and magic. They took it all—spelling songs, storybooks, folios of poetry, scientific dissertations, blueprints of architectural innovations, even the events of the past themselves—leaving only empty husks behind: nonsense rhymes, irreproducible inventions, citadels so complex that without records to show how they were constructed, no one could figure out how to replicate them.

Under the direction of the Master Scribe, they gutted history of every trace of reading and writing— except the Guard. Someone needed to protect the written word, to preserve the memory of what had happened when it went unchecked, and to ensure that it would never run rampant over the world again.

But there was one bastion of literacy still to be eliminated, a place dedicated to the most perilous magic of all, a place too dangerous to exist.

The abbey of the Scribes.

To prevent anyone from ever finding them, the Scribes erected towering walls of ice around the entirety of the Northern Reach, so steep and formidable they obscured even the memory of the white lands beyond.

Then the Scribes laid down their quills, or whatever arcane instruments they used for their craft, for the last time. They would rewrite the world no more.

Alone in her office, the Master Scribe continued the work. Her quill raced across the lands of the Northern Reach, blotting out roads and isolated villages, snowshoers and sled dogs and infants lying asleep in their baskets.

And when her magic reached her own abbey, she destroyed that too.

She brought down the pointed roofs and frosted eaves. She caved in the chimneys and roaring fireplaces, the walls, the windows, the tiled ceilings. The furniture splintered. The floors split.

As the Master Scribe worked, she could hear the noise of her own quill striking out every room in the abbey, from the cellars to the attics, snuffing out the lives of all her Apprentices, all the men and women and children who served in the abbey.

In a world without literacy, there could be no Scribes, who wielded the most powerful magic of all—the power to rewrite the Illuminated world. So she sacrificed them.

She could hear the approach of her own ruin, could hear it come thundering down the hall in explosions of rock and powder, and when it reached her, she severed the line of her own life with one last flourish.

All was still.

Kelanna had been stripped of the written word. Only five divisions of the Guard remained, protectors of the First Book, a last line of defense between the word and the world.

Chapter 33

Poison on Her Tongue

Sefia had asked how to help Archer escape his fate, and the Book had answered.

If you want to save him, you can't keep him.

To prevent the people of Kelanna from ripping each other apart, the Master Scribe had sacrificed her purpose, her beliefs, the people entrusted to her care. She'd even stricken her own life from the world.

To save Archer, all Sefia had to do was leave him.

She'd known he was a killer since the day they'd met, but now he was a warrior, and a leader, and if he didn't stop himself—if *she* didn't stop him—the Guard would claim him, and their war would kill him.

And Sefia was not going to let that happen. She could still change his destiny. If she could save him from himself, and from the Guard.

If she left him, he wouldn't have the Book to guide him to the impressors anymore. But if she left him, he'd be more vulnerable to the Guard.

She had to stop them from seeking him out ever again. She had to take him out of their plans for good.

A couple of the bloodletters had left, including Mako, the youngest, but nineteen remained. As they prepared for the voyage to Oxscini, selling off their horses and carts for the provisions they'd need during their weeks at sea, a plan began to take shape in Sefia's mind.

It wasn't a great plan. She'd be giving up the Book, her freedom, maybe her life, and all the lives that might be lost in the Red War.

But Archer would be safe. He'd be happy.

Because she had the one thing the Guard wanted more than they wanted the boy from the legends.

She checked the Book to make sure, saw herself making the bargain, knew it would come to pass.

She knew better than to trust that everything would go smoothly after that, but she also knew that however risky her plan was, it still might work. And she had to take that chance.

Her secret was like poison she held on her tongue. One false word, one whisper of what she knew about his future or of her fragile plans, and she might accidentally break her silence . . . and force him closer to his own death.

So she kept it to herself, between her teeth, and poisoned only herself.

On the day of the *Brother*'s departure, Sefia stood on the

cliff above the flooded quarry as the wind nipped at her hair and clothing, like it was trying to rip her out to sea.

Her pack lay at her feet, and in it, the Book.

"Sefia?" Archer asked from behind her.

She turned. In his rolled-up shirtsleeves and well-worn boots, he was a rugged kind of handsome—tall in height and broad in the jaw and shoulder, with the grace and swiftness of a jungle cat. He was more confident than the boy she'd met over four months ago, more at ease in his own skin.

But he was damaged. Up close she could see it—the hairline scars from the knife fight on the *Current of Faith*, puckered bullet wounds, scrapes, blemishes, fading bruises, crescent-shaped cuts on his face and knuckles, and a look in his gold eyes that told her no matter how many dreams he dreamt or fights he fought, he'd never be able to forget what he'd done, the people he'd killed.

"Are you ready?" he asked.

No. But she placed the mate's wand, made from the same timbers as the *Current* itself, in his palm.

He blinked, struggling to understand what it meant. Then his eyes widened. "You're not coming?"

The wind stung her cheeks as she whispered, "No."

He gripped the wand and said in a small voice, "I thought you were with me."

"I can't watch you do this to yourself anymore. It's like you're killing yourself, and you don't even know it."

"I'm trying to make up for the things I've done."

She smiled sadly. "I think you're trying to justify what you're *still* doing."

347

A muscle twitched in his jaw.

She almost told him. She almost spilled her entire plan. Maybe, just maybe, things could be different. Maybe they could be together. "Come with me, please," she said, reaching for his wrist. "Just come with me. Tell them you're not going. Tell them it's over. Together, we can run. Together, we can be free."

For a second he hesitated, and she thought he might go with her, might give up the bloodletters, give up the mission, give it all up to be with her, wherever she went.

But then he balled his fists and looked away. "I'm not free," he said.

And Sefia swallowed her secret once and for all. "So . . ." she said. "I guess this is—"

Suddenly, Archer grabbed her and pulled her to him—his hands finding her waist, her spine, her shoulders.

He thrust her back again, staring into her eyes. "I love you," he said. "I should have told you sooner. I love you."

The words took the breath out of her.

Love?

Love.

Of course.

She didn't say it back—couldn't, or she'd never be able to leave—but that didn't stop her from hurling herself against him, crushing his lips with hers, fingers knotting in his hair. Their bodies came so close even their breath was mingled—the desperate in-out of air between them as they found each other's mouths over and over again.

It *hurt*. Her chest was so tight every kiss was an arrow, and her heart the quivering string.

At last, Archer took her face in his hands and brushed his thumbs over her cheeks. "Don't leave," he whispered.

"Leave *with* me."

He found her lips again. And again. And each time it seemed like the last, and each time it wasn't.

"Where will you go?" he asked.

"Corabel," Sefia answered softly. "But I don't know where after that."

"Will I ever see you again?"

"I don't—"

He stopped her with his mouth. "I love you," he breathed between kisses. "I love you. I love you."

She closed her eyes, memorizing the sound of his voice, the shapes of his words against her lips. She locked them up deep inside her. Because she didn't know if she'd ever see him again—not for years, maybe, if she made it out at all—and she'd need those words in the days to come.

Finally, they parted for the last time, their skin flushed, their faces radiant. The sea breeze tore at them, whipping the grass into a frenzy.

Collecting her pack from the ground, Sefia got to her feet.

Archer stood beside her. He didn't seem to know what to do with his hands. They roved aimlessly over his pockets, up his chest and to his throat, where he removed the leather cord from around his neck.

Sefia blinked. He hadn't had it when she'd read his future in the Book, but she'd assumed he'd thrown it into the sea. Crushed it beneath his heel, maybe. Anything to forget her.

Instead, he placed it over her head. Still warm from his skin, the piece of quartz nestled in the open V of her collar, below the hollow of her throat.

"Thank you," she whispered.

He almost looked as if he were about to reply, but he only pressed his lips together and nodded.

Sefia took a step back. Grass crumpled beneath her boot heel. Then she turned, beginning the long hike southeast to Corabel, with the weight of the Book against the small of her back.

It rained the first night, and she huddled miserably inside her tent, watching her meager fire hiss and snap in the drizzle.

Of course, the weather was the least of her miseries.

Her hand kept straying to the crystal looped around her neck, until the stone was warmer than her stiff fingers. She held it tight in her fist as she opened her pack and began to burn her possessions.

Embroidered handkerchiefs. Bandages. Spools of thread.

Nothing she brought to Tanin could be marked by her time with Archer and the bloodletters, for any Illuminator worth her salt would be able to glean information from a rip in a shirt-sleeve, a dent in a cup.

And Sefia couldn't risk them learning anything about Archer. Or where she planned to hide the Book.

Along the way, she traded what she couldn't destroy. Forks. Pots. Knives. None of it in the same place. Always for objects of lesser quality.

She began to steal again, taking to pickpocketing like she'd never stopped. Thievery was easier with Illumination. With a flick of her fingers, she could topple a stack of tin plates or send a scarf flying in a nonexistent breeze, using the distraction to unpin jeweled brooches or snap strings of pearls.

She bought a horse a few days after leaving the coast and traded it for another a day later. Every town she passed, every merchant she crossed, she gave something up, until her belongings were scattered across southern Deliene like dandelion seeds in the wind.

On the last night, she rented a private room at an inn in Jahara and sat down before the little woodstove with her last four possessions lined up on the floor like letters.

The Book.

Nin's lock picks.

Her green feather.

Archer's worry stone.

Sefia opened the stove's iron door, and a puff of heat kissed her cheeks. With a sigh, she lifted the packet of Nin's old tools to her nose, inhaling the smell of the leather. It smelled like nights spent stargazing at the rail of a ship, like hours running traplines in the Oxscinian jungle, like sweat and dirt and the pickling solution Nin used to treat hides.

Unrolling the case, she plucked out the tools, which she'd drop into the Callidian Strait on the ferry to Corabel. Then she fed the case into the stove.

Dark stains like bruises appeared on the oiled surfaces, and there was the smell of charred leather. She watched the case shrivel until it was as hard and black as charcoal.

Dashing tears from her eyes, she plucked up the feather next, smoothing it with her fingers until it almost looked as it had the night Archer had presented it to her.

The fire ate it quickly, in a gasp of smoke.

Then Sefia picked up the worry stone on its leather cord. It flashed in the light of the stove, its black and gold rutilations sparking like fireworks inside the crystal.

Wiping her cheeks, she took a deep breath.

But she couldn't give it up. Not this.

Placing the piece of quartz around her neck again, she closed the stove and pulled the Book into her lap. With her back against the side of the bed, she unfolded the waterproof wrapping and ran her fingers along the edges of the cover.

It might be years before she saw it again. *If* she saw it again.

The only thing she had left of her parents.

She traced the ⊖ with one damp fingertip. The circle for what she had to do. *Give it up.* The straight line. *For Archer.* A curve for Nin. Two curves for her parents.

Lon and Mareah, whom she'd never see again after this.

Closing her eyes, Sefia found the clasps and flicked them open. The gilt-edged pages were smooth as satin under her fingers.

"Show me my parents," she whispered. "One last time."

Theft

Lon & Mareah
—SUMMER?
—Main Branch
—21 years ago

In the bedchamber, Lon was just pulling on his shirt when there was a knock at the door. Gulping down half a cup of cold coffee from the night before, he stepped around the books that littered his floor. He must have accumulated half the Library by now, studying Fragments late into the night, jotting notes on scraps of parchment while the electric lamps buzzed at his bedside. All in preparation for his and Mareah's departure, as he concocted a plan to steal the Book and disappear from the Guard without a trace.

The knocking sounded again.

He managed to tuck in half his shirt before he opened the door.

Mareah stood there in full Assassin's garb—all black, with her bloodsword at her side. Tanin hovered behind her, looking from Lon to Mareah with wide gray eyes.

The smile faded from Lon's lips. *Have we been found out?*

"Good morning, Mar—" he began.

"Don't use that name," she snapped.

He closed his mouth with an audible *click*. He may have been discovered, but if Mareah was distancing herself from him, she hadn't been implicated yet. She must have been summoned to escort him. Despite the circumstances, he felt flattered that the Guard thought him so dangerous.

"Director Edmon has requested your presence in the Administrator's Office," Tanin said, almost apologetically.

Goose bumps rose on Lon's arms. The Administrator's Office was buried deep in the mountain, below the primary levels of the Main Branch, so embedded in the rock that prisoners held there couldn't be heard screaming.

The Administrator's Office meant that whatever Edmon suspected of him, it was serious. Something worthy of the dungeons.

"What for?" he asked.

Mareah's gaze met his for a fleeting second before she fixed her stare on the wall above his bed, where they'd hidden the key Nin had made them—a copy of the one Erastis wore around his neck.

We have *been found out.* Nervously, he ran his hands through his hair. They weren't ready. They hadn't made a cast of Director Edmon's key yet. They didn't even know where he kept it.

Whatever happened next, he had to trust Mareah.

Tanin led the way down the corridors, deeper into the mountain, down spiraling staircases and slanted corridors. The carved columns, statuary, and fine silk carpets of the upper levels disappeared, replaced by faceless walls and stone floors. The passages narrowed. The air grew cold and moist.

Every so often Tanin glanced over her shoulder, a wrinkle between her brows.

Lon wished he didn't have to worry her. Tanin had been like a younger sister to him and Mareah ever since her induction. He'd tutored her. He'd snuck out at night with her, exploring the mountainsides by starlight. But when he and Mareah left the Guard, they'd have to leave her behind too.

At last they reached the Administrator's Office, a cylindrical stone room with electric bulbs flickering along the windowless walls. To their left, a metal door led to the laboratories, where the Administrators conducted experiments and took down notes over cauldrons and glass beakers. To their right lay the entrance to the detention center.

Administrators made sure all the Guard's plans ran smoothly. Among other things, they were tasked with crafting poisons for political assassinations and interrogating prisoners.

And sometimes those interrogations involved torture.

Letting out a slow breath, Lon approached the wooden chair in the center of the room. Opposite him, Dotan, the Master Administrator, sat behind a table. He was as dark as molasses and as thin as a rail, his clothing neatly pressed, a tiepin piercing his silk cravat.

Tanin's Master had always unnerved Lon. His tranquillity, maybe, how unmoved he was by others, even as he was skewering them with spikes.

In contrast, Director Edmon, pudgy and jittery as a pudding, paced back and forth along the left wall, his shoes tapping on the rough floor. He was an effective if not visionary leader. For a long time, Lon's greatest wish had been to succeed him.

But that had changed as soon as he'd been left alone with the Book.

"I don't know how to say this, Lon . . ." With a sigh, Edmon halted. "Erastis found something while studying the Book last night."

Lon's gaze flashed over Edmon's embroidered coat, wondering where he kept his vault key. "Oh?" he said, trying to sound nonchalant.

Giving his lower lip a pull, the Director scowled. "We know what you're planning to do."

Briefly, Lon met Mareah's gaze, as impenetrable as a black sea.

"Come now. You have plans to steal the Book,

don't you?" Edmon pressed. He glanced at Dotan, who blinked once, the whites of his eyes seeming to glow. "It'll be better for you if you talk."

"Try to make me," Lon said. "We'll see how you do."

"How could you do this, Lon? We had such high hopes for you." Edmon stuffed his hands in his pockets and resumed pacing. "I'm afraid I—"

Mareah moved so quickly Lon barely saw her strike. With a wave of her hand, she whipped the Director against the wall, knocking his words back into his mouth.

The Master Administrator stood, raising his arms.

But Mareah was faster. For decades, they'd been training her to be faster.

She grabbed at the air. Dotan's face hit the tabletop. He slid to the floor unconscious.

"Go," Mareah ordered through gritted teeth. "Stop Erastis from telling anyone else. I'll meet you in the Library once I have the second key."

Lon glanced at Tanin, standing there like a lost little girl, and nodded.

As he raced from the room, the Apprentice Administrator finally found her voice. *"Mareah, what are you doing?"*

• • •

With a twist of her fingers, Mareah slammed Edmon's head against the wall and let him drop, stunned, to the ground.

"Are you mad?" Tanin grabbed the collar of Mareah's shirt. "*Stop* this!"

Reaching across her chest, Mareah twisted Tanin's hand away from her. The girl cried out in pain.

Inwardly, Mareah cringed. But Tanin had to be driven off. She couldn't think they were still family, or she'd be branded a traitor as well and executed. With a wave of her hand, Mareah opened the door to the laboratories and palmed the air, sending Tanin staggering out of the room.

"No, Mareah, wait! Don't!"

Flicking her wrist, Mareah slammed the door, leaving herself alone with the unconscious Master Administrator and the Director to whom she'd answered for so many years.

But this was what she had to do. For Lon. For *her*.

"Where's the key to the vault?" she asked. Her voice was a wire. A garrote.

On his knees, Edmon shook his head.

"It'll be better for you if you talk."

He waved at the air. She dodged easily as bits of rock exploded behind her.

Tanin began pounding on the door to the laboratories, but Mareah held it firmly shut with the power in her right hand. With the other, she flung Edmon against the wall again. He struck it like a rag doll and collapsed. While he lay groaning on the floor, she turned out his pockets—empty.

Next she stripped him, ripping away his robes, his trousers, his underclothes, until he lay cowering and naked on the ground, his ample flesh quivering.

"Where is it?" Mareah asked.

The Director glared up at her with as much pride as he could muster.

So she tortured him. She didn't have much time, so she did it quickly, in the most painful way she knew how.

She was no Administrator, but she knew a lot about pain. Her time as an Assassin had taught her that.

The room filled with Edmon's screams. His shrieks and gibbering wet sentences. But no one heard.

No one except Tanin. The pounding and rattling on the door grew more and more frantic as Edmon continued to squeal. But Mareah was the finest Manipulator in generations. There was little Tanin could do against her.

Mareah jabbed and twisted, pulled and wrenched, until pieces of him separated and went splattering across the walls, the floor. Then she'd pause just long enough for him to shake his head.

No. He would not give in.

Then she'd go at it again, until parts of him were so mangled they were unrecognizable.

Finally, he yielded, pointing a broken finger at his discarded pile of clothing. "The waistband of my trousers. The key. Sewn in."

While he lay on the floor, hands shaking over parts

of him that were too raw to touch, Mareah found his trousers and flicked her fingers. The threads sprang apart, flinging buttons through the air.

There, exactly where he'd said, was the little skeleton key. She snapped it up in her palm. "I'm sorry it had to come to this."

She drew her sword and stepped over the slabs of flesh and bone. The air hummed with the scent of metal, and she struck Edmon's head from his body in one clean stroke.

Sheathing her blade, Mareah waved her hand at the Master Administrator's table. It flew across the room, barring the door to the laboratory where Tanin was still crying out for her to stop.

"Good-bye, little sister," she whispered. Without a backward glance at Edmon's corpse or Dotan, groaning on the floor, Mareah raced up the corridors toward the Library, where Lon was waiting.

• • •

When Mareah burst through the Library doors, Lon had pinned Erastis to one of the chairs and was kneeling in front of his Master, head bowed. Flicking the dead bolt, Mareah summoned a bound manuscript from the shelves and wedged it between the door handles. The covers bent. The pages creased.

Lon winced at the damage, but he didn't stop her. "Did you get it?" he asked.

Mareah held up the key she'd taken from Edmon, which winked in the light, and strode to the vault.

"What have you done to the Director?" Erastis asked. "To the Master Administrator? To Tanin?"

Neither of them answered. Signaling to Mareah, Lon lifted the copy of Erastis's key, which he'd retrieved from its secret compartment in his bedchamber.

As one, they inserted their keys and began the complicated dance of twists and turns needed to open the vault.

To the left. To the right. A pause. All the way around again.

Behind them, Erastis struggled against his invisible restraints. Mareah flung out her free hand, throwing him back in the chair. Lon let his hold on the Librarian dissolve.

The heavy steel door swung open.

From deep in the vault, a gust of cool air reached him, like an exhalation. He breathed in the faint odor of leather, paper, and stone.

There was a shout from the corridor. The Library doors buckled inward. Narrowing her eyes, Mareah thrust out her hand, stilling the movement.

But she couldn't hold the doors for long.

"Go on," she said.

Lifting his chin, Lon entered the vault. It was seamless, hewn perfectly out of stone, but all along the walls were glass cases with carefully preserved texts inside. Pages. Folios. Other talismans and sacred objects passed down from previous Guardians.

And in the center, inside a crystal case, was the Book.

He almost wanted to leave it. It was how the Guard kept tabs on the world, how they maneuvered people into place like pieces on a game board. It was how they were going to incite the Red War, which would unite the kingdoms and create an empire so stable it would last for centuries.

But with it, the Guard would be able to find them.

Stuffing the Book into a waterproof wrapping, he returned to the Library, closing the vault behind him.

Erastis tried to lean forward. He was begging now, twisting at his invisible bonds as tears leaked from the corners of his eyes. "Please, my Apprentice, don't."

He was Lon's teacher. His confidant. His friend. Lon hated to imagine what the Master Librarian would think of him after this.

"I'm sorry, Master."

Lon raised his arm. With a twitch of his fingers, he sent the doors of the Library exploding outward in a cloud of rubble, splinters, and dust. The walls shook. Cracks appeared in the marble.

Waving her hand, Mareah picked up a sheaf of papers from the table and flung them into one of the electric lamps. The glass burst, and the papers caught fire.

"No!" Erastis cried.

She threw the burning pages into the bookshelves, where they flared, catching Fragments and Commentaries, eating decades of work in the space of a few seconds.

Erastis was free. He stumbled over his chair, his arms outstretched to quench the flames.

Lon almost wanted to go to him.

Then Mareah touched his elbow, and his grip tightened on the Book. In the hallway, Tanin and the servants she must have summoned were struggling to stand, their bodies bruised, their faces covered with blood and dust.

"Ready?" Mareah asked.

Lon nodded.

They ran. Leaping over rubble and into the corridor, ignoring Tanin's frantic cries. From the doors of the Library, smoke flooded the hall.

The chase was on.

CHAPTER 34

Full Circle

Ever since Lon and Mareah betrayed them twenty-one years ago, Tanin had tried to avoid the Administrator's Office. The very smell of it—chemicals and decay—dredged up memories she would have preferred remain buried.

Edmon's raw screaming and the tackiness of the varnished door under her cheek.

The flayed hunks of flesh and the shape of a broken tooth against the sole of her shoe.

The blood pooling inside the iris of Dotan's right eye like wine filling a glass.

Mareah had been right. Tanin *hadn't* wanted to see it. And now she couldn't forget.

Plucking at the scarf that covered her scar, she crossed the Administrator's Office, tiptoeing over the stone floor as if she could still feel Edmon's viscera slick under her boots.

She stepped into the laboratory corridors, searching for Administrator Dotan.

Now that she had taken the measure of her allies and enemies, it was time to retake control of the Guard.

The Master Assassin, known simply as the First, was essential to her plan. She'd give him the opportunity to kill Sefia and the boy, who had murdered his Apprentice on the *Current of Faith*. He'd retrieve the Book for her. After that, she could turn him on Stonegold.

No one would know. Covering their tracks was what Assassins did best. And Tanin would be Director again.

Control of Everica would fall to Braca, the Master Soldier, who would remain loyal as long as she didn't suspect Tanin of treachery.

But the First was out of reach for the time being. The only person who knew how to reach him was Dotan, her old Master, the Administrator with his poisons and contraptions and dungeons and spies.

She found him in the apothecary, measuring herbs with a weighted scale.

Perfect. She needed him to concoct a draught for the Lonely King as well, in case Detano's nerve failed him. A little something to add to the king's melancholia and tip him over the edge into darkness.

As ever, the Master Administrator was so impeccably dressed it was almost painful. Everything about him, from his pointed shoes to his narrow shoulders, was so well-balanced that you could have halved him with a mirror and you wouldn't have been able to tell the difference.

Except for his right eye, which had been damaged when Mareah had slammed his head into the table. Like a wisp of cloud against a starless sky, a milky scar obscured much of his iris, marring the perfect symmetry of his features.

"Tanin," he said, tapping herbs onto one side of the scale. A whiff of hemlock wafted through the room. "I've been expecting you."

She fought the urge to straighten her scarf. The Master Administrator had an eerie stillness about him that made you want to fidget, and ramble, and run. Even as his Apprentice she'd found it unnerving.

Instead she gave him a little bow. "Master."

"Call me by name, or call me nothing," Dotan said. "I haven't been your Master since you surpassed me in rank."

"I have no rank anymore."

He said nothing. He didn't even blink. Behind him, the scale swayed.

"Will you help me be your Director again?"

"What do you need?" he asked.

"I need your loyalty, and I need your spies. Sefia and the boy have taken the *Artax* and I need to know where."

When he spoke, the Master Administrator barely moved his lips. "Stonegold may have his own plans for the children."

"Letting them loose with the Book isn't a plan." Inadvertently, Tanin began fretting with her scarf.

Again, Dotan said nothing.

"I also need to get a message to the First in Kelebrandt. I need—"

"You need to give it a rest, dear," a soft voice interrupted her.

Tanin went almost as still as the Master Administrator. She didn't even breathe as Darion Stonegold, King of Everica, swaggered into the apothecary.

The Master Politician had the look of a fighter in his old age, a once-fit man swallowed by his own fat. Like gobs of clay, it stuck to his hands, his midsection, his jowls and cheeks. But his brown eyes were as keen as ever.

"You're a slippery little thing, aren't you?" He smiled sourly. "Never where you're supposed to be."

Dead, he meant. She was supposed to be dead. Tanin's first instinct was to fight. Politicians had always been light on Illumination. She could have stuffed his own tongue down his throat in a matter of seconds.

But the fact that he was here, now, eavesdropping on her conversation with her former Master, meant that she had been wrong. She didn't have Dotan's loyalty. Which meant she didn't have access to the First.

And three of the five Masters were against her.

Behind Stonegold, the Master Administrator hadn't moved at all. The gaze of his distorted eye seemed to bore into her.

"Predictability is tiresome," was all she said. At her sides, her fingers twitched. She might have been able to fight both of them at once. She'd been tutored by Lon and Mareah, after all.

But then General Braca Terezina III, the Guard's Master Soldier, settled, smirking, against the door frame. Her face was badly burned, as was much of her body—a tactic the Administrators had used decades ago to camouflage her features, so she could assume the identity of a soldier in Darion's army—same age, same build, same coloring—who'd died in a fire. Since then, she'd risen through the ranks, and now her coat of blue suede winked with brass bars and silver stars—marks of her many victories.

Tanin's hands went limp. One, she could have dispatched. Two, she could have managed. Against three, she could not win.

And unlike the others, Braca, who wore two gold-tipped guns at her sides, knew how to fight.

"I said it when you were selected, and I'll say it again: You're rash. You're compromised. You're full of sentiment," Stone-gold said. "A sniveling sycophant to those traitors, and now to their witch of a daughter." He licked his lips, as if savoring insults he'd been withholding for years.

She swallowed a retort. She wouldn't be baited. "Every one of us has a vice that will compromise the mission," she said, measuring her words carefully.

He grabbed her arm. "*My* people never broke their vows. *My* people are dedicated to the cause."

There wasn't a shred of doubt in his eyes. Detano hadn't confessed his weakness for the Lonely King.

Good. Another weakness to exploit when she regained her ground.

If she regained her ground.

Tanin glared at him as his fingers found pressure points between her muscles. Pain lanced up and down her arm. But he would not make her scream.

"You're lucky you still have friends here, or I would have

done away with you long ago," he said. "They've convinced me you're more valuable alive than dead."

Friends. Erastis. Rajar.

Over his shoulder, her gaze met her former Master's.

Dotan?

"How?" she asked.

"The First needs a new Apprentice."

The Second. Tanin wrenched her arm out of his grasp and took a step back, measuring the distances between herself and the others.

For years, the position of the Second Assassin had been a constant reminder of the family she'd lost, of the hole in her life she could never seem to fill. And now she had the chance to fill it herself. She could take the place of the person she'd sent to her death on the *Current*. The place she'd wanted for Sefia.

Everything under the sun came full circle, didn't it? It was almost poetic.

"You'd keep me alive?" she croaked.

Stonegold smirked. "Usefulness will keep you alive. But if you won't allow yourself to be used . . ." His sentence trailed off, as if he were too lazy to finish it.

She'd already been stripped of her rank, and now she'd be stripped of her name too. She'd be a shadow of a person—deadly, feared—but nothing more than the whisper of a knife in the dark.

Tanin would have liked to think she was the kind of person who didn't need power, titles, renown, who believed in the cause so strongly she'd give up everything for it.

But she wasn't. And in that moment she knew it.

She blinked, and motes of golden light exploded across her vision. She raised her arms.

By the door, Braca tensed, her trigger fingers twitching. But Tanin didn't want to fight. She wanted to live. On her own terms. Sifting through the currents of light as one would sift through sand, she searched for the only place she could turn to now, the only place that still felt like home.

In the Illuminated world, she saw mountains rush past her, waves and islands and vast waters.

There it was—a black point on a wide blue sea.

With a flourish, she swept herself into the streams of light, out of the apothecary, out of the Administrator's Office, through the rock of the mountain and into the bright clean air.

But not before Stonegold's lazy voice reached her: "Don't take too long before you give me your answer, dear. I'm not a patient man."

CHAPTER 35

Captain of the *Black Beauty*

Captain Reed heard about the *Black Beauty* long before he laid eyes on her: a black ship with a charging horse for a figurehead and a speed matched only by the *Current*. While he was still swabbing decks, she was racing sea monsters, outpacing storms, and committing sundry acts of piracy in the southeast, robbing shipments of bullets and gunpowder coming out of Roku.

She was the only ship who'd sailed into the ever-present rains of Zhuelin Bay, raised a flag in the ruined, waterlogged city of Ashrim, and gotten out again.

The day Reed met her captain, she was chasing dragons through the volcanic Rokuine islands, harpoons glinting at her prow. When he and the *Current* interrupted her hunt, she was livid. He remembered her standing on deck, her black hair all a-tangle, and her voice, furious, ordering the *Beauty* to fire on the *Current*.

They'd crossed paths many times in the years since—during high-stakes games of chance and skirmishes between pirates; she'd even been the one to fish him off that island where Dimarion had abandoned him nearly six years ago—and to Reed, the *Black Beauty* was everything an outlaw should be: too wild to be tamed, too big in legend to be contained.

Ships like that didn't belong in a shrinking sea.

After meeting with Adeline and Isabella, Captain Reed and the *Current of Faith* spent months scouring the Central Sea for other outlaws. Some refused Haven. Others, chased out of the east by the Alliance, gladly came. They brought in the *Crux*, Captain Bee and the *One Bad Eye*, mercenaries, treasure hunters, and merchant brigs that had taken one illegal job too many to remain among civilized folk.

Some, they were too late to save, sailing in upon the wreckage of outlaws who had died fighting back. They collected the stories of survivors and the names of ships that had been lost.

The *Current* went out again and again, but it wasn't until mid-autumn that they finally found the *Beauty*.

The fear that had been knotting in Reed's gut since they'd started the search for outlaws eased. The *Black Beauty* was intact. She wasn't moldering somewhere at the bottom of the sea.

But when her captain boarded the *Current*, leaving her lieutenant Escalia aboard the *Beauty*, Reed almost didn't recognize her. She was thinner, paler than he remembered, her silvery gaze wandering over the decks. She blinked too often to be sure of herself.

For a moment she knelt, pressing her palm to the deck.

Over her shoulder, the chief mate shrugged.

When she stood again, she offered no explanation. That, at least, was familiar.

In the great cabin, she paced along the shelves of relics Reed had spent his life collecting. She reminded him of an animal, probing the bars of her cage for weaknesses.

While he poured her a few fingers of whiskey, she laid a slim hand against the case that held the Thunder Gong, which he'd fished out of that maelstrom nearly six years before.

"You ever get this to work?" she whispered.

"Nah." He offered her a glass. "Reckon it's broke."

Like your voice, he thought. Once smooth and strong as steel, now it was harsh as brushfire and quiet as ash.

She ignored the proffered glass, relieving him of the crystal decanter instead. Prowling past him, she swigged directly from the bottle and flung herself into one of his armchairs, sprawling out in a way that was both perfectly poised and totally nonchalant at once.

"The world's broke, if you ask me," she declared.

Reed raised his glass. "That's why I been lookin' for you. Where you been, Tan? Dimarion and I expected you on our tails months ago."

Captain Tan removed the scarf at her throat, revealing a thin scar that curved across her throat like a scythe. "I ran into a couple problems in Oxscini," she whispered. "And Jahara, once I got there."

In one smooth movement, Reed set his glass down and bent to examine her neck. "Who did this?"

To his surprise, tears beaded at the corners of her eyes.

He almost stepped back. The captain of the *Black Beauty* didn't *cry*.

"What happened out there?" he asked.

"It's a long story," she said, pushing him away, "and not one I'm willin' to tell." She took another drink from the decanter.

Reed took a seat opposite her on one of the benches. "Lemme spin you a yarn, then, unbelievable but true," he said, and began to tell her about the Alliance between Everica and Liccaro, the *Crux*, Haven.

Tan didn't look impressed. Then again, he hadn't thought she would be. He'd seen her load five bullets into a revolver and spin the chamber before turning the gun on herself. Folks like her didn't play it safe.

"That mean you found the Trove?" she asked. He felt her searching his skin for new tattoos.

"This seemed more important."

She lifted from the chair so gracefully it was like she was floating. "That's all well and noble of you, Cannek, but you don't just give up a lifetime of chasin' adventure to settle down and raise hogs. That isn't—that ain't you." Hooking her finger into his collar, she tugged his shirt down so hard he nearly fell forward.

"*This* is you," she whispered. Her gaze traveled over his neck and down his tattooed chest. "You got more of these since I last saw you shirtless."

Heat flowered in his face. A long time ago, they'd been lovers for a night. When he awoke in the morning, Tan was gone and the rudder chain on his ship had been cut.

"Lettin' you get me naked is a mistake I'm never makin' again," he said, detaching her fingers from his shirt.

Captain Tan scowled. "Don't flatter yourself. Seein' you naked was a mistake I ain't fixin' to repeat either."

He grinned as she flopped down beside him on the bench, her legs stretched out before her. For a few minutes, they drank in silence.

Finally, she said, "You been workin' your whole life to get yourself a little bit of immortality." She waved the bottle of whiskey at his tattooed arms. "Don't know why you'd give up when you were so close."

Reed shrugged. "I let that dream die when Jules did."

She lifted an eyebrow. "Dreams don't die, Reed. Family, friends, lovers . . . they rot like anything else. But not dreams."

"I tried, Tan." He sighed. "No one can say I didn't try."

"Then why are you givin' up when you've almost got it?"

Low though it was, the tone of her voice made him sit a little straighter. "It?" he asked.

"The Resurrection Amulet."

Resurrection. The word called to him. *Immortality.*

"The what?"

"The Resurrection Amulet." Tan pronounced the words slowly, as if he'd misheard her. "It's supposed to be hidden somewhere in the Trove. One of the king's most precious treasures."

A treasure that could cheat death. The cursed diamonds of Lady Delune had been a bust. Just like everything else he'd ever tried. But maybe . . . Maybe he *could* escape the fate that awaited him—that awaited them all—at the edge of the world. Maybe he didn't have to end up like that. Maybe he *could* live forever, and not just in name.

Reed narrowed his eyes at her. "Why're you tellin' me this? What's the catch?"

"No catch." She shrugged, though she couldn't hide the bitterness in her voice. "But *some* of us oughta get what we always wanted."

Immortality.

He'd told himself he didn't need it.

Didn't want it.

But Tan was right. Dreams didn't die. Dreams were always there, deep inside you like a flame in the dark, waiting for fuel.

"You ain't kiddin' me," he said, still afraid to hope.

Captain Tan plunked the crystal decanter on the table. "Do I look like I'm in a kidding mood?"

And as she spun Reed a tale of death and ancient creatures made of stars, of desperate smiths and something called a *soul*, the flame inside him roared into a blazing fire. Hot enough to burn all thoughts of Haven to ash. Bright enough to light the way, no matter where this adventure took him.

He was Captain Reed.

He'd find a way to cheat death—or die, gloriously, trying.

Account of the Impressor

I didn't want to believe the stories. They were just boys, you understand? Boys *we* captured. Boys that were *ours*. Our prisoners. Our possessions. Our creations. How bad could they be?

But these weren't boys.

They were bloodletters. Like something out of a nightmare.

Can you imagine all your worst deeds made flesh? Your own monsters unleashed against you?

I thought I recognized one of them. This boy with white markings on his face. He killed one of ours half a year past. He pissed himself when they added a burn to his count.

But he wasn't that boy anymore. He was fast. Skilled. He would've finished me if I hadn't gotten off a lucky shot. That was all that saved me. *Luck*.

And he wasn't even the worst of them.

No, that was their leader—Archer. That was his name. *ARCHER*.

I'm telling you, Serakeen can stop looking. Someone's already found his boy.

I've never seen anyone fight like that, like it was second nature. Like he'd sooner stop breathing than stop fighting.

He killed his own lieutenant—did anyone tell you that? Beat him to a bloody pulp then shot him between the eyes. You should've seen the lieutenant. He *loved* Archer. You should've seen the love in his eyes. And Archer put him down like a rabid dog.

He's the one, all right. The boy with the scar.

And he's coming for all of us.

CHAPTER 36

In the Lair of the Enemy

The warehouse seemed smaller in daylight, not mysterious but ordinary, with a plain wooden facade and dingy salt-encrusted windows. Casting a glance over her shoulder, Sefia tested the door.

Locked.

Out of habit, her hand went to her pocket, although of course the lock picks were gone, probably carried away by the swift Callidian Strait by now. Ignoring the twinge of regret in her chest, she slid a hairpin and knife into the lock and, with a few twists of her fingers, opened the door.

Inside, the warehouse was all echoing ceilings and dusty light. Hefting her pack, which almost seemed empty without the Book, Sefia wound among the wooden pallets and lengths of rope to the far wall near the foreman's office.

She wondered if it had been too much of a gamble, entrusting the Book to a Jaharan messenger. But she had to do this quickly, before the Guard found out where Archer was going and hunted him down, and messengers were bound by oath as well as the promise of severe punishment to carry out their duties. And she had no one else she could trust to deliver it to Captain Reed, with instructions to bury it deep on one of those hidden islands only he seemed to be able to find.

Facing the wall, Sefia summoned the Sight. Over and over, she watched the porter touch the stones in sequence as he ushered countless candidates into the tunnels.

Like shadows, her hands followed his movements, and soon the door slid aside, revealing the darkened corridor beyond.

There were no guards in front of the door this time, but the ⟨🌕⟩ had not changed—a promise that after she crossed the threshold, nothing would ever be the same.

She gripped the symbol and began to turn.

As the door opened, she was struck by how familiar it all was: the tapestries on the walls, the portraits of stern-faced subjects, the leather armchairs, and Tanin, standing behind her marvelous ebony desk.

Just as the Book had foretold.

Tanin looked up from what she was scribbling, hurriedly, on a sheet of parchment. Her silver eyes flickered with recognition.

"Sefia." Her eyes narrowed, and she returned to her writing. "Come to finish me off, have you?"

Sefia closed the door behind her. "Just to talk," she said.

Heating a stick of wax over a candle flame, Tanin sealed her letter with a brass stamp. "I'm afraid I'm not much of a conversationalist these days."

Sefia had read about Tanin's damaged voice in the Book, but

she was still surprised at the rasp of it, like a wood file, so unlike the clear commanding tone she remembered from nearly three months before.

Tanin propped the letter against a bottle of ink. "What do you want?"

"To strike a bargain."

"Oh?" Tanin twirled a cloak around her shoulders and clasped it at the neck. Her gaze roved over the room as if checking for items she might have left behind.

"The Book for Archer's life."

Tanin froze. She blinked, like she was seeing Sefia for the first time. Her gaze darted to Sefia's pack. "Don't tell me you brought—"

"I've hidden it. Not even my father could find it now. But I'll tell you where it is, if you abandon all your plans for Archer. Get another captain for your armies if you have to. But leave him out of your war."

She could almost see the wheels turning inside Tanin's head. She swallowed, waiting for the future she'd seen in the Book to come to pass.

Slowly, Tanin sank back down. With a flick of her fingers, she unfastened her cloak. "If it's written, we won't need to find him," she whispered. "He'll come to us."

Sefia almost smiled—it had happened exactly as the Book had said. "Then you'll turn him away," she said, already knowing how the argument would unfold. "He lives, and you get the Book back at the end of the war, or you'll never see it again."

Tanin raised an eyebrow. "What does your boy say to this?"

"He doesn't know I'm here."

"Your sacrifice is touching."

Sefia ignored the twist in her heart. "Do we have a deal or not?"

"The war could take years."

"You've waited decades. A few extra years won't make much difference now."

Tanin steepled her fingers, probing Sefia with a gaze that was suddenly sharp again. "You'd have to remain in the Guard's custody, as insurance. The two of you might be separated for a long time."

"I know. I'm willing to stay."

"Even knowing what we do? What we did to the Locksmith?"

Sefia smiled. It was smile or cry at this point, and she refused to let Tanin see her cry again. "I'm not signing up to be tortured, if that's what you're asking."

"You'd be a prisoner, essentially. You might not have a choice."

"I'd have Illumination."

"What if we took your eyes?" Tanin asked idly. "Illumination relies on one thing . . ."

Though Sefia had known this was coming, actually hearing the threat in Tanin's broken voice still made her skin prickle. "The Sight," she said. If she couldn't see, she couldn't access the Illuminated world. She'd be powerless.

Balancing the tip of her letter on one corner, Tanin spun it beneath her finger.

"You wouldn't," Sefia said.

"I would. But maybe not to you."

"Why?"

"Sentiment." A bitter smile curved Tanin's lips.

Sefia twisted her pack straps. "We have a deal, then? The Book for Archer's life?"

Lifting the letter, Tanin ran it over a flame. The paper caught, burning at the edges. As fire crawled up the face of the page, she flicked it into the waste bin.

"Deal," she said.

This was as much foresight as the Book had given her. Now Sefia had to trust her own wits and skills to see her through the next few years.

Taking a candle and a box of matches from her desk, Tanin led Sefia through the hidden back door of her office, past the tapestries into the sloping corridor behind. Candelabras lined the walls, and the rough stone was black with scorch marks. They passed ornate wooden doors, long hallways, and twisting staircases that spiraled up into darkness.

Sefia wondered if they climbed all the way to Corabel above.

At last they came to a room—a cell—with a bench hewn out of stone and a soiled bucket in the corner. Though she didn't show it, Sefia couldn't help but feel afraid.

As she removed her pack, Tanin held out her hand. "Your lock picks too," she said.

"I don't have them anymore," Sefia replied, sliding her knife and hairpins into the woman's palm.

Surprise flickered in Tanin's eyes, but she said nothing. Placing the candle on the stone bench, she lit the wick. Light flared in her silver eyes.

"I have to consult with my Director," she said.

Doubt passed through Sefia like a draft. "I thought you were—"

"I was." Tanin raised her ink-stained fingers to her throat. "Until you did this to me."

The Book hadn't shown her that. Had it tricked her? *No.* She could still change the future. She could still save Archer. She had to. She blinked, summoning the Sight, readying for a battle. "I came to you thinking you could give me this. If you can't—"

"If I haven't returned by the time the candle burns out," Tanin interrupted suddenly, pressing the knife and pins back into Sefia's hands, "run."

Run?

Before Sefia could ask what she meant, Tanin swept out the door and locked it behind her.

Sefia climbed onto the bench, hugging her knees. If things didn't go as planned, if the new Director, whoever that was, didn't agree to their deal, Tanin had given her a chance to escape.

Was it a trap? A test?

Would it cost Tanin, if her Director found out?

Beside Sefia, a bead of wax slid down the candle, pooling on the cold stone. Swallowing her doubts, she leaned back against the wall to wait.

T he candle had almost burnt out by the time Tanin came to collect her.

"You got your Director's approval?" Sefia asked.

At the use of the title, the woman shot her a glare and blew out the flame, leaving the wick smoking in a mound of wax.

She led Sefia to another room, empty but for a full-length mirror on the opposite wall.

Sefia studied their reflections as they approached: their black hair, their dark eyes. In the windowless room, Tanin's creamy complexion appeared sallow, but Sefia's sun-weathered skin seemed to glow golden, like her mother's had.

As if echoing her own thoughts, Tanin whispered, "You look like her."

Sefia leaned in to study the mirror frame. It was decorated with readers hunched over desks, poring over manuscripts in such exact detail that if she leaned close enough she could read entire passages from their immobile pages. The artistry of it all was so exquisite she was almost sure the figures moved when she wasn't looking, their quills skittering across golden sheets of parchment.

"Why are you showing me this?" Sefia asked.

"This is the way to the Main Branch." Without further explanation, Tanin stuck her hand through the mirror, disappearing up to her wrist in a pool of silver and light—a portal.

She gestured Sefia forward.

Squaring her shoulders, Sefia stepped through it with the barest shudder, like a stone sinking into a still pool. A ripple of cold went through her, and then she was appearing from the other side of the glass.

This room was lined with black and green marble laid out in

complex geometric patterns, with lamps along the walls that let off a glow unlike any Sefia had ever seen. She'd read of electricity in the Book, of course, but she still found it hard to believe.

There were four mirrors in this room: one edged with silver waves, one with gold, another with ramparts of stone and turrets with metal flags poised in an invisible wind, and the one they'd just left, with a frame of lighthouses and cliffs and a walled city—Corabel.

Tanin appeared behind her and crossed to the only door in the room, where she removed the scarf around her neck, revealing a scar like a sickle moon. She gestured to Sefia.

There was no turning back now.

She allowed Tanin to tie the scarf over her eyes. Darkness closed in around her.

There was a jingling of keys, and then Tanin took her arm, leading her through the door. The air opened up around her. Light touched Sefia's lids through the silk.

"Is this the Main Branch?" she asked as their footfalls echoed around her. The room must have been huge, because her voice carried, magnified dozens of times.

Tanin said nothing. They passed onto a carpeted floor—a hallway—and the light from Sefia's left told her where the windows were. *Unless they're more of those electric lamps,* she thought, making a note on the map forming in her head.

She was led down steps and through other corridors. The air grew cold as they descended into the heart of the mountain. Their footsteps began to echo on the rough stone floors.

"You're taking me to the Administrators." She almost jerked out of Tanin's grasp.

"Director's orders," the woman whispered. "But don't worry. They won't harm a single hair on your pretty little head. You have my word."

"How can I trust you?"

"I think we have to learn to trust each other."

When Tanin finally untied the scarf, they were standing at the threshold of a simple, unadorned bedchamber. It had a set of drawers and a wardrobe for clothing, a chest at the foot of a narrow bed. The only sign that they were in a dungeon was the fact that there were no windows and there was no way to unlock the door from the inside.

As Sefia's eyes adjusted to the sudden light, she realized with a start that they were not alone. A tall man dressed in white stood beside her, unnerving in his stillness. Though he barely moved, she got the feeling he was studying her with every fiber of his being, watching her with his mismatched eyes—one nearly black, the other clouded—listening to her movements, smelling her with every silent breath.

"Sefia, meet Dotan, my former Master," Tanin whispered.

He didn't speak, and neither did she. This was her jailer, and perhaps one day, her interrogator. His scarred eye bored into her like a white-hot drill, burning as it went. There was such malevolence in his expression that Sefia knew immediately that he'd kill her if he ever got the chance. He may have been planning it even now.

She just hoped Tanin's deal would be enough to protect her—at least until she found ways to defend herself among her enemies.

Tanin gestured her into the room. "You'll stay here for now.

The lamps have power, and there's running water in the taps."

"Some dungeon," Sefia said.

"If you'd prefer more ascetic accommodations," Tanin replied tartly, "I can have that arranged."

"Is that her?" someone asked eagerly, peering through the doorway like a spectator at a traveling show. "The traitors' daughter?" He was just a boy, not much older than her or Archer, with brown skin and large eyes, made larger by a pair of thick spectacles he kept pushing up on the bridge of his nose.

"Away, Tolem," Dotan said in a voice sharper than Sefia had expected. Tugging the boy by the collar, he ushered him away. The sense of malice in the air dissipated like smoke.

"Was that the Apprentice Administrator?" Sefia asked when she was sure they were gone.

"Yes."

"He's so young."

Tanin looked almost regretful. "It took Dotan a long time to replace me."

"How long will I be here?" Sefia asked.

"Until I send someone for you."

She crossed her arms. "I'm going to need proof that you're keeping your end of the deal."

At the door, Tanin turned. A smile flitted across her features. "Everything in good time," she murmured, and shut the door.

Sefia shuddered. She was in it now. No changing her mind, no going back.

She began to explore the room. Fascinated by the lamps, she flicked the switches on and off, on and off again. She tested the taps and was rewarded by a rush of steaming water.

She took a bath—the first hot bath, it seemed, she'd had in years, in a real bathtub under a real roof. Layers of grit and trail dust sloughed off her in ribbons while she scrubbed her hair.

Later, a servant came by with a tray of food and a leather-bound book. Hesitantly tasting her dinner with a gold spoon, Sefia traced the title with the tip of her finger.

OSTIS GUIDE TO TALISMANIC BLADE WEAPONS

She read. Most of the text was bewildering to her, talking of magical methods that were beyond her comprehension, but here and there was an underlined word, a scribbled sentence, diagrams drawn in the margins, that helped her to understand.

This was how bloodswords were made.

She read, and when her eyelids grew too heavy to read any more, she turned off the lamp at her bedside. The dungeon seemed to close in around her while she lay under the covers, tracing the worry stone that lay warm against her neck.

Chapter 37

Far from Home

When Archer showed up on the beach without Sefia, the bloodletters were full of questions.

"Where's she going?"

"You mean she didn't say good-bye?"

"Did she take the Book?"

"Why'd she leave?"

He blinked, trying to focus, but his attention kept wandering toward the cliffs, like Sefia would be standing on the edge, looking down at him.

"Chief," Scarza said.

"It wasn't her mission," Archer answered.

The bloodletters shifted uneasily, and in their silence, Archer could hear the gravel grinding and settling beneath their feet. The tide lapped at the boats.

"What are we going to do?" someone asked.

Archer glanced at the bluffs above the quarry again, but Sefia was gone. He turned back to the others. "We carry on. It'll be harder to locate the impressors without her, but it can be done." He paused. "If you're still with me."

Scarza took hold of a boat with his one hand. "We're with you, Archer."

As they rowed out to the *Brother*, Frey turned to him. She'd gotten sharper since they'd lost Versil and Kaito, and her eyes glinted like arrowheads. "You should have gone after her," she said.

Archer's gaze traveled past her to the shrinking cliffs. *I could still go after her.* For a second, he imagined turning them all around, paddling madly back to shore, where he'd stumble into the surf and go running after her, dripping water, until he found her walking through the fields, pack on her shoulders, hair whipping around her face.

He shook his head. "I couldn't have made her stay."

Frey stopped rowing. Her gaze was so critical it was like she was peeling him open, revealing his raw, wounded heart. Seawater slid down the blade of her oar and dripped softly into the waves. "I know," she said.

D ays passed. They sailed south.

    At night, Archer dreamed.

And woke alone.

He missed Sefia. Missed the heat of her body against his side. Missed her hands on his back and her voice in his ear. He missed her ferocity, her impatience, her lips, her laughter. He missed happening upon her curled up with the Book, and he missed passing the watches together while the sun climbed over the yardarm or the moon sank into the sea at night.

He began sleeping less, to avoid the dreams, the guilt, the knowledge of what he'd done. But he could never escape them entirely.

A battle, he knew, would have helped him forget, for just a little while, and every so often he found himself staring at the horizon, hoping to see Serakeen's scouts bearing down on them, seeking retribution.

The bloodletters began to fight during the evening dog watches, but Archer didn't join them. How could he, after what he'd done to Kaito?

No one challenged him.

He spent most of his time in the crow's nest, watching the sky. Thundershowers came and went. Day became night became day again. Sometimes he'd imagine Sefia beside him, telling him stories about the Great Whale or the other constellations that swam through the dark. Sometimes he'd imagine Kaito walking along the yards, daring the wind to take him.

He missed them. He missed them so badly it was like parts of him had been carved away, and all the places where they should have been were bright with pain.

But they were gone. Because of him. Because he hadn't been able to stop. He still couldn't.

And without a battle to fight, he couldn't forget either.

So he looked south toward Oxscini, and hoped for battles there.

When they reached Epigloss, a city of bays and bridges, he sent out bloodletters. They wove among the buildings painted saffron, emerald, vermilion, and fuchsia in search of information on the impressors.

Everyone came back with the same news.

The impressors were finished in Oxscini. Over the past month, Serakeen had bought all the branded boys that remained and withdrawn his support from the operation. The arbitrators had closed shop. The crews of impressors had disbanded or moved on to other crimes. There were no more candidates in the Forest Kingdom, or, if the rumors were to be believed, anywhere in Kelanna.

Had they found the boy they were looking for?

A small part of Archer was relieved. *It isn't me.* Another part was angry. He'd let Sefia go for nothing.

But the greatest part of him was disappointed. That the mission was over. That he had no more enemies to fight.

Archer paced the captain's quarters of the *Brother*, treading over and over the stained carpet while his bloodletters idled away the hours belowdecks, waiting for instructions.

Once, he'd lost everything—his memories, even his name—to the impressors. It wasn't until he met Sefia that he'd begun to piece the shards of his identity back together.

But somewhere in Deliene, he'd gotten lost again. Maybe it was the moment he decided to become a hunter. Maybe it was later, bit by bit, on the road, or during those evening skirmishes.

Or when he killed Kaito.

When he didn't go after Sefia on the cliff.

The only home he'd known in the two and a half years since he'd been kidnapped, and he'd let her go.

Now he was adrift, and in need of a mooring.

He could stay on with the bloodletters. They could find someone to fight. There would always be someone to fight.

But he didn't know if he wanted to anymore.

Didn't know if he could, after what he'd lost.

"We thought it might come to this," Frey said when Archer told them.

They were gathered on deck—all nineteen of them—like shadows in the twilight. His bloodletters.

"You did?" Archer asked.

"This is your kingdom."

"I didn't plan on—"

Aljan took him by the shoulders. Up close, Archer could see that the white paint the boy applied to his face every morning had begun to crack. But the mapmaker showed no signs of doubt when he said, "Go home. Go see your family. Tell them you love them."

Archer looked guiltily at Scarza, Griegi, Keon, the others. How could he have taken them all this way, only to leave them?

"If you don't come back," Aljan said, "we'll know you stayed."

"I'm not going to—"

"You should," Frey interrupted, echoing the words he'd spoken to them so long ago, "if you can."

Could he?

He'd been telling himself for so long he couldn't go home,

not after what he'd done, he was too different, he didn't belong there.

But without the mission, without Sefia, where else did he belong?

"What about the rest of you?" he asked.

"Don't worry about the rest of us," Scarza said, clasping Archer's hand in his. "I'll get us home safe."

They'd acquired a horse for him, as if they'd already known what he'd do. He embraced them all, one by one.

"Go home, brother," Scarza murmured before they parted. "Be at peace."

Archer mounted. The horse's hooves sounded hollowly on the dock. From the deck of the *Brother*, silhouetted by stars, the bloodletters saluted him. A sign of respect. A farewell.

He rode west.

Toward home.

He arrived at the lighthouse as the last embers of sunset died away. He rounded the wooden walkway, hands passing over the railings as he glanced up, watching the transparent storm panes of the lantern room and the light racing out to sea.

Behind him, in the arc of the bay, the village of Jocoxa glimmered, the houses lit up by lanterns, the windows warm and orange. The calm waters were a blue so deep it was almost black, tipped with crests of gold.

It was peaceful, this place he used to call home.

He passed beneath the lighthouse tower and descended the

narrow steps to the family quarters, where the old green door greeted him, both familiar and foreign at once. He paused. The smell of seared beef and tomato sauce was in the air.

He could have entered without knocking. He used to, when he'd lived here.

Archer's knuckles struck the wood—once, twice.

After a moment, the door opened, and his aunt Seranna stood there, her short plump form almost filling the doorway. She frowned at him for a moment, as if she didn't recognize him.

Archer moved to speak.

Her eyes widened. She threw her arms around him, crying, "Emery, it's your boy! Your boy is home!"

She hugged him so tight the breath went out of him.

He hugged her back.

There was a clatter from the kitchen, and Archer's mother came rushing to the door. At once Seranna relinquished her hold on him, shoving Emery into her son's arms.

His mother.

Emery had always been stout, like her sister, and strong. But she seemed more fragile now, as if she were made of flour, liable to burst apart at the slightest touch. She smelled the same, though, like spices and machine grease.

His mother.

Archer rested his head against hers. Her tears wet his cheek.

Over her shoulder, he saw his grandfather and his cousin Riki watching him. His grandfather, looking stern and proud; Riki, taller and ganglier than he remembered. What was she, twelve now? She'd been ten last time he saw her.

"My boy," Emery said again and again, "my boy."

"Hi, Mom," he murmured.

When she finally released him, she took him by the hand and dragged him into the kitchen, barely allowing him time to hug Riki, who clung to his waist like she'd always done, and his grandfather, who clapped him firmly on the shoulder with a gruff, "Good to have you back."

Seranna dashed up the stairs to the lighthouse, calling, "He's home! He's home!"

"Sit." Emery pushed him into a chair and plopped down beside him, smiling and wiping her eyes. "How are you? What happened to you? You're so tall! Tell me everything."

Archer's grandfather began setting hot dishes on trivets in the center of the table—a steaming red stew of beef, tomato, and eggplant; a bowl of white rice drizzled with oil; smaller bowls of fresh herbs and flatbread.

Riki climbed into the seat beside Archer, leaning back in her chair and balancing herself with her knee against the edge of the table. "Was it impressors?" she whispered.

"Riki!" Grandfather snapped, like he was reprimanding her for being impolite.

"Sorry," she grumbled.

"Yeah, impressors. They had me for a long time . . ." Archer glanced at his mother, whose eyes welled with tears as she bravely tried to smile. "But then I was rescued."

"By who?" Riki asked.

"By a girl. Her name's Sefia. She . . ." He shook his head, straightening the faded cloth napkin beside his bowl. "I owe her everything."

397

Emery glanced toward the front door, as if looking for Sefia. "Where is she?"

"She's not—"

"Is she pretty?" Riki interrupted.

"Yeah." Despite the twinge in his chest, Archer smiled. "Dark and beautiful, like water at night."

"The water's dangerous at night," Grandfather said.

"Yeah."

Emery shoveled his bowl full of rice and stew, sprinkling a handful of green herbs on top. "My boy," she said, "always a lover. Eat. The others will catch up."

"Mom, please," he said, taking the dish from her. "I can serve myself."

She smiled so brightly it hurt. "But now that you're home, you don't have to."

As she set his bowl in front of him, two men descended the steps from the lighthouse. One of them was his uncle Rovon, slender like his daughter, Riki, with thick black hair. Archer stood, and Rovon embraced him, firmly, as if to reassure himself Archer was really there.

"Calvin," he said. "We thought you were dead."

"I didn't," Riki chimed in faithfully.

He hadn't heard that name in years. It didn't even feel like it belonged to him anymore—like a pair of shoes he'd long since outgrown. Still, Archer clasped his uncle's arm as they released each other. "I felt dead, at times," he said.

The other man stepped forward then. He was paler, softer, like soap, with the gentle paunch of middle age. Among his freckles, his kind blue eyes crinkled at the corners.

Archer didn't recognize him.

The man extended his hand. "Calvin. We haven't met. I'm Eriadin." His palm was damp, but warm and strong.

"This is my new husband," Emery interjected quickly. "Eriadin, this is my boy."

New husband? Archer stepped back. His father had been killed a long time ago in service to the Royal Navy, and his mother had never remarried after that. It was hard to think of her as married. "Oh." He hesitated. "Welcome to the family."

"She was lost without you," Eriadin said, moving to a chair on her other side. "I can't tell you how much it means that you're home."

They sat and began eating again—except for Emery, who continued to watch Archer like she would never get enough of him. Beside her, Eriadin smiled.

"Seranna's watching the light for us," Rovon said, taking a fistful of flatbread. "Says she got to see him first, and one look's enough to last her through dinner."

"Not for me," Emery said. "Forever won't be long enough for me."

Archer squeezed her hand.

Her gaze passed over his scars, lingering briefly on the blistered collar of skin at his neck. "You look . . . well."

"Strong," Eriadin added. "Emery always said you were strong. You must have spent a lot of time fighting your way back, huh?"

The food suddenly felt like glue in his mouth. They all looked so hopeful. "Yeah," was all he said.

"Eat," his mother commanded. "You're too skinny."

They tucked into their meal. He avoided most of their questions, but in truth they didn't ask that many, their conversation turning quickly to what had been going on in the village while he was gone, how Riki had grown, Grandfather's arthritis, and Seranna's headaches. And it was a strange feeling, fitting in here again, because despite all that had happened, *this*—his family, and him included—hadn't changed. Even with Eriadin, who laughed and joked as easily as the rest of them.

But there were some things he couldn't say. Things that had happened to him. Things he'd done. Things that would break their hearts, if they knew. He couldn't do that to them.

And more than that, he was afraid. That if he started talking about the mission, the bloodletters, he wouldn't want to stay. With every silence, every unanswered question, he built up the wall between that life and this one and hoped it would not break.

"Have you been in Oxscini the whole time?" his grandfather asked near the end of their meal.

"No." Archer shook his head. "I ended up in Deliene for a while."

Rovon helped himself to another serving. "Did you run into any of those bloodletters while you were up there?"

Emery shot him a glare, but Riki sat forward in her chair eagerly.

"You've heard of the bloodletters?" Archer asked. He'd known the Delieneans had stories about them, but he hadn't known the stories had traveled so far.

"Everyone's heard of them," Riki said, like he should already know. "They're heroes."

"Heroes?"

"They're the reason the impressors are gone."

Emery dug her fingers into Archer's hand. "I wish we would've had some of them around when you were taken. Those impressors never would have gotten away with it."

Archer tried to smile, but he felt it falter on his lips.

"So, did you meet them?" Riki asked.

"Meet who?"

She rolled her eyes impatiently. "The *bloodletters*. I heard they've all got scars on their necks, like you, except they've got these tattoos on their arms that make them invincible."

"Riki, no one's invincible," Rovon corrected her.

"The bloodletters are. I heard they've got a sorcerer with them who casts enchantments to make them bulletproof. And their leader, Archer, is so tough he even killed his own lieutenant for disobeying him."

Archer cringed, remembering Kaito—the bullet puncturing his skull, the light dying in his eyes.

"A good leader protects his own, if you ask me," Grandfather said.

"You never have to take a life, Riki," Rovon said very seriously, looking into her eyes. "You always have a choice."

Archer folded his napkin. Almost picked a fight with his uncle. Almost walked out. Rovon had worked in the lighthouse since he met Seranna. He'd never even served in the Royal Navy. The Oxscini-Everica conflict had always been a distant nightmare to him. Even now, with the Everican-Liccarine Alliance, the war must have been little more than a rumor.

A choice?

Sometimes the choice was kill or die.

Noticing Archer's silence, Eriadin cleared his throat and tossed his napkin into his empty bowl. "Anyway," he said, "I don't suppose you met those folks, right, Calvin? It sounds like you'd know if you had."

Archer's hand went to his neck, but the worry stone wasn't there. His fingers brushed his scar instead. "Yeah," he said. "I guess I would."

Later, he stood in his old bedroom, surrounded by tokens of the boy he used to be. A woven blanket his grandmother had given him the day he was born. His father's crimson uniform, hanging in the corner. A brass telescope on a tripod. A collection of seashells on the windowsill. One of Annabel's hair ribbons tucked beneath his pillow.

The boy who'd lived in this room had never killed a man, an enemy, a friend, a brother.

The boy who'd lived in this room hadn't known that kind of loss, grief, guilt. He hadn't resented his own family because their lives hadn't been touched by violence. He hadn't hated himself for what he'd done.

Could he live here, even if he'd never be that boy again?

He leaned against the window, pressing his forehead against the cool glass. Far below, the base of the cliffs was white with ravenous waves.

Emery joined him. "You've gotten taller," she repeated, almost accusatorily.

"I've been gone over two years."

They were silent for a moment, looking out into the dark.

The spur of the headland had claimed over a hundred ships before the lighthouse was built to warn them off the rocks. The Aurontas family had been manning the lights for generations. Archer was supposed to have taken over the operation from his grandfather, also named Calvin.

"What do you think of Eriadin?" Emery asked.

He didn't answer. "How'd you meet?"

"He was shipwrecked off the Dragon's Nest."

The Dragon's Nest was a cluster of rocky spines a few miles out. But no one had wrecked there since Archer could remember.

"The lighthouse?" he asked.

"It was my fault," Emery said flatly. "After you were taken, I . . . I was lost. I let the light go out. Eriadin was on a lumber barge—the only survivor. He washed ashore in Calini Cove. You remember the place?"

Yes. He'd gone there with friends on his sixteenth birthday.

He remembered his skin wet and sticky with salt. Annabel had been splashing him. He remembered legs and knees and arms, the backs of her hands dappled with sand. And her voice, a ripple of light in the hot thick air.

He had touched her elbow.

There had been a kiss. Lips and tongues.

"I remember," Archer said.

"Some kids found him and brought him back. I went to apologize, to explain, to beg his forgiveness . . . and he gave it." Emery sighed, a fondness in her voice Archer had never heard except when she talked about his father. "I don't know how anyone could do that, after what I'd done, the deaths I'd caused, but Eriadin did. He said we've all done things we're sorry for."

"Do you love him?" Archer asked.

"Yes." She leaned back and smiled, cheeks dimpling. "Very much. He loves us too. He even took our name."

Eriadin Aurontas—a lumberman turned lighthouse keeper. How easily names changed. How easily people slipped from one identity to another.

Or . . . maybe not easily.

Maybe you had to go through a lot of tragedy. Maybe pain and death wrung you out over and over, until your old self bled away.

He'd become Archer because he couldn't remember who he'd been, and once he'd remembered, he'd stayed Archer because being Calvin didn't seem right anymore.

And deep down, he didn't feel like he deserved it.

"Have you been to the village yet? You'd better say no, you came straight home to your mother."

"No," he said, "I came straight here to my mother."

She pinched his chin lightly, though the look in her eyes told him she'd noticed he didn't call it *home*. "Good boy," she said.

Would she still think he was good, if she knew how many people he'd killed?

And not all of them because he had to?

He didn't think she'd ever be able to look at him again, if she knew.

Archer squeezed her hand, still clasped over his forearm.

The light passed over them.

"You should go, though," Emery said. "Tomorrow, if you feel up to it. She'll want to see you."

She.

Annabel—soft and light as cream, with blond curls and a quick laugh. He remembered her slippers leaving soft prints on the floured floor of the bakery. She'd creep up to him while he was browsing the shelves, and when she was near enough she'd let out a laugh and clasp her arms around his waist, and instead of flinching, he would gently place his hands over hers.

"She's with someone." His mother's voice interrupted his thoughts. "Aden Asir. You remember—"

Archer watched his breath fog the window. "Yeah." Aden had been one of his friends: handsome, popular, honest eyes and black hair continually falling into his face when he laughed.

Emery smiled through closed lips. "I thought you should know before you went down there, so you wouldn't be expecting—"

"I wasn't."

She looked at him knowingly, the way only parents and people who've changed your diapers can. "I just didn't want you to have that kicked-dog expression you do right now."

"I don't—"

"Anyway," she said briskly, "it sounds as if you've moved on too, haven't you? Sefia, is that her name?"

"Yeah."

"You didn't say where she was."

Archer's hand went to his neck again. "I don't know."

"Oh." Emery's voice fell. She folded her hands, trying to hide her disappointment. "Well, I'd like to meet her one day. To thank her for saving my boy."

Archer nodded, though the lump in his throat made it difficult to breathe. "I'd like that too."

They stayed there a while longer, mother and son standing side by side while ships passed at sea, before Emery shuffled him off to bed, tucking him in and planting a kiss on his forehead. "Sweet dreams, my boy."

As he lay there staring up at the ceiling, he hoped his mother's touch would be magic, like in the stories, and with a single kiss she'd erase all his nightmares, all his memories of the worst parts of himself, and he'd be washed clean again.

But when he finally drifted off to sleep, in a bed that no longer felt like his own, the dreams returned. He woke, drenched in sweat, arms and legs twisted in the sheets, reaching for a worry stone that wasn't there.

As she'd done countless times when he was younger, Emery ran in. She sat on the edge of his mattress and tried to hold him, murmuring, "Shh. Shh."

But he wouldn't let her. Didn't want her strong pillowy arms or her pity or her assurances that everything was okay, that he was home. Nothing was okay. And he was far from home.

CHAPTER 38

The Traitors' Daughter

A servant arrived in the morning, or what Sefia thought was the morning—without natural light, she couldn't be sure—with a tray of steamed breakfast buns, tea, and a glass of fruit juice. She had little appetite, however, and picked fitfully at the meal, wondering what would happen next.

Would Tanin and the Administrators question her?

Keep her in isolation?

Torture her? She shuddered to think what Dotan, with that cold simmering rage, could do to her.

Instinctively, she straightened. Whatever they did, they would not break her.

Soon she heard voices outside. As the door opened, someone whispered, "Run along, Tolem. Your Master doesn't want you around her."

Sefia caught a glimpse of the Apprentice Administrator's black hair and thick spectacles before he dashed off.

An old man shuffled into the room, his long robes dusting the floor. Sefia recognized him from the Book—his hair white as snow, with liver spots speckling the backs of his arthritic hands.

"Erastis?"

"My dear," the Master Librarian said warmly, clasping her hands. "You look just like your mother. Though I suspect you've something of your father to you as well."

Unlike Tanin, when Erastis mentioned her parents, she could detect no twinge of sadness, no regret, only the fondness of memory. Sefia was grateful for that.

"Are you ready to be out of these stuffy chambers?"

"Tanin told me to wait."

For someone who looked so fragile, Erastis's grip was surprisingly strong as he tugged her toward the door. "And you will," he said, leading her into a cold stone corridor with bare electric bulbs fastened to the walls, "in the Library with me."

"No blindfold?" Sefia asked.

"Would you like one?"

"No, but won't Tanin—"

"The Second will indulge me." He patted the back of her hand.

The Second? Her mother's title. Had Tanin been demoted to Apprentice? Of another division?

Did she still have the authority to hold up her end of their deal?

"Tell me," Erastis interrupted her thoughts, "did you enjoy the book I sent over?"

"That was from you?"

"Of course it was." He chuckled. "Did you enjoy it?"

"I didn't understand most of it," she admitted.

"Ostis is a complicated text."

"Then why did you—"

"That was the book your mother was holding the day she met your father. Their notes are all over it."

Sefia couldn't believe she hadn't remembered. The diagrams, the underlined passages, the commentaries that trailed along the margins like vines. They'd been written by her parents? She fought the urge to go racing back to her room, to snatch up the book and run her finger over the words, tracing every letter, every line her parents had written so many years ago.

"They weren't supposed to write in the books," Erastis continued, "but they were so brilliant I didn't stop them."

They wandered through the winding halls out of the Administrator's Office to the upper levels of the Main Branch, where at last they reached the Library. Sefia had read about it, of course, but nothing in her imagination could have prepared her for *this*.

The steps fanned from the center of the room, beckoning her toward alcoves into which she felt she could disappear for hours, days, even months—wandering among the shelves like an explorer, tracking her parents' writings as if they were elusive, legendary creatures, always disappearing just as she thought she'd found them. She could imagine withdrawing a volume from the shelves and curling up in an overstuffed armchair, while the bronze statues of past Librarians read over her shoulder. Or, on particularly good nights when the reading wouldn't let her go, perhaps she might light one of those electric lamps and sit alone at a curved table, awake long into the night while the rest of the world dreamed around her.

It's the perfect place for a reader, she thought. Then, guiltily, *It's the perfect place for* me.

"Well, my dear?" Erastis asked.

"It's marvelous."

At one of the tables in the center of the room, a young woman stood. She had light brown eyes and round cheeks, with a pinched face that made her look a bit piggish. "Master," she said.

"Ah, June. Please meet Sefia, the daughter of my Apprentice before you."

June's expression puckered. "The traitors' child?"

Sefia flexed her hands. Did June know why she was here? That she was still keeping the Book from them?

"Be civil, June," Erastis chided gently. "We can't be held responsible for the mistakes of our parents."

Sefia glanced toward the chalkboards and the closed vault beyond.

"Have you brought it back?" June asked, undeterred.

"She's here," the Master Librarian said before Sefia could answer. "That's a start."

June went to fetch him a cup of tea, and Sefia trailed her finger along the edge of the table, where an old book had been laid out like a scientific specimen, its cover stripped off, its bindings bare.

"Curious, are you?" Erastis asked.

"What are you doing to it?"

"Making repairs." He accepted the cup June brought him, inhaling the steam as he watched Sefia lean over the volume, hands clasped behind her back. "You're cautious too, I see. More cautious than your father was at your age. You know he used to sneak in here at night to meet your mother? He didn't think I knew, but of course I did . . . Come. Would you like to observe as June and I repair this Fragment?"

The Apprentice Librarian scowled.

"You mean I can—"

Tanin wouldn't have wanted her to. But Erastis seemed to operate according to his own rules. "You may browse instead, if you wish," he said.

"No, I'd like to watch." After a moment, Sefia added, "Thank you."

She studied the Librarians as they bent over the book, scraping glue from the spine, flattening creased edges with a folding bone, their movements swift and sure. Once that was done, they summoned their magic, and as their hands passed over the speckled paper, blots of mold dissolved and disappeared.

Quickly, Sefia blinked. In the Illuminated world, she could see them disentangling strands of gold from the pages, drawing them away as gently as if they were pulling sugar. As they left the book, the streams of light dispersed into the shifting sea of gold.

"Is this Transformation?" Sefia asked.

"Indeed," June answered in a clipped tone. "And it's rather difficult, so please be quiet. You've interrupted my lesson enough already as it is."

Transformation, Sefia had learned from the Book, was the third tier of Illumination, used to change the properties of different objects, turning salt into gold, imbuing swords with a thirst for blood.

She squinted, trying to distinguish threads of ink from threads of mold. "What happens if you remove the wrong thing? Or too much?"

"Poof." Erastis flicked his fingers.

"I see."

"Yes, you do, don't you? I knew there was something of your father to you."

She almost smiled, until she remembered her father had *betrayed* Erastis. Before her emotions could work themselves out, however, the Master Librarian took her hand. "Would you like to try?"

It seemed like there should have been a rule against teaching outsiders Illumination. Apparently, that didn't matter to Erastis. "Yes," Sefia said eagerly.

June blew a loose strand of hair from her face. "Master, she's the *enemy*."

"Once she was, but perhaps she won't always be."

Despite June's glowering, Sefia joined them at the book. Under Erastis's guidance and his Apprentice's snippy corrections, she was soon excising strands of mold from the pages and returning them to the ocean of light, which washed them away like footprints in the sand.

She was so good at it that after an hour, June no longer glared at her whenever she spoke, and when the Apprentice went to fetch the tea, she returned with a cup for Sefia too.

Sefia had never had a teacher before, never had anyone she could share her magic with. It was challenging and thrilling, and she wondered at how like a family these Librarians were, how ordinary in their affection for each other, despite their extraordinary talents.

She could have hated them for what they'd done, for being part of an organization that had hunted her for her entire life.

But how much hunting had they done, really?

Apparently, Erastis hadn't left the Main Branch in over a decade, and June, as devoted to him as a granddaughter, never left his side. How much responsibility did they share for what Tanin had done to her father? For what Rajar's impressors had done to Archer? For the war against Oxscini?

She shook her head. She couldn't allow herself to think about that. If she did, she might waver. And wavering was something she couldn't do. Not now. Not *here*, in the heart of the Guard. In one clean sweep, she lifted a patch of mold from the page in front of her and was pleased to note June's admiring glance.

If she could only stay like this, a few years wouldn't feel long at all.

CHAPTER 39

Reasons to Stay

The bakery had not changed. Flour dust still collected in the corners of the windowpanes. The door still had a cracked lower edge where unwary customers stubbed their toes on the threshold. Archer smiled. He'd stumbled through the doorway too, the first time he'd come to the bakery.

Riki nudged him. "Go in already."

This time he didn't trip.

Annabel sat behind the counter, weaving knots into a set of counting strings. Her golden curls were tied back with a blue ribbon that matched her eyes. "I'll be with you in a moment . . ." But when she looked up, her voice died away on her lips. Her eyes filled with tears as her gaze passed over him: his neck and shoulders, his hands flecked with scars, down to his feet and back up to his face. The counting strings cascaded from her fingers as she rushed out from behind the counter and flung herself into his arms.

Automatically, Archer's hands went to her waist, and it was as if they'd never been separated, they fit together so perfectly.

Because even after all this time, he knew her. He knew her shapes and the smell of her hair. And from the way she clung to him, he knew she knew him too.

For the first time since coming back, he felt like he was home.

Dashing tears from her eyes, Annabel released him. "Calvin," she said. "I can't tell you how many . . . Every time someone walked through that door, I thought . . . for *months* . . ."

By the windows, Riki stood with her hands behind her back, watching them delightedly.

"I'm sorry," he said.

"You have nothing to be sorry for."

Archer winced. He had *everything* to be sorry for. But that part of his life was walled up inside him, and he could never share it with her.

He could feel her studying him, assessing his differences. He shifted his weight. "You look well."

Annabel pursed her lips. Taking a step closer, she reached up to cup his face in her palm. He almost leaned away, but didn't.

"What happened out there, Calvin? You're—"

She'd done this, exactly this, so many times before. He remembered the pressure of her fingers, the pillows of her hand, her skin silky with flour.

"Different," he finished for her.

"Yeah. But not as different as you'd like everyone to believe."

He caught her hand and brought it down. "How's Aden?" he asked.

Annabel stuffed her hands in her apron pockets. "He's fine. I guess you heard . . ." She glanced over at Riki, still beaming at them from the windows. "I waited for you. I waited. But everyone was saying . . . Even your mother . . . They talked about you like you were already dead."

"You don't have to explain. I *was* dead."

Drawing a curl behind her ear, she tilted her head at him curiously.

"I came back, though." He smiled. "This girl, Sefia, she—"

"A girl?"

"Sefia," he repeated. "She saved me."

For a moment Annabel looked unsettled, but she composed herself quickly, courteous as ever, smoothing her expression with a smile as she peered out the window. "Is she here?"

"She didn't come."

"Oh."

"He says she's pretty," Riki added unhelpfully.

Archer glared at her.

But Annabel just smiled as she sashayed behind the counter again. "He deserves a pretty girl, I think. Can I get you anything? Are you here for your usual order?"

Riki nodded as Annabel pulled loaves from the shelves. "And a cake! For Calvin."

"Of course! Dad can whip one up by tonight. I'll drop it off myself, if you like."

"You don't have to—" Archer began.

"It's no trouble."

At the same time, Riki nodded eagerly. "Why don't you stay for dinner too?"

Annabel blushed. "Oh, I couldn't—"

"Sure, why not?" Archer said.

They looked at each other, confused.

Then she laughed, and her laughter reverberated inside him, shaking loose the dusty corners of his memory. How comfortable his little life had been. An apprenticeship in the lighthouse. A family. A girl at the village bakery. Would it be so hard to make this his life again?

"Okay." Annabel finished pulling bread from the shelves. "I'll tell Aden I'm busy."

"Why don't you invite him?" Archer asked.

With an exaggerated sigh, Riki loaded the loaves into their basket and headed for the door.

Annabel flattened her hands on the counter. "He usually works nights at the tavern, but I can see if he's available."

"Great." Archer began counting out coins.

She laughed again. "I am *not* taking your money, Calvin Aurontas. It's not every day a boy comes back from the dead."

He backed up to the door, fumbling for the handle. "Should I pick you up?"

"I'll be perfectly safe. It's not like it was . . ." She trailed off. "Actually, if Aden's coming, he'll want to catch up with you."

"I'd like that."

Opening the door, Archer and Riki turned to go, but before they could leave, Annabel came out from behind the counter and caught him by the arm. He tensed, but she drew him into another embrace, whispering, "I'm glad you're home."

Her curls brushed his ear, his cheek. "Me too," he murmured. And he was surprised to find that he meant it.

When Archer returned to the bakery at dusk, Annabel had changed from her apron and flour-dusted dress into a skirt and blouse. A glint of green shone in her hair.

For a second he thought it was a feather. But no, it was just an enameled pin.

"No Aden?" he asked.

"No." She avoided his gaze. "He couldn't come."

As they walked, they exchanged talk of what Archer had done that day, the people he'd seen, how the bakery had been, even some news of the war and the reinforcements being funneled from Epigloss to her sister city, Epidram, in the east.

But about halfway there, Annabel's walk slowed. She sniffed.

Archer recognized that sound, had heard it dozens of times in the past, when she burned her hand on the ovens, when her grandmother had died, when one of her favorite love stories ended in tragedy.

"What's wrong?" he asked.

"It's my fault. If you hadn't snuck out to meet me, you never would have crossed paths with those horrible impressors."

He passed her a bandanna to dry her tears, the same one Horse had given him when they'd parted ways in Jahara. Sefia had one just like it.

"I loved you," he said quietly, frankly. Then, "I regret a lot of things, but not that."

Annabel gave him a searching look, but when he didn't add anything more, she looped her arm through his. "I loved you too," she whispered.

Together, they walked the rest of the way to the lighthouse, and at dinner, it was almost as if things had gone back to normal. While Annabel chatted gaily with his family, who welcomed her to the table as if she were one of their own, everything seemed easy again. She smoothed over wrinkles in the conversation. She didn't probe him for answers when he went silent. She accepted him with the same unquestioning trust she'd always had.

Soon—too soon, it seemed, for all of them—Annabel had to return home. In comfortable silence, she and Archer walked back along the trail until they reached the jungle, when she sighed happily. "I've missed your family."

Archer cocked his head at her. "Don't you see them all the time?"

Annabel trailed her fingers through the undergrowth beside the path, the backs of her nails tapping softly against the stiff leaves and autumn flowers. "I did at first, after you disappeared . . . But then your mom found Eriadin, and Aden and I . . ."

He looked away. "Right."

"You found someone too, didn't you?" she asked. "Sefia?"

Found her and lost her. He nodded.

Annabel gave him the simple, curious smile that used to make him spill all his secrets—who'd given him a black eye, what he'd gotten for her birthday. But he was not the boy he'd been—now his secrets were deep and painful.

But he wouldn't think about that. He wasn't the chief of the bloodletters anymore. He was someone different, he told himself, someone who wanted to stay.

"Why isn't she here?" Annabel asked.

They stepped from the path, wandering through the trees until they found the cliff, where they could see the village of Jocoxa along the eastern curve of the bay.

"It's . . . complicated," Archer said.

Annabel sat down among the sprawling roots of an old tree, which made a sort of bench near the edge of the bluff.

"With her, nothing was ever easy," he continued. "Not like it was with—"

"Us."

"Yeah." He shrugged. "Except there is no 'us' anymore."

"Could there be?"

He looked out toward the village, where the lamps glowed yellow through the curtained windows and the sailboats bobbed softly at their moorings.

This had been home once. Could it be again? If he could forget Sefia, the bloodletters, the guilt, the violence, the way his longing for it remained kindled even now, like a candle flame floating in the vast black ocean?

"I don't know," he said.

Annabel bit the inside of her cheek. "I didn't invite Aden tonight," she confessed.

"I figured."

"You did?"

Archer chuckled. "You haven't changed a bit, Bel. I can still read you like a book."

"Like a what?"

"Sorry. Nothing."

"Where is she, Sefia?" Annabel asked.

He sighed and sat beside her, placing the empty cake box

between them. "Deliene, I think. I don't know for sure." Again, he felt the absence of the worry stone at his throat.

"Do you want her to come back?" Annabel pleated the folds of her dress, not daring to look at him.

"Bel . . ." he began.

She leaned over, mimicking him. "Cal . . ."

He almost didn't say anything. But he must not have been as immune to her charms as he thought, because the wall inside him cracked. "That's not my name," he said, surprised to hear the truth on his lips.

"That's always been your name," she chided him.

"Not anymore," he said, holding her gaze, needing her to believe.

"That's okay." A smile dimpled her round face. "I don't mind getting to know you again."

He buried his face in his hands so he couldn't see her bright-eyed earnestness anymore. "I don't think you'd say that, if you knew."

"Knew what?"

And because he couldn't resist her, even now, the wall he'd so painstakingly built came crumbling down. "I've killed people, Bel," he began, and once he started it was like he couldn't stop. It all came flooding out of him, all the things he'd tried to keep hidden, all the things he'd tried to forget. "I've killed so many people I've lost count. Some because I had to. Some because I wanted to. Some because I couldn't tell the difference anymore. I couldn't stop. I'm afraid I still can't. I'm not *Calvin* anymore. I'll never be him again."

"I know," Annabel said, so matter-of-factly, he looked up,

surprised. She bit her lip. "I mean, I didn't know all of that, but I knew you weren't the same. How could you be? But I still believe in you, whatever you've done, whatever your name is now."

He swallowed. "Archer."

"Archer, then." She extended her hand. "I'm Annabel."

He took it.

"Nice to meet you." She leaned in, and for a second he thought she was going to kiss him, and it scared him, because he wanted it. Missed it. Longed for it. Although he could not help thinking of Sefia and their last kiss on the cliff, with the wind buffeting around them.

Wild.

Complicated.

Thrilling.

Instead, Annabel kissed him on the cheek, her soft pink lips lingering on his skin. And he wanted so badly to turn, to put his mouth on hers, to gather her up in his arms.

Maybe that would drive out his memories of Sefia. Maybe that would help him let go. Maybe if he kissed Annabel, they'd slide back into the love they used to share, simple and straightforward. Maybe with her, he wouldn't need walls, and he could be all the different boys he'd been, all of them at once—the lighthouse keeper, the animal, the killer, the captain, the commander, the lover—and maybe . . . maybe he'd finally be home.

But he didn't.

Annabel leaned back suddenly. "I'm sorry. I shouldn't have—"

"No, it's okay." He touched one of her curls.

And it was. Things weren't simple between them anymore. But maybe, one day, they could be.

They got up, wandering back along the path to the village until they reached Annabel's door.

"If you need time, you have it," she said, toying with her keys.

"Aden?"

"How could there be an Aden when there's even the slightest possibility of you?"

He embraced her. "Okay," he whispered, and he almost believed it.

O n the way back to the lighthouse, there was a rustling in the shadows. Archer tensed. For a second, he was fifteen again, and his kidnappers were upon him—the snapping of branches, the quick scuffle of feet, the dark shapes lunging out of the jungle. He felt the pinioning of his arms and the burlap sack being thrust over his head, heard the sound of his own voice against the fabric, begging for help.

But he wasn't that boy anymore. His nerves sang. His senses opened up. The sounds were sharper; the shadows darker. The world was *new* again—urgent and perilous and beautiful.

How he'd missed this.

He was weaponless, but he didn't *need* weapons. He crouched in the darkness, waiting, as the rhythmic clopping of hooves reached him.

"Who's there?" he called.

"Chief?" Frey's voice, soft and high.

The white spots of paint on Aljan's dark face seemed to glow like eyes as they rode out of the trees.

The tension eased in Archer's limbs as he stood. "What are you doing here?" He couldn't keep the note of disappointment out of his voice.

"I didn't want to come, but it wouldn't have been right to keep this from you," Frey said.

"Keep what from me?"

"Hatchet is in Epigloss. He's working security for a tavern by the docks."

Archer's fingers went to the scar at his throat. *Hatchet*— stout build, ruddy skin, scabbed knuckles.

He'd killed Oriyah.

He'd turned Archer into an animal.

"He's just one man. You don't have to come," Frey said. "You can stay here."

In the dim light, Aljan looked eerily like his dead brother. "Or, if we leave now, we can make it by tomorrow night."

Archer's hands curled. There were so many reasons to stay—his mother, his cousin, his grandfather, his aunt and uncle, Annabel, *Annabel*, the girl he once believed he'd marry if only they'd had more time together—and only one reason to go.

In the distance, he could have sworn he heard thunder.

"Let me get my horse," he said.

CHAPTER 40

The House on the Hill
Overlooking the Sea

Although at night Sefia was locked in her windowless room, in the custody of the Administrators, during the day she toured the galleries and corridors, visited the kitchens, which smelled of browning pastries and sauces simmering in pots. She conversed with gardeners and groundskeepers, and explored passageways deep within the mountain.

Sometimes she noticed Dotan watching her from the bottom of a stairwell or the end of a corridor, and though he never said a word to her, she could feel his hatred following her through the Main Branch like a shadow. His Apprentice Tolem, she never got the chance to formally meet.

She was always accompanied by an escort—one of the servants, or June, sometimes Erastis, but more often than not, Tanin—the Second—herself. She was waiting for the return of the First, so she could begin training. "A merciful decision by our esteemed Director," she said bitterly.

"You'll get a bloodsword?" Sefia asked.

"Yes."

"But to earn their bloodswords, Assassins have to kill their family."

Tanin shrugged. "What family?"

Often, they talked of Sefia's parents: Tanin recounting their days as Apprentices, Sefia telling her about their life in the house on the hill overlooking the sea.

"I'm sorry I wasn't there for Mareah's last days. I heard she was ill. She probably contracted it before she betrayed us, from one of her victims. It must have taken years for her symptoms to show," Tanin said once, idly ripping a square of flatbread into soft pieces. "I loved her, you know, even after she turned on us . . . I would have liked to know why she did it."

"You mean you don't know either?" Sefia asked.

"How could I? She kept pushing me away."

Sefia prodded the lumps of rock sugar the kitchen servants served with her mint tea. "Then why would you still care about them? After all they did to you?"

"They were my family."

"*I* was their family." Sefia glowered down at her cup, where the leaves had begun to brown. "You killed one of them. You would have killed them both if you'd found them before my mother died."

"Perhaps I've already earned my bloodsword, then."

Sefia almost felt sorry for her. They'd spent so much time together over the past week that to anyone else they might have looked like friends.

Tanin swept the pieces of flatbread into a small pile. "Have you ever been back? To the house?"

"No." Sefia twisted her napkin in her lap.

"Do you want to?" The woman leaned forward, suddenly eager. "I can take you. We can go tomorrow."

"How long will it take to get there?"

Tanin smiled. "Not long."

The next day Tanin brought Sefia to the south side of the mountain, overlooking the snowcapped range. Rocks slid into the gorge below as Sefia toed the edge. Granite ranges like this only existed in Deliene's Szythian Mountains and on the west coast of Everica—so she had to be in one of those places. She filed that information away for later use.

"What are we doing here?" she asked, glancing around. "Are we going to fly?"

A corner of Tanin's mouth twitched. "Not exactly." She smoothed her hair away from her face. "Do you remember how many tiers of Illumination there are?"

"Four," Sefia said. The first two levels, Sight and Manipulation, were commonplace enough among the Guardians, but Transformation was rarer, and the final tier was only attempted by the most advanced Illuminators. "Oh. Teleportation."

"Teleportation is the most complicated and dangerous form of Illumination. With it, you can transport yourself instantaneously across great distances." Tanin blinked, and her pupils contracted. Sefia summoned her Sight as well, her vision filling with gold.

"The Illuminated world is like a living, breathing record of the physical world. With our limited senses, we can only see a small fraction of it at a time—or risk losing ourselves—but it's all there. We could see a city as distant as Braska if we could sift through such a prodigious amount of information." As if to illustrate her point, Tanin trailed her hand through the swirling currents, which trickled between her fingers like water and re-formed again.

"So you can go anywhere?" Sefia asked.

"Only to locations we know so well we can recall every detail. As with the Sight, if we don't have a clear referent, well . . . imagine what would happen if someone tried teleporting to a place that doesn't exist."

The wind blew over them, cold and smelling of snow. "You mean you'd die?"

"Do you remember what happened to the mold the Librarians were extracting from their manuscript?"

It had disappeared like raindrops in a river. Was that what would happen to her, if she made a mistake in Teleportation? "You knew about that?" Sefia asked.

"Erastis shouldn't have included you in his little lesson, but Erastis does what Erastis wants." Tanin opened her arms wide, as if she were parting drapes to let in the sunlight.

Sefia watched her sift through the Illuminated world. "Is this a lesson too?"

"Consider it a test run. You do want proof we're leaving the boy alone, don't you?"

She could see Archer. She'd know he was safe. Her heart clenched. She might also see him with Annabel.

But that was better than watching him die.

Tanin's eyes narrowed. "Take my hand."

"Why?"

"I've found your home."

Sefia slid her hand into Tanin's. "You're not afraid I'll learn how to teleport too?"

Tanin laughed. "Didn't I say Teleportation was the most complicated and dangerous form of Illumination? You're talented, Sefia, but not even your father was clever enough to figure out Teleportation by himself."

Eagerly, Sefia watched Tanin sweep them forward, carrying them through the turbulence of gold and light. Then her feet touched grass. Sea air filled her lungs. For a moment, Sefia reeled. Releasing Tanin's hand, she slumped onto the stairs in front of the door. The boards were cracked and covered with grime, but these were the same steps on which she'd stood so many years ago, the morning she'd found her father dead on the kitchen floor.

Tanin looked down at her pityingly. "You should know Lon's body isn't here," she said. "We gave him a proper burning."

"When?"

"Two days later."

Long enough for the animals and insects to have found him first. Sefia balled her fists.

As if she realized she'd said something wrong, Tanin plucked at her scarf, looking anywhere but at Sefia—the cliffs and the rocky coast, the chimneys half-collapsed, the garden gone wild with brambles.

Finally Sefia stood. Placing her hand on the knob, she opened the door.

The last time she'd been here, the house had just been ransacked by the Guard. Now it was a ruin. Shards of glass littered the floors. Most of the furniture was missing. The curtains lay crumpled and rotting beneath the windowsills. The pots and knives were gone, the plates smashed, the blankets soiled.

With Tanin behind her, Sefia picked her way through the debris.

"Why'd you bring me here?" She knelt, turning over a piece of a broken vase.

"I thought you'd want to see it . . . " the woman began uncertainly. "I thought you'd want to come back."

"There's nothing to come back to."

A wrinkle appeared in the center of Tanin's forehead. "I'm sorry. I thought . . . We can leave."

As Sefia turned, her footsteps smeared in the dust. She'd almost reached the door when something in the corner of the room caught her eye—a flickering, as if something was hidden there, just out of sight.

She went to the wall, running her hands over the dirt and cracks.

"What is it?" Tanin asked.

Sefia found something round and hard—a doorknob, invisible to the eye. She leaned forward, tracing the carvings encircling the knob.

Words.

Summoning the Sight, she saw them engraved in the wood:

Invisible.

Entirely invisible. The words brought back memories of darkness and bilgewater, of lamplit nights and cramped quarters, of sleeping next to Archer, knees touching, his breath warm on her cupped hands.

Entirely invisible had been carved into their crate, keeping them safe from the uncanny senses of the chief mate.

Who had done this? Her father? Her mother?

Taking a shard of pottery from the floor, she drew it across the words, scoring them out of existence.

The invisible door flickered once or twice and appeared in the wall, hinges and all.

Tanin gasped.

As Sefia tested the knob, the woman leaned down to examine what remained of the letters. "Lon's writing. We didn't know it was here," she murmured. "We searched . . . We even came back after we found out you existed, but no one ever saw this."

Then how did I? Sefia wondered.

"Do you have a knife?" she asked.

Tanin slid a blade from her boot and passed it to Sefia, who used it to tinker with the lock. "Clever," the woman whispered.

If Sefia hadn't known better, she would have thought Tanin was being sincere.

After a few seconds, she opened the door. They both leaned in to see what was inside, what was so precious it had to be protected by magic.

Tears wet Sefia's eyes.

Inside were all their most valuable possessions: her mother's jewelry box, her father's telescope inside its black leather case, packages of dormant seeds, coins from every kingdom, ingots of gold and silver.

Ignoring the currency, Sefia lifted the jewelry box into her lap. Gently, she pulled out each of the little drawers, disturbing the tarnished chains and bracelets of semiprecious stones with the tip of her finger.

After a few minutes of searching, Sefia found what she was looking for, tucked away behind a tangle of glass beads—a silver ring set with sharp black stones.

"Mareah's ring." Tanin held out her hand. "May I?"

Sefia almost drew back. Their enemy didn't deserve any part of them.

But Tanin hadn't always been their enemy, had she?

She passed the ring to Tanin, who took it in her slender fingers and twisted. The setting unhinged, revealing an empty pocket inside.

"I knew about the compartment . . ." Sefia murmured as Tanin flicked a hidden latch. A tiny blade, no thicker than a spear of grass, popped out from between the stones. "But not the blade."

"This was given to her by a Liccarine jeweler," Tanin said. "For poisoning her enemies." Closing up the ring again, she extended it to Sefia.

"I thought Assassins didn't have personal effects." Sefia slipped the ring onto her middle finger.

It fit perfectly.

"I think we both know Mareah was no ordinary Assassin."

Nodding, Sefia got to her feet and took up her father's telescope case. Outside, she stood on the steps, listening to the sea crashing against the coastline—a sound woven throughout the whole fabric of her childhood. "So you can travel anywhere in Kelanna with Teleportation?"

Beside her, Tanin raised an eyebrow. "As long as I've been there before."

Sefia touched the ring on her finger. Her parents had hidden the closet from sight. Had her mother done the same with the crate on the *Current*? The sailors outside had spotted a girl there, someone who'd looked like Sefia, but older. "Could you travel through time?" she asked.

"Why? Planning to go back and stop me from killing your father?"

Sefia's eyes narrowed. "Could I?"

Tanin sighed. "*Theoretically*. But the only accurate referents we have are pages from the Book. You see the problem with that, don't you?"

"Yes." Sefia's voice was small. You'd need two pages to teleport through time: one for your destination and one for your return.

But her parents had had the Book in their possession. Hard as it was to navigate those infinite pages, her mother just might have been able to find the exact two pages she needed . . .

"Could you teleport with a Fragment instead of the Book?" she asked.

"You could *try*." Angling around her, Tanin descended the steps. "But Fragments are copied by hand, and even the best copyists make mistakes. If they were wrong in even one detail, you'd be lost."

Sefia followed, murmuring, "But it's possible." They clasped hands again, and she studied Tanin carefully as she swept her arms wide. In a whoosh, the magic carried them from the Delienean coast back to the Main Branch. Among the mountains again, Sefia was keenly aware of the weight of her father's telescope on her back, of her mother's ring on her finger.

She now had something to remember them by—something she could keep.

"Thanks for bringing me home," she said quietly.

Beckoning her toward the entrance to the Main Branch, Tanin smiled, and this time Sefia was sure she was sincere.

CHAPTER 41

One of the Wolves

Archer, Aljan, and Frey found Hatchet exactly where they expected to, outside a little tavern at the end of a neglected alley. He seemed bored, leaning against the flaking wall as he picked at the scabs on his knuckles.

Dismounting, Archer handed the reins of his horse to Frey, who waited at the mouth of the alley while he and Aljan advanced.

"Hatchet." Archer drew his gun. Behind him, he could feel the two bloodletters watching, listening. But no movement stirred in the windows facing the alley. None of the doors opened.

Hatchet squinted at him, ignoring the revolver. "Is that you, boy?"

At the sound of his voice, Archer went cold. *Boy. Bootlicker.* The names they had given him.

Lifting a hand to his mouth, Hatchet pulled at a scab with his teeth.

Archer had to swallow a few times before he could force the words out. "I go by Archer now."

The impressor's eyebrows went up. "That's quite a name these days. I thought it might have been you who wrecked all those crews up north. You've come a long way since I caught you back in Jocoxa. Easy prey for a predator like me." He looked Archer up and down, much as he'd done when Archer was his prisoner, his candidate, his *boy*. Like he was appraising livestock. "Only . . . you're a predator yourself now, aren't you? One of the wolves."

Archer's trigger finger twitched.

The gun was heavy in his hand.

While he hesitated, a smile crossed Hatchet's face and curled up there like a self-satisfied cat. "But even wolves are game to the hunter."

Archer felt a thrill of fear. Or excitement.

It was a trap.

A fight.

Gunshots exploded behind him. At the entrance to the alley, Frey cried out.

Glass burst in the windows above. Archer twisted out of the way as a bullet skimmed his arm.

Smoke rose from the revolver in Hatchet's hand.

Archer shot him. Almost without thinking. Almost without feeling. It was easy. Natural. Like breathing.

Hatchet gasped. Blood flowered in his gut. He buckled, stumbling into the wall.

Archer didn't wait to watch him fall. Pivoting, he fired through the broken window above. A spatter of red hit the curtains. He turned toward the mouth of the alley.

But before he could rejoin his bloodletters, Serakeen emerged from the tavern.

Archer recognized him immediately: scar on the side of his face, sad eyes, two silver-tipped guns at his thighs.

His aubergine coat flared around him as he lifted his arms.

"Frey!" Archer whirled. "Aljan!"

But they were too slow. Serakeen's magic caught them and swept them both into the wall.

Frey crumpled. Aljan's face collided with the stonework. Blood mixed with the white paint at his eyes. He dropped beside Frey.

Were they breathing?

Barely.

Neither of them got up.

"I was wrong about you, Archer." Serakeen's voice rumbled through him, just like it had three months ago in the Guard's office beneath Corabel. "You're more killer than I gave you credit for."

Archer fired.

With a wave of his hand, the pirate sent the bullet whizzing into the wall—a move Archer had seen Sefia use dozens of times before, now used against him.

Archer blinked. The fight unrolled in front of him like a length of silk—quick and slippery.

Serakeen's fingers clenched, trying to pin him. Archer dodged. Felt the magic close like a net around the place he'd been standing moments before.

The pirate advanced.

Near the tavern door, Hatchet lay against the wall, clutching the wound in his stomach.

From the ground, Archer let off two rounds so quick they sounded like one explosion. Fire and the black smell of gunpowder.

Anyone else would have been killed. But not a Soldier of the Guard. Serakeen sent the first bullet into the wall. But the second got him in the shoulder.

He hissed and wrenched at the air.

Archer spun, but Serakeen's magic caught his arm. The gun was wrested from his grip.

He crouched, sliding one of his hunting knives from its sheath. As Serakeen neared him, Archer drew the blade across the pirate's thigh and jammed it between his ribs.

Serakeen bellowed and flung out his hand. Archer leapt aside. The ceramic pots behind him shattered.

He attacked, striking Serakeen in the face, the side, wherever he could land his fists.

Under the onslaught, the pirate yanked the blade from his side and flung it. Archer skidded backward as the knife flew toward him, narrowly missing his ear.

Serakeen drew a curved cutlass, gleaming, from its sheath. "I'm sorry. I know she made a deal for you, but my Director thinks you're too dangerous to let go."

She. Sefia? The mere thought of her quickened Archer's blood. Was that why she'd left? To make a deal with the Guard?

He flicked Harison's sword from its scabbard—familiar and deadly in his hand—and attacked, lunging, jabbing, slashing, while Serakeen parried, his boots scuffling over the cobblestones.

Their swords sheared against each other as they circled. Archer drew blood again and again. Serakeen's leather coat split under his blade.

With a wave of his hand, the pirate flung Archer back and lunged. The cutlass kissed his arm, his leg, before Archer could dance out of range.

That magic. Sefia's magic. Archer was good, but he wasn't a match for it.

Again the shining arc of Serakeen's cutlass came down. Archer lifted his sword. The edges met.

In a split second, he knew: He could deflect the blade. They could go on fighting like this, winnowing away at each other's defenses until he was too tired to dodge and the magic got him like it'd gotten Frey and Aljan.

Or he could take the hit.

He twisted his wrist, and instead of curving away, the cutlass slid inward. It bit deep into his side, bringing them close.

Close enough for Archer to see Serakeen's nostrils flare.

Close enough for Archer to smell him sweat.

Their gazes met. In that instant, Serakeen's eyes widened. His expression was a mixture of horror and admiration. His cutlass was trapped at Archer's side.

But Archer's sword was free. He swung.

The blade met little resistance as it severed Serakeen's hand from the rest of his arm.

He wouldn't be using magic again—not with that hand.

Howling, the pirate staggered back, yanking his sword from Archer's flesh. He hoisted the blade onto his shoulder.

Archer was quick enough to see Serakeen press the latch on the hilt of his cutlass.

He wasn't quick enough to avoid the flash powder that exploded from the pommel. His vision went white.

He stumbled. He couldn't see.

Serakeen's sword clanked against the cobblestones.

Then came the magic.

Archer's limbs were pinned. He felt himself lifted off the ground, felt the air go rushing past him, felt his body hit the wall. Pain flared along his back and limbs. Spots burst before his eyes.

He collapsed, groaning.

As his vision cleared again, he saw Hatchet, not ten feet from him, lying dead against the wall. A half-picked scab still clung to the knuckles of his left hand.

CHAPTER 42

Long Live the King

Eduoar had been true to his word. Arcadimon Detano now had the support of all the major houses. He had the deadly draught—the same one the Suicide King had taken all those years ago—in his pocket. Everything was set.

Outside, the shadows lengthened along the inner courtyard as the sun crowned the castle walls. With a glance up at the lighted windows of Eduoar's tower, he hurried along the first-floor corridor. He thought he saw the king behind the curtains, rubbing his sad, tired eyes.

Reflexively, Arcadimon swallowed.

This was it. The last obstacle between himself and total control of Deliene.

His king.

His friend.

Arc bounded up the steps to the second floor two at a time. When he reached Eduoar, he'd kneel, bow his head, and present the vial in his palms like a knight offering his sword. The king would take it from him, touch his shoulder in a tender act of absolution and gratitude, and turn to the window, where the last light of day would graze his fine features. He'd look, once more, over his castle, his city, his kingdom, as Arcadimon withdrew, having delivered the killing blow.

This was it. His Master—his Director—had ordered it.

His loyalty to the Guard demanded it.

Eduoar had requested it. He'd been wanting it for years, and at last he'd have it: the end of his life, the end of his line, the end of the curse.

The hour was upon them. Arc's hand froze over the knob.

And then he wasn't thinking anymore of how to pull it off but of how to stop it. Throw open the door. Relish the look of surprise on Eduoar's face. Take him by the collar and pull him in, bringing their lips together so quick and hard they'd feel it for days afterward.

Another body. Arcadimon would need another body. It was the only way.

But how would he fool his Master, or any of the other Guardians, who could read the marks on a corpse like passages in a book?

I love him. I love him. I can't kill him. I love him.

He flung open the door.

• • •

When Arcadimon burst into the room, his face was flushed. His blue eyes were bright. He looked handsome, and eager. In the pocket of his coat, his hand shook.

Eduoar felt a flash of pain, panic, longing. "Is it today?" he asked, starting up from his chair.

Arcadimon closed the door so hard Eduoar's wine shivered in its glass. "No. Not today." His gaze was so intense it almost burned. "Not ever, if I have anything to say about it."

Eduoar recoiled.

Arc extended his hand—it was empty.

Eduoar backed toward the window. "But this is the only way we both get what we want."

Arcadimon caught Eduoar's face between his hands. "I want you to live," he whispered. His thumb skimmed Ed's lower lip.

Eduoar almost leaned in, wanting Arc's mouth on his own, wanting a kiss as urgent as a bruise and as bright as a scream.

Instead, he retreated until his back hit the windowsill. "I want to be free."

"You can be." Arcadimon's voice was pained. "If you leave. Right now."

"And go where?"

"Away. Far from here. Go somewhere no one will recognize you. Start over." Arc inched toward him. "You won't be a Corabelli anymore. You won't be cursed. You can do anything you want."

Fumbling behind him, Eduoar found the window latch. "That's not how this works."

" 'Not until your family has been stripped of everything will the curse be broken,' " Arcadimon recited. " 'Not until you are bereft and begging for mercy.' "

The words made Ed pause.

He'd lost so much.

He'd begged for mercy.

But he hadn't been stripped of everything. Not his title. Not his kingdom. Not his name.

He twisted the signet ring on his finger. *Not yet.*

He'd believed in the curse for so long he couldn't remember a time when he wasn't standing in its shadow. It had taken his mother, his father, his aunts, uncles, cousins. He'd been terrified it would take Arcadimon.

For so long, he'd been sure death was the only way to break the curse.

Arcadimon pulled him from the window. Their faces were so close they nearly touched. "You're not dying, Ed, not while I'm here." He smelled of glaciers and wild places. "I'm sorry it took me until now to realize it. I'm sorry it got this far. I should have told you a long time ago."

Ed froze. "Arc, don't."

For as long as he lived—and he didn't know how much longer that would be—he'd remember the shapes of Arcadimon's lips, sending the words like smoke rings into the air.

"I love you," Arcadimon said.

Something in Eduoar's heart flared up, something he hadn't felt in a long, long time.

Want. Hunger. For more of *this*. For life.

It was little more than a weak flame flickering under the weight of his melancholia, but it was there. A splinter of possibility. Maybe he didn't want to die.

Maybe, just *maybe*, he wanted to live.

It didn't burn away his sadness. It didn't make his future appear any less dark.

But it was there—hope, perhaps, or something like it—and it was enough.

"Okay," Eduoar whispered.

Arcadimon dragged him toward the door, and stumbling into the hall, they began to run.

They ducked through the castle, using empty passageways they'd discovered as children, rooms no one had set foot in for years, lower and lower into the cellars, where Arcadimon pulled him into an alcove so tight they were crowded thigh to thigh, chest to chest.

Again, that want. He could see Arcadimon's pulse jumping at his throat, and he was overcome with the desire to trail his fingers down his neck, tracing veins coursing with life.

Arcadimon pulled a hook on the wall, opening a secret stairwell. Cool air, tasting of salt, passed over them.

Eduoar followed him into the dark. Down they went, until they must have been well below the city.

Arc squeezed his hand. "Come on. There's a ways to go yet."

When they reached the bottom of the well, Eduoar could hear the ocean clearly—the gasp of the tide and the soft knocking of moored boats.

Arcadimon led him along the slick corridor until they reached a long low cavern filled with blue water. At the far end, there was a glimmer of golden sunset, barely visible.

A hidden dock.

Arc began untying the mooring lines. "The current will take you out, and dusk will cover your escape."

Eduoar swallowed. "Where do I—"

"I don't know. Just get out of here. If they find out you're alive, they'll have both our heads."

"Who's they?"

"It doesn't matter. But they have a plan for Deliene, and that plan doesn't include you."

Something about Arc's tone made Eduoar pause. "Arc," he said.

"What?"

"Did you kill Roco?"

Arcadimon balked. "What? No. Ed. I'd *never* . . . Look, you wanted it. He didn't. I've done a lot of rotten things over the years, but not that."

Eduoar wanted to believe him. Needed to believe him, despite the doubt that pooled in his stomach.

Chose to believe him.

"Okay," he said.

Arc held out his hand. "Your ring, please."

Eduoar rubbed his thumb over the Corabelli crest. What would he be, if he gave up his name?

The answer came to him on the whisper of the tide. *Free.* He'd be *free*.

Tugging the signet ring from his finger, he placed it in Arcadimon's palm. Arc's fingers closed around his, smooth and strong.

Want.

Eduoar pulled him in so suddenly Arcadimon's chest struck his. Staggering under the impact, he turned Arc's face to his own.

Hard. Clumsy, teeth knocking.

And bright. Bright as he'd imagined, the flame inside him roaring to life, licking at the edges of his sadness until he could feel light burning in his palms, in his eyes, at the back of his throat.

Beneath his fingers, Arcadimon's heartbeat was just as quick as his own.

Breathless, they parted.

"Go, Ed," Arc said. "Go now."

Dizzy, Eduoar stepped into the little wooden boat and released Arcadimon's hand.

The current drew the dinghy through the cavern, and Arc's figure was swallowed by the shadows.

Then Eduoar was free—in the sunset and among the rocks—and as the sails unfurled, carrying him out to sea, he saw the towers of his castle flash pink and gold in the dying light.

Except it was no longer his castle. And he was no longer Eduoar Corabelli.

The Lonely King was dead.

And only he remained.

CHAPTER 43

The Many or the Few

That night, in her room in the dungeon, Sefia opened her father's telescope case. Inside, the tubes and brackets gleamed, unspoiled by time. Reaching out, she touched the eyepiece, imagining Lon's hands flitting over the instrument, turning knobs, adjusting counterweights until the distant images grew sharp and close.

Though the telescope was pristine, the velvet lining was peeling in places, and it tore as she removed the tripod, revealing yellowed sheets of paper beneath.

Frowning, she slid the delicate pages, barely thicker than onionskin, from their hiding place.

The handwriting was Lon's. It matched the script she'd seen in texts taken from the Library shelves.

She bit her lip. Were these words for her? Some message transmitted to her across time, overcoming even death?

She read the first line—

Master,

—and swallowed her disappointment. The letter wasn't for her at all.

Master,

Please know I wanted to tell you. I wanted to tell you as soon as I found out. I think you, of all the members of the Guard, might have understood why I have to do this.

Then I remember our oaths:

Once I lived in darkness, but now I bear the flame.
It is mine to carry until darkness comes for me again.
I shall forsake all ties to kin and kingdom,
and render my allegiance unto the service of
*   the Guard.*
It shall be my duty to protect the Book from
*   discovery and misuse,*
and establish stability and peace for all the citizens
*   of Kelanna.*
I shall fear no challenge. I shall fear no sacrifice.
In all my actions, I shall be beyond reproach.
I am the shade in the desert. I am the beacon on
*   the rock.*
I am the wheel that drives the firmament.
For today I am a Guardian, and so shall I be to
*   the end.*

I wanted to let you know that I haven't stopped believing. I guess it would be easier if I had. Although there's nothing easy about what Mareah and I plan to do.

I'm afraid

I'm sorry I couldn't be the Apprentice you deserved.

Here there was a series of scratched-out words, paragraphs stopped and started.

How do I begin?

If I had to

Once

I want to believe that our choices make a difference.

I need to believe it.

Do you remember the first time you left me alone with the Book? I'd been looking forward to it for years. It was as if I knew there was something I was supposed to see, something important. Did you feel this way too, when you were an Apprentice?

"Be warned," you said. "The Book likes to surprise new readers."

"How did it surprise you?"

You told me the Book showed you your family. When you were inducted, your parents thought you were dead. They were bereft. They mourned for years . . . until one day, they had another son.

Though they never forgot you, with your younger brother there, every day they thought of you a little less. And every day, they hurt a little less too.

When he grew up, your brother married a fisherman's son. Together they took in an orphan girl and raised her as their own.

"My parents, my brother, the niece I'll never meet . . . they were fine without me. They were happy. Seeing that, I knew I'd made the right choice, joining the Guard."

I asked if the Book would show me my own family.

"Everyone's relationship with the Book is different," you replied, "for the Book is not a static history but a living story, full of intent. Sometimes it is a beacon, illuminating your path when you have fallen into darkness. Sometimes it is an oracle, prophesying greatness or hardship. Other times it is a trickster, telling partial truths."

"What's your relationship with the Book?" I asked.

You laughed. "I like to think of the Book as an old friend. Faithful, with a good heart."

Then you left, and I was alone in the vault. I flipped open the Book.

~~I wonder if I hadn't been so eager, that would have changed what I found.~~

~~If I~~

When Sefia reached for the next pages, she found the familiar lettering of the Book, the ragged edges where Lon must have removed them.

The Reader

Once there was, and one day there will be. This is the beginning of every story.

Once there was a world called Kelanna, a wonderful and terrible world of water and ships and magic. The people of Kelanna were unremarkable in many ways, but in their storytelling they could not be matched. They told their stories with their voices and bodies, repeating them over and over until the stories became a part of them, and the legends were as real as their own tongues and lungs and hearts.

Some stories were picked up and passed from mouth to mouth, crossing kingdoms and oceans, while others perished quickly, repeated a few times and never again. Others, like secrets, were kept within a single family or a small community of believers, whispered in the dark.

One of these rare tales told of a mysterious object called a *book*, which held the key to the greatest tragedies Kelanna had ever known. Some people said it contained records of the worst atrocities ever committed: mutilations, brandings, murders, massacres, rapes and abuses, every form of torture ever perpetrated against another person. Some said with long hours and a little dedication, you could even learn to do such terrible things yourself. The accounts differed in the details, but on one thing they all agreed: Only a few could use the book. Some people said there was a secret society trained precisely for that purpose, toiling away generation after generation, poisoning themselves with power and methods of domination.

But stories are curious things. They change with the telling—multiplying, transforming—until the story you think you know becomes one among thousands.

Incomplete.

Or false.

One such story told of a reader who would change everything. She would be the daughter of an assassin and the most powerful sorcerer the world had seen in years, and she'd grow up to surpass them both in greatness.

But there'd be a cost.

There's always a cost.

She would be young, only five when her mother died and nine when her father was murdered, and her childhood would be steeped in violence. She'd grow up to be a formidable force in a formidable world, and one day she would be responsible for turning the tide in the deadliest war Kelanna had ever seen. She would demolish her enemies with a wave of her hand. She would watch men burn on the sea.

And she would lose everything.

Her parents. Her friends. Her allies.

The boy she loved.

And by the time it was over, she would still be standing—but she'd be standing alone. She'd survive, all right, but survival is a hard and terrible thing to live through. You do things you never thought you could, and some you wish you'd never had to.

She'd survive, all right, but with the bones of ships and soldiers at her feet. With blood on her hands and nothing inside.

We're going to have a daughter, see? Not now. Not anytime soon. But one day. The Book showed me my family after all.

"Five years," Mareah whispered when I gave her the pages. "That's all I'll get with her. And you, only nine."

"Maybe not," I said. "Maybe things can be different. Better."

We're taught that what is written comes to pass . . . and we take great pains to ensure it. The Book says there's going to be a famine? We don't tell the provinces to stock up on sacks of grain. We plunder their food stores for ourselves and when the people starve, we shrug and say it was written. The Book says war is coming? We don't negotiate for peace. We teach the smithies to make better weapons and call it being prepared.

It's treason, I know. But maybe if we tried to change destiny instead of running toward it with open arms, maybe what's written wouldn't be set in stone.

Mareah and I would have to turn our backs on everything we'd been trained to do. On everything we believe—the good of the many over the good of the few—and we still might fail.

The only thing I knew, the only thing I know, is if we stay, my daughter won't be able to escape this fate. You know the Guard will want her for the war. They'll do everything they can to make her into the weapon the Book says she's going to be. Powerful. Hollow. Alone.

And I want better for her than that.

That night, we began planning our escape. Getting out

455

of the Guard would be easy. We could teleport. Mareah could cover our tracks. Getting the Book would be impossible. But it would lead you right to us if we didn't.

I've considered telling you a hundred times. But this choice was forced upon me: our mission or our daughter. I can't make you choose as well. (And perhaps I'm afraid. If all goes according to plan, Mareah and I will escape with the Book and no one will be hurt. But if something goes wrong . . .)

Maybe when this is all over, I'll find a way to tell you.

Maybe if I'm not too much of a coward, I'll even deliver this letter myself.

I'm sorry, Master. I'm sorry for betraying you. I'm sorry for not trusting you. I'm sorry for taking the one thing most precious to you.

~~Please forgive me.~~

Always your pupil,

Lon

Sefia blinked tears from her eyes.

Her parents had tried to beat the Book too. They'd tried to cheat destiny.

And they'd failed. Her mother had still died when Sefia was five. Her father was still murdered when she was nine.

She didn't know about Mareah, but Lon might have lived if they'd abandoned her. He could have hidden her away somewhere in an obscure corner of the world—the Paradise Islands, a sulfur mine in Roku. They wouldn't have been together, but he might have lived.

Instead, they'd chosen a handful of years *with* her over a lifetime without her. They'd chosen the hope—however faint—that they could outsmart fate, and find more time.

The few or the many. Their family or their mission.

The stone walls seemed to close in around her. Her parents had never wanted her to end up with the Guard, and yet here she was—their willing prisoner.

What is written comes to pass.

It wasn't the Guard she needed to defeat. It was destiny itself.

Had she been running toward it with open arms?

In leaving Archer, had she forced him to do the same?

The boy from the legends.

The boy she loved.

It *was* him. It had been him when she found him in the crate . . . or *because* she found him in the crate. It had been him when Rajar cracked open his memories. It had been him when he killed Kaito, when she saw him with Annabel, when she left him on the cliff. It had been him all along.

Sefia touched the piece of quartz at her throat, her fingertips sliding over the crystal as if it were made of ice.

Did it *have* to be him?

Maybe not, her father had said. *Maybe things can be different. Better.*

But Lon and Mareah, with all their combined power, had failed. How could she do what they hadn't?

Her hand closed over Archer's worry stone, which warmed in her palm until she could no longer tell what was crystal and what was her own flesh, her bones, her blood.

How could she live with herself if she didn't try?

Carefully, she refolded the letter and placed it inside her vest pocket. Then, settling the tripod inside the telescope case again, she slung it across her back.

She had to believe they could do it together. That they could escape, together, and live out their lives, together.

The few or the many, and she'd always choose the few. She'd always choose Archer.

Would love and cleverness and nerve be enough to beat the Book?

And change both their fates?

She had to find him. And to do that, she couldn't stay here.

Blinking, Sefia summoned her sense of the Illuminated world. Gold sparks burst before her eyes.

She palmed the door open, wrenching it from its hinges, and paused in the empty hallway. But Dotan and his Apprentice must not have been around to hear.

Soft as a whisper, Sefia sneaked through the corridors to the Library, where she found Erastis sitting at one of the curved tables with a manuscript in front of him. When he noticed her in the doorway, he looked up, blinking over the tops of his spectacles. "Sefia? What are you doing out of . . . Oh. I see."

"I'm sorry," she whispered.

Erastis sighed as he stood. "Like father, like daughter, I suppose."

She reached into her vest for the letter. "I found this in my father's telescope case. He kept it all these years, even though it would have put them both—all of us—in danger."

Erastis unfolded the letter with trembling fingers. "Indeed?" As he read the first lines, he sank back into the chair, his gaze skimming over the words. After a moment, he paused. "Why are you showing this to me?" he asked.

Sefia twisted her mother's ring on her finger. "It's yours."

"Aren't you, like your father, afraid I'll raise the alarm?"

"I don't think you will."

Erastis didn't answer, holding the letter to the light again. She watched him read, the planes of his face shifting as Lon's words reached him through the years. By the time he got to the last page, he was crying.

"He loved you," Sefia said.

"He loved *you*." The Master Librarian extended the letter to her.

"It's addressed to you. Keep it."

Sniffling, Erastis pressed the pages into her hands. "If you're going to do this, my dear, you'll have to be more careful."

Sefia tucked them into her pocket again. "Would you tell Tanin . . ." She bit her lip. History had made them enemies, but if things had gone a little differently, at a dozen different times, they might have been allies, friends . . . even family. "Would you tell her I'm sorry?"

"I'm sure she's sorry too. For everything." He hesitated. "Wait here. I have something for you."

She shifted the telescope case on her shoulder as he shuffled into the stacks, his voice drifting to her through the bookshelves. "I knew you before I met you, my dear. Your skill, your courage, and your capacity to love." Soon he reappeared, clutching a manuscript in his arms. Setting it down, he turned the pages, carving the air. Then, taking a straight edge, he pressed it to the book and ripped out a single page.

Sefia gasped at the sound. "What is it?"

"Your way out," he said, passing it to her.

She skimmed the page and looked up in confusion. "You want me to teleport? Based on a Fragment? Tanin said—"

"It's dangerous, yes. But don't you recognize this place?" He tapped the page. "Don't you know where you have to go?"

She looked down again. "I've never teleported before."

"You'll make it. It's been written, and what is written always comes to pass."

I hope not, Sefia thought. Aloud she said, "Is that why you're helping me? Because you already have?"

He nodded. "And because I'm a sentimental old fool."

"You might never get the Book back."

"I made peace with that possibility a long time ago." Erastis smiled sadly. "If your parents taught me anything, it's this: Love what's in front of you, right now, because now is all you have."

She knew he was speaking of more than the Book. She nodded. "How do I get back?" she asked. "*Do* I get back?"

He patted her kindly on the shoulder. "Some of the ancient Masters believed that Teleportation was not a matter of remembering the places you've been, but of finding your way back to the stories that had such a powerful impact on you that they'd become entangled with your own."

Sefia frowned. "What does that—"

"There are some people we can always get back to, no matter how far they are from us."

She swallowed her questions. "How much do you know about what's going to happen? How much have you already read?"

He shook his head. "Good-bye, my dear. I'm afraid the next time we meet, we'll be bitter enemies."

She clasped his hand. "Then I hope we never meet again."

Stepping back, she glanced once more at the words and tucked the page into her vest. She could do this. She had already done this. Blinking, she raised her arms as Tanin had done earlier that day, parting the sea of light. As if she were skimming for a passage in a book, she skimmed the golden crests until she found what she was looking for. Then, with a wave of her hands, she vanished.

CHAPTER 44

What Is Written
Comes to Pass

Sefia landed, staggering, on a dock. The air smelled of salt and tar, and the wind was full of the creaking of boats, the cries of gulls. Dinghies and tall ships surrounded her, and a rickety old cutter lay at anchor nearby. At the far end of the pier, a wooden column topped with a metal statue of a songbird—a canary—rose above the throng of sailors, servants, and war orphans scrambling for scraps.

She was back in Epidram, the city where she and Archer had fought Hatchet on Black Boar Pier and stowed away on—

Then she saw it. A green hull and a figurehead shaped like a tree: the *Current of Faith*. Laughing, she hoisted the telescope higher on her back and charged forward. Captain Reed was supposed to be somewhere in the Ephygian Bay, searching for treasure. What was he doing here?

She had almost reached the gangplank when two figures

appeared at the rail. The chief mate looked just as she remembered, his strong rectangular face weathered with age, but the boy beside him . . .

It couldn't be. Black curls soft as satin, big ears, an easy smile. A red bird perched on his shoulder.

Harison?

Sefia drew back. Harison was dead. She'd been there when it happened. She'd watched him die. She'd *felt* him die. She'd mourned as his body was sent burning onto the ocean. He couldn't be alive.

Which meant only one thing.

She was in the past. Over four months before she'd left Erastis in the Library.

For a moment, she allowed herself to feel the full weight of her disappointment. Her mother *hadn't* carved those words onto the crate after all. She *hadn't* returned from the dead to save her daughter.

Sefia ran her thumb over the sharp black stones of Mareah's ring.

She couldn't buckle now. She had work to do.

With a stealthiness she hoped her mother would have been proud of, she sneaked toward the stacks of supplies yet to be loaded onto the *Current*. Among the chests and kegs, she hunkered down to listen.

There it was—a murmuring from inside one of the crates. She crept closer.

It was only one voice—her voice, higher and more childish than she'd expected. She couldn't make out all the words, but she remembered what she was saying.

"I'm sorry. I should have been more careful. I should have noticed . . . I just couldn't control my vision . . ." Then, "Hatchet said you were supposed to lead an army."

How little they'd known back then.

Sefia blinked and drew her knife. Glancing around once to make sure she wasn't being watched, she began to carve.

In the Illuminated world, the words blazed beneath the tip of her blade. She hoped she was doing this right. The most she'd ever achieved with Transformation was removing mold from a book. Making something disappear was entirely out of her depth.

The voice inside the crate went silent, the air hushed and tense. She wished she could reassure her younger self. They were going to the *Current of Faith*, where she'd meet Captain Reed and the chief mate, Meeks and Horse and Jules . . .

In her mind's eye, she pictured the way the crate had seemed to flicker in and out of her vision, the way the mate kept touching it to reassure himself it was still there. The way the door in the house on the hill had done the same thing.

She didn't have much time. The crew of the *Current* were coming. She knew they would. She remembered their voices.

"You there!"

She looked up, blinking. Theo and Killian were heading toward her, readying the ropes that would swing the crate onto the green ship.

But her gaze was drawn by movement farther down the dock.

From the deck of the old cutter, a woman in black leapt onto the gangplank. Sefia's breath rushed out of her. She knew that pale pockmarked face, that curved sword.

Another corpse risen from the dead.

And just a few feet ahead of her, Tanin.

Cursing inwardly, Sefia sheathed her knife and dashed into the crowd. Her attempt at Transformation had to work—it had been written, and it had already come to pass.

Escaping with her life was another matter.

She dodged through the throng, knocking aside merchants and burly stevedores. She leapt coils of line and gleaming chests waiting to be loaded.

Behind her, she heard startled cries and Tanin's annoyed hiss.

She had to get out of there, had to find a way back to her own time. What was it Erastis had said?

There are some people we can always get back to, no matter how far they are from us.

Some people's stories were so entwined with your own that you'd find your way back to them again and again.

Archer.

Archer was her referent. Her anchor. Her home.

She blinked. The Illuminated world swept over her, turning her vision to gold, and she could see her way through the groups of passengers and stacks of kegs, past the cannons ready for the warships and the discarded fishing nets stinking on the docks.

But she needed to see more than this.

Racing down the pier, she ducked around a cart, wincing as her elbow struck the hard corner.

Archer. His face. His scars. The color of his hair in the lamp-light and the feral glow in his eyes. The strength and gentleness of his hands.

Where was he? As she ran, she searched the Illuminated world for him. For the boy she'd saved, the boy she loved, the boy she'd gladly join her life to—in this story or any other.

Oceans of time slipped past her as she ran. Days in the blink of an eye. Months in a breath.

And she still couldn't find him.

She was nearing the end of the pier, looming before her with a stack of crates like steps into the sky.

Archer.

Where are you?

She was out of space to run. Teleport or be caught. And she already knew she wouldn't be caught.

Though it made her a target for Tanin and the Assassin, she bounded up the crates and flung herself into the air. She spread her arms wide, like wings, hoping, desperately hoping, to see him at the other end of the parted sea of gold.

He wasn't there.

The water rose up to meet her.

Pain seared through her arm as a knife flew past.

She wouldn't make it. She'd end up stuck in the past or in some far-flung future. Worse, she'd end up nowhere. Dissolved into nothing but dust, all the pieces of her carried off by the currents of history. She'd never be able to tell Archer she'd been wrong. She never should have kept him in the dark. She never should have left him. She should have stayed, and they should have faced this, together, whatever came for them.

Then, seconds before she hit the water, she saw him. Flawed. Perfect. Surrounded by a tapestry of light so dazzling it nearly blinded her.

She waved her hands, sweeping herself through the sea of gold. And then she was gone.

CHAPTER 45

Always

Sefia hit the ground and rolled, coming up in a low-ceilinged storeroom crowded with kegs and dark barrels of wine.

Archer was tied to a wooden chair, his head lolling forward, his hair matted, his clothing torn.

Archer. Her heart dented. Bruised, bleeding, groaning, golden *Archer*.

By the door, two guards were already drawing their weapons. Bullets sped toward her. Blinking, Sefia sent them back. One of the guards cried out, clutching his throat as red spattered his lips.

Swiftly, almost casually, Sefia lifted her hand. The remaining guard catapulted toward the ceiling, where she struck the beams and went limp, falling to the ground again like a sack of bricks.

There was shouting outside.

Someone thrust the door open. Sefia got a glimpse of eyes and steel before she shut them all out with a sweep of her arm.

"Sefia," Archer whispered. He was so hurt, bleeding everywhere. A gash yawned in his side, deep and black.

Keeping her hold on the door, Sefia went to him, kneeling as she pulled her knife and cut his bonds. The ropes pricked her fingers.

A gunshot split the door. Splinters flew into the storeroom. Sheathing her blade, Sefia swept barrel after barrel in front of the door, barricading them inside.

"Sefia," Archer kept saying—just her name, like the word was a lifeline and he was drawing himself to shore.

Gently, she loosed the ropes, easing them from his wrists and ankles. "What happened? Who did this?"

Archer slumped forward. She barely caught him before he hit the ground, his skin sticky, his hair smelling of sweat and thundershowers. "Serakeen," he said. "He—"

Sefia's grip tightened. "Serakeen's here?"

Tanin lied. She'd said all those things about trust, about family, and Sefia had believed her, had even felt sorry for her.

But Tanin had been lying all along. The Guard would *never* stop hunting them.

Archer shook his head. Blood dripped from his lips like strands of molten sugar. "We've got to get them," he mumbled.

Tanin, she thought, Serakeen, whoever else was responsible for doing this to him. "We will," she said, "but we can't stay here."

Bullets came flying through the door, puncturing the barrels.

Burgundy wine poured onto the floor. The sour smell of fermentation filled the storeroom as Sefia looped Archer's arm over her shoulders.

Summoning the Sight, she swept her arm wide, searching the currents of light for the only safe place she knew of.

There.

The vault of sails and rigging and the length of the deck before her.

As the sounds of banging and bullets grew dim around her, she gripped Archer tight and teleported them from the storeroom . . . onto the deck of the *Current of Faith*.

Her telescope hit the floor as she and Archer collapsed in a heap. He was heavy and half-conscious in her arms, but he was alive. And they were together.

Exclamations of surprise exploded around them like fireworks.

"Sefia? How did you—"

"Is that Archer?"

"He's injured." She sat up, cradling Archer's head in her lap. "Get the doc!"

Footsteps scampered across the deck as the news of their arrival went through the crew.

"Sefia," Archer murmured.

Laying her palms on his cheeks, she leaned over him, memorizing his face: the contours of the bones beneath his skin, his bruises like sunsets, and the deep bloody cleft in his side.

"You were right. I should never have left," she murmured. "I'm so sorry. I'll never let them take you again. I won't let you die. I promise, I promise . . ."

"You came back," was all he said.

Sefia nodded. Tears spilled from her eyes.

"Did you get Frey and Aljan out too?"

She froze, frantically trying to recall the details of the store-room. Archer. Two guards. No one else. She was sure of it.

"Were they supposed to be with you?" she whispered.

He nodded.

She leaned back, ice forming in the pit of her stomach. *Serakeen still has them.*

"Move, girl." The chief mate pulled her aside as Doc arrived with her black bag.

"Hey, Sef," Horse murmured, patting her shoulder with one of his enormous hands. "I dunno how you got here, but I sure am glad to see you both."

Doc's keen gaze flicked over Archer. "How did this happen?"

"I don't know. I wasn't there." Sefia squeezed her eyes shut, trying to conjure up the storeroom in her memory. It had been dark, with clay floors, kegs stacked in the corners. What color were the walls? How high was the ceiling? Was it lighted with torches? Lanterns? Candles? She couldn't picture it. She hadn't been there long enough.

And if she couldn't remember it clearly enough, she couldn't teleport back there. She couldn't save Aljan and Frey.

While Doc examined Archer's wounds, the other crew members gathered around. Meeks swept her up in a hug, crying, "Sef! Sef! You came back!"

For a moment she buried her face in his dreadlocks and gripped him tight.

The safest place she could think of.

As the second mate let her down, she caught sight of Captain Reed—his blue eyes bright beneath his wide-brimmed hat, looking quite the hero with the sun blazing behind him.

Sefia straightened. "Cap."

"Sef." He tipped his hat at her. "I don't know how we keep meetin' like this."

"Sorry, Cap, I guess I should've sent a messenger."

"You're always welcome on the *Current*, kid. You know that. In fact, we been lookin' for you—" He paused.

Quick as lightning, he grabbed her hand.

"Cap!" Meeks shouted.

Reed's fingers dug into her skin. Pain shot up her arm. She blinked—clouds of gold burst across her vision. It took all her self-control not to fling him across the deck.

He ignored the cries of his crew, studying her ring with the same intense focus he'd had when he first saw the Book.

No, when he saw the words inside. When his anger had exploded out of him like a bullet from a rifle.

In a flash, Sefia understood: He'd seen the ring before. Somewhere on his adventures, he'd met Mareah. And it hadn't gone well for him.

She wrenched out of his grasp.

"Where'd you get that?" he asked quietly.

"It was my mother's."

"Your—" His gaze went from the ring to her face and back again. "I thought she was—"

"She is," Sefia said flatly. "I found this when I went home."

Captain Reed rubbed his eyes. "Kid, I think we've got a lot to talk about."

472

Before she could reply, Doc stood, motioning to Horse. "He's taken quite a beating, but he'll recover with time. Get him down to the sick bay."

As Archer was lifted from the deck, he reached for Sefia.

"Are you back?" he asked, the plaintive note in his voice a heartbreak all its own. His grasp tightened, as if he was afraid she'd slip away like water through his hands. "For good?"

In answer, Sefia crossed her fingers, one over the other.

They were together. And nothing, not even fate itself, would part them again.

"For always," she said.

Chapter 46

Of Oaths and Prophecy

When Sefia fled the dungeons, Tanin assumed she'd have to run as well—run or die. By helping the girl escape, Erastis, her only remaining supporter, had betrayed her. She no longer had allies in the Guard, and without the girl, without the Book, she had little chance of ousting Stonegold before he killed her.

Then Detano had come to her, begging for help. He'd failed his Master. He'd failed the Guard. He'd let the Lonely King live.

Sentiment.

Detano had found a body, he'd said, a boy with an ailing mother, a host of younger siblings to provide for, and a striking resemblance to the missing king. But the Apprentice Politician didn't have the talent to fabricate an assassination, not when the other Guardians could detect the means of murder from the marks on the body.

Desperate times call for equally desperate allies, and Detano was offering her the one thing she needed to stay.

Hope.

Together, they'd arranged it: the darkened royal chamber—the boy curled up in the corner, beyond the reach of the light—a dram of poison that would discolor and distend his flesh, obscuring any revealing scars—a signet ring that would have to be cut from the bloated finger—a stench of rotting flesh that would warrant a swift burning, before the body could divulge any secrets.

Soon after, Detano had been elected regent of Deliene.

Stonegold and the rest of the Guard remained unaware of his failure.

And Tanin had not run.

Her fingers flexed on the marble banister of the highest gallery as she watched the ceremony below. The Hall of Memory was a magnificent five-story chamber where historians worked to remember and repeat, preserving the world's history. Although every village, town, and city in all the Five Kingdoms employed historians, Corabel was the only place where hundreds of them gathered, making the Hall the second-greatest repository of knowledge in all Kelanna.

Now, historians, councillors, advisers, and representatives of the major and minor houses had assembled on the grand floor of the Hall for the oath-taking of the regent.

Standing before a set of engraved mirrors, bedecked in his black-and-silver regalia, Arcadimon Detano lifted his eyes.

For the briefest of seconds, his gaze met Tanin's.

She'd keep his secrets. He'd keep her alive.

As long as she survived the next few minutes.

Behind her, she heard two sets of footsteps on the thick carpet. It took all her nerve to appear nonchalant as she turned to face her enemies.

"Come to kill me, Stonegold?" she purred. The more arrogant she acted now, the more effective her remorse would be later, if she didn't accidentally get herself gutted first.

At the derision in her voice, the Politician's nostrils flared with displeasure. He strode to the balcony beside her, his girth pressing against her as if to prove he deserved more space on the landing than she did. "I half-expected you to be running for your life by now," he said.

"I've been working toward this moment for more than a decade," Tanin replied. "I would not have missed it." As she spoke, Braca flicked back the tails of her blue suede coat and leaned against one of the velvet chairs, her gold guns gleaming in the afternoon sunlight. Such bravado. The Master Soldier wouldn't dare use such disruptive weapons at a public event.

No, the attack, if it came, would be silent and swift.

Deliberately, Tanin turned her back on the Soldier.

"It's stupid, valuing sentiment over survival." Spittle flew from Stonegold's lips. "At least this time, your soft heart will cost only yourself."

"You should have told me you were setting a trap for the boy. I would've been more careful with Sefia if—"

"The only thing I should have done was execute you as soon as I became Director," he interrupted.

She trailed her finger along the railing. *Yes, that* was *a mistake,* she thought. *One you'll regret when you see my blade protruding from your chest.*

The Politician couldn't contain his smugness. "No quippy retort? No scathing insults? I'd at least hoped you'd beg."

Tanin glanced over her shoulder at Braca. "Begging is for dogs," she snapped.

As soon as the words left her lips, she felt the Soldier's invisible grip on her throat. Braca closed the distance between them so fast Tanin didn't realize she'd drawn a gold dagger from inside her coat until the blade was digging into her neck.

"Then beg, bitch," the Soldier growled, her burned face inches away from Tanin's.

Tanin could feel her neck bruising, but she forced herself to smirk. "Here?" she wheezed. "In front of all these people? A murder would be a stain on the celebration."

Braca's dagger slit open her scar. Blood dripped down her neck. "*Your* murder would be an excellent way to celebrate."

Tanin's head spun with lack of air. Here it was—the only way Stonegold would believe he'd earned her allegiance. Repent or die. If she wanted to kill him later, she had to put herself at his mercy now. She looked to the Director who had taken her place.

"Please," she croaked, "don't."

He sneered at her. "Say that again."

"Please, let me live. Let me serve the mission to which I've dedicated my entire life."

"Serving the mission means serving *me*."

"I will. I'll serve you. I—I swear."

"Prove it. Give me a token of your allegiance."

Tears slid down her cheeks. "The outlaws," she whispered.

"Parasites from a less civilized age. We've been exterminating them with extreme prejudice. The others will disperse and die like the roaches they are." The Politician flicked his fat fingers at her dismissively. "Go ahead and kill her, my general."

A smile wormed across Braca's lips, pulling at her scarred skin. Tanin felt her throat opening up again, felt her life seeping out of her.

"They're organizing," she managed to whisper. "They're at least a hundred strong by now."

Stonegold balked at her.

Tell her to let me go, you asinine old pig. Spots swam before her eyes.

With a nod, he ordered Braca to loosen her grip.

Air flooded back into Tanin's lungs. Blood rushed to her face. She fell to her knees, clutching her neck.

The Politician loomed over her. "Know where they are, do you?"

She nodded, trying to suck air down her damaged throat.

"Where?"

"An island they call Haven." She could see her own reflection in Stonegold's polished shoes. She looked thin. Better, she looked *weak*. "Impossible to find unless you already know the way."

"And you know the way, do you?"

She nodded again.

"This will cost you your precious pirate captain."

Reed.

She'd liked being the captain of the *Black Beauty*, his one-time lover and perpetual rival. But they all made sacrifices for the greater good. "I know."

She felt Stonegold's hand descend onto the top of her head. "Good girl."

Below, Detano's rich voice began to fill the Hall as he took the oaths that would make him regent of Deliene, with control over the White Navy and the power to declare war.

The Historian of the Corabelli Era took an ivory crown from a velvet pillow and nestled it among Detano's curls.

The third phase of Lon's plan for the Red War was complete. The Guard controlled Everica, Liccaro, and now Deliene.

Stonegold hauled Tanin up by her hair as the Hall of Memory erupted in applause. "Let me handle the outlaws," he whispered, his breath in her ear. "You, my Assassin, have only one task now, to earn your bloodsword and secure your place in the Guard."

The spring had been tightened. The trap was ready to be sprung.

"Kill the girl. Kill the traitors' daughter. Kill what remains of your precious *family*."

Soon the Red War would begin in earnest, and all their plans and prophecies—the bloody battles, the fall of Oxscini, the military triumph of a boy-commander and his tragic demise, the victory decades in the making—would finally come to pass.

CHAPTER 47

The Boy from the Legends

For days, Archer slept.

He dreamed, of course. The dreams were a part of him now. He was a boy who'd had terrible things done to him and who'd done terrible things himself. He was a boy who nightmared.

He was also a boy who awoke, and when he opened his eyes, Sefia was there, mending sails with Doc or playing Ship of Fools with Horse and Marmalade, her very presence all the reassurance he needed.

Only once, early on, did he awake alone. He'd been dreaming about Frey and Aljan—the angle of Frey's arm beneath her unmoving body, the way the blood ran into Aljan's eyes—and found himself alone in the sick bay. The setting sun flamed in the portholes, and Doc's dried herbs swayed overhead like hanged men.

Down the corridor, he could hear the crew talking, the faint, halting notes of a mandolin.

Though Archer wasn't supposed to move about by himself, he staggered from the cabin, up the hatchway. He could feel the stitches in his side pulling, blood seeping into his bandages. But he had to find Sefia. To be sure she was still here.

She was standing at the rail, silhouetted by the light reflecting off the water, brilliant and gold. She looked beautiful . . . and pensive. Maybe even guilty.

But he felt that guilt too, for all the mistakes he'd made, for not going after her when she left, for Frey and Aljan falling into the Guard's hands. Maybe he always would.

After a moment, Meeks joined her. Their murmured conversation was too quiet for him to hear, except for the sound of the second mate asking if it was written. As darkness slid over the sky, they lapsed into silence, and Archer slipped belowdecks again, clutching his injured side.

When he awoke next, the bandages had been changed, and Sefia was curled beside him in the narrow bunk. He did not ask her to move.

It was during these times, when they were alone, that he began to tell her, hesitantly, in fits and starts, about the past he'd kept from her: the acts of viciousness he'd witnessed, the ones he'd committed, the family he could not return to, no matter how much he loved them. He showed her his guilt, his anger, his self-loathing, his insatiable desire for violence. He began to peel himself open for her, layer by painful layer, revealing his raw and wounded heart.

He didn't tell her everything. How could he? There was so much to tell, and there was so much that was still broken inside him. But it was a start.

In turn, she told him about her deal with Tanin, her return to the house on the hill overlooking the sea, her father's letter.

"You left to save me," Archer murmured, touching the worry stone where it rested between her collarbones.

She swallowed. "I came back to save you."

His fingers trailed up the side of her neck to the back of her head, where they twined in her hair. Pain streaked along his side, but he chose to ignore it, bringing his mouth so close to hers he could feel her breath on his lips. "You always save me," he whispered.

He kissed her.

And in that second, kissing her was *everything*. An explosion—a downpour—a secret. A sigh—a bolt of lightning—the feeling of flight before the fall.

His hand slid beneath the hem of her shirt, fingertips grazing her ribs.

Sefia gasped, and it was such a sweet sound it made Archer's head spin and his bones ache with desire.

"I love you," she whispered as his lips found her jaw, the lobe of her ear, her throat.

He didn't know how badly he'd been wanting to hear the words until she said them, but there they were, turning slowly in the air like crystals in sunlight, and they were the best words and the only words and he would pin them to his heart until his dying day.

He was a boy who was loved.

One time when he awoke, Captain Reed was sitting in the sick bay, peering through the portholes at the swells outside. He had a new gun, Archer noted—a long-nosed revolver with a jet-black grip—and somehow, in the light through the glass, the captain's eyes looked bluer, hungrier.

He looked how Archer felt when he was fighting.

But that life was behind him. It had to be—he knew that now—if he wanted to live.

As Archer sat up, a smile softened the harshness in Reed's eyes. "Hey, kid." He pulled up a stool beside the bunk. "Sef's been tellin' us what you were up to in Deliene. What'd I tell you? You don't got a ship, but you sure as shootin' are an outlaw."

Archer smiled. "Thanks, Cap."

"So you do talk." Reed chuckled. "Hard to believe 'til I heard it myself."

"It took me a while."

"That's okay." Captain Reed's eyes got that starving look to them again. "Some things are worth the wait."

Archer cocked his head, his hand going to his temple, but before he could ask what Reed meant, Sefia burst into the cabin with a heaping platter of sweets. Her face brightened when she saw him, with a spark he wished he could bottle for dark nights.

Placing the plate on his shins, she grabbed an egg custard and sat on the end of the bunk. "So there was writing on the inside of the bell, huh?" she asked Reed.

He passed her a folded sheet of parchment and scratched his chest. "I'd know those marks anywhere."

She watched him sadly for a moment. "I'm sorry they did that to you."

It had taken them a while to see all the ways their lives were connected, but once Reed had told her about the Resurrection Amulet inside the Trove of the King, and Sefia had told him about the missing page her mother had removed from the Book, they'd realized Lon and Mareah had given him his first tattoos. They'd hidden the location of something Tanin wanted: the last piece of the Resurrection Amulet, a magical object that could conquer death, an object Reed now wanted too.

"It don't matter now." The captain shrugged, though Archer could see his anger—and his disappointment. "Those words are long gone. We ain't gonna find the last bit of the Amulet that way."

"The Book can tell us where to find it."

Archer frowned. "I thought we couldn't trust the Book."

"We can't," Sefia said as she unfolded the paper Reed had given her. "But we need it to rescue Frey and Aljan. And find the Amulet inside the Trove."

It was all too connected, too convenient, too coincidental.

And as Tanin had said, *There are no coincidences.*

"What if that's what it *wants* us to do?" Archer asked.

Reed shook his head. "You talk about this thing like it's alive."

"Erastis did say the Book was a living story, full of intent," Sefia replied, skimming the charcoal rubbing in her hands.

The captain traced a set of interconnected circles on the worn edge of the bunk. "Maybe it's a livin' story because we're still livin' it, and our actions ain't foregone conclusions after all."

She smiled grimly. "Let's hope so." After a moment, she began to read:

> *The brave and the bold may find Liccarine gold*
> *Where the stallions charge into the spray.*
> *Where the sidewinder waits, the heart lowers its gates,*
> *And the water will show you the way.*

Archer watched Reed carefully as the captain listened to the words he'd been waiting months to hear. There it was again—hunger and hope.

"Do you know what it means?" Archer asked.

Captain Reed grinned. "I know where to start." A place on the outer curve of Liccaro where the cliffs formed the shapes of mustangs: teeth and heads and hooves. "It's called Steeds. Don't know about the rest yet, but we'll figure it out when we get there."

What are we going to do?" Sefia asked later, when they were alone again. "We go to Jahara to get the Book back. We rescue Frey and Aljan. We help Reed find the Amulet. And then? What do we do after?"

Archer scratched at one of his bandages. Some things they couldn't do without the Book, like find Frey and Aljan, wherever they were. They were his bloodletters. He would not leave them to Serakeen.

But after? After they'd wrapped up their obligations to the bloodletters and to Captain Reed?

He couldn't lead the bloodletters anymore, that was for sure, couldn't go near a battle without kindling his thirst for bloodshed. Even now, he could feel the urge to fight stirring in his half-healed limbs.

But he didn't want to be that boy. He *couldn't* be that boy without letting Sefia down again.

He bit his lip. "It's me, isn't it?"

The boy with the scar.

The boy from the legends.

The boy the Guard wanted.

"Yes," she whispered. "And it's me too."

"The reader." He looped a strand of hair behind her ear.

She made a face.

"It suits you."

"I'd rather be an outlaw, thanks."

Archer kissed the top of her head. "Okay. Let's be outlaws."

He tried to imagine it: They'd stay on the *Current*, becoming adventurers and treasure hunters who harbored at Haven while the kingdoms battled for land, and they'd give no more thought to the Red War than some half-remembered dream. What a life they'd have. A life of salt and gunpowder. Of friendship and love and boundless horizons. A dangerous life, but a *life*.

But he could not entirely ignore the storm brewing inside him—dark and brimming with violence—the unquenchable desire to fight, to lead, to conquer.

With a shiver, Sefia tucked herself into the crook of his arm, and he held her, hoping she couldn't feel the thunder in his chest.

They could beat the Book.

They could.

They had to.

For a moment, they watched the stars glimmering in the portholes as the constellations swam across the lampblack sky.

"What about the Guard?" he asked. "Won't they still be hunting us?"

Sefia shrugged. "If we can change destiny, we can outwit the Guard."

"You really think we can beat the Book?"

She looked up at him then, with that dark gaze he knew so well—focused, determined, daring. "Together, we can do anything."

Acknowledgments

Around this time last year, I wrote that "books are magic because *people are magic*." This is as true today as it was then, but I also understand now, with deeper clarity, that magic isn't easy. It takes more than an incantation, a sprinkle of fairy dust, and a little hand-waving to make a book. It's a Herculean feat, a labor of love, a headache, and an incomparable joy, and *this* book wouldn't have made it into the world without the time, skills, and continued support of a vast community of people whom I could not thank enough in a hundred pages, much less four. The fact that I even have the pleasure of writing this, right now, as we near the end, is both a privilege and a gift. Thank you, thank you, thank you.

To Barbara Poelle, the fiercest agent-warrior I could have ever hoped to work with (for?)—thank you a thousand times for your panache, your wit, and, despite what I said above, some arcane quality I still can't explain as anything except "agenty-magic." (This is why I do the things.) Thanks also to Brita Lundberg and everyone at IGLA—I am so grateful to be one of your authors.

To Stacey Barney, who still shouts and backs away at the faintest suggestion of spoilers—please accept my deepest thanks for your insight, your patience, and your faith. You are an artist with a flawless vision and a sharp pen. It is a true honor to be working with you.

Immense gratitude to all the talented people who worked so hard on these words and the design of this book. Thank you to Chandra Wohleber—I always look forward to your copy edits with glee—and to Clarence Haynes for your keen eyes. To Cecilia Yung, Marikka Tamura, and David Kopka, who take on all my wild ideas with courage and style—thank you for turning this story into a precious, multifaceted object brimming with treasures. I am repeatedly impressed with your inventiveness and your attention to all the details that anyone else would overlook.

To the cover design team, Deborah Kaplan, Kristin Smith, and Yohey Horishita, who have outfitted this book with such an arresting exterior—you have outdone yourselves. Thank you. Special thanks to Kristin for every revision and for every extraordinary piece of detective work.

To all the members of the incredible team at Putnam and Penguin—thank you for accepting me into the Penguin family and always making me feel so welcome here. I am especially grateful for Jen Loja, Jen Besser, David Briggs, Emily Rodriguez, Elizabeth Lunn, Cindy Howle, Wendy Pitts,

Carmela Iaria, Alexis Watts, Venessa Carson, Rachel Wease, Bri Lockhart, Kara Brammer, and all the amazing hardworking folks from Sales, Marketing, Publicity, and School & Library whom I've met over the past year and whom I've yet to meet. Extra buckets of gratitude to Kate Meltzer for your endless patience with me, and to my publicists Marisa Russell and Paul Crichton, who manage a million spinning plates with so much aplomb.

Many, many thanks to Kim Mai Guest, Arthur Insana, Orli Moscowitz, and the lovely people at Listening Library and PRH Audio, who turned a book about storytelling into a magnificent storytelling experience.

Overflowing amounts of gratitude to Heather Baror-Shapiro, who has brought Sea of Ink and Gold to so many new lands and new languages, and to my foreign publishers, who have poured so much enthusiasm into this series, spreading the words to readers across the world.

To my earliest readers, Diane Glazman and Kirsten Squires, thank you for braving the sulfurous fires of my first drafts and helping me pull a story from the flames. Thank you to Jess Cluess and Emily Skrutskie, who valiantly rode in to herd my most stubborn and meandering subplots back into line; to Kerri Maniscalco, my beautiful friend with whom I am so grateful to share this wild ride; and to Renée Ahdieh for taking the time to tell me yet again to turn up the romance. Thanks to Mark O'Brien, Mey Valdivia Rude, K. A. Reynolds, Mara Rutherford, Gretchen Schreiber, RuthAnne Snow, and Nick Oakey-Frost for helping me breathe life into these characters. They are deeper, sharper, and more complex because of you. Special shout-outs to Parker Peevyhouse and Jonathan Vong for taking my panicked phone calls about increasingly complicated Easter eggs and patiently spending the wee hours of the morning trying to solve my impossible puzzles.

To my friends and family, who have shown up in truly magnificent ways this past year—I am constantly astounded by and grateful for your support and your love. Thank you for coming to my events, talking up my book to your friends and coworkers, posting bookstore sightings of *The Reader* on Facebook and Twitter, and generally going out of your way to be the awesome people who have shaped my life into what it is today. Additional gratitude to Tara Sim—the Tony Stark to my Pepper Potts—and to the Table of Trust.

To Mom and Auntie Kats, who have always been my heroes—your hard work and your selflessness are inspiring. Thank you for feeding me when I was sick, watching the dogs when I was traveling, and supporting me in a thousand small ways for which I can never thank you enough.

And to Cole, who has more patience and good nature than I could ever hope to match—thank you for being there every time I need to laugh, rant, cry, nap, brainstorm, and celebrate. This journey would not have been possible without you—my referent, my anchor, my home.

Can Sefia and Archer outrun their fate
and beat the book?

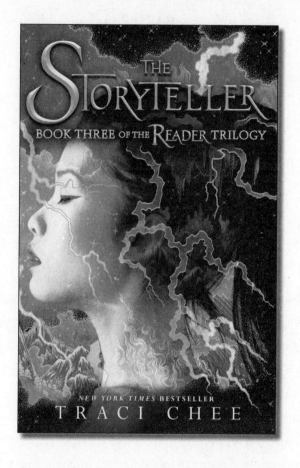

Turn the page for a preview of
The Storyteller, the conclusion to

THE READER TRILOGY

CHAPTER 1

Fine as Gossamer,
Hard as Iron

Sefia sat up in the shadows of the sick bay, startled out of some half-remembered dream.

The ship rocked and plunged beneath her, making the jars of ointment and bottles of tonic rattle on their shelves. Outside, rain spattered the portholes, blurring her view of the waves, high as rolling hills.

A storm. They must have come upon it in the night.

Sefia shivered, hugging her knees to her chest. In the four days since she'd returned to the *Current* with Archer, she'd had the same dream again and again. She was back in the house on the hill, and ink was seeping—no, *flooding*—from the secret room in the basement where her parents had kept the Book, the dark waves reaching across the floor to grasp them by the ankles and crawl up their calves. In the dream, Lon and Mareah scooped her up. In the dream, they shoved her out the door. But they were always too slow to save themselves, always too slow to escape the growing pool of ink that drew them, screaming, into its black depths.

Destiny. Her parents had been destined to die, their futures recorded in the Book with everything that had ever been or would ever be, from the flicker of a mayfly's wings to the life spans of the stars overhead.

Somewhere in the Book was the passage where her mother got sick.

Somewhere were the paragraphs that described her father being tortured.

It had been written, so it had come to pass.

But they'd fought it. They'd betrayed the Guard, the secret society of readers to which they'd sworn their undying allegiance. They'd stolen the Book, the Guard's most powerful weapon, to protect their daughter from her own future. They'd run.

They'd lost, in the end, but oh, how they'd *fought*.

As Sefia had to fight now. Fight and *win*, or she'd lose Archer to destiny too.

Beside her, he lay curled beneath the blankets, hair tousled, fingers twitching in his sleep. He always slept so little, his dreams haunted by memories of the people he'd killed.

He felt *fractured*, he'd told her a few days before. At all times, he was the same small-town boy he'd been before the Guard's impressors took him, and yet, at all times, he was an animal, he was a victim, he was a killer, he was loud as thunder, he was the boy from the legends, with a bloodlust that could not be slaked.

Lightning forked in the distance, pulsing like veins in the restless sky.

As if in response, Archer's body spasmed. He let out a wordless gasp.

Sefia shifted out of his way. "Archer. It's okay. You're safe."

His eyes opened. For a moment, he seemed to have trouble coming out of his dreams, seemed to have trouble recognizing where he was, *who* he was.

But the moment would pass. It always did. And then—

The smile. It spread across his face like dawn racing over water—his lips, his cheeks, his golden eyes. Every time, it was like he was seeing her for the first time, his expression full of such hope that she longed to see it again and again for the rest of her days.

For a second, the storm abated. For a second, the ship was still. For a second, Sefia's whole world was light and soft and warm.

"Sefia," he whispered, tucking her hair behind her ear.

She bent closer, drawn to him as a hummingbird is drawn to a flower, her mouth gently landing on his.

He leaned into her kiss, responding to her lips and wandering hands as if her very touch was magic, making him moan and arch and yearn for more.

He laced his fingers in her hair, like he needed to be closer to her, like he couldn't get enough of her, but as he tried to sit up, he let out a sudden hiss of pain and reached for his injured side.

"I'm sorry," she said.

"Don't be." Propping himself up on his elbows, he grinned. "I'm not."

Her cheeks warmed as she pulled aside the blanket to examine his bandages. Doc had stitched and dressed the wound twice now: first when he'd arrived, half-conscious, with the gash below his ribs black and nauseatingly deep, and a second time when Archer had torn his sutures trying to help Cooky dump a pot of potato peels overboard. Sefia would never hear the end of it if Doc had to redo the stitches again.

"I'm fine." Archer tried batting her away.

"You almost died."

"Only almost." He shrugged. He'd told her about the fight with Serakeen. There had been the smell of cordite and blood. A gust of magic that had swept Archer's lieutenants, Frey and Aljan, into the wall of the alley before dropping them, unconscious, onto the cobbles. The resistance of bone as Archer severed Serakeen's hand at the wrist.

"I should've been there," Sefia said, not for the first time. If she'd been there, she could have protected him. She had the same magic as Serakeen—a magic the Guard called Illumination—she might have even matched him, in a fight. *After all,* she thought bitterly, *I'm the daughter of an assassin and the most powerful sorcerer the world has seen in years.*

No. She didn't want to believe in that future. She wouldn't become a weapon in some war for control of the Five Kingdoms. She wouldn't lose Archer, the boy she loved.

"You're here now. That's what matters," Archer said quietly. "Without you, we wouldn't be able to rescue Frey and Aljan."

His bloodletters, his *friends,* had followed him into the fight with Serakeen, and Serakeen still had them. The Guard's Apprentice Soldier, known to Sefia's parents as Rajar, had once been their friend and collaborator. Together, they'd orchestrated the war that was supposed to claim Archer's life.

How many of Lon and Mareah's mistakes would Sefia have to fix? She'd loved them, but they'd made *so many*.

"Frey and Aljan will be all right," Sefia said.

"You really think so?"

She trailed her fingers down his arm, over the fifteen burns that marked his kills in the impressors' fighting rings, and took his hand. "Yes," she said.

The plan was to return to the bloodletters, organize a rescue, and meet up with the *Current of Faith* again at Haven, an island in the unexplored reaches of the Central Sea—one of those places you could get to only if you knew how to get there. Reed had set it up months ago to take in outlaws on the run from the widening scope of the war. If Sefia and Archer got there with the bloodletters, they would all have a place to wait while the fighting—and destiny—passed them by. If they got to Haven, Archer would live.

But first, they needed the Book. Sefia couldn't teleport to the bloodletters without a clear image of where they were, and only the Book, with its infinite pages of history, could provide that.

She'd hidden it in the safest place she could think of: the Jaharan messengers' post. The messengers' guild dealt in all kinds of secrets—delicate packages, incriminating information—and they never broke their trust. They were respected and powerful, and with them, no one could touch the Book.

Not even the Guard. She hoped.